Author's Note

The Deceit is a work of fiction. However, I have drawn on many real, historical, archaeological and cultural sources for this book. In particular:

The *Sacred Magic of Abra-Melin the Mage* is a book of spells and curses, compiled by a Jewish Kabbalist, Abraham of Worms, in fifteenth-century Germany. Various versions of the text survive in libraries across Europe. In occult circles the magic of Abra-Melin is regarded as the most 'dangerous' of all hermetic rituals.

Aleister Crowley (1875–1947) was a British mountaineer, adventurer, drug-addict and black magician, and for a time a member of the Hermetic Order of the Golden Dawn, alongside artists such as the Irish poet, and Nobel laureate, W B Yeats. In 1924 a disciple of Crowley's died in Crowley's house in Cefalu, Sicily – allegedly after Crowley had fed him the blood of a cat.

The little town of Akhmim is possibly the oldest

inhabited site in Egypt. Regarded as the cradle of alchemy, and as one of the birthplaces of Gnostic and Coptic Christianity, Akhmim also, in antiquity, enjoyed a reputation as being home to the greatest magicians in Egypt. Despite its extraordinary history, Akhmim has never been properly excavated by archaeologists.

THE DECEIT

TOM KNOX

HARPER

Harper
An imprint of HarperCollins*Publishers*
77–85 Fulham Palace Road,
Hammersmith, London W6 8JB

www.harpercollins.co.uk

A Paperback Original 2013
2

ISBN 978 0 00 745919 3

Set in Meridien by Palimpsest Book Production Limited,
Falkirk, Stirlingshire

Printed and bound in Great Britain by
Clays Ltd, St Ives plc

Acknowledgements

I have read many books for the purposes of researching this novel. My thanks therefore go out to all the authors: Robert Sattin, Jan Assmann, Nicholas Reeves, Georg Dehn, Andrew Smith, Erik Hornung, D M Murdock, Burton J Bogitsh, Thomas Cheng, Paul Newman, Lawrence Suttin, Claude Combes, Richard Wilkinson and Carl Zimmer. I must thank Glenys Roberts for allowing me to use her excellent essay on Crowley, and the estate of John Heath-Stubbs for allowing me to quote his verse about West Penwith; a particular debt of gratitude is owed to Marvin Meyer and Richard Smith for their marvellous and mind-blowing *Ancient Christian Magic, Coptic Texts of Ritual Power*.

Thanks are also due to my tireless agent Eugenie Furniss, and my erudite and indispensable editor Jane Johnson.

Mostly, I want to thank the many people of Egypt

– Muslim and Christian, Arabs and Nubians – who have shown me so many corners of that fascinating country, and for being so hospitable every time I came visiting – even when Egypt was in violent political turmoil.

I am grateful to Al-Tayyeb Hassan, who drove me to the remotest parts of Middle Egypt. I am also grateful to Ethar Shalaby, who showed me around the home of the Zabaleen in Moqqatam, Cairo. Finally, I am enormously indebted to the Zabaleen themselves for allowing me a glimpse of their lives.

This book is dedicated to the nuns of the fourth-century Coptic monastery of St Tawdros, near the Valley of the Queens, Luxor.

'And the LORD brought us FORTH out of EGYPT, with a mighty hand.'

Deuteronomy 26:8

1

Cairo, Egypt

The taxi stopped in the City of the Dead. Victor Sassoon stared out of the dusty cab window, adjusting his spectacles, and cursing his seventy-five-year-old eyesight.

Ranked on either side of the unpaved road, that led directly through the cemetery, was a monumental parade of Mameluke shrines, yellow-painted mausoleums, and enormous white Fatimid graves; in front of the larger tombs, young children played obscure games in the ancient dirt.

Sassoon stared, a little deeper: he could glimpse shrouded Arab women in the unknowable interiors; he could also see the blue and orange of charcoal braziers: the women were cooking chicken claws and flatbreads amidst the corpse-dust.

The cab engine idled. The women gazed, from behind their veils. Sassoon wondered if the denizens of the City of the Dead could tell he was Jewish. *Anglo*-Jewish.

He leaned and tapped the cab driver on the shoulder.

'Why have we stopped?'

Silence.

'Why?' he repeated.

The driver shrugged, not turning; the violet prayer-beads hanging from his rear-view mirror shivered in the breeze of the Cairene winter.

A kid in a grimy *djellaba* – the long Arabic robe worn across North Africa and beyond – wandered over to the taxi. The boy was smiling at Victor, as if he knew something Victor didn't.

'Why? Tell me.' Victor raised his voice, a hint of panic therein. He didn't want to be stuck here in the cemetery with the *fellahin*. The City of the Dead, one of Cairo's direst slums, was a dangerous place to linger.

'*Aiiii*.' The cab driver squinted at Victor via the mirror. '*Afwan, khlass, ntar—*'

'Stop!' Victor snapped. 'I know you speak English!'

Not for the first time, Victor condemned himself for his inability to speak much modern Arabic – despite speaking dead languages by the dozen.

The cab driver sighed.

'You are from England, yes? *Inglizi?*'

Victor nodded once more.

'So I see you do not understand.' The driver smiled, patiently. 'I will explain. You want to go to Manshiyat Naser?'

'Yes, you know that. Moqqatam.'

'*Aiwa*. Moqqatam.'

The wind was picking up as the winter sun weakened:

2

it made Victor cough, and reach for his handkerchief. The breeze was carrying a hateful dust: the residue of the dead.

Victor wiped his mouth and spoke.

'We agreed you'd take me there.'

The driver shook his head.

'Look and see. Thief and drug-seller live here. In the tomb.'

'So let us go. Please. Quickly.'

'*Ahlan sadiqi*, you are not understanding. Even the people *here*, even the people in City of the Dead will not go to Moqqatam.'

'I don't care. You said—'

'No.'

'But—'

'You walk now. Is just a walk? One or two kilometre. That way.'

The driver was pointing at a raised freeway thick with frenzied Cairo traffic, and beyond that a mighty cliff, grey and gloomy in the impending twilight.

Under that cliff, as Victor knew, was the abandoned quarry which was home to Cairo's poorest of the poor: the Zabaleen.

The Zabaleen suburb, Garbage City, had a terrible reputation – worse, perhaps, than that of the City of the Dead. But Victor did not care. At the back of Moqqatam was, apparently, an ancient church, the Monastery of the Cave. And in that monastery was an old priest who could tell him whether the Sokar Hoard really existed. And whether it could be deciphered.

And right now the archaic documents that comprised the Sokar Hoard meant more to Victor than his own dwindling life. The faint but persistent rumours in London, in Egyptological circles, were too startling to ignore.

The Copts have discovered a cache of documents in Middle Egypt. Parts are written in Arabic and French, as well as the most ancient Coptic. The Arabic and French commentaries imply that the Coptic source texts are revolutionary: they could alter our entire understanding of religion.

Of course these rumours were probably exaggerated. But even if you stripped out the hyperbole, the prospect was extremely enticing. Not least because the supposed provenance of the Sokar Hoard – Coptic Middle Egypt – made it all the more plausible that someone had indeed found *something*.

Coptic Middle Egypt was one of the historically richest yet least explored areas of the Middle East. Middle Egypt was where, in 1945, two farmers had unearthed an old earthenware jar which turned out to contain the famous Gnostic Gospels: heretical Christian writings which had since radically altered the conception of Christianity's evolution.

And yet this new prize, the Sokar Hoard, was said to be *vastly more significant*?

Victor *had* to find it. It was his final calling, his allotted task, his Jewish destiny. He was probably one of a handful of scholars who could translate the source text, the Ur text in old Coptic.

But right now he was stuck in a rusty Cairo taxi, surrounded by dirty kids who lived in tombs.

The cab driver sighed, again.

Belatedly, it dawned on Victor what the driver wanted. *Baksheesh*. More money. *Of course*.

He reached in the pocket of his blazer, pulled out his wallet and handed over a fold of new notes.

'Two hundred Egyptian pounds. Now take me to Moqqatam!'

The driver stared at the money in Victor's hand as if it was something utterly repugnant. Then he took the cash and jammed it in the sweat-stained pocket of his nylon shirt. And started the car.

The drive took merely ten minutes, past the last of the Fatimid ossuaries, past the final tombs of the Abbasid nobles, past an Ottoman mausoleum adapted into a car-repair workshop. They made a quick dash and a violent U-turn on the angry motorway with its angry taxis, and then the smell hit.

A smell of apocalyptic grime and aching misery.

This was it: Moqqatam. Ahead of them was a road which led to a kind of mock gate made of mud-bricks, old tyres and crushed metal.

The taxi stopped again. Victor reached reflexively for his wallet. But this time the driver waved a dismissive hand, and his frown was sincere.

'*La*. You are here, mister. Manshiyat Naser.'

'But—'

'I am a Muslim. I cannot go in there . . . Not with . . .' He nodded in the direction of the gate. 'Not with the *Christians*.'

The last word was expressed with utter contempt, as if the driver was spitting on a rat.

There was no arguing for a second time. Victor Sassoon accepted his fate. He grabbed his walking stick and climbed stiffly out of the taxi, which reversed in a cumulus of dust, then accelerated back up the hill into real Cairo, where the Muslims lived.

Victor regarded the gate, and the suburb beyond.

Even the people in the City of the Dead will not come here.

Leaning on his walking stick, Victor said a quick Jewish prayer. This was his greatest scholarly adventure, the fitting culmination of a life spent untangling the truth of Jewish history and Jewish faith. This was the moment towards which his entire existence had been building. But he was ageing and ill, and time was short. Stick in hand, Victor Sassoon walked towards the City of Garbage.

2

The City of Garbage, Cairo

The first thing that he saw as he passed under the gate was quite unexpected: two beautiful, unveiled young Coptic women walking past in embroidered robes, laughing as they made their way through the mud and the stench. He glanced at them, warily, but they ignored him. Just another stooped old man.

Victor sighed stoically, and walked on. A plastic Christian icon, suspended above the road, swung in the chilly breeze.

The main street was lined on both sides by enormous sacks of rubbish. Faces gazed, perplexed and blank, from dark windows and doorways. These stares certainly weren't friendly. Yet neither were they necessarily hostile. They possessed a kind of desperate inertness.

Victor advanced. He knew from his research that the Monastery of the Cave was somewhere at the other

7

end of the suburb, right under Moqqatam Hill, carved out of the cliffs. He could be there in ten minutes. If he wasn't stopped.

To quell his anxiety, he went over what he knew.

The name Zabaleen meant, literally, 'the rubbish collectors'. But fifty years ago they were called the Zarraba, or the pig people, because that's what they had once been: peasant swineherds dwelling in the region of Assyut and Sohag, two hundred miles south of Cairo. In essence, they were just another tribe from Egypt's ancient Coptic communities – Christians who had been living in the Middle East since the second century AD, long before the Muslims arrived.

No one knew why the Zabaleen had suddenly decided to migrate to Cairo. Their lives in Middle Egypt had certainly been poor, and Assyut was a dusty and sometimes violent region: home to many Islamists, who had grown in power and audacity – and hostility to Christians – in the last fifty years. Yet, still, why did they move *here*? Victor Sassoon found it difficult to imagine that any peasant life in the sticks could be worse than that now endured by the Zabaleen in Cairo.

He'd reached the main street of the City of Garbage. Looming beyond the lofty and toppling houses of the township were the limestone cliffs that delimited Cairo's eastern suburbs. Directly behind him was the vastness of the City of the Dead and the urban motorways.

The whole neighbourhood was cut off and excluded.

It was also situated in a hollow – a great and disused quarry – which made it invisible to the rest of Cairo.

A young man stepped across the road towards Victor. He had a cheeky, Artful Dodger-ish grin.

'Hey. Hello? Mister? You tourist? Take photo of us? Fuck you.' The lad laughed, flicking his chin with his hand, and then sauntered away down a darkening alley.

Victor walked on. He was nearly there. He was trying not to look left or right but he couldn't help it. The scene was so extraordinarily medieval. No, *worse* than medieval.

Groups of women were sitting on stinking heaps of rubbish *inside* their own homes. The women spent their days herein, picking over the rubbish brought into Moqqatam by the men with their donkey carts. The women were looking for rags, paper, glass and metal: anything that could be recycled. Because this was what the Zabaleen did, this was their daily toil, and the sum of their existence: they sifted and recycled the garbage of Cairo, in the City of Garbage.

Pigs and goats scuttled between the tenements. Children played among bales of hospital waste; a toddler had been placed on sacks of refuse. Her smiling face was covered with flies.

Compassion pounded in Victor's heart. He wanted to help these people, shut away in their claustrophobic ghetto. Yet what could he do? He'd heard that some brave charity had opened a clinic here a few years ago, dispensing rudimentary medicine to deal with the wounds and infections the Zabaleen contracted from their repellent environment.

Yet some also said the Zabaleen mistrusted modern medicine and refused help, preferring their traditional solace: religion. It was *God* that made the lives of these people bearable. If the Zabaleen were notorious for their bellicosity, for their sad or drunken desperation, they were also famous for their religious fidelity and devotion. The churches around here were thronged every Saturday, the Coptic Sabbath.

Even now Victor could see two women on a street corner kneeling to kiss the fat gold ring of a lavishly bearded Coptic priest. The black-cloaked priest smiled serenely at the purpling sky, while the women kneeled and kissed his jewellery, like supplicants in front of a Mafia godfather.

A priest? A priest meant a church. He needed to find the Monastery of the Cave.

Ahead, the main road, such as it was, forked left and right. On the left a man was butchering a pig in the gutter. The other lane led to a wall of distant rock. That was surely the route. And yes, through the dust and the bustle of Moqqatam, Victor could make out the arch of a monastic gate: probably the only noble piece of architecture for miles.

Victor Sassoon approached a wooden kiosk erected beside the gate. Inside, a badly shaven man sat scowling on a stool. The interior of the kiosk was decorated with lurid pictures of the Virgin Mary, with farcically huge eyes. Like a seal-pup.

10

'*Salaam,*' Victor said, as he leaned to the open window of the kiosk. 'Ah. *Salaam aleikum*, ah – ah—'

'I speak English.' The middle-aged man spat the words. 'What do you want?'

This was less than friendly.

'I am a visiting scholar from London. I am keen to meet Brother Wasef Qulta, in the monastery.'

A definite sneer lifted the gatekeeper's face.

'Many peoples want to see Brother Qulta. You need permission.'

'I have emailed and telephoned but I have been unable to get a response from the Coptic episcopate. Please. I only need a few minutes of his time. I have come a very long way.'

The gatekeeper shrugged. *No.*

Victor had expected this; and he had a plan.

'Perhaps I can explain better. I am . . . happy to make a very considerable donation to the monastery. I will entrust it with you?'

This was the entirety of Victor's plan: bribe his way in, bribe his way through every problem. It was crude but it was effective in a poor country like Egypt – especially in one of the poorest parts of Cairo. And Victor had plenty of money to spare.

Yet the gatekeeper was unmoved. He gazed at the dollar bills that Victor was discreetly flourishing and this time the sneer was angry. '*La!* No! *Ila jahaim malik!*'

But his anger was interrupted: by shouting. Victor turned. A slender, white-robed adolescent, perhaps a

11

novice monk, was yelling from the steps of the monastery, yelling at no one – and everyone. The shouting was loud and wild. Victor could not translate the words, but the meaning was clear – something terrible had happened. Some kind of crime?

The gatekeeper was already out of the tatty little kiosk, running towards the porch of the monastery; others pursued. Victor took his chance and joined the anxious people. He strained to see over the shoulders and arms. What was going on?

The crowds were too thick. Shameless now, Victor used his stick to lever himself between the onlookers. There! The monastery door was open – and Victor brazenly stepped inside.

It took a second for his eyes to adjust to the darkness within. There was a knot of people in the shadowy hallway: they were pointing at the stone stairs beyond. Victor caught the word 'police' – *shurta* – and then the word *qalita*.

Murder?

A noise came from the stairs, where a makeshift stretcher was being hauled along by sweating hands. The agitated Zabaleen stretcher-bearers lowered their burden, as they pressed towards the door. And then Victor gazed, quite appalled.

The man on the stretcher was pale and stiff. His robes had been wrenched open, revealing his white chest, where he had been stabbed brutally in the heart. The pools of blood were lurid. The crossguard of the dagger, still lodged between the ribs, gave the impression the monk had been stabbed with a crucifix.

Victor recognized the silent face of the victim. It was Brother Wasef Qulta. Maybe the only man who knew the truth about the Sokar Hoard. And now he was dead.

3

Zennor, Cornwall

The year was gone; the party was over. Malcolm Harding wandered, unsteadily, through the detritus of their New Year's Eve merrymaking. He marvelled at how much booze ten people could manage to drink in seven hours.

The vodka bottles clinked at his feet; an entire army of empty beer cans stood to attention in the corner of the sitting room. Jojo was fast asleep on the sofa, cradling a wine bottle in her delicate hands.

He resisted the urge to look up her miniskirt.

She was so beautiful though. Even now, with her make-up mussed, sprawled dissolutely on the leather sofa, she was just lyrically pretty: perfect and blonde and twenty-one years old. Oh yes, he adored Jojo. Ever since they had arrived here on Christmas Eve in this grand and spooky old house, perched between enormous rocks in the wild west of Celtic Cornwall – which

14

was itself the wild west of England – he had tried to hook up with her, in as subtle a fashion as he could manage.

And he had failed. Maybe he hadn't been subtle enough? Maybe he had been too subtle? Maybe he could try again when they were all back at university. The holidays were nearly over. It was January the first, and it was – what? – three a.m.

Three a.m.!

Malcolm sat on a table and swigged from his bottle of beer. Amy Winehouse was still lamenting all the drugs that would kill her from the stereo. The music was so boomingly loud it was probably annoying the dead in Zennor churchyard, half a mile away.

Beer finished, Malcolm wondered vaguely, and groggily, where everyone else had gone. Rufus was presumably in one of the many bedrooms, with their amazing views of the sea, sleeping with Ally, as they had been doing ever since they had shared a bottle of vintage port on Boxing Day. Andrei had crashed with his girlfriend immediately after midnight. Josh and Paul were probably smoking upstairs, or chopping out a line. Or flaked out in their clothes.

Jojo turned over on the sofa, half-stirring, but still asleep. Her little denim skirt rode up as she did. Manfully, Malcolm resisted the temptation to linger; instead, he stood up, walked across the room, then wandered through the *enormous* mess that was the kitchen (they would have to hire some kids from the village to clear this up) and opened the kitchen door to the large gardens that surrounded this great old house, Eagle's Nest.

The night was cold. The garden seemed empty. Then a dark and sudden figure loomed into view.

'*Jesus!*'

Freddy laughed, and casually dropped his glowing cigarette onto the grass, not bothering to crush it underfoot.

'Sorry, old boy. Did I frighten you?'

Malcolm was half-angry, yet half-relieved.

'Yes you did. What the fuck are you doing, skulking out here?'

'Well I came out to chuck up into the bushes, as is traditional on New Year's Eve.' Freddy smirked. 'That last joint was a bit of a serial killer. But the air revived me.'

Now the two of them stood together in the cold, looking out to the distant waves. The house, Malcolm recalled, had once been owned by artists. You could see that its position might inspire.

'So? Do tell. Did you manage to ravish Jojo yet?'

Malcolm sighed.

'Not exactly.'

'Ten days and not even a kiss? This is potentially worse than the Holocaust.'

'Maybe. I'll survive.' Malcolm gazed down, once more taking in the magnificent view, the vast granite rocks and the moonlit fields below, which led down to the Atlantic. 'Anyway, Freddy, mate, why are you still out here? You've been gone hours. It's freezing.'

Freddy put a finger to his lips.

'I wanted to sober up, as I said . . . and then . . .'

'Then what?'

Even in the semi-darkness he could see the sly frown on Freddy Saunderson's face.

'Then I heard something.'

'Duh?'

'Something weird. And I *keep* hearing it.'

'That's Amy Winehouse. She's dead.'

'No. Not the music. Something *else.'*

'But—'

'There it is again! Listen.'

Freddy Saunderson was, for once, not joking. From way up on the moors there came a wild and very loud scream. No, not a scream – a feral chorus of screams; yet distorted and shrieking, mingling with the howl of the wind.

Malcolm felt an urge to step back: to physically retreat.

'Jesus Christ. What is *that*?'

For a moment the noise abated, but then it returned. A distant choir, infantile and hideous. What the hell would make a sound like that?

At last, the noise ceased. The relative silence that followed seemed all the more oppressive. The thudding music in the house; the waves on the rocks below. Silence otherwise. Malcolm felt himself sobering up *very fast.*

Freddy pointed.

'Up there.'

He was surely right. The noise appeared to be coming from the moors *above* them: from Zennor Hill, with its great granite carns and its brace of ruined cottages.

They'd walked around that forbidding landscape the day before, in the driving rain and blustering wind. The hilltop was druidic and malignant, even by day.

Freddy's eyes flashed in the dark.

'Shall we go and have a look?'

'*What?* Are you nuts?'

'No. Are you *gay*?' Freddy laughed. 'Oh come on. Let's *investigate*. It'll be *fun*.'

Malcolm hesitated: quite paralysed. He was seriously unkeen on investigating that noise, but he also didn't want to appear a wuss in front of Freddy; he was wary of Freddy's cruel sense of humour, his lacerating jokes. If he didn't show he was up for this, Freddy might just humiliate him the next time he was feeling a little bored at the union bar.

Malcolm tried to smile.

'All right then. Let's see who's the real gaylord.'

'Excellent.' Freddy rubbed his hands together. 'We'd better get coats and stuff. This is like Enid Blyton, only with ritual murder.'

When they went back into the house, they found that Jojo had disappeared. Probably gone to bed? Malcolm was glad, in a protective sort of way. They turned off the music, grabbed their coats, boots and a pair of torches.

The path up to Zennor Hill began just outside the grounds. It had been treacherous the previous day; in

18

the moonlight it was even trickier. Ferns and brambles dragged at them, tussocks of grass tripped every step. Above them, the imponderable carn glowered, framed by myriad stars.

But the horrible noise had stopped.

For five, ten minutes they ascended the silent, narrow path up the hill. The view of Zennor village below, its Christmas lights twinkling in the wind, was beautiful and sad. Malcolm began to wonder if they had imagined it. Maybe it had been some curious sound effect, perhaps the fierce January wind whistling through the rocks: there were many strange rock formations up here.

But then it came again, and this time it was even worse. The sound curdled the thoughts in his mind. This scathing and animalistic wailing was surely the sound of somebody – or some*thing* – in terrible and angry pain?

Freddy turned, just ahead, his face a blur in the gloom.

'Pretty sure it's coming from the ruined cottage, the big one, Carn Cottage. Is that a fire inside?'

Malcolm desperately wanted to go back now. This had been a daft idea; and yet he was still scared of Freddy's put-downs. He was stuck.

The noise came, and went. This time it was so close it was like an exhalation – you could *feel* the scream on your face.

'There, look!' Freddy pointed his torch beam excitedly. 'Scoundrels!'

Figures. There were people walking away – no, *running away* – down a lane across the top of the hill, dark shapes. How many? It was too difficult to see. Who were they? *What* were they?

Freddy was laughing.

'Do you think it's devil-worshippers? We might be turned into newts!'

The figures were already out of sight, swallowed by the darkness. Had they been spooked by the noise? Or by the fire? Or by Malcolm and Freddy?

Malcolm waved a desperate hand. 'Look. Please. Can't we just go? This is dangerous. Let's just go, please. Call the cops.'

His protestations were futile; Freddy simply vaulted the low garden wall of the half-ruined cottage, and ran across the garden; he was followed by Malcolm, much less briskly.

As they neared the cottage, Malcolm could see there was indeed a fire burning inside the building. And it was a large fire, too, casting eerie orange shadows on the windows. The heat from within was palpable in the cold winter air.

'Freddy – wait – don't—'

It was too late. His friend was kicking at the old door; even as the infernal shrieking went on, and on.

'C'mon – open up!' Freddy laughed, 'Open up, in the name of all that's holy!' Now Freddy stepped back and kicked even harder at the splintering door, and at last it succumbed. The lock snapped and the old door swung open, revealing a roar of heat and howls and *things*, strange black burning shapes, racing out at them, fleeing and burning—

A flaming creature leapt at Malcolm's face, and its claws sank deep. Malcolm's scream echoed down from the lonely carn, carried on the freezing wind.

4

La Bodega bistro, Zamalek, Cairo

Victor Sassoon sat in a darkened corner of the darkened bar, cradling a glass of Scotch and water, his fourth of the afternoon, and maybe his fortieth of the last four days. It was his last afternoon in Cairo. The whisky tasted like the bitter herbs of Seder: the taste of defeat.

The monk was dead. The Sokar Hoard, if it had ever existed, would probably never be found. His one last hope, that he might meet Albert Hanna, was about to come to nothing.

Hanna was a Coptic antiquities dealer. He was also notorious for his serpentine skills in fulfilling the desires of museum curators and billionaire collectors across the globe. The mummy of a concubine of a Rammeside Pharaoh? *But of course*. An intact and entire Fayum portrait rescued from the black mud of Antinopolis? *Please allow me*.

His methods were obscure, and probably illegal, but

he got results. Albert Hanna knew every rumour of every new find from every sandy corner of Egypt. If anyone knew anything about the truth of the latest gossip – the whispers of the Sokar Hoard that had brought Sassoon to the polluted streets of the Egyptian capital – it would be Hanna.

But Hanna was an elusive quarry. He didn't answer his phone; he didn't answer emails; like many Christian businesses, his office in central Cairo was closed because of the recent and ongoing riots.

So, La Bodega bistro was Sassoon's rather desperate and concluding bid. Many of Cairo's antiquities dealers were middle-class Copts like Hanna, and nearly all of them liked to drink discreetly – and many of them were regulars at the Bodega, not least because it was increasingly *dangerous* to drink everywhere else. Some of the bars near the Coptic quarter were getting trashed and gutted by Islamists. Christian grocers who still dared to sell beer were being forcibly closed.

Pensively, Sassoon inhaled the aroma of his Scotch, and remembered a time when it had been much easier to drink in this city. He remembered drinking good German beer in Shepheard's Hotel, with that keen young American Egyptologist, Ryan Harper.

Victor wondered what had happened to Harper. But then, he wondered that about many people these days. Friends died like flies when you reached your seventies, as if there was an Old Testament plague, the Great Pestilence of Egypt. Now, which book of the Bible was that?

His aged thoughts were wandering, again. Sassoon sipped the solacing bitterness of his Johnnie Walker, walked to the heavy velvet curtains, and gazed down at Zamalek.

The street outside was a parodic vision of its own history: this part of Cairo, situated on an island in the Nile, had been built in the early twentieth century as a place of European elegance, with boulevards and plane trees, and chic apartment blocks – even a palace for Princess Eugenie, wife of Napoleon III. But now all the trees had been chopped down, the apartment blocks had been turned into tatty shops and crowded flats, and the traffic was, of course, endless and polluting.

Yes, the smoke and scuzz of Cairo disgusted Sassoon. It was time to go home, and to give up. It was never going to happen; it had all been a foolish dream.

'You can positively *smell* the smoke from the TV centre. *N'est ce pas?*'

Sassoon swivelled, letting the velvet curtains fall.

Standing behind him was a slightly paunchy man in his mid-forties, wearing a perfect yet worn Savile Row suit, with a beautiful faded Milanese silk tie, and a moustache that curved down to a goatee.

It was Albert Hanna.

The man was unmistakeable. Sassoon had seen this face in Egyptological websites. It was his first stroke of luck: five tedious days of patient waiting had paid off. At the very last moment.

'The Islamic students, in their vulgar fury, are burning

everything. One can only pray that the Sphinx is inflammable.' The man sighed, and pulled himself a seat. 'You know the Arabic name for the Sphinx, Mister Sassoon? It is *Abu al-Hol*, the Father of Terror.' The dealer smiled, politely. 'And yes, of course I know who you are. You are quite famous.'

Sassoon slumped into his own chair, and set down his Scotch. He realized his demeanour probably seemed defeated, yet inside he was secretly delighted.

'I also know, Mr Sassoon, that you have been searching for me. My apologies if my delay in contacting you seems rude: I have been distracted by the troubles. Soon the fundamentalists may make it impossible for us Copts to *live*, let alone *drink*.' Hanna swirled his glass of cognac. 'You know Egypt was once renowned for its wines? Tutankhamun was buried with several jars of a fine dry white. But now, ahhh, *où sont les vins d'antan?*'

He stroked his dyed goatee, which had indubitably been dyed pitch-black, and added, 'There is no hope for us, there is no hope for the drinkers, for the Copts. But we will stay here anyway! We are the true descendants of ancient Egypt, after all. Now tell me. Why are you in Egypt? A famous Anglo-Jewish scholar like you, visiting Egypt amidst this turmoil, when Tahrir is engulfed in flames? Why do you want to talk to me?'

This was Victor's chance. 'The Sokar Hoard.'

Hanna looked at Victor, darkly, and his eyes flashed with thought. 'Why did you not mention this in your emails? I might have responded sooner.'

'Because . . .' Victor paused. 'Because this is a delicate issue. I know there are severe laws regarding antiquities. If the Sokar Hoard exists it belongs to the Egyptian state and people.'

'You were being discreet? That is well advised.' Hanna picked up his balloon glass of cognac and swirled it again. 'So. The Sokar Hoard. Hmm. The rumours are ripe, are they not? Exuding a heady perfume of promise? Just imagine: a cache of ancient documents that make Nag Hammadi look like . . .' Hanna closed his small and sparkling brown eyes while he summoned the words '. . . like a cheap photocopy of *Harold Potter and the Prisoner of Azkaban*. Yes, the Sokar Hoard, if it exists, would be an unexampled prize. If you could decipher such a thing, this would eclipse your spectacular work on the Dead Sea Scrolls. You would finally have your statue in the sunlit plaza of greatness, for pigeons to soil.'

Was he trying to insult? Or merely provoke? Sassoon didn't care. 'I'm not hunting for academic glory, Mr Hanna. As I understand it, the Sokar Hoard contains evidence that alters our perception of Jewish history. The exploration of Jewish history and theology has been my life's calling. As such, if there is a deeper truth, I want to know it – before . . .'

'It is too late?'

'What do you know, Mr Hanna?'

'Call me Albert. Like the German–English prince. You know he used to couple with Queen Victoria three or four times a day? It is a surprise she looks so grumpy in her photos.'

26

'Please. What do you know of the Sokar Hoard?'

Hanna smiled his moist and thoughtful smile. 'First tell me what *you* know of the Hoard.'

Victor Sassoon finished his whisky, and impatiently recounted his own story. 'It all derives from Wasef Qulta. Brother Wasef Qulta was something of a fixture in circles of Egyptology and biblical history. For instance he corresponded, occasionally, with a colleague of mine in London, a professor at the Flinders Petrie collection.'

'Ah yes, one of the finest, the Flinders Petrie, a very excellent museum – I always loved that adorable faience cat from Amarna. I have sold similar.'

'Last month my London friend got a rather emotional email from Qulta. Telling him that the Coptic church was in possession of an astonishing discovery of crucial early Christian texts which had been unearthed in Middle Egypt. Qulta claimed the texts were comparable to the Dead Sea Scrolls or the Oxyrhynchus papyri: maybe even more important, more exciting. My friend told others, and the rumours and speculations spread.'

'Indeed. I have also heard these rumours. The late Wasef Qulta started quite a *fracas.*'

'A week later Qulta emailed again. He told my friend the Coptic church was keeping the Hoard close and hidden, and that he was being told to say no more, and stay silent. And then the emails stopped.'

Hanna was quiet.

Victor concluded, 'I felt I had no choice but to come

to Cairo and seek out Qulta for myself. Last week I went to the Monastery of the Cave in Moqqatam.'

'You went alone to Moqqatam?'

'Yes.'

Hanna tittered. A couple of ex-pats – white businessmen – glanced over. 'Well, well. How did you deal with the Zabaleen, Mr Sassoon? Did you fight them off with your walking stick?'

'Sorry?'

'The Zabaleen are perfectly mad. The poorest of our Coptic brethren. They brawl and they fornicate and they live in their palaces of swine and rubbish. They say life there is getting worse, the madness and the diseases, the mental afflictions, the suicides, all that horrible trash.'

'I saw Qulta. I saw his body. *I know he was murdered*.'

Hanna stroked his goatee. Patiently waiting, like a cat that is confident of being fed.

Victor went on, 'Do you know *why* he was killed, Mr Hanna? Albert? I *know* you have intimate connections across Coptic society. Was the Hoard stolen, is that why he was killed? Was it a violent robbery? The papers say nothing.'

The ex-pat white men were telling coarse jokes; and chortling.

At last Hanna spoke, leaning close. 'Ah, but Mr Sassoon, does the Hoard even exist? What can I say? I can barely speak. My throat is quite dry. Parched as the Qattara Depression.' Hanna looked at his empty glass, then at Victor.

28

The message was clear. Sassoon ordered the most expensive cognac for his companion.

Hanna accepted the glass, and sniffed the liquor, and tasted it with a wince of pleasure. Then he gazed around the quiet old bar. 'God bless the old Bodega. One of the very last oases of civilization in Cairo,' he said. 'You know the British Satanist Aleister Crowley had his famous thelemic revelation here?'

'In 1904, the Book of the Law.'

'Quite so! You really are the scholar of your reputation. Crowley's wife saw the so-called stele of revealing, the stele of Ankh-ef-en-Khonsu, in the Bulaq Museum.'

'Item number 666.'

'Then she began raving, and he repaired to his apartment, probably in this building, and had his moment of intimacy with the divine, his theophany – or perhaps some more opium? Crowley was so very fond of opium. My grandfather knew him. Apparently he liked to be sodomised by Nubians. But this is true of many.'

'I don't have much *time*, Mr Hanna. Please tell me: how much do you know about Qulta and the Sokar Hoard? I can pay, and I have a lot of money.'

The correct switch had evidently been thrown. Hanna's evasive smile disappeared and he gazed directly at Sassoon. 'Five thousand dollars and I will tell you all I know.'

Sassoon didn't even bother to haggle. The sum was large, but he was too old and tired, and too eager and

29

excited, to haggle. And he had enough money. A life-time's savings.

'I have it here. In cash.' He reached in his blazer pocket, opened his calfskin wallet and took out a wad of new, one-hundred dollar bills. He briskly counted out twenty notes and arranged them in a neat and tempting stack. 'Two thousand now. Three thousand if your assistance is as valuable as I hope.'

Benjamin Franklin stared at the ceiling.

Hanna snatched up the notes and thrust them in his pocket, his expression businesslike.

'From what I understand, Monsieur Sassoon – and this may or may not be true, but my half-brother is quite senior in the Coptic church, and he knew Qulta – yes, the Sokar Hoard *does* exist. And yes the documents are said to be, potentially, a revelation. Some of them are in French and Arabic and quite legible, but the oldest, most crucial and, unfortunately, most incomprehensible, documents are in Akhmimic. Qulta was a scholar of Akhmimic, so it was hoped he could translate these most opaque Coptic documents. And so he was allowed to take the Hoard to his monastery in Moqqatam for further scrutiny.'

'That's why he was killed, someone stole it? Theref—'

'Wait.' Hanna frowned. 'Brother Qulta's indiscretion did not meet with the approval of his superiors. The emails to your friend, the rumours he allowed to spread – they were attracting unwelcome attention. He was ordered to shut his foolish mouth.'

'The Hoard?'

'Furthermore . . . when the latest *troubles* began in Cairo, the riots, the strife, the threats against Coptic communities, the Pope himself – our own Coptic pope – decided that the Hoard should be taken somewhere safer. So it is alleged.'

'But where? Where did it go?'

The bar was getting even darker, as the winter evening finally descended on Cairo's grimy streets. Hanna shook his head gravely. 'Who can say? These things are occult. But I have heard this: a few days before his death, Brother Qulta took a trip to the Monastery of St Anthony.'

'The oldest monastery! By the Red Sea. Yes. Of course. Remote, untouched. A perfect place to keep a treasure.'

'And a tiresome journey across the eastern sands. Why did Qulta do that? Why do that if not for some serious reason? He must have taken the Hoard with him, to hand it over. That is what I believe.'

Sassoon was confused. 'But if the Hoard was not in Qulta's possession, why was he killed? You mean it wasn't a robbery?'

Hanna picked up his glass, and swirled the cognac. 'Perhaps he was killed because of what he knew, perhaps because of what he said. Perhaps he was secretly canoodling with the belly-dancer mistress of a major-general in Heliopolis. It is a mystery. And there it is. *C'est tout.* Would you like something else while we are? Here. Look. I have a precious jar of Mummy Violet.' Like a cardsharp, Hanna flourished a small silvery, seemingly antique steel jar from a pocket of his suit jacket, and carefully unscrewed the top. 'It is a pigment used by painters, made from the decayed corpses of the Egyptian dead, from mummies, *mummiya*, hence its name: Mummy Violet. I believe the Pre-Raphaelite artists were very fond of it, the hue it offers is intense, though of course some find the concept, *eheu*, politically incorrect, and a touch Hitlerite, like those lampshades. Consequently it is very rare, I can sell it for two thousand US dollars – a pigment made from the desiccated flesh of the ancient dead – imagine what your exciting London artists could do with that!'

Sassoon stood up. He had his information.

Hanna raised a hand, looking up at him. 'Please, Monsieur Sassoon, I did not wish to offend. The Jews are a great people, and I know you are a great believer, as well as a great scholar. Allow me to say one more thing.'

'What?' Sassoon was impatient to get going.

'Mr Sassoon, please be careful.'

'You mean it is dangerous? The journey?'

'No. Yes. A little. But it is more that . . . you might be careful of what you wish for. My half-brother told me that when he saw Qulta . . .' Hanna's face was almost invisible, the velvet-draped bar was now so dark. 'The poor monk was quite deranged. It seems the contents of the Hoard are, in some form, sincerely devastating. Really quite calamitous.'

But Sassoon didn't care to listen; he was already

walking to the door. The idea had entirely seized him with its romance, its intense biblicality. To find his prize, his promised treasure, he had to cross the Egyptian wilderness, to the very shores of the Red Sea.

Like Moses.

5

The Monastery of St Anthony, the Red Sea, Egypt

It took Sassoon two days to find a taxi driver who was willing to make the journey. The driver who finally agreed was fifty, and shifty, and hungry, and desperate, and he said he would charge Sassoon five hundred dollars for the job. He spoke a slangy Arabic so accented it sounded like a different language, but Sassoon certainly understood the figure '500' when the man wrote it with a stubby pencil on his tattered map of Egypt.

They left at dawn to avoid the rush hour but got caught in traffic anyway. It took two hours for them to crawl out of the final dreary suburbs of Cairo, past the last shuttered Coptic grocer, with its defaced sign advertising Stella beer; and then they headed into the grey austerity of the Eastern Desert, the rolling dunes and stony flats, stretched out beneath an overcast sky.

The driver played loud quartertoned Arab music

all the way, music that sent Sassoon half crazy. It felt like the music of delirium. But he was also glad that he didn't have to talk to the driver. Talking would be pointless anyway: they couldn't understand each other.

Six hours later they attained the outskirts of Suez, and the driver made an extensive detour, avoiding the centre of the city entirely. Sassoon guessed why: the Al Jazeera English news had told him last night. Central Suez was in uproar. Riots were wracking the city, several youths had died and, even worse somehow, several people had been *blinded* by plastic bullets aimed deliberately at their eyes. The televised image of one protestor, his sockets empty yet filled with blood, had stayed with Sassoon for half the night.

The hours droned past. The wailing music droned on. The desert became emptier and dustier. It was now clear they weren't going to make it in a day, so the driver pulled into a scruffy truckstop with a village attached.

What looked from the distance like a public lavatory turned out to be their designated resting place. A 'hotel' with cracked windows, five rusting beds, and one shared and fetid bathroom. Sassoon drank whisky, alone, in his bare cement room, to force himself to sleep. The mosquitoes danced around his face, drunkenly, as he nodded out.

Morning cracked blue. The sun of the desert had won. And Sassoon's spirits rose as the driver slowed, and turned the music down, and Sassoon caught his first glimpse of the Monastery of St Anthony, lost in the fathomless depths of the desert.

It looked enchanting: a complex of spires and tiled arches and archaic chapels, tucked into a fold of red desert rocks. This was it, the oldest monastery in the world, founded by St Anthony in 250 AD.

The car stopped; Victor disembarked. '*Shukran*,' he said, handing over the dollars.

The driver took the cash, shrugged, gave Victor a faint smile of pity; then he turned on the hollering music, and sped away.

Hoisting his heavy bags, Victor stumbled across the road and under the arch. At once he was engulfed by the silence, the silence of silent worship, of punitive adoration, the silence of the endless Red Sea sun.

And then a monk came out from a darkened chamber, squinting at this sweating old man in his ludicrous blazer with his walking stick, and the young monk smiled quietly and said, in accented English, 'Hi, I am Brother Basili. Andrew Basili. This way please. You are a pilgrim? You can stay here, no worries. There are no other visitors, they're all too scared of the troubles. You must be pretty brave. This way. Over here. Guess you'll want some refreshment? You are in time for breakfast.'

Breakfast turned out to be austere plates of olives and flatbread, and carafes of water, consumed at a long table in the refectory in almost total silence, apart from a monk intoning the psalms.

During the morning Victor was left to do as he pleased. In the central courtyard, the sun blazed. The monastery was mute. One youthful monk was hurrying about his business, keeping to the shade of the stumpy colonnades.

Victor approached. '*Salaam—*'

But the monk shook his head. When Victor tried again, the young monk blushed and fled.

Victor sat on a stone bench, rubbed his aching chest and read his guidebook.

'The body of St Justus the monk is kept in a passage by the Church of the Apostles . . .'

In the afternoon he located the monastery library, domed and white, and delicately frescoed with images. A reverential hush pervaded the eight-hundred-year-old room: it felt wrong to talk. But Victor had to try, and Brother Andrew Basili was at the other end of the library, immersed in at least three open books.

'Hello,' said Victor.

Basili's smile was brief and a little cold. He evidently didn't want to be interrupted. But Victor had to try.

'This is a fine library.'

Basili's nod was terse. 'Used to be better. Then the Bedouins raided it, in the eighteenth century. They burned many of our volumes as cooking fuel.'

Victor listened, finally placing the accent. *Australian.* This was not unexpected; Sassoon knew that many young men from the Coptic Diaspora – in Australia, Canada, America – were returning to Egypt to renew their church, in defiance of the troubles and the hostilities. Many Coptic monasteries were, paradoxically, flourishing for the first time in centuries.

'You're from Sydney?'

'Nah. Brissie.' Basili sighed. 'Now, sorry, if you'll excuse me, I've got my studies.'

Supper was the same as breakfast, apart from a single beaker of vinegary wine.

The next day it became apparent that no one was going to speak to Victor, not properly, not *ever*. Most of the monks shrank at his approach. The few who did linger were so shy and kind and virginal it was emotionally impossible to ask about the Sokar Hoard. The only time he did mention the terrible phrase, to an elderly, English-speaking monk from Port Said, the man scowled and stalked away.

As the days passed and shortened in their repetitiveness, their mesmerizing and beautiful dullness, Victor found himself giving up. Wandering out of the monastery gate, into the sunburned desert, he sat under the thorn trees, and stared at his absurd leather shoes and his absurd twill trousers and he felt like a fraud, just a dying and childless narcissist. Maybe he was seeking mere glory, and he deserved to fail. Maybe it was all just spiritual vanity.

On the fifth day Victor was woken as usual by a softly tolling bell, even before the darkness had dispelled. Opening the thin cotton curtain, he gazed at the first tinge of the sun, still hiding behind Sinai, just a roseate rumour at the dark edge of heaven.

'The heavens declare the glory of God; and the firmament showeth His handiwork.'

Crossing the silent square at the centre of the monastery, Victor creaked open the door to the church and joined the thrumming tranquil hubbub of the monks in their daily Matins: the *Agbeia*.

'Khen efran em-efiout, nem Epshiri, nem Piepnevma ethowab ounouti en-owoat.'

The pew was painful to sit in for so long. Victor shifted and listened. The hour of prayer passed slowly, and hypnotically. And then the last of the prayer was intoned.

'Doxa Patri, ke Eyo kai Agio epnevmati ounouti en-owoat. Amin.'

The words were bewildering, and lovely, in their strangeness, their syncretism. You could hear all of religious history in these Coptic words: maybe a touch of Aramaic, more than a hint of Greek, and certainly the very syllables of ancient Egyptian – it was like a Pharaoh sitting up in his tomb, and turning, in a nightmare, and talking to Victor. Blood seeping from his decaying mouth.

A sudden coldness swept up his limbs, and into his heart, and Victor fell to the floor.

Darkness. Darkness.

And the light shineth in darkness; and the darkness comprehended it not.

The next thing he realized, he was in some kind of kitchen staring at the kindly young faces of half a dozen monks. They were daubing his forehead with water.

'I . . . What happened?'

'You fainted.' It was Andrew Basili. 'Are ya OK? We can get a doctor . . . in a day or so.'

'I am so very sorry,' Victor said. He was acutely embarrassed, as if he had publicly soiled himself. 'I am an old fool. I shouldn't have come. I am so sorry.'

The other monks dispersed, black cloaks whispering, leaving him alone with Brother Andrew. The sun was up now.

'So, why did you come?'

'I came to find out something. Something very important to me. I want to know about Brother Wasef Qulta. A monk murdered in Cairo. He came here, about two weeks ago. And I want to know why.'

Andrew Basili said nothing. For a long, long time. Then he nodded. 'Look, I don't really know anything about that stuff. Sorry. If you are feeling better, maybe you should go back to Cairo?'

Once more, silence filled the sparse monastic kitchen.

In his desperation, Victor Sassoon decided to do something quite terrible. Something he had never done before in his life.

'Brother Basili, the reason I ask all this is that I believe Brother Qulta was carrying documents which relate to the history of my Jewish faith. I am a scholar of this area. The texts may be written in a language few can understand. I may be one of those few.'

Brother Andrew said nothing. Victor went on,

'The history of my faith is very important to me. Because . . . you see . . .' Very slowly, Victor Sassoon pulled up the cuff of his blazer, unbuttoned his shirt and revealed the markings to the Australian.

The monk's eyes widened. He gazed at the small, faded tattoo on Victor's left arm. 'You were in the *camps*?'

Victor nodded, suppressing the fierce rush of shame. How could he use this as blackmail, as emotional bribery? It was the worst of sins: the Shoah as a bargaining device.

But he didn't care.

'Auschwitz. I was a tiny boy, one of the last, from Holland, we were taken there in 1944, but the Russians saved us. Then . . . well, we had a British side to the family, they took me in after the war. My mother and father died in the . . . in the camp. All my Dutch family. They died. That's when I resolved to keep my faith alive, my Jewishness.'

The ensuing silence was different. Brother Basili sighed, rubbed his face, shook his handsome young head. Then he pulled up his own wooden chair and sat next to Victor. For a moment, Basili stared at the wall.

Victor could see the confusion in his profile. Finally, Basili spoke. 'I guess there is no harm in telling you what I know. 'Cause I don't know much.' He made a weary gesture. 'Brother Qulta visited his mentor. Brother Kelada. A scholar, an anchorite. Qulta had documents on him, I have no idea what they said, I know they were old and valuable.'

'How valuable?'

Basili turned, and his young face flushed with a tiny hint of pride.

'Priceless! The Coptic church is the source of everything. We are the original church! The church founded by St Mark the Evangelist. The church of the gospel of St John.' He shook his head, then continued, with real passion. 'Even the very oldest copy of the Bible in the world is Coptic – the Codex Sinaiticus!'

Victor nodded.

'I know the story. Stolen by a German from St Katherine's in Sinai. Then given by Stalin to the British, yes?'

'Yes!' Basili said. 'The Brits keep it in London, but it's *ours*. We won't let *that* happen again. Whatever these documents are, I am pretty sure we shall keep them. God has entrusted us to be the curators of the Christian faith, of the original church.'

'So where *are* the documents now?'

Basili frowned. 'Sohag, I think? Does it matter? Brother Kelada didn't want them here, I don't know why. So he told Qulta to take them back where they came from, where they were found – some cave in the desert. That's what I heard. That's all I know.'

Again, the frustration returned, but also the excitement. Sohag, *Middle Egypt*. The Red Monastery, or the White, or the Monastery of the Martyrs, the Monastery of the Seven Mountains. Which? But it made sense. Sohag was not far from Nag Hammadi, where the Gnostic gospels were found.

'Where in Sohag? There are many monasteries. Please let me speak to Brother Kelada. He can tell me.'

The Australian monk shook his head. 'Impossible.'

'What?'

'He died three days ago.'

'But how?'

Basili looked faintly contemptuous.

'We had to bury him outside, near the trees. Suicide is the worst of sins.'

6

Carnkie, Cornwall

The walk to the Methodist chapel for her mother's funeral took Karen Trevithick past grey, pinched, tin-miners' houses that probably once belonged to her extended family. She was descended from generations of Cornish tinners. And Cornish wreckers, smugglers and fishermen, for that matter.

Cornwall was her homeland, this was her home. Carnkie was the hearth of that home.

Yet she didn't feel at home. Not at all.

'All right, Karen, my dear? So sorry to hear about Mavis.'

'Yes, thank you.'

'How is the littl'un?'

'Ellie is OK, staying with Julie, my cousin's wife in London – they have kids.'

'Ah yes, nice for her to have playmates. 'Specially now.'

'Yes. Yes it is.'

Who was this polite elderly Cornish gentleman who had stopped her in the street? Karen ransacked her memory. She couldn't place him: some distant third cousin? A friend of her mother's? The man smiled at her, kind and gracious, and laid a consoling hand on her elbow. She thanked the nice old gent once again, and walked on, around the drizzly corner, to the chapel, a dour grey granite pile, a building of deliberate and penitent ugliness.

Karen's mother, a widow since her fifties, had returned to this old village, Carnkie, a few years back: retreating from an increasingly lonely London to the emotional comforts of Cornwall.

At the time, Karen had confessed mixed feelings about this. She was glad her mum was retiring to the country she loved, but she was selfishly sad her mother was leaving as that meant less free childcare for Ellie; she couldn't work out why her mother chose Carnkie of all places, even if it was the ancestral hamlet.

Much of Cornwall was lovely, from the sheltered yachting harbours and languid creeks of the south, to the rawly beautiful cliff-and-thrift coasts of the north; but Carnkie was in the brutal, ugly *middle* of Cornwall, a place of wind-scraped moorland – and dormant, decaying mining townships. Like Carnkie.

The mourners were gathered at the gate that led to the chapel door.

'Hello Karen.'

'So sad, so very sad. So young as well.'

'I tell 'ee, sixty-two?'

Barely listening, Karen took one last look at the view. A typical Cornish fog, half-drizzle, half-mist, was rolling down from old Carn Brea, shrouding the rocky moorland above the village. It murked between the granite-built tin-mine stacks, making them look, even more than usual, like classical ruins.

Karen turned, and entered. The interior of the chapel was notably better than the façade: it was airy and spacious. But the spaciousness underlined the fact there were so few people here. At least she could see her cousin Alan at the front, in a pew; he saw her, too, and waved her over.

'All right, Kaz?'

'Yes,' she sighed, sitting down next to her cousin. 'Fine. I mean. *Ish.*'

Apart from Alan there were maybe ten or eleven people, their paltry numbers exaggerated by the vastness of the chapel. This was a place built for hundreds of lustily singing miners and their ruddy-faced wives and many, many kids, a place built at the height of the tinning boom in the nineteenth century, when places like Carnkie were churning out more copper and tin than anywhere else on earth, when places like Redruth, Carnkie and St Just were allegedly the richest square miles on the planet, though all the real money disappeared to London with the owners and the landlords.

Now it was all dead. The chapels were empty, the mines were closed, the people were old and the children had gone. And now even her mother had been taken and swallowed by the mizzle, reducing her immediate family to just two people: herself and her six-year-old daughter.

She realized, with a kind of surprise, that she was crying.

'Hey now, come on.' Alan handed her a tissue.

'Sorry. Look at me. Train wreck.'

'No need to apologize. Just remember, you're nearly through. The crem is usually the worst bit.'

'I'm glad we did it first.'

'Yes.'

The cremation had been yesterday: this was the service. Karen already had her mother's ashes in her car, sealed in a faintly farcical pot, itself in a supermarket carrier bag. She had no idea what to do with them. Scatter them at sea? But her mother had distrusted the sea. Like many older Cornish people she had never even learned to swim, even though she lived in a peninsula surrounded by the churning Atlantic.

Where then? Up on Carn Brea, next to the castle? That was better – the view across to St Agnes Beacon, and the sea beyond, was immense and glorious; but the grieving wind hardly ever stopped.

Incongruously, Karen considered the disaster that might ensue if she scattered the ashes in a typical blowy Carn Brea morning.

'We are gathered here to celebrate the life of Mavis Trevithick.'

The vicar was doing his thing. Karen barely listened.

She imagined her mother's reaction to the news that her mortal remains had been ritually distributed across a bank of Lidl shopping trolleys.

She'd surely have laughed. Like many Cornish people, her mum had possessed, or inherited, a wry and salty sense of humour: that kind of wit was the only way to deal with tough lives down the mines, or on bitter moortop farms.

'Can we all sing Hymn 72, "Abide with Me"?'

Oh God. *'Abide with Me'*? Karen was entirely immune to religion; she believed none of it – that's why she'd left Alan to arrange the service – but this one hymn always got her. Something in the tune – it mined her soul, found the motherlode of human grief, every time.

The organ hummed, the frail voices joined in. Karen put the scrunched-up tissue in her fist to her trembling mouth and closed her eyes. Hard.

> *Abide with me; fast falls the eventide;*
> *The darkness deepens; Lord with me abide.*
> *When other helpers fail and comforts flee,*
> *Help of the helpless, O abide with me.*

It didn't work, the tears were falling lavishly now. Along with the memories of her mum, before Dad died, making jokes and pasties, with flour on her fingers, when everyone was alive, when she had cousins and uncles and parents, but so many were gone, all gone—

I fear no foe, with Thee at hand to bless;
Ills have no weight, and tears no bitterness.
Where is death's sting? Where, grave, thy victory?
I triumph still, if Thou abide with me.

Karen stifled her sobs. If only she could believe that was true, that there was something beyond, a loving God for all, a brother for the lonely, a father for the orphaned, an embracing and eternal Lord, gathering the anguished. But whatever Nonconformist fire had once filled this big ugly chapel was long ago extinguished; all the tin was mined out. *She* certainly hadn't inherited any faith.

The grave was victorious, after all. And yes, death stung.

Thankfully, the next hymns were more bearable. A few prayers were mumbled, the vicar talked of Mavis's vivacity and gardening. Then everyone – all twelve or so of them – filed out of the chapel, and repaired to her Uncle Ken's house for Cornish bread, saffron cakes and pots and pots of tea, thick protection against the cold and drizzle outside. There was no alcohol. The Nonconformist tradition of teetotalism lived on, even as the religion itself had expired.

At three o'clock Karen got a call. She stepped out of her uncle's front room into the hall to take it. The number flashing on her phone was unknown.

'Hello?'

'Karen?'

'Hello – is this . . .? Is this . . .?'

'Yes. Sally Pascoe. Your second cousin! Remember?'

'Sally!'

Karen was genuinely pleased to hear her voice, and also a little perplexed. She and Sally had been great friends as kids, during those childhood Cornish holidays they spent hours hopscotching in Trelissick or building sandcastles at Hayle. Later on, their adult lives had diverged, yet continued in parallel: Karen had become a detective chief inspector in London, Sally a policewoman; but she had stayed in Cornwall. Busy careers and lively kids meant they hadn't met in years.

'Karen, I'm so sorry I couldn't make your mum's . . . you know. So sorry.'

'Sal, it's OK.'

'But work is, well, it's very busy. I'm sure it's a lot more hectic up in London, but we have crimes down here too.'

'Don't worry. It's fine.'

'Anyway I just wondered if you might . . . well, I mean, you have quite a reputation in London, as a DCI . . . I wondered if you . . .'

'Sally, spit it out!'

'Do you want to drive over to Zennor, maybe later, or tomorrow? I mean, if you have the chance, it might, uh, distract you. You see, we have a strange case, a cottage on the hill.'

'I can come over right now. To be honest I'd like an excuse. The funeral was . . . intense. And now my Uncle Ken is trying to overdose me with scones.'

Sally laughed gently. 'We like our carbohydrates down here.'

'I'm on my way. Meet you there in forty minutes?'

The drive took less than forty minutes. Karen drove fast, with her mum in the back, in a carrier bag. She parked at Zennor church and followed the winding path up to the hill to the ruined cottage. Her destination was obvious: there were two police Range Rovers parked next to the derelict building, their yellow-and-blue insignia garishly conspicuous on top of the grey-green, stony hill. The drizzle had abated but the January wind was keen.

A constable greeted her. 'You must be DI Pascoe's friend?' He opened the door of the cottage.

Karen stepped inside. Her reaction was reflexive. *'Oh my God!'*

7

Sohag, Egypt

Victor Sassoon saw the smoke of the second small bomb from his hotel window. The fifteenth-floor balcony of his hideous 1970s concrete tower gazed across the Nile, from the dense and frazzled streets of Muslim Sohag, to the smaller, ancient, more Coptic, west-bank town of Akhmim. The smoke from this latest bomb rose like a long-stemmed lotus flower above the dense medieval streets.

Then came the sirens, harsh and plaintive in the noonday heat. Had the Muslims attacked the Copts again? Or was it the Copts attacking the Muslims in return? The only thing anyone knew for sure was that the violence was worsening. The papers had informed him this morning that the Zabaleen were also rioting in Cairo. Egypt was truly roiled.

Yet this very morning the poor people from the countryside had tethered their shallow boats to gather reeds from the side of the Nile, much as they must have done in Pharaonic times. This was Egypt, turbulent and tumultuous, and also unchanging.

Turning from the balcony, Sassoon sat on his bed and unscrewed his precious bottle of Johnnie Walker Red Label and filled a tooth mug with half an inch, slugging it in one go. It gave him courage for the day ahead, and it dulled the pain. The pain in his lungs and in his legs; and in his heart.

Lifting up the bottle, Sassoon examined the liquor that remained. Five inches maybe. And it would be hard to buy more: Sohag was a dry city. Islamist.

Everything was running out. Time and whisky, and life.

He rose, buttoned his blazer and picked up his stick. In the street he hailed an old, pale blue fifties Ford taxi and got in the back seat to negotiate the day. The driver, Walid, spoke a little English and asked Victor if he knew his brother Anwar who lived in Manchester and worked in a car showroom.

Victor confessed that he had never met Anwar, despite living in the same country. Walid seemed very disappointed by this, until Victor told him what he wanted: to be driven to all the nearby ancient Coptic monasteries, for the next two days; and then Victor added that he would pay a hundred dollars for his time and gasoline.

This was an absurdly generous offer, but Victor was infinitely beyond caring. He had tens of thousands of dollars in his account – the product of a lifetime of academic salaries and scholarly frugality – and he had no family. What better use could he find for the money than discovering a great and final truth?

But he needed to be quick. The pain in his lungs was like a murderer had stabbed a sharpened crucifix in his chest.

'Please.' Victor gestured at the donkey cart blocking their way. 'Let's go.'

Walid smiled a tobacco-stained smile and slammed his horn, frightening the donkey, as they screeched out into the Sohag traffic.

They talked about the bomb as they made their slow way through the chaos of trucks and cabs, and old Mercedes minibuses full of Egyptian matrons, in vividly coloured headscarves.

'Much bad,' said Walid. 'Very bad. Soon they will make the Coptic leave Egypt. Sadat, Mubarak, they protect the Copt. But now . . . No good. No good.' He made a chopping gesture with his hand.

Sassoon gazed at the rear-view mirror, and the absence of dangling prayer-beads. 'You are a Christian?'

'La.' Walid shook his head and ignited his third Cleopatra-brand cigarette of the morning. 'Muslim. But I having many Coptic friend. We are all Egyptian, all People of the Book. The bad men want to . . . make hate. You smoke?'

Victor demurred. He had once been a smoker. Forty years a smoker, then he'd stopped. Evidently he had given up too late: the lung cancer was very advanced. He listened placidly as Walid smoked and sighed and cursed and swore at the politicians and chattered away about his eight children, and his annoying new wife, until at last they reached the desert.

The transition was sudden, as always in Middle and Upper Egypt. The fertile valley of the Nile was a vivid and glorious sash of green across the ochre of the Saharan wilderness, but when the desert began it did so with a painful severity: in a second one travelled from emerald to grey, or from city to nothingness.

Ahead of them, in the first desert sands, was the White Monastery. In truth it looked quite unprepossessing, like an ugly and very humble pile of mud bricks and cracked pillars, yet it was one of the oldest church buildings in the world.

'I wait here. You take time. Plenty time.' Walid parked, with a brisk spin of the wheel, at the steel gates of the monastery complex.

Victor ejected himself from the taxi, his chest and his knees complaining at the effort. Two bored-looking Coptic men greeted him, and frisked him, then allowed the harmless old man beyond the gates. He was instantly greeted by a young, anxious-eyed Copt called Labib – a 'server', not a monk. Labib spoke good English and wore badly-fitting jeans and poignantly cheap shoes; he carried a large bunch of keys. It seemed he single-handedly ran the White Monastery complex.

First, Victor made a generous offering to the monastery coffers, and then Labib spent the next tedious hour showing Victor the remnants of the old monastery, the Armenian brickwork, the fifth-century apse and the huge monastic graveyard, and then he showed his visitor all the exciting *new* buildings: the grotesquely ugly new church with its glass elevator, the bizarrely fresh murals of Adam and Eve painted in red and green on the perimeter wall, and then, the greatest triumph of all, a six-metre-wide animatronic statue-fountain of Christ's Miracle of the Watered Sheep.

'Look,' said Labib, sighing slightly. 'I can show you the miracle.' He stepped behind the huge, cement-and-plaster sculpture. Victor leaned on his stick with a grasping sense of despair. He heard the squeak of a metal tap being turned.

The water duly cascaded from a fake cement rock and ran past the smiling plaster Jesus who lifted his holy plaster hand and the animatronic sheep bent their animatronic heads in the manner of sheep drinking at a miraculous stream in the desert.

Victor flushed with faint embarrassment, and looked away. He had at least five more monasteries to visit. And then what? Victor felt the full futility of the exercise. Even if he found the right monastery, how was he going to get into the archives? Was he going to burgle them at night? Climb through the mud-brick windows? Hire a tractor and smash the walls down?

Labib emerged from the back of the automated Jesus, and gestured at the sheep. 'It is a good miracle. Do you think?'

'Yes. Ah. It's marvellous.'

Labib gazed at Victor, and smiled forlornly, and shook his head. 'No it is not . . . It is stupid. You know this.'

'Erm . . .'

'I can see you are intelligent man.' Labib turned, and gestured at the wide-eyed Jesus. 'Look. This is what we are reduced to, the Copts, making stupid miracles out of toys. But what can we do? We are in prison.' He exhaled, with enormous weariness.

There was nothing to be said. Sassoon gazed at some crumbling, pitiful heaps of mud brick as they began the trudge back to the gates. He tried to change the subject to something more fruitful. 'The White Monastery was much bigger once?'

'Yes it was,' Labib answered. 'Many times bigger. We had kitchen and churches, and the great library. A thousand monks lived here in Saint Shenouda's time. Fourth century.'

'You know a lot of the history.'

'I was a history teacher, at the university, Sohag. But they closed the department. Islamists did not like us teaching Coptic history. Now I have three children to feed, so I do this. I make the sheep drink from the miracle water. Twice a day.'

Victor paused. And daubed his sweating forehead with a handkerchief. 'Tell me about the library.'

'It was famous. The Codex Borgia came from here, and the Gospel of St Bartholomew, the Acts of Pilate, Gospel of the Twelve – many, many texts. But it was all scattered: Arabs burned some of the books; people stole them, Germans and French and English. Many times monks hid the books – in the caves in the hills. Now we are trying to rebuild the collection.'

'What hills, Labib?'

The young man pointed at the desert cliffs beyond the gate, to the west. 'The Sokar cliffs.'

Victor gazed at the wall of daunting rock.

Labib muttered, 'I think Sokar is the name of an Egyptian god? There are many caves.'

Victor thought the puzzle through. There were probably a thousand places in Egypt named after Sokar: a god of the sands, of the western afterworld, of cemeteries and canals. But the coincidence of this and the library? He had surely found his goal. He stared at Labib. Gentle, sad, helpful Labib, a scared and unhappy young man, with a family he was desperate to feed.

It was time. Victor Sassoon abandoned his last shred of morality. 'Labib,' he said, 'do you ever think about emigrating?'

The eyes of the young Copt glanced upwards, as if God might disapprove of his answer.

'Yes, yes of course. Many Copt thinks of this. I want to go to Canada, take my wife and children . . . I have cousins there already. But I do not have any money.'

'How much money would you need?'

Labib laughed, long and bitterly, in the desert sun. 'Five thousand dollars. Ten? It is just a dream.'

Victor opened his arms as if offering the world.

'I will give you ten thousand dollars if you do something very difficult for me.'

The sun burned down on Labib's astonished face. 'Do what?'

Victor took him by the arm and explained. Labib

stared. And stared. And stared. And the plaster Jesus behind him lifted his mechanical hand, and blessed the miraculous waters.

They arranged to meet the next evening, in Victor's hotel, at nine p.m. Ten minutes before the designated time, Victor took the clattering hotel elevator down to the lobby, where he sat and gazed at the headscarved women drinking Lipton's tea; then he looked at his watch, on and off, for two hours.

Then he went to his room and drank whisky. Labib had not shown up.

At midnight he got a cryptic text message:

Cannot get in. I will try again one more time. If I succeed I see you in hotel tomorrow 21:00 at your room. Labib.

Precisely twenty-one hours later, Victor heard a furtive knock at his hotel-room door.

Labib.

Labib was out there in the twenty-watt darkness of the landing, carrying a cheap plastic shopping bag. Mutely, full of shame, the Copt handed it over.

Victor grabbed the bag. An urgent glance inside gave him confidence. The contents looked authentic. Victor strained to contain his agitation, and his jubilation.

Now it was his turn. From the inner pocket of his blazer he took a thick envelope.

Labib didn't even bother to count the thousands of dollars therein. Instead, he just smiled, very regretfully; then turned and walked away down the landing.

Alone in his room Victor sat on the bed, trying to

quell his excitement. But his hands were trembling as he opened the bag and gazed at the frail documents bound in even frailer goatskin.

The call to prayer echoed across Sohag, across darkened Akhmim, across the moonlit reaches of the Nile, as Victor Sassoon took out the crumbling papyrus sheets of a very ancient document, and began to read.

8

Tahta, Middle Egypt

'But where are we going, *effendi*?'

'It doesn't matter.'

'I am not understanding?'

'Please, just drive on.'

Walid shook his head, and lit a Cleopatra cigarette. The smoke filled the taxi as they drove through yet another dusty, sunlit Egyptian village, with metal shacks selling palm oil and soap powder, and minarets soaring into the dusty sky. Dark-skinned boys played naked in the canals.

The cough came again, a hacking, savage cough; Victor Sassoon saw Walid checking him, anxiously, in the rear-view mirror.

'I sorry, *effendi*, I smoking, sorry, I stop.'

Walid threw his half-finished cigarette out of the taxi window, even as Victor made vague protestations: because it really didn't matter, not any more. There were specks of blood in Victor's handkerchief, tiny sprinkles of scarlet prettily arrayed. He quickly stuffed the handkerchief back in his pocket and clutched the shopping bag close to his aching chest.

Inside the bag were the Sokar documents. They were far more revelatory than he had expected; more explosively challenging, more conclusive. The first pages of Gnostic spells and curses were interesting, but the next codex in the most obscure dialect of Akhmimic Coptic was quite remarkable, and the Arab gloss, by Abd al-Latif al-Baghdadi, was astonishing. And what about the tiny concordance – that brief note in French, probably early or mid-nineteenth century – written by whom, and how, and why? It was perhaps the most killing evidence of all.

Who had hidden these documents? And who had compiled them? Seen the connection? Who had put them together? Some renegade monk? A Copt from the White Monastery? Why not then destroy them?

Sassoon's first urge had certainly been to destroy the Hoard, to burn the books. But he just *couldn't*. Burning books was the antithesis of everything his life had been about: burning books was what the Nazis did, the men who killed his mother and father, his entire family. So Victor had decided to preserve the books, and he was going to take them with him.

An hour passed. Walid smoked and then apologized for smoking. The scenery grew ever more bucolic, losing the last ugliness of urban Egypt, reprising its timeless rural beauty. A side channel of the Nile lay alongside the road, where egrets flapped and dived, dazzling white in the sun. Reeds of green and hazy gold surrounded mud houses; yoked donkeys stood patiently under African palms, drowsing in the heat.

Sassoon tapped on the glass. 'Where are we?'

'This next village –' Walid pointed with a tobacco-stained finger – 'this Nazlet, I think. End of road, into desert. Or we go on to Assyut.'

Nazlet Khater? Victor recalled a fragment of history. The earliest Egyptian skeletons were discovered here. In caves.

'So we stop.'

'Sorry?'

'Here,' Victor said. 'This is where we must stop. I need to go and look at something.'

Walid turned and frowned. 'Here? Is nothing here! Camel shit. Peasant people.'

'It's all right, Walid, I know what I am doing.'

The driver shrugged. 'OK. I wait you here. How long?'

'A few hours.'

Another stubborn shrug; Walid was clearly unhappy, but in a protective way. Perhaps it was because Walid was a Muslim, and Victor was, in a way, his guest; Walid's faith demanded he look after him. Momentarily, Victor considered this paradox, the paradox of Islam – a faith capable of great violence, and yet tenderly hospitable and sweetly generous, and truly egalitarian, too. But all religions were paradoxical, more paradoxical than Victor had ever imagined.

As he walked away from the car he could sense his driver staring after him, at his old Jewish passenger, regretful and sympathetic and frustrated. Victor ignored this; flicking stones with his walking stick, he turned a corner by a scruffy little mosque and saw that the road really did end.

Two camels were tethered by a rusty lamppost at the broken edge of the pavement. The last of life. Beyond them was rock and plains and level sands and nothingness.

Victor kept on walking. The road immediately turned into desert rubble. The sun was hot. He had water and some food in his shopping bag along with the Sokar documents. He wondered how strange he must look: an old Englishman in a blazer, carrying a shopping bag, just walking out into the emptiness.

But there was no one here to see him. Victor walked and walked, with the last of his strength. He felt the sun weaken as he went, beginning to set behind the mountains of the western desert. As the true darkness ensued he sat on a boulder in the cooling shadows. An eagle wheeled in the twilight. The silence was enormous: hosannas of quiet surrounded him.

He slept in his clothes, under a ledge. The pain in his chest was so intense it was like a lover, clutching him too tight. He remembered being a student, sleeping in a tiny single bed with his first wife. Intensely uncomfortable and yet happy. Cambridge. Bicycles. His wife dying in the hospice. There was dust in his mouth. A memory of a young rose by a leaded window.

When he woke the sun was already warm and he drank the very last of his water. He had no idea where he was: just somewhere in the desert. Dirty and dishevelled and dying. But that was where he wanted to be, somewhere no one could find his body: not immediately, anyway.

Two or three more hours of shuffling across the sands brought him to an outcrop of orange-red rock, hot in the sun. Shadows of birds on the sand told him that vultures were circling above. He'd thought that only happened in movies. But it was true. The birds sensed carrion: a body. Food.

But they were going to be disappointed. Victor crept around the rocks, then down the adjoining cliff, looking for a cave. His tongue was cracked with dehydration, his eyesight was failing. But at last he found a cave, and it was dark and long and cool.

Victor got down on his aching knees and crept inside. At the very end, where it became too narrow to even crawl, he laid his head on a rock and stared into the infinite blackness of the darkness above and around. He was clutching the Sokar documents to his chest, and gazing into the darkness of deep time. Maybe one day someone would discover his corpse: another body mummified by the Egyptian desert; and with him the codices and the parchments in their plastic shopping bag.

Maybe one day someone would, therefore, recover this astonishing truth, once again. And maybe, just maybe, they wouldn't. It was right to let God decide.

If there was a God.

The wind whirred outside, at the end of the long cavern. Victor thought of his wife and of the children they never had; he thought of her on that bicycle, that holiday, a spaniel puppy, a car journey somewhere, a cottage with a well in the garden, a photo of his dead parents, snow falling on the Polish camps, and then his wavering and failing mind considered one final thought: the blessed name of Jerusalem, derived from Shalim, the Canaanite God of Night; the God of the End.

And here was that same spirit, coming into the cave like the cool desert wind: Shalim, the God of the End.

9

Zennor Hill, Cornwall, England

Cats? The cottage was full of cats: or rather the *corpses* of cats. Some skinned, most of them charred. Charred and burned and scorched and roasted. Piles of dead cats in one corner. Piles of dead cats in another. The stench was intolerable. They had begun to rot.

'Jesus Christ.'

DI Sally Pascoe nodded, grimly. The white shirt of her police uniform was smeared with greasy soot. The stuff was everywhere. The burning fur and cat flesh had thickened the air and blackened the walls. The floor was actually sticky: Karen shuddered to think why that was, though she could guess – the heat must have been intense as the cats burned, so intense that the fat in their flesh had liquefied, had turned to oil or tallow, now congealing. Like candles.

These cats had been burned like candles.

She resisted the urge to vomit.

Sally pointed, and Karen followed the gesture. 'That must have been where some of them were burned. A spit roast, but others appear to have been doused in petrol, and burned alive. We found some petrol canisters at the back, and firelighters too, used for kindling.'

'They stink. Are you going to move them?'

Sally shrugged. 'We don't quite know what to do, I mean, who do we go to, Forensics, Pathology?'

'Or a vet.'

'Yes, maybe.'

Karen gazed around the awful scene. One cat was only half-burned: so they hadn't all been burned at the same time. They had been torched one after the other. Ritualistically. And this ritual had not been completed.

Ritual?

Ritual.

She turned to Sally. 'Maybe you should speak to an expert on witchcraft.'

'Yes! That's what I thought, some kind of terrible witchcraft. That's one reason I asked you over, Kaz. Didn't you handle a case in London, last year, African voodoo?'

'Yes. A Congolese couple decided their kid was possessed, and they beat him to death.'

Sally shuddered visibly. 'OK, OK, so this is just amateur night here, just a house full of barbecued cats.'

'It's quite bad enough, Sally. Properly Satanic.' She stooped to one sticky, charred heap of corpses. Using a pen, she flipped one small corpse upside down. The mouth of the cat was open, agonized and screaming.

Karen shook her head. 'The noise must have been unbelievable. Right? Dozens of cats, being burned alive. Through the night? You know how cats yowl. I get them outside my house in London. Caterwauling. Imagine the appalling noise if you . . . burned them like this.'

'Yes, that's how we were alerted, someone heard the noise.' Sally was backing away to the door as if she wanted to flee. Her face was pale. 'Sorry. I've had enough for the moment: the smell. Can we get out, and speak in the car?'

'Sure.'

The door was opened; the fresh air – cold and faintly drizzly – was unbelievably welcoming. Both women inhaled, greedily. Then they both laughed, very quietly.

'Hey, I haven't even said anything about your mum . . . Sweetheart, I'm so sorry. Karen, I'm so, so sorry. Come here.' She hugged her friend.

Karen welcomed the embrace: human warmth. She missed her daughter; she missed her friends; at this moment, she missed her mum most of all.

A silent constable standing at the door watched them, perhaps slightly embarrassed by their open emotion.

Karen and Sally walked to the Range Rover and got in. Sally spoke first. 'Look at us, two important police-women. Or one slightly important and one really impor-tant. I mean, Detective Chief Inspector at the Met? What happened to little Karen Trevithick? A DCI at thirty-two? Go girl!'

Karen waved away the compliment. 'It's easier for

women in some ways. We have a different way of looking at things. Changes perspective.'

'Yes I find that too . . . Sometimes.'

'Hard work too though; and it's pretty tough on Ellie.'

'Your daughter must be, like, six?' Sally's smile faded. 'The father—'

'Still isn't really involved. But that's my choice.'

'You were never one to get married and bake scones, Kaz.'

'No. I guess not. Not like Mum.' She looked out of the car window, at the distant, yearning sea, way down the hill, beyond Zennor. 'You know we used to come here, to Zennor. On holidays. We'd take a picnic and sit on the cliffs. Dad would always say the same thing – the same bit of history. He loved Cornish history. You see them? Those little fields, down there?' Karen gestured towards the intricate labyrinth of tiny, vivid green fields, surrounding the granite village. 'You see the stone hedges dividing them? The big boulders. They're Neolithic. My dad told me those were the oldest human artefacts in the world still being used for their original purpose.'

Sally peered down Zennor Hill. 'OK . . . Not a history fanatic, how old is that? Neo . . . lithic?'

'We're talking 3000 BC – five thousand years old. The first farmers moved the huge stones they found in the fields to make hedges. And they're still using them now.'

Sally nodded, absently. 'I never liked it here. Penwith, I mean – this part of Cornwall. Creeps me out a bit, the tin mines and the standing stones, it's all so brooding.'

'Which is why people come here, right? Hippies and druids. Bohemians and artists. And Satanists. Which brings us back to the cats. You said the noise alerted someone, so you have a witness?'

Sally shook her head. 'There was a bunch of rich kids, uni students, staying for Christmas and New Year. They rented Eagle's Nest.'

'Sorry?'

'That big house down there.'

Karen stretched to see: a large handsome building, with extensive gardens, in a spectacular position hard by the highest sea-cliffs. '*Must* be rich, to rent that place. So they heard the noise? Of the cats being tortured?'

'Yep, in the middle of the night, and they came up to have a look.' Sally Pascoe frowned, expressively. 'I guess they were drunk. They kicked open the door – and got *way* more of a fright than they expected. One of them was badly clawed by a cat, a burning cat, trying to escape. Must have been terrifying.'

'They saw no one?'

Sally reached for a stick of Nicorette chewing gum. 'I've given up for New Year,' she explained, unwrapping. 'So, yeah, where was I . . . yes, the two boys – Malcolm Harding and Freddy Saunderson – they both say they saw people running away, but it was dark. That's all we know at the moment. No other witnesses, nothing. But it must have been those people who burned the cats.'

71

'The kids aren't involved?'

'No.' Sally's negative was firm. 'I'm convinced they have nothing to do with it.' She chewed the gum methodically. 'So we're maybe looking for a gang of Satanists out on the moors of Penwith who like to torment cats by the hundred. How sweet.'

Sally's phone rang. Karen raised a hand to say *I'll be outside* and opened the Range Rover's door. The wind was so gusty it almost slammed it shut against her fingers. Raising the collar of her raincoat, Karen walked around the cottage.

It was half-ruined. A shed of some kind, with a clear plastic roof, was attached to the rear. Most of the windows were broken. It obviously hadn't been inhabited for many years, maybe decades. That in itself was odd, Karen thought: the cottage was spectacularly situated. It had the kind of view that you could rent to summer holidaymakers for two thousand a month. Even in winter it would attract arty types, who liked the rawness, the stern and brutal beauty of the West Penwith landscape. Why let it fall into ruin?

She turned a further corner and peered in through one of the few unbroken windows. The interior was dark, but there was still enough light to see the piles of contorted and tormented little corpses. What a ghastly thing. She shivered in the wind. Her mother had loved cats . . .

'Karen, come over here!'

Stepping over tumbled bricks and shattered window-glass she saw Sally, in the Range Rover, gesturing.

'Get in the car and shut the door. Listen to this!'

Karen obeyed. Sally could be a little bossy; she hadn't changed all that much. But that was fine, it was actually reassuring.

'What?'

Sally's face was stern. She lifted up the phone, significantly, pointing it Karen's way. 'I just got another call, from my Detective Sergeant, Jones.'

'And?'

'They found a body.'

'Where? Here? Zennor?'

'No, down a mine, Botallack, you know that one, on the coast, over Morvah way.'

Karen's thoughts whirled into confusion. She wondered aloud, 'An accident? Falling down a mine shaft? I don't see the connexion. How . . .?'

'The owners found the body this morning, at the bottom of the shaft. They say it was covered in a weird grease, black soot and stuff.'

The Atlantic wind buffeted the window of the Range Rover. Karen looked at the charred and open door of Carn Cottage. It was covered with grease and soot.

10

Morvah, Cornwall, England

What was that line of poetry her father used to quote, about the West Penwith countryside?

> *This is a hideous and a wicked country,*
> *Sloping to hateful sunsets and the end of time,*
> *Hollow with mine-shafts, naked with granite . . .*

The poet was right.

DCI Trevithick steered her Toyota carefully along the narrow Penwith roads; to her left, the moors rose abruptly, scattered with enormous rocks, oddly deformed. To the right, the pounding and merciless sea, assaulting the cliffs. And in the narrow strip of flat land between, there lay the wind-battered farms and the grey mining villages. Ex-mining villages.

Just ahead was Morvah. *Morvah.* Karen mouthed the vowels, silently, as she slowed the car. There was another line, by some writer, her dad would quote: 'the fearsome scenery reaches a crescendo of evil at Morvah'. It was so very true.

And yet people loved this country, too, which was why it got so many artistic visitors who adorned it with these famous quotes. Even on a raw and hostile January day, like today, it had a powerful and hypnotic quality that made you want to linger.

Who killed the cats? She had to find out. The case was starting to obsess her.

At Botallack Karen took the last turning, onto a winding, rutted track that seemed to lead past a farm, directly over the cliffs and straight down to the crushing sea three hundred feet below. But at the last moment the track veered right and opened up to a tarmacked car park at the very edge of the precipice.

And there below was Botallack Mine. Just seeing it made Karen shiver.

It was one of the oldest mines in Cornwall, three or four centuries old at least, though tin streaming and tin mining had been happening here for three *thousand* years. That was why the entire Penwith coast was riddled with tunnels and shafts and adits, like a honeycomb under the sea-salted grass. There were so many mine-workings that people occasionally fell down unsuspected shafts to their deaths; dogs disappeared quite frequently.

Yet within this ominous world Botallack had an especially sinister quality, not because of its age, but because of its position: right by the sea, halfway up an almost-vertical cliff. The mine had been built here to exploit the tin and copper *under the ocean*. The shafts were famously deep and the tunnels famously long: extending out under the Atlantic.

Imagine the life of the men who worked here every day . . .

Karen got out of the car and cringed from the cold fierce wind.

Yet, working here every day is precisely what her ancestors had done. Her father's family ultimately came from St Just, and her great-great-grandfather, and no doubt the men before him, had been miners right here. At Botallack.

It must have been a horrible existence: they would have risen before dawn, often in a ferocious Atlantic gale, then walked in the wintry dark from their cottages along the coast and down the cliffside to the minehead, where they descended deep underground. In Victorian times they would have had to climb down half-mile-long ladders, deeper and deeper into the darkness. And after an hour, when they reached the bottom, they had to crawl for a mile under the sad and booming sea in terrifyingly narrow tunnels to the rockface.

Only then did their shift officially begin, hewing and drilling the vile, wet rocks to get at the precious black tin; only then did they begin to earn the pittance that paid for their families' subsistence. When did they find the time or energy to live and pray and sing and make love to their wives? No wonder they died so young: at thirty or thirty-five. Apart from Sundays, they wouldn't have seen the sun from October to March.

Karen locked the car, thinking. The word Sunday must have had a special resonance then. The only day they saw the sun. *Sunday*.

An image of her father flashed before her. They had come here once and he had told her all this mining history, trying to make her proud of her Cornish heritage. In reality, the sight of awesome Botallack had just made seven-year-old Karen rather scared.

Slowly, she made her way down the perilous cliffside path, towards the handsome stone stacks of Botallack engine house, and the small cabins surrounding it.

She was greeted by a tall dark-haired man in a yellow hard hat and hi-vis jacket. He extended a firm handshake and shouted above the buffeting sea-wind, 'Stephen Penrose. You must be Karen Trevithick?'

She shook his hand. 'Can we go inside?'

The peace inside the great, cold, stone-built engine house was almost a shock after the stormy noise of the wind.

'Hell of a day! Yes, I'm DCI Trevithick, from Scotland Yard.'

The man looked her up and down. Karen didn't know whether to feel patronized, or flattered, and didn't particularly care either way: she was just eager to crack on. She'd had to fight for permission to be assigned to a case so far from London; indeed, she'd had to use a little emotional blackmail with her senior officer at the Yard, expend some capital. But this strange case intrigued her, and distracted her from gloomy and interior thoughts.

She was also distracted by the great void just a few metres from her walking boots. *The shaft.* It dominated the stone chamber. A black circle of nothingness, much bigger than she had expected: a great mouth that swallowed men daily, with a gullet that went down for miles.

'In the old days, when they were tinning,' Penrose said, as if he sensed her thoughts, 'you would see steam coming out of that shaft.'

'Sorry?'

'Steam, from all the men, the miners breathing deep underground, the steam from their exhalations, would rise up the shaft.'

It was another jarring concept.

'Have you ever been down a mine, Miss Trevithick?'

'No.'

He tutted, sympathetically. 'With a good Cornish name like Trevithick?'

'The stories put me off,' she said, staring at the shaft. 'My dad would tell me stories of my family. Working in these places. One of them died when the man-engine collapsed at that mine, along the cliffs: Levant. And my great-grandmother was a bal maiden at South Crofty.'

'Ah yes, the girls, breaking the rocks and sifting the deads, standing in the wind. What a job that must've been.'

'They were tough women.'

'Very true, Miss Trevithick, very true. Here. You'll need this.'

She took the hard hat, put it on, strapped it under her chin and smiled briskly. 'So, where is the body?'

'Right at the bottom of the shaft. You'll need this overall too. 'Tis very wet down there.'

Karen slipped on the blue nylon overalls. They covered her like a nun's habit. Properly attired, she followed Stephen Penrose to the other side of the shaft and a metal cage suspended over the void. Once inside the cage, he slid a wire metal door, pressed a fat red button, and they began the long descent. The sensation was distractingly unpleasant. Going down underground, to the tunnels under the Atlantic. She could hear the grieving boom of the sea as they descended.

'Who found the body?'

'I did, yesterday.'

'What were you doing here? Botallack has been closed for decades.'

He shrugged.

'We're exploring the, uh, possibility of tourism. Opening a mine museum, you see, like Geevor up the coast. We have some EU funding. We've just finished draining the main tunnels. That's one of them: one of the oldest, eighteenth century.' He pointed down a tunnel that flashed past them as they plunged further in the rattling cage. The whole mine was dimly lit with strings of electric lights: frail and exposed against the threatening dark.

It was surely a haunted place. As the cage neared

the bottom of the chilly shaft, Karen remembered more stories: of the knockers – the spirits of the mine, strange poltergeists the miners would claim to hear. Auditory hallucinations, presumably, from hunger and stress.

'OK, here it is. Watch your step.'

The body was crumpled at the bottom of the shaft, next to the enormous metal winch that controlled the cage. Beyond it was the main tunnel, a narrowing corridor that extended that long, long mile under the Atlantic Ocean. The moaning sea above them was still audible, but now muffled, stifled even: like someone in another room dreaming bad dreams.

Karen knelt and looked at the broken form. The victim was young, white, male, twenty-something, in a shredded anorak and dark jeans. Covered in blood and blackness.

Penrose spoke, his voice not quite so confident now. 'Nasty, isn't it? Quite gave me the frighteners when I saw it. Poor bastard. Then all that weird stuff on him . . . Soot and grease and . . . cat fur, right?'

'How did you know it was cat fur?'

'I didn't. It was my boss, Jane. She came down a few minutes later, she keeps cats, she recognized these might be –' he pointed – 'scratches. Cat scratches. See there. On the neck and the face. Then we worked out that maybe all this stuff . . .' Penrose knelt beside her. It was as if they were praying in front of the corpse. 'This weird stuff on his clothes must be fur, burned cat fur, because she'd already heard the reports, on the radio news, the cats burned on Zennor Hill.'

'Uh-huh.'

Penrose stood up, abruptly, as if he really didn't like to be too near the corpse. 'What is it, Miss Trevithick? Something to do with witchcraft? That's what they're saying on the internet.' He tilted back his hard hat and scratched his head, frowning. 'Because it's not good for business. We don't want people associating Botallack with anything like *that*, not if we're going to make a go of this museum. And we need the jobs round here. Sorry to sound selfish, but . . .'

'No, no. I quite understand.' Karen gave the shattered body one last scrutiny in the faint damp light given out by the pitiful bulbs. 'I'm sure it will be fine, you'd be amazed how quickly people forget. I've seen it all before.'

She gazed at the sad, pale, slender face of the cadaver, scratched, and badly bruised, and with one long horrible gash by the left ear. There were several other terrifying scarlet gashes distributed across the body, as if someone had attacked the man with a mighty sword. The legs were the worst: they were virtually pulped. The flesh had *melted* into the clothing; you could only just tell he was wearing dark indigo jeans. 'Pathology will confirm, they're coming here in a minute. But these injuries, they must have been from his fall.'

Penrose said nothing: he was looking in his canvas bag.

In the end, she answered her own question. 'Yes . . . That makes sense. The wounds look terrible but that's because of the enormous drop. You'd bang against the sides of the shaft on the way down. Ripping and tearing, shattering the bones.'

Karen stood and stared up. The tiny hole of light half a mile up there was the sky and the wind. She resisted the sudden urge to panic and escape this unnatural, inhuman prison, to fling herself in the cage and press every button.

Soft distant booms echoed down the tunnels. The sea was talking in its sleep, fighting a nightmare. The sea was also *above* them, weighing everything down: an unbearably oppressive sensation. What a place.

She turned. Penrose was holding something in his hand. It was an iPad. He spoke, as he switched it on. 'We know the injuries are from the fall, Miss Trevithick, because we have him on CCTV. Uninjured.'

'What?'

'They didn't tell you! We found it a couple of hours ago. Jane emailed it to me and to . . . DI Pascoe?'

'I've been out of contact. My mobile is recharging. You have it?'

'Yup. Here, look.'

He opened up the iPad and clicked on a stored email. The light given out by the computer seemed unearthly in the gloom. A magic oblong in ancient darkness.

The CCTV footage was grainy but good enough. The two of them stood in the echoing blackness, with the baffled noise of the sea all around, and watched the silent movie.

'There he is.'

Penrose's indication was unnecessary. A young man

in dark jeans was climbing a fence surrounding the mine-head. It was dark, but the moon was full. The victim was unmistakable. *And he was alone.* So this was no murder?

'That's him all right. No injuries. Looks perfectly OK.'

The footage jerked and the scene changed. Now they were gazing at the interior of the engine house.

'We have a CCTV camera inside as well. It's much darker, but you can still see him.'

The ghostly image of the man moved to the shaft. What was he looking for? His movements were edgy, jerky, and odd. As if there was a problem with the film-speed, and yet there wasn't. Where was he going? How did he accidentally fall down? Karen watched the figure climb very close to the big black hole. Why was he going so stupidly close to the shaft? She almost cried out: *Stop, you're getting too close!*

Her hand went reflexively to her mouth.

He *jumped*.

11

Abydos, Egypt

'It is estimated there are maybe *half a billion* mummies still lying in the dust of Egypt.'

This was one of Ryan Harper's favourite factoids: he always wheeled it out when the students' attention started to wander. Today the students remained mute, and unresponsive. Had they even heard?

'I said, it is estimated there are half a billion mummies in Egypt.'

He looked at the young faces before him. There were just three kids in this study group: the renewed Egyptian troubles – would they ever end? – had begun to scare away the students, as they had already scared away the tourists.

This was a pain. Ryan relied, very heavily, on this part-time weekend teaching to supplement his meagre income from the charity. If the teaching disappeared, he would be properly impoverished.

At last, the keenest of the trio, a bright spark from Chicago, offered a response: 'Half a billion? You're joking, right?'

'No.' Ryan stood tall, and gestured across the beige and rubbly levels of the Abydos cemeteries. 'Remember the eternity of Egyptian life . . .'

Just at that moment a blaring Arab pop song shrilled out from a café down by the main temple. Ryan sighed. The screeching music didn't add to the mysterious atmosphere he was trying to evoke. And this was the one thing about teaching that Ryan really enjoyed – the chance to instil some mystery into these kids, to give them a glimpse of the grandeur of Egypt; to make these gum-chewing twenty-year-olds share a little of that soaring rhapsody that he had once enjoyed, in his first season's digging at Saqqara, as he unearthed the tombs of the Apis bulls – the sense that he was an historical scuba diver, floating above so much translucent and fathomless archaeology it could give you vertigo.

'Mr Harper—'

'Sorry?'

It was the Chicago kid again, Tyler Neale.

'Explain the figures, maybe?'

'Sure.'

''Cause I don't see it. There's, like, no way you could bury that many mummies: they'd be turning up in your lunch.'

Harper gestured across the flooded tomb of Osiris, the Oseirion, where he spent much of his working week. 'In a sense, you just have to do the math. But

85

let's go through it. First, as I say, you need to appreciate the profundity of Egyptian time. Let's make a comparison. How long has America been around?'

He gazed at the students. Daniel Melini seemed to be asleep standing up. The pretty girl, Jenny Lopez, was texting on her phone. And Tyler Neale, in his scruffy jeans and baseball cap, simply looked tired. Fair enough. The students had a right to be tired and maybe a little irritable: they'd spent five straight hours wandering the epic site in the endless sun, listening to him explaining styles of epigraphy in the Abydos King List and the problems of rising water tables across Middle Egypt. He liked to give them value for their money: he'd probably said *way* too much.

Well now they could have some fun, at least for the last thirty minutes. And after that, as the sun set over the Rameses temple and the forts of Zebib, Ryan Harper could go back to his lonely bachelor apartment in the town and spend the rest of the evening smoking *shisha* outside the tea-house downstairs with the Arabs who somehow tolerated the slightly dishevelled, thirty-eight-year-old American with no wife and no kids, whose once-famous career had turned to humble toil.

Harper quietly cussed himself. No need for self-pity. He liked his work, the charity and the teaching. He was lucky, in a way.

'Two hundred and fifty years.'

He was startled by another student answering. It was the cool one with the Italian heritage, Melini.

'That's the answer, isn't it, Mr Harper? America has

been a political reality, a nation, a country, almost two hundred and fifty years. Since 1776. Right?'

Neale shook his head. 'But the Pilgrim Fathers came in 1620, so that's like, nearly four hundred. You could say America began then, no?'

Lopez looked up from her smartphone. 'Whoa! Racist much? You're saying America has only existed since the first Caucasians were there? Since Columbus? Where, like, did the Navajo live in 1200, then, fracking limbo?'

At least this was zesty, at least they were engaging; but the argument was going entirely the wrong way. Ryan raised a hand. 'OK. Guys. Let's say America has been a *political* entity, in the European sense, for about three hundred years. Can we agree on that? Well, from beginning to end, ancient Egypt lasted approximately –' he paused, for effect – *'ten times as long.* Excluding more primitive cultures like the Badarian, the first true Egyptian civilisation began in 3200 BC.'

'But half a *billion* mummies?'

'I'm getting there! Remember, most ancient Egyptians would have sought some kind of mummification if they could, such was their obsession with making it to the afterlife. And of course mummification is not hard out here: the desert naturally mummifies bodies, it is so dry. That is probably, in fact, how the ritual began, in about 3200 BC, when the First Dynasty Egyptians realized that human corpses were curiously preserved by great aridity.'

Lopez was toying with her phone again. Or maybe

she was checking his sums. He fought the desire to compare her feisty beauty to his wife's, or even his dead daughter – would she have looked like this? He banished the thought and continued, 'You don't need a calculator to do the equations. Let's say Egyptians died at the rate of a hundred and fifty thousand a year, which is about right for a population of three million on average, with a life expectancy of twenty or so. Take a hundred and fifty thousand deaths a year and multiply it by more than three thousand years and you get . . . at least four hundred and fifty million dead. That is to say, *half a billion mummies*. Some estimates go even higher.' He pointed at the western cliffs, behind which the sun was reluctantly declining. 'Basically, when you walk on Egyptian soil, you are walking on the dust of the dead.'

Lopez looked up. 'Eww.'

Harper laughed. 'Yes. Maybe I won't mention the way we have used human and animal mummies in the past: as fertiliser, medicine, machine oil, pigment and fuel.'

'Medicine?'

'OK, we're done, guys.' Harper liked to end the day with a question hanging in the air. Politely he dismissed the tiny study group, who seemed just a bit too keen to get back to their rented apartments and have a clandestine beer. But then he shrugged. So what? Good for them. They were young.

Ryan's walk home was agreeable in the cooling twilight: this was his favourite hour of the day. Boys played football under ragged, sun-bleached posters of a long-deposed president. Little girls skipped happily next to their mothers, carrying wicker shopping baskets way too big for their tiny hands; their mothers were shrouded entirely in black niqabs.

And of course the old men with the white *keffiyehs* were smoking their *shisha* pipes outside the dusty tea-house. One or two raised a hand or an eyebrow in greeting, as Ryan keyed his latch. But then he saw an even more familiar face. It was Hassan, sitting outside on the terrace.

Ryan waved hello. 'Hassan. *Ahlan!* I'll be down in a minute.'

His apartment was welcomingly cool and dark. As he splashed water on his face, Ryan considered Hassan. Their revolving lives.

There was a time when Hassan Elgammal had been Ryan's assistant: a keen young student aiding the rising young American Egyptologist. Now, fifteen years later, Hassan was in charge of all Egyptian antiquities in the Abydos region, and he was therefore, by a distance, Ryan's superior.

Ryan didn't much care about this inversion in their roles. Ambition had left him when his wife had died in childbirth. It had literally flown his soul, like the living spirit – the *ka* – that fled the corpse of an ancient Egyptian when they died. And when he had finally given up his Egyptological career altogether, and taken on the charity job, he had felt a sincere moral relief.

His employers – the Abydos Project – were dedicated

to saving Egyptian antiquities, such as the Abydos temple complex, from flooding and decay. This meant that Ryan spent his days giving something *back* to Egyptians, rather than always taking stuff away, as Westerners had done for centuries. That was a good feeling.

And Ryan also enjoyed the sheer physical labour: he often spent entire days down there in the Oseirion with the Egyptian workers, rebuilding walls, shifting rubble, digging new drainage canals; toiling in the Egyptian sun, like a mindless slave building a pyramid. Then in the evening he quenched a mighty thirst with sweet hibiscus juice. And he slept soundly. And didn't dream. And the days went by. And the years went by.

Towelling his hands dry, Ryan descended the stairs, opened the door, and took a seat besides Hassan. His friend's affable face was grave, yet also excited. 'They found him, Ryan.'

'Sorry?'

'A goatherd found the body yesterday. Your old tutor Sassoon. In the desert, north of Sohag.'

Ryan blinked. Emotion surged.

Hassan added, 'And they say he was found with a bag. Of documents.'

12

Middle Egypt

Ryan resisted the idea, at first.

'What has it got to do with me?' He shook his head. 'I work for you guys now, I'm not an Egyptologist. That was a decade ago.'

'Please.' Hassan gently raised a hand in protest. 'You have done enough here. At least take some proper time off, a month at least, three months better.'

'But—'

'When did you last have a holiday?'

Ryan watched the café owner drop a glass of tea on their table. The smell of apple *shisha* hung in the frowzy air. 'Six years ago.'

Hassan smiled. 'Exactly. This is too much: you have done Egypt great service. We owe you money! And really –' another languid gesture – 'are you going to spend the rest of your life carrying bricks, like a peasant? Is this all that is left? Sassoon was your great friend.'

'Yes.'

'And you know the rumours of what he found.'

'Yes.'

Everyone in Egyptology, anyone remotely *connected* to Egyptology, had heard or read these rumours. Ryan's heart had secretly raced at the notion. The Sokar Hoard! And then, the absurd thought had occurred: what if he, Ryan Harper, found the Sokar Hoard once again, and deciphered it? Of course he had crushed this outbreak of ambition as soon as it was born; but here was his boss *telling him* to seize the moment.

Again, Hassan smiled. His dark suit looked expensive on the terrace of the shabby Tetisheri tea-house; Ryan's jeans were still covered in dust.

'So. Ryan. Please will you go? I will make the arrangements. Give you letters. Holiday pay. Go now. Go and find the Hoard. Go and be an Egyptologist again.'

'Hassan—'

'This is an order! I am your boss, Ryan. Remember I can have you shot at dawn, under the temple of Nectanebo, if you disobey.'

This was a joke, of course. But there *was* a steeliness in Hassan's voice. And the sternness of the order was answered by a corresponding yearning in Ryan to obey. He wanted to go: maybe there *was* still a scientist inside him, despite the calluses on his hands and the sand in his sun-bleached hair.

Hassan pressed his point. 'There is no teaching work here any more. Maybe even the charity will have to close, because of the disturbances.'

'Really?'

Hassan frowned, heavily. 'Really. It is very bad, very bad . . .' He sighed. 'But at least I can help a friend come to his senses. Your dear wife would have wanted you to do this. To be the Ryan Harper she knew, once more. After ten years, I think, it is time. No?'

The moment was tense. Ryan drank his tea, and said nothing, and watched the moon rise over the Temple of Seti. He remembered Rhiannon. Her fever, the last days, the terrifying and inundating sadness. Maybe it was time to let this go.

The moon stared at him. Shocked at his decision. But the decision felt entirely right.

He took leave of absence that very night, hastily packing a bag, then jogging straight to the teeming Abydos railway station.

Time was strictly limited. Ryan was very aware that others would be on the trail. He had to get to Nazlet as quickly as possible. But *quickly as possible* was not an Egyptian state of mind.

The ticket queue was full of sweating men in *djellabas*, all shouting angrily at the narrow-eyed man behind the cracked-glass reservations window. The man behind the glass was dispensing his tickets with a reluctant and painful slowness, as if they were his personal inheritance of Treasury bonds. Harper growled with impatience. They'd found the body of Victor Sassoon!

Sassoon was his old tutor, his mentor, a man Harper had once admired and revered: the great Jewish scholar of the Dead Sea Scrolls, one of the greatest men in his field. What had happened that he should be found dead, alone, in a cave? What could have driven him to do that? To walk into the wilderness, alone, two months ago? Poor Victor.

It had to have been something extraordinary to invoke such a response. That meant the bag found with Sassoon's body *must* contain the Sokar Hoard, the great cache: the cache Victor had illegally bought in his final days of life, or so the lurid rumours had it. Sassoon had, it seemed, read these documents, then killed himself. Or been murdered. Why? What had Sassoon retrieved at the White Monastery? *What was in those texts?*

The mysteries were arousing, energizing, tantalizing. They pumped the blood in Harper's heart. Hassan was right. All these years the keen and ambitious scientist in Ryan Harper hadn't entirely gone away, but had merely slumbered. And now the long-buried Egyptologist was being resurrected.

If Ryan could find the Sokar Hoard, then he would have *done something* with the scholarly skills he had disregarded for a decade. Something *amazing*.

Did you hear about old Ryan Harper? Oh, he found the Sokar Hoard.

Ryan Harper?

'Effendi!'

'Maljadeed!'

The queue in front of him seemed to be getting *longer* as half of Abydos barged in. Harper resisted the urge to punch his way to the kiosk. But it was hard. Trying to buy a ticket in an Egyptian railway station was always a hassle – like trying to change nationality during a hurricane – and he knew he had to exercise patience. But he *couldn't* exercise patience tonight of all nights. The next Sohag train – the *last* Sohag train of the day – was leaving in fifteen minutes.

'*La – ibqa!*'

'*Jagal – almaderah – incheb!*'

What could he do instead? He crunched the equations, frantically. Perhaps he could hire a car and driver and just take the road? But no. That might be possible by day, but at night – not a chance. Security was tightening up and down the Nile; a Westerner in a cab without a very special permit would be immediately halted at the edge of town and summarily returned whence he came – that or detained and questioned. Or worse.

No, a train was the only way to get to Sohag tonight. Then he could head on to Nazlet tomorrow. And he needed to get there tonight. Because, if the reports of Sassoon's body being rediscovered had reached Abydos, then they would have reached elsewhere, too; and other people would have reached precisely the same conclusion.

'*Haiwan!*'

'*La! La!*'

There were men apparently *fighting* at the front of the queue.

Harper abandoned any hope of getting a ticket in

time. Instead he reached in the zipped pocket of his fleecy climber's jacket – the desert night was cool, even down here in southern Egypt – and pulled out a wad of US dollars. *Baksheesh* might just work where patience was exhausted. He had to try, or his quest would be finished before it began.

Ryan sauntered over to the concrete arch that led onto the platforms. Like almost every official threshold in Egypt it was barred by an airport-style detector, a boxy doorway of metal: a detector that served no purpose as it wasn't plugged in.

But the security guard was real enough. He eyed Harper. '*Men fethlek? Aiwa?* Tick-et!'

The voice was curt; this was far from promising. But Harper had no choice. Subtly as he could, he offered a twenty-buck note – a day's wage – to the security guard, folded between his fingers.

The guard glanced for a moment at the money, then clasped the cash with a practised grace, like a concierge at the Carlyle, and ushered Ryan through.

He was on the platform. Now the train.

There!

The train was *pulling out*. Barging past some smoking soldiers, he reached for the receding metal handle, but it slipped from his grasp.

Now the train was really grinding into life – and speeding up. He wasn't going to make it; but this was the last train of the night so he *had* to make it! Breaking into a sprint, he jumped and tried again, and at the edge of his strength he grabbed the escaping handle, swung himself violently in through the open door, and with all the strength of a decade of carrying rocks, somehow tugged himself and his rucksack safely inside.

He was in the train. He was in. He'd done it! There was an advantage to being a peasant who hodded mud bricks in the sun. It made you fit and strong.

The Nileside express hooted merrily, as if in appreciation of Ryan's gymnastic achievement. Then it accelerated out of Abydos, past a straggling Muslim cemetery, past the last neon-lit minarets, spearing the darkness, and then the cooler air told him he was in the Nilotic countryside.

For two hours he stood in the vestibule between the toilet and the broken carriage door, waiting, nervously, for the collector, dollars for *baksheesh* in hand. Yet the collector didn't even show up.

The chaos of Egypt could sometimes be beneficial.

Only the tea-boy interrupted the rattling journey down the Nile valley, carrying a silver tray of little glasses as he patrolled the carriages, calling out, '*Shay, shay, shay!*'

Harper bought a cup of black tea, heavily sugared.

'*Sefr, men fadlak . . .*'

Gratefully, he sank the tea, then chased it with mineral water, as he opened his notebook and examined the scribbled document that Hassan had given him before he'd departed Abydos. The name was written in Latin letters as well as Arabic:

MOHAMMAD KHATTAB.

The head of police in Nazlet, and a cousin of Hassan's.

The fact he was related to Hassan came as no surprise to Ryan. Everyone who ascended through the bureaucracy of provincial Egypt – from the police to the army to the civil service – did so because they were related in some complex manner to someone else.

'*Shukran.*' He handed the tea-glass back to the tea-boy, who had returned to collect the empties. The drained glasses chinked on their steel tray as the train switchbacked, closing in on Sohag. The boy steadied himself, and his tray, and pressed on.

'*Shay! Shay! Shay!*'

Harper looked at the note again. The rest of it was in Arabic, which he could barely read, even though he spoke it pretty well. But Harper knew the contents: Hassan had already explained. It told the director of the Nazlet police that Ryan was mightily important and a great friend of Egypt, and Hassan of Abydos would be lavishly grateful if any assistance could be offered to his VIP American acquaintance.

Exactly what that assistance might be, how the hell he was going to get his hands on the Sokar documents, and how he was going to stop others from doing the same, Ryan did not know. But he was going to give it his best shot. His last shot. Late in the day, he'd been offered a break and he was going to take it. For his wife. For Victor. But mainly for himself. After ten years of giving everything to Egypt, a little selfish ambition was excusable. Wasn't it?

The train hooted in the dark, and this was accompanied by the squeal of its brakes: the dusty yellow

98

stain in the midnight sky confirmed that Sohag was near. He'd made it as quickly as he could in the circumstances. Would this be the crucial factor?

Quite possibly. The body of his old tutor had only been discovered yesterday. Harper might just be the first person on the scene with a real sense of what treasures could be contained in the bag found on Sassoon's body.

A row of shuttered shops flickered under dirty streetlights. The train clattered, and then halted, with a juddering wrench.

The station forecourt was chaotic. This time Ryan gave up any pretence at politeness and shunted his way through the mêlée. And as soon as he reached the street, he accepted the first offer of a cab – *Jayed!* – chucked his rucksack in the back seat, and sat in the front, like an Egyptian, alongside the driver.

Another half a mile brought them to the biggest hotel in town: an ugly concrete tower that loomed over the elegant eternity of the Nile in a forbidding manner. As he checked in, Ryan wondered if Sassoon had stayed here, during his final nights alive on this earth.

The night passed fitfully. Barges hooted on the Nile. His room smelled of toilet but the toilet smelled of woodsmoke. He tried to sleep but had bad dreams, for the first time in years. Dreams of his dead wife mixed with dreams of dogs, headless dogs, running down canal towpaths. Endless, sweaty, malarial dreams that made Ryan all too ready for morning: he rose before his alarm.

As the first pink intimation of day tinted the horizon he was already dressed and hailing another taxi.

The drive to Nazlet took several hours. By the time he reached the impossibly rural remoteness of the desolate town on the very edge of very serious desert, it was noon and fiercely hot. Dogs lay whimpering in the shade of the biblical palm trees.

He had to find the police station.

A handsome youth in a clean *djellaba*, riding a Japanese dirt-bike, was negotiating his way down the rutted road, avoiding heaps of camel dung. Ryan waved him over. The lad pulled up and stared, in blatant astonishment, at a Western face. Presumably Nazlet saw very few Euro-American visitors: maybe *none*. This was about as remote as settlements got on the frontiers of Middle and Upper Egypt.

Ryan asked in his clearest, slowest Arabic where the police station could be found.

The boy paused. Then he answered, in Arabic, 'Not far, half a kilometre past the old houses. Just up there.'

'Thank you.'

The youth nodded, and smiled his handsome white smile, then kick-started his bike again. As he drove off he shouted, 'But be careful. They are arresting everyone!'

This gave Ryan serious pause. Arrests? What could he do? Maybe he should go back to Sohag and wait. But that was absurd: he had come this far, and he was so near. The Sokar Hoard was within his grasp: he could sense it.

Resolved, Ryan turned. And saw a policeman.

The cop was standing three metres away. With a gun. Pointing at Ryan's chest.

'Come with me.'

13

Museum of Witchcraft, Boscastle, Cornwall

'Roasted cats?'

'Yes.'

'Hmmm.'

The owner of the museum paused, staring thoughtfully into space. Above him was a decorative wooden sign saying: THE MOST FAMOUS MUSEUM OF WITCHCRAFT IN THE WORLD.

Karen Trevithick would normally have dismissed this as tourist-attracting whimsy, or indeed as bullshit, but everyone she had spoken to had assured her: *No, go there, the guy who owns the place really knows his stuff. The museum is serious.*

So she had made the long drive to the beautiful stormy cliffs of far-north Cornwall and the fishing village of Boscastle, sequestered in a cove between those cliffs, staring out at the furious waves that attacked the stone harbour. The day was blustery and bright, and very cold. The village still had its Christmas lights dangling across the wet and narrow cobbled roads; they looked melancholy now Christmas was over.

Karen was glad when Donald Ryman, the late-middle-aged owner, closed the door to the salt-scented air, silencing the seagulls.

Again he stared at nothing, then he turned. 'Let's go into the museum, and think about cats. Roasted cats, yes, a little strange.'

Another door led into the museum proper; a series of small, low ceilinged rooms: fishermen's cottages knocked together. There was a big glass box in front of Karen: inside was a perpendicular stuffed goat wearing a dark scarlet robe.

'The goat of Mendes,' said Donald. 'An avatar of Satan, the Horned God, worshipped for thousands of years.' He pointed at a large rack of little glass jars, some full of vegetable matter, some containing ghastly wax dolls; naked, grimacing figurines. 'These are herbs for witchcraft, the real thing. Gerald Gardner collected them decades ago. The wax figurines are poppets, little models of people for sticking pins in, to cause injury or death.'

She waited for an explanation but Donald's eyes were now fixed on something over her shoulder. She turned to see what he was looking at. The exhibits were many: a dried old stoat, a hag stone for cursing, a rabbit's heart pierced with a thorn – and a stuffed cat, chasing a stuffed rat.

He gestured at the mangy old stuffed cat. 'Taghairm! Yes, yes. Taghairm!'

'What?'

'I believe what you witnessed was Taghairm! A truly *ghastly* ritual, often associated with the Celts, especially in Scotland.'

Karen gazed at the cat, as Donald went on, 'Cats, why didn't I think of this before? Yes! Cats are so important to magic. In medieval England cats would be buried alive in walls, as charms against rats or mice. These are surprisingly common – they come as a nasty surprise to homeowners, ah, renovating their lovely period cottage. A dead cat in the walls!' He chuckled. 'Cats are intrinsic to magical ritual. The idea of them as creatures of supernatural power dates back to Egyptian times, of course. The Egyptians worshipped the cat. The fear and veneration of cats has continued ever since.'

'Taghairm? What is that?'

He was interesting but her time was short: they had a suicide now, a dead body, linked to the atrocious ritual on Zennor Hill. *Speed the case.*

'Sorry, witchcraft is my passion, I can be a little discursive. Taghairm is a Celtic rite also known as "giving the Devil his supper". It's a ceremony where a series of cats is burned alive, one after the other, sometimes over a period of days. The animals would be roasted on, ah, spits, or drenched in liquors and oils and burned that way.'

'But why?'

'To summon the Devil! Or least a highly important demon. It was believed that the horrendous shrieking of the cats would disturb the Devil, and invoke him, and eventually he would be forced to reveal himself and do the bidding, at least temporarily, of the coven or the wizard.'

A ritual for summoning the Devil? Karen walked around the darkened rooms with their glass cabinets and their morbid contents: a naked mandrake in a jar, inscribed with a screaming face; a knitted poppet woven with real human hair and stuck with a vicious pin; a medieval wooden carving of a woman tearing open her vagina, leering. The silence was claustrophobic. She turned to look at Donald, who was sorting through some keys.

'The museum.'

'Yes?'

'Why is it so empty?'

'Because we're closing today you see, closing for the winter.' He brandished the keys. 'We open from April to October, for the tourists. In the winter we reopen for Christmas and New Year, but that's it. The village is largely holiday homes, half are empty in winter: there's really no point after New Year.'

The village had seemed strangely deserted. A bit like Zennor. Karen filed the thought away: holiday homes? That was a thought, but she didn't know why: it was a useful object she could not yet find a use *for*.

'OK, tell me more about Taghairm. This really happened? How do we know?'

'Because it is attested by reliable historians.' Donald smiled. 'The last known certain case of a Taghairm was

105

in Skye, Scotland, at the so-called False Church – a large rock by a cave – some time in the eighteenth century. Though there are reports of it happening since.'

'What reports?'

'Rumours, as it were. No more than that. Satanists, Wicca practitioners, you know.'

Karen felt she was missing something. Cats. All those cats. Screaming. She walked between the glass cases, examining the noisome objects. A selection of moles' feet; a human skull strapped in a leather harness 'for placing on an altar'; glass spirit houses – pieces of animals and plants trapped in ancient glass bottles.

The collection was impressive, and disturbing. Karen had no time for superstition, no more than she had for religion, yet there was a real quality to this display; the weighty evidence of human credulity, and human malignancy, was itself unnerving. People actually believed all this stuff: to curse and kill, bewitch and invoke. And people roasted dozens of cats, on Zennor Hill, *just last week.*

Cats. Again the cats. What obvious piece of the puzzle was dangling in front of her face, hidden in plain sight from her mind?

Karen had reached the back of museum. It was very dark here, and cold. The wind moaned at a small window. These cottages were badly lit. But the walls were thick and strong, to withstand the winter gales.

A passing shaft of frail sun illuminated a SPECIAL EXHIBIT OF SEA WITCHCRAFT: a mermaid's purse for capturing ghosts, a lobster claw inscribed with a spell, a glass ball for warding off evil from the oceans, and something very odd: a kind of ugly, fragile grey cloth. What was it?

Leaning closer, Karen read out loud the small explanatory sign: 'One of the museum's prized possessions, this is a human caul, a membrane that sometimes covers a baby's head at birth. Dried and preserved, these were much sought after by seamen as they were supposed to prevent drowning.'

Karen winced. A baby's caul? Wretched.

She turned to ask Donald a question but he was nowhere to be seen: locking up his business, perhaps.

'Hello?' she called.

The museum was silent. The skull with the leather harness stared at her. The sacred seahorses on their little strings swung gently in some unfelt breeze. The darkness was palpable now, the winter twilight falling at four p.m. She thought about her mother, burned in the crematorium. The burning of the corpse. This was stupid; yet it was so dark. She could barely see the way through the maze of exhibits to the door.

The door was shut.

'Hello?'

Silence. Karen felt a rising and absurd panic. Where was Donald Ryman?

'Miss Trevithick.'

She jumped as if she had been scalded. He'd appeared from nowhere – or at least, from a little open side door she hadn't even seen.

'*Jesus!*'

'My apologies, ah, did I scare you?' He lifted the keys again. 'I was locking some of our most valuable cases, the Golden Dawn collection. In the side room.'

'The Golden what?'

'Dawn. They were a group of bohemians and writers, poets and aristocrats, in the 1900s, in London. Yeats was a member, the Irish poet. The Order of the Golden Dawn. They revived Western occultism. We have some of their more exquisite paraphernalia here, very valuable. And actually . . .' His smile was scarcely visible in the gloom, but he was definitely smiling, a man with a secret, or a revelation.

'Go on.'

'I have had an insight that might entice you. The library angel has visited!'

Donald began the walk back to the main door, swinging the keys, annoyingly. And talking over his shoulder. Karen followed, listening.

'One of the most famous members of the Golden Dawn was Aleister Crowley, of course. Interestingly, he was also closely associated with the use of cats for ritualistic purposes. He was known as the wickedest man in the world, the Great Beast 666.'

Karen was mystified. She followed Donald into the museum shop, and watched as he locked the door behind them. She was glad to be in the brightness of the shop. With its plastic skulls and its fake poppets. 'I don't see the relevance of this Crowley guy, apart from the cats.'

'Come over here. I have a book for sale. *The Tregerthen Horror*, by a fine local writer.'

He plucked the book from a wire rack and handed it to her. A storm seemed to be picking up outside, dark rain flaying the shop windows.

'There are several links between Crowley and far-western Cornwall. As this book explains: links between him and Zennor, and Penzance, and Newlyn, that whole area. I also believe there is some connection between him and Carn Cottage – wasn't that the cottage where you found the cats?'

Karen nodded. She had one more question. 'But who was Crowley?'

Donald was turning off the lights, one by one. 'Oh, a great Satanist, or a great lunatic, take your pick. A very controversial figure. In the 1920s he rented a villa in Sicily, which he devoted to sex magic and such, a very notorious place. He had his wife raped by a goat there. And he is said to have performed Taghairm, which killed someone.' Ryman switched off the final light, so that they were drenched in sudden darkness. 'That's interesting, isn't it?'

14

Nazlet, Egypt

They didn't even get in a car.

The policeman just walked him five hundred metres up the road, to a large office tiled white and blue. What was happening? Why was he being arrested? Was this the police station? Ryan gazed around, repressing his panic.

The place was certainly governmental – one of the few buildings in this broiled and dusty town not made of mud brick and straw.

Inside the stuffy office were three more Egyptian cops, irritable and tired. The men were sweating in the afternoon heat and waving at the sandflies. A non-dusty oblong on the otherwise dusty wall showed where the latest portrait of the lately deposed president must have hung until very recently.

A cop invited him to sit. The police didn't seem *that* hostile. More dutiful. But dutiful could easily turn to vengeful with the Egyptian security forces. And they weren't averse to beating up the odd foreigner.

Ryan steeled himself.

They questioned him for two hours. What was he doing here? How did he get here? Why come to a place like Nazlet Khater? Why did he speak good Arabic? Did he have a permit to travel? Ryan knew his best hope of avoiding a much nastier complication was honesty, or something close to it. So he was honest. Almost.

'I am an Egyptologist, an American academic. I live in Abydos; here is my passport. I am an old friend of Victor Sassoon, and I heard that his body had been found. I do not have a permit to travel, but I only travel by day . . .'

But it wasn't his answers the saved him from further harassment: it was Hassan's letter.

When he produced it, the senior policeman read the contents and broke into a wary smile.

'Ah, Hassan Elgammal. A great friend. I know his father.'

He handed back the letter, and nodded, with a faint expression of apology. 'We have had a lot of trouble here. Many people wanted to find this Victor Sassoon, I do not know why. Anyway, his body is already buried, in accordance with Islamic law, so you have no further need to concern yourself.'

Every part of Ryan's soul was yearning to ask: what about the Sokar documents? What was found with the body? But he knew he couldn't do that: this would only provoke their suspicion once again, and then their wary acceptance of his story would certainly revert to something much nastier.

Taking Egyptian antiquities unlawfully was a serious offence, in any circumstances: the Sokar documents technically belonged to the Egyptian people and the Egyptian state. The police could put him in jail for years if he confessed what he was really doing, without any kind of permission. It would be like admitting intent to steal the golden death mask of Tutankhamun.

Ryan felt defeated. The entire exercise had been valueless. Now he could go back to hodding his bricks in the Oseirion, back to the life of a Pharaonic slave. But something in him rebelled at the idea: Hassan had been right, Ryan had done enough labouring now. He wanted to be a scholar again. To be the Egyptologist he was. To think. Use his brain.

The police officer stiffly gestured: 'You can wait in here for a while, then we will take you to the buses and you can go home.'

A door was opened to a side room. Two other people were sitting on bare chairs therein. A white woman in her late twenties, and a light-skinned Egyptian. Both looked weary and bored; both gave him a brief glance, then looked away, staring at the floor, or at the barred and grimy window.

What was a Western woman doing here? Ryan had no time to find out, or even ask a question. Minutes later, a fifth policeman entered the room. He escorted them silently out into the blinding sun, with their bags.

The woman had a hefty rucksack, like a backpacker. They were squeezed into a police car, which rattled down the muddy road, to a bare and windy square. Dented minibuses waited here. Egypt's rural public transport. The policeman gestured at one empty bus.

'These will take you to Tahta. From there you can get a train.'

The police car drove off. The light-skinned Egyptian looked nervously around, then immediately climbed on board the minibus.

Ryan was about to follow when the woman spoke, very quietly. 'You're Ryan Harper. The Egyptologist. You knew Sassoon.'

He paused, almost frightened. She continued.

'I've seen you in photos. With him. I know a lot about Victor Sassoon.' Her English was perfect but she had a definite accent: Dutch, or German. A blonde European woman in Nazlet who knew who he was: what the hell?

Now she lifted two stiff fingers to her mouth like a boy pretending to blow smoke from the muzzle of a gun. As if to say: *Wait, be quiet, listen, say nothing.*

He said nothing. She spoke again. 'You came looking for something, didn't you?'

The wind whirled across the sandy square. The place was deserted, apart from a stooped old woman in black shrouds, walking in the shadows towards a little shop. Ryan nodded and replied, very quietly, 'Yes.'

The young woman's face was expressionless. She seemed to be assessing him. 'I have something you need to see, later. We can talk later. In the town.'

He climbed on the minibus, and calmed himself as best he could.

The journey was staccato and uncomfortable. The road to Tahta passed endless little villages identical in their poverty: the repetition was like an hallucination, as if Egypt had hired a handful of extras on the cheap to appear in every scene. There was the wall-eyed man sitting on a stool smoking *shisha* outside a tea-house, there was the dog with three legs dragging itself towards a reeking heap of rubbish. And there they were again.

Through it all the European woman texted messages from her phone. Occasionally she made, or took, furtive calls, whispering and inaudible. Glancing at Ryan as if she was deciding something.

What did this woman have? What was going on?

'Tahta!'

The minibus had drawn to a halt in a nondescript square with a perimeter of tea-houses with *shishas*, and a blue Co-op gas station, trailing a queue of rusty taxis. Everyone climbed off, dragging their bags. Ryan looked around. The sun was going down, turning the eastern cliffs, fifteen kilometres away, to mauve. The city of Tahta was straggled along the Nile valley.

The light-skinned Egyptian disappeared at once. The other passengers dispersed. Soon it was just him and the woman.

Abruptly, she extended a hand. 'Helen Fassbinder.'

Perplexed, Ryan shook her hand.

For the first time, she allowed herself a small and anxious smile. 'You must have questions.'

114

'Just a few million. Nothing too demanding.'

'Come. Let us have tea.'

The Dutch or German accent was definitely there: come – *komm*. Brusque and forthright.

His curiosity *burned*.

Ryan followed as Helen led them to the dirtiest possible tea-house at the corner of the square. Despite its impoverished exterior, it was busy with men smoking *nargilehs*, sipping thick sweet coffee from small dirty cups, playing *sheshbesh*, arguing. Some of them glanced at the Western couple, then returned to their games and caffeinated debates. Obviously Tahta still got a few tourists, thanks to its train station: tourists heading south for Abydos and Luxor, or north to Coptic sites, like the Monastery of the Bones.

Helen ordered tea for them both in clumsy Arabic, the tea-boy looking almost paralytically fascinated at the idea of a woman ordering for a man. Or maybe it was her hair that astonished him. The boy kept looking at her unveiled blonde hair. Stealing glances at it, rapt with repressed desire.

Helen was apparently either oblivious, or very accustomed, to the effect she was having on the boy. 'Let me tell you my story. Yes?'

Ryan disguised his urgent curiosity. He nodded calmly.

Between brief and rapid sips of tea, she told him she was a German film-maker, freelance; she lived in London, or sometimes Berlin. Or sometimes she just travelled. She made documentaries by herself, with her own camera. Just her and a camera. Her living was precarious, but exhilarating.

'Sometimes I get lucky, sell a film. To German TV or the BBC or America. That feeds me for a while. I made a documentary two years back about Gilles de Rais. *The First Serial Killer.* You have heard of it?'

'Sorry. No.'

'A medieval mystery, a Frenchman who was a murderer. I tried to solve it. I did not. But at least I sold it. My movies try to answer historical or modern puzzles.'

'What were you doing in Egypt?'

'I think you can guess. You are beginning to guess? No?'

'Am I?'

'I was in Egypt making a film about Tutankhamun. It was not so good. Boring. But then I heard about Victor Sassoon.' She sipped her tea. 'I heard about his disappearance, and all the other rumours. This was much more exciting for me. A great possibility, a real modern mystery. What did he find in the desert? The Sokar Hoard? Why did he disappear? Walk off into the wilderness? So for these last weeks I have been tracing his steps across Egypt. Cairo. The Red Sea. Nazlet.'

Ryan stared into the deep red tea in his glass; then he looked into her clear blue German eyes. 'But how do you know who I am?'

'I began with lots and *lots* of research. I did not sleep for days! Learning everything I could. In a lot of Cairo

116

internet cafés.' Her smile was very brief. 'I now know many things about Sassoon. Who he taught, who he knew, who he met. You were one of his more famous pupils when he taught at UCL. What happened to you? You used to be famous, then, *pfft*!'

The question was so direct it was beyond rudeness. Maybe it was just Teutonic and efficient? Ryan shook his head. 'Something happened. It doesn't matter. Tell me more about . . . Nazlet.'

Helen Fassbinder paused, and looked past him at the doorway and the street, and Ryan took the opportunity to assess her. She was beautiful, but in a very severe way; indeed it was so severe her beauty bordered on plainness. Her blonde hair was too-tightly tied back, her blue shirt was stainless, despite the rigours of the day. Her black jeans were quite immaculate. But there was also a real nervousness there, a vulnerability, a flaw in the ice-blue of her eyes.

'I came to Nazlet and stayed for three weeks. I rented a house. A hovel. I rented a motorbike. I scoured the desert, I made a friend. But of course it was impossible. The desert is too big.'

A text pinged on her mobile phone. She broke off the conversation and read it, without apology. A wordless nod. Then she looked back at Ryan. Blue eyes fierce, judging him. 'Then a Bedu, a camel herder, came into town, from the western desert.'

Ryan nodded. The old trading routes, from oases like Kharga and Farafra, often made shortcuts straight across the wilderness. Modern Egypt had long since

117

abandoned such three-thousand-year-old thorough-fares but Bedouin would still use them.

'The Bedu man was bubbling. Gossiping. He told everyone in Nazlet that he had found a body, a white man, in a cave. Apparently his dog had wandered off, into the cave. The Bedu followed. Found the body. I knew it had to be Sassoon. A body wearing Western clothes? Of course it was Sassoon.'

'And he had a bag with him?'

Helen didn't answer. 'I made my move immediately. I knew that as soon as the news spread, the police would come. Treasure hunters. Journalists. I paid the Bedu to come with me, two hundred dollars. We got another motorbike. He led me into the desert, and I found Sassoon. Lying there, in the cave. He had already begun to mummify.'

A tiny ripple of emotion made Ryan bite his words away. Helen's voice softened, just for a moment. 'I am sorry. He was your friend?'

Ryan Harper fought the sadness.

'Victor Sassoon wasn't just my friend, he was an *exemplar*. The amazing work he did on the Dead Sea Scrolls, they were an inspiration to me, one of the reasons I took up Egyptology. He was maybe the greatest scholar of ancient Semitic and Egyptian languages. And he was . . . generous with his time, a great man – it's difficult to explain . . .'

The softening in her voice disappeared. 'So your friend Sassoon could understand the Sokar documents? And maybe you can too.'

Ryan's excitement returned. He leaned forward, urgent. 'What did you find in the cave?'

She paused. Then she hauled her rucksack onto her lap. And answered plainly, 'The Sokar Hoard.'

15

Tahta, Egypt

Ryan stared at her. 'You have the *Sokar Hoard*?'

She nodded. 'Yes. Or rather, I have part of it. I found some of the documents. They had been scattered. The bag was ripped open. A jackal maybe. Or just wind, I do not know. They were everywhere, in chaos. I picked up a few pages, and then . . .'

'Then what?'

Helen glanced over her shoulder, and nodded in greeting. Then she looked back at Ryan. 'Ryan, meet Albert Hanna.'

The name chimed a bell in Ryan's mind, but he was so full of questions and puzzles that he couldn't recall it. Helen hurried on, as the dapperly dressed man pulled up a chair and sat down.

'Albert has been helping me. I met him during my weeks in Cairo, when I was researching Sassoon. I have promised him a share in the profits, of the film, if we solve the puzzle.'

This was enough. Ryan chopped the air with a hand. 'So tell me, show me the *texts*.'

Helen Fassbinder shook her head. 'There is one more chapter to the story. Then I will show you.' She blinked, and hurried on. 'You see, I picked up some pages, when I was in the cave. But then, as I was gathering these pages, I heard noises outside. I realized the Bedouin had gone, so it was not him. And the noise was . . . loud, deafening. It was *whump whump whump*.'

'Sorry?'

'A helicopter. Landing outside. That distinctive noise. *Whump whump whump*, just landing in the desert.' She shrugged. 'Soon as I heard the helicopter, I knew it was serious. Dangerous. I found a place to hide, in the cave. Right at the back, it was . . . not nice. Frightening. I had to just lie there in the dark. Then the men came in. The soldiers.'

'Egyptian soldiers?'

She shook her head. 'Israelis.'

'*What?*'

'They spoke Hebrew. They must have been Israeli soldiers. Or police. Mossad. I do not know.'

The tea-house seemed to have darkened; everything seemed to have darkened. He leaned closer, as she continued.

'They gathered all the other pages of course, everything I had not got. They took the bulk of the Sokar

121

Hoard. But they left the body. And then they ran out. Just like that, to their helicopter. *Whump whump whump!'*

'They didn't find you?'

'I was well hidden. And maybe they saw the Bedouin running away, on his bike, so they thought everyone had gone. They were in a hurry, too.'

'But how did they know where to go? How did *they* find the cave?'

'Following our bike trails? A satellite? Probably. We did try to hide our tracks at the end. My motorbike was concealed, five hundred metres away. In case.'

'Smart, very smart.'

She ignored his remark. 'I waited for a while, to make sure they were gone, but then the Egyptian police came. Suddenly it was like a rush hour. And still I hid. I had to stay there. For hours. I thought I was going to die. I had one bottle of water. Then at last they left with the body. And I got on my bike and drove back to Nazlet in the dark.'

Ryan gazed at her with admiration. She had real courage; it was quite a story.

She didn't seem to notice, or care. 'But the next morning the police did a sweep. Arresting anyone foreign or suspicious in Nazlet. Like you. Of course the Israelis were long gone. But they did it anyway. They took me too. I was getting ready to leave town. I told them I was a tourist, an academic on holiday.'

'In Nazlet?'

'A decade ago they found some ancient bones here,

thirty thousand years old. In the caves. So I pretended I had an interest in palaeontology.'

'OK . . .'

'My story made sense. To them. They do get the occasional scientist. So they questioned me for a while, then held me. In that room where we met.'

The last corner of the puzzle was revealed.

'They never searched you. Wow.'

'They did not search me. They had no suspicions. So, I still have them in here, the pages I collected. The Sokar Hoard, or part of it. Here. Let us go outside. And now you can see. I think I need your help to decipher the texts.'

The hitherto silent Mr Hanna waved over the tea-boy, and paid the minuscule bill. As he did so, Ryan clocked his accent: middle-class, Cairo, probably Coptic. What was he doing here? But that question was swamped by the bigger desire, the impending revelation. *The Sokar Hoard.*

Together and in silence they walked to a discreet street corner, deserted apart from a water-seller sleeping in the dusk, his back to a bare unplastered wall. The nocturnal traffic of Tahta buzzed in the background.

Reaching into her rucksack, Helen Fassbinder pulled out a file. She opened it in the mosquito-ridden street-light, and showed the first precious page to Ryan.

He took it, his fingers slightly trembling.

It was unquestionably old. It was written on papyrus, fragmented at the edges but still essentially intact. The calligraphy was faded yet legible; the script looked like ancient Coptic demotic, Akhmimic, certainly extremely archaic. Dating from maybe the sixth or seventh centuries.

With a juddering sense of bitter defeat, Ryan Harper realized that he couldn't understand a single word.

16

Carnkie, Cornwall, England

'Look, Mummy, I can do the giraffe dance!'

Karen stared at the laptop screen, and the image of her six-year-old daughter twirling. 'That's brilliant, sweetheart.'

'And the llama dance. Like a llama. We're doing llamas at school, Miss Everest says.'

'I love it. So how *was* your first day at school? . . . Ellie?'

No answer.

Her daughter had disappeared. All Karen could see was the wall of her cousin's spare bedroom back in London. She waited for her daughter to realize that her mother was still here, at the other end of this video call, at the other end of the internet, at the other end of the country. But nothing.

'Ellie . . . darling. Eleanor? Sweetheart? Hello?'

Suddenly her cousin Alan appeared on the screen.

'Sorry, Karen, she's run off with the twins. They're counting how many cracks we have in the ceiling. I think we may have to decorate. But at least they're having fun. Lots and *lots* of fun.'

Karen smiled even as she felt the fierce pang of separation from her daughter. She was pleased that, as an only child, Eleanor had somewhere close to go, with cousins the same age; but selfishly, ludicrously, she didn't want Eleanor to have *too* much fun, not without her.

'How did her first day at school go?

Alan shrugged. 'Oh fine, fine. She's got some party invitation, and a gold star for reading about the Fire of London. She's absolutely fine, Kaz.'

Karen shook her head. 'God I feel guilty. Her first day back at school and I wasn't there. I'm a terrible mother.'

The kind eyes of her cousin stared at her, unblinking. 'No, you're a *single* mother, Kaz. And it's *tough*. And you have an important job and you just lost *your* mother; don't beat yourself up.'

'I should be back in a few days, it's just that I've been assigned to this case – they reckon I have some expertise, after the Muti killing in London. But if we—'

'Karen! Shush. Ellie can stay here as long as she likes, the twins love her, they go to the same damn school, it's not an issue, please don't stress. But look, I have to go.' He was gazing away from the camera, but laughing. 'Ah. I think they're trying to climb in the tumble dryer. That's not good. Skype you soon!'

'But—'

The screen went dead.

Karen stared at the blackness, then shut the laptop and shivered. A window was open across the room: she was airing out her mother's old house, getting ready to sell it. She had spent the last two days packing away her mother's things: binning most of them, with pangs of guilt. The paraphernalia of an entire life. Tipped into a black plastic bag.

The job had been painful and troubling, and Karen had distracted herself by working the case in her mind. But she hadn't got far.

As Karen made one last sweep of the house, closing the windows, picking up the last knick-knacks, throwing away the final detritus, she did the sums again. Maybe this time an answer would miraculously evolve.

As she locked the kitchen window, she thought about a story her dad once told her, of miners in their thirties, even twenties, dying of silicosis: they would stand at these same windows in Carnkie and suck at the fresh air, desperately trying to fill their dying lungs. Killed by just a decade of drilling hard rock.

Mining was so tragic.

Mining. Yes. *Mining.* She focussed on Botallack mine, once again.

The boy in the main Botallack shaft had yet to be identified. He'd had nothing on his person that could name him. He matched no missing person on the Scotland Yard files.

They also believed, now, that the cat-burning on

Zennor Hill had probably been some Satanic rite, Taghairm, but this guess was just about *all* they had to go on.

So who were the people glimpsed running away from the scene? Maybe a group of in-comers: people who had rented a house, or stayed in Cornwall for Christmas, or longer – blow-ins, as the locals called them. The Truro police were right now asking every owner of every hotel and apartment and holiday cottage in western Cornwall for the identities of every tourist and visitor on the books for the last two weeks.

But this was a long shot, and an arduous task. There were thousands of hotel beds and thousands of holiday lets in West Cornwall: the region lived off tourism. And the cat-burners could have stayed in various different addresses, to hide their traces, or they could have used a base just over the River Tamar. Or maybe they had driven in from Dorset, or London, or France, or China.

No, they needed more than this dragnet to find these cat-burners, and to unravel the reason for the boy's suicide in Botallack. That's if it *was* suicide. Maybe something he'd seen had driven him to kill himself? They appeared, after all, to have been trying to summon the Devil. By burning cats.

Of course the Devil had not appeared on windy Zennor Hill, on New Year's Eve, but to go to those lengths meant these people believed they could do it, which meant they could believe anything. So maybe the victim in Botallack jumped because of some terror, of something he had seen – or *imagined* he'd seen?

Alternatively, the horror of that night might have tipped an already unbalanced mind to suicide.

Karen shuddered, feeling the absence of something, like a faint ache. Something hidden from view, like her daughter hiding behind the sofa, laughing.

She went into her mother's old bedroom. The wardrobes were empty, the bed was stripped, the life had gone. She bit her lip to scare the tears away, and checked the chest of drawers for anything left behind. Nothing there. It was all gone. Just one framed photo, of her mother and father, on their honeymoon, stared back at her. She'd saved this for last: it was so symbolic of the past. The past now gone.

Picking up the photo, Karen stared at her mother. She could see the obvious resemblance with herself: slightly pretty, perhaps, but certainly no beauty. Someone had once said Karen's mum was 'sturdy and determined', and it was true – and true of Karen, too. They were, after all, descended from those bal maidens who worked the deads at South Crofty. All those generations of tough women.

Slipping the photo in a bag, Karen turned away.

Focus on the case. Sort the deads.

She walked back into the living room and sat at the table. Next to the laptop was the book Donald Ryman had sold her. *The Tregerthen Horror*. She picked it up and squinted at the pages as the winter daylight faded outside.

She'd spent the last two days reading the book between bouts of house-cleaning; reading it with increasing frustration. It told a complex story of links between the Satanist Aleister Crowley and Cornwall, but the links, however interesting, were tenuous.

The title itself referred to a mildly notorious death that had occurred at Carn Cottage, in the 1930s.

The victim – a local artist, Ka Cox – had previously been linked with bohemian circles, including Crowley, before the Great War. In her middle age she seemed to have renewed some of those links – she got to know a couple performing Crowleyan magic. This couple had then come to stay at Carn Cottage, near Cox's own house, Eagle's Nest. And it was at Carn Cottage, one dark winter's night, that Ka Cox suffered a fatal and unexplained seizure.

But what did all this add up to? The story was tantalising enough. But there was no *real* proof of anything. It was all gossip, and supposition.

Karen flicked through the pages of the book, one more time. Since Cox's death the cottage had housed artists and writers. In the sixties a man had gone mad there after taking mescaline, ending up in Bodmin asylum. Ghosts had supposedly been seen in the vicinity. The local consensus was, unsurprisingly, that the cottage was haunted, or hexed in some way. Hence its ruinous state. You could therefore see why someone might select it as a venue for summoning the Devil, with all its morbid history, and that spectacularly brooding location.

But the direct Crowley connection with Carn Cottage was weak. If anything the links between this strange man and Cornwall were stronger a few miles across the moors, on the *south* coast: he had definitely stayed in the old fishing town of Newlyn in the thirties, but he had also stayed in lots of other places, some of them with the vaguest of descriptions: a 'seaside inn', a 'Victorian hunting lodge', a 'guest house in Penzance'. It was a maze of seemingly pointless information, with no exit.

The room was very dark now; it was time to go. Karen didn't want to linger: the sadness was too much. She had a hotel room booked in Truro.

Turning to leave, she realized there was one last thing she had to do. Kneeling on the worn grey carpet she checked under the leather sofa. Something was there, among the dustballs. Straining and squeezing, Karen reached and pulled it out.

A tiny little china cat. Her mother collected them.
Jesus!

Karen cursed in the silence of the house. Jesus Christ. The cats!

She swooped on her mobile, and called Sally Pascoe.

'Hello? Karen?'

'Cats, Sally. The cats!'

'What?'

Karen was excited, almost babbling. 'You've checked for missing cats?'

'Yes, but—'

'Sal, they needed *hundreds* of cats for this: where would they get them? You wouldn't transport them far, not if you could help it. A van-load of cats!'

'Of course we checked, across Cornwall, took us days – we were hoping for some witnesses, suspicious characters, someone seen taking a cat, but we didn't get very far. Cats are lost all the time, the pattern is random.'

'We need to map them properly, and this time we need to *look for houses*.'

'What?'

'I'm coming over. Thirty minutes.'

Karen grabbed her bag and stuffed the book and photo inside. She was leaving her mother's lonely house for maybe the last time. She had to do it quickly, like this, or she would burst into tears. Determined and firm, she shut the lights, and marched to the door; the latch clicked behind her and she practically ran to her car. Fleeing the past.

A faint drizzle was falling: a regular Cornish mizzle. The windscreen wipers whirred and washed with her urgent thoughts as she sped into Truro, the pretty little cathedral city – the capital of the county. And the home of the big, grey, concrete Duchy of Cornwall Police HQ.

Four hours. It took four long hours and six bitter black coffees for Sally and Karen to re-analyse the records: to note every missing cat from the last six months in West Cornwall, and then to pin those locations onto Google Maps.

Finally, the two policewomen examined the completed map. The only noise was the late-night traffic, the hiss of cars on wet streets. Sally spoke first, stating the obvious.

'There's nothing, no pattern, it's really just . . . random. As I said.'

She was right: it was a chaotic mess of virtual pins.

'Bollocks.' Karen said, reaching for her coffee, and walking away from the desk in frustration. It was horribly cold. 'Bollocks. Bollocks. Bollocks.'

'Except . . .'

She turned. 'What?'

'Here.' Sally said. 'Look, see, there is a bit of a concentration here, *but it's a circle*. Inside it there are fewer pins.' She gestured at the centre of the screen. 'See – Kaz – here. Like a kind of halo effect. Hmm. Is that something?'

Karen leaned close to the laptop. As she scrutinized, she listened to her friend, explaining her thoughts.

'If they were stealing cats, they would have tried to disguise it by *not* stealing cats close to where they were holed up, so . . . so they'd maybe drive a few miles, in every direction – *then steal the cats*. No? So that might explain why there is a concentric circle, like a halo. And the centre of that circle . . . is where they were staying?'

Karen felt a tremor of excitement; she was so close to the screen she could almost kiss the computer. Tapping briskly on the laptop keys she expanded the map.

'OK, so let's see – here's the halo – and what's in the centre, here . . . just north of Penzance, Mousehole, the B3315. There's a wood right at the middle, Trevelloe . . . and here, Trevelloe Lodge. Looks like a big house. Or rather, a big *lodge*?'

133

Karen dived for her book. *The Tregerthen Horror*. She found the bookmarked page and read it out to Sally: '"Before the First World War, Crowley allegedly stayed in a large hunting lodge in the Penzance district, and conducted black magic rituals in the adjoining woods."'

'Well there are certainly woods, right next door, could be, could be . . . let's see, I'm googling it now.'

Sally Pascoe brought up an image on the screen. It showed a rather handsome Victorian hunting lodge. She clicked a key. '*And it's a holiday let*, Karen, look – it says the owners rent it out: "Available for rent on a monthly or weekly basis, with extensive gardens, in the beautiful district of Kerris."'

'Where do they live? The owners?'

'Here, in Truro, there's a number. We can call first thing tomorrow.'

'No. Let's wake them up.'

'Kaz, it's midnight!'

But Karen was already out of the door, racing down to her car. The drive took three minutes. They pulled up in front of a large expensive Georgian townhouse on Lemon Street with a fine view of the cathedral.

The second long buzz of the bell summoned the late middle-aged householder. He opened the door warily, dressed in silk pyjamas and a paisley dressing gown, looking shocked to see two women, and even more shocked when Sally showed him her ID.

'Devon and Cornwall Police, and this is Karen Trevithick, a detective with Scotland Yard.'

The man paled. 'Has something happened? My daughter?'

Karen realized belatedly how terrifying this must be, a police visit at midnight: obviously awful news. 'No, please, it's nothing serious, we hope. We just want to know about Trevelloe Lodge. You own it, yes?'

'Yes, we do, but, ah, we don't live there, we live here in town, we lease it.'

'You rent it out?'

'Well, yes, is that—'

'Who were the last people to stay there?'

The man frowned, anxious and maybe scared. 'A group of, er, young people. They rented it for the whole month, all of December. They left on New Year's Day.'

Sally asked, 'Do you have a list of the names?'

'No, not all of them. The booking was made in one name, we're not a hotel.'

Karen reached in her pocket and pulled out a photo of the dead kid from the mine. 'Do you recognise this face? Was this young man one of the party that rented your property?'

The flustered householder reached in the pocket of his dressing gown, and extracted some spectacles. He looped them over his ears, and examined the photo for half a minute. Then he said, very quietly, his voice quavering, 'I think so. Yes. He's the young chap that collected the keys. What is going on? What is this terrible wound on his face?'

Karen ignored the question.

'Was there anything odd about him, his manner – anything? Please think.'

'Ah . . .'

'Depressed, distracted, anything?'

'No, he seemed perfectly happy, ah, cheerful even.' The householder looked as if he yearned to shut the door on the cold night and these intrusive and pointless questions. 'Look, ladies, can't this wait until—'

'No,' Karen replied abruptly. 'Who was he with? You said you have the name of the one who booked the house. You recall it?'

The dressing-gown cord was tightened, defensively. 'Yes, it was Rothley, um, Mark Lucas Rothley.'

'Describe him.'

'Late twenties and intelligent, well spoken, presentable. I remember the name because he said it with such certitude. Yes. When we first spoke on the phone, and when he signed the rental agreement, he was the same.'

'What?'

'The way he stared at me, was . . . it was odd.'

'Odd? Odd how?'

The man was blushing. Sally was suddenly using her phone to browse the internet.

'Well. This is a little foolish. But, yes, it was the way he stared into my eyes. Rather rude in truth. I almost cancelled their rental. I was quite unsettled.'

Karen started to speak but Sally nudged her, brandishing her smartphone.

'There. I knew I'd heard the name. Rothley. I was cc'd an email from Bodmin police yesterday.'

'And?'

'A constable in Bodmin town centre arrested a girl yesterday, Alicia Rothley. There *must* be a connection.'

'What did she do?'

'Nothing much, apart from frightening shoppers. It wasn't an arrest as such. She was taken into custody *for her own protection*. She's up at Bodmin Secure Unit.' A pause. 'The old lunatic asylum.'

17

Sohag, Egypt

'It has often occurred to me that the women of Arabian Egypt have evolved so as to resemble the camel – the preferred sexual partners of their menfolk.' Albert Hanna gestured towards the end of the lobby, at a matronly woman swathed in a black niqab sipping tea with a young, similarly-shrouded woman. 'I mean, look at that poor mother, is she not camel-like? Isn't there something faintly Bactrian about her, the undulation, the humps—'

'Albert, shut the hell up.'

The beautifully suited Hanna turned and tightened the tiny knot of his exquisite silk tie. 'I am just whistling in the dark, Ryan. And, believe me, for Copts in Egypt now it is very, very dark.'

Ryan Harper grunted his ambivalence to this remark. Hanna was right, in a sense, of course: the news coming out of Cairo, and Assyut, and the Delta, was increasingly grim: Egypt's troubles were taking a sectarian turn – Muslim versus Christian – and with eighty million Arabs outnumbering eight million Copts there could only be one loser if everything really kicked off. But Ryan had very good Muslim friends and very good Coptic friends, many friends on both sides of the divide: the ordinary people, the workers, the real Egyptians who wanted nothing but peace. And casual, offensive bigotry like Hanna's was not going to help.

Moreover, what the hell was he doing here anyway? All through their train journey to Sohag, Ryan had been wondering this. He wondered it this morning, again, after a welcome night's sleep in the hotel that smelled of toilets.

He understood that Hanna was an expert in Coptic history and in Egyptian antiquities; he also understood that Hanna was one of the last people to see Victor Sassoon alive. But was that reason enough to recruit this annoyingly loquacious and faintly sinister man to the cause? Perhaps his barbed wit would play well on camera. Perhaps he could be a fixer, as Helen said. But he had fixed nothing yet.

A female voice interrupted his thoughts.

'OK, guys. I am ready. We will try again? Now?' Helen Fassbinder had returned from the rest room. She picked up her tiny movie-camera and raised a questioning glance at Ryan. He sighed but stood up: he had agreed to help make her movie.

Besides, they were all pooling resources so as to solve

the puzzle: they got to use his Egyptological talents, he got access to the Sokar documents.

But how were they going to solve the puzzle? The Sokar Hoard – or the small parts of it that Helen had retrieved from the cave – were opaque when they weren't bizarrely inconsequential.

Picking up the file of documents, Ryan followed Helen into a little room adjoining the lobby, which they had secured for its privacy. Albert Hanna remained in the hotel foyer.

After adjusting her digicam, Helen looked up, with an expectant gaze. Quietly and obediently, Ryan spoke to the camera, clutching the first sheet of papyrus.

'This is the most cryptic and perhaps significant of the Sokar documents that we possess. Unfortunately at the moment we are unable to translate it.' He paused, waiting.

Helen asked him, off-camera, 'Why? Tell us *why*. I can edit out the questions later. Do not speak to me, speak to the lens. Now.'

He stared at her, half-smiling. 'Are you always like this?'

She gazed back, unblinking. 'Yes. I am always like this. When I am working. Why waste time saying please and thank you? The lens, look in the lens.'

Ryan smiled, and faced the camera. 'Coptic is a very ancient language. The most archaic forms of it stretch directly back to the tongues of ancient Egyptian, that is to say, the language of the Pharaohs. This is because the Copts *are* the ancient Egyptians, to all intents and purposes; the word Copt is cognate with the word Egypt, hence the similarity. Both derive from the name Ptah, the founding deity of Egypt, first named in history perhaps five or six thousand years ago.'

He lifted up the papyrus, to show it to the camera.

'Coptic is, in a sense, ancient Egyptian simply written in a new alphabet, incorporating some Greek characters, and retaining, fascinatingly, a few hieroglyphs. Therefore the great age and venerability of Coptic makes it of serious interest to scholars. But it also makes it fairly impenetrable. It is essentially a dead language: perhaps only three hundred people speak it these days, mainly monks in the more remote areas of the country, who use it liturgically.'

Helen circled a hand, from behind the camera. A *hurry-up* gesture.

Again, he obeyed, feeling irritated. He'd never done this before; he didn't know what to do. But he tried. 'The problem with *this* text is that it is written in a very ancient and obscure form of Coptic. The Coptic language is divided into several dialects, like Fayyumic, Bohairic, Sahidic. This text is written in a form of Coptic known as Akhmimic, which makes sense, as the ancient, historically important city of Akhmim is just here, just across the Nile from where we are now, in Sohag, Middle Egypt.' Ryan pointed to his left, as if the camera could zoom in on Akhmim, through the hotel walls. 'The Gnostic gospels, famously discovered in a sealed jar in a cave in the desert a hundred miles from here, were written in Akhmimic. They shed new

141

and amazing light on the origins of Christianity at its inception. They tell us how some strange ideas were excluded from the Christian faith, and how certain heresies in turn became accepted beliefs. They provoked, and are still provoking, enormous arguments among historians and theologians, and great interest around the world.'

Ryan gestured at the papyrus sheet, in a way he hoped was eloquent.

'There is a strong chance this text, from the Sokar Hoard, could be *even more* explosive. But at the moment we cannot read it. Why? Because this codex has been inscribed using a peculiar form of sub-Akhmimic, also known as Lycopolitan, a form so ancient and difficult there have been just a few people in modern times who could decipher it. One such man was, of course, Victor Sassoon. But when he finished reading what is in this document, and those that were compiled alongside it, he walked out into the desert, and took his own life. Why? Was it something to do with what he read here, on this papyrus? That is what we are going to find out.'

He finished. Helen Fassbinder lifted her camera again, and instructed, 'Now go on to the other papers. The ones we *can* read.'

'Yes. OK.'

Ryan cleared his throat and picked up the newer pages, the only other documents Helen had retrieved. 'These more robust papyrus documents are maybe a little less intriguing, yet we *can* read them. They probably date from the eighth century. The Coptic is newer: mostly Sahidic, the standard form. These brief pages seem to be a list of Coptic spells and curses. Early Coptic Christianity was a peculiar mix of beliefs, doctrines and ancient traditions, strongly coloured with what we would call magic or sorcery. For instance, Copts and Gnostics thought nothing of citing Jesus as a kind of avenging demon, who could be summoned at will by the magician or spell-caster. At the same time, they would pray for aid from Egyptian gods, or Hebrew angels, or Assyrian djinns. Here, for instance, is a Gnostic fire baptism, citing Jesus, but also the demonic names of God.' Ryan turned the papyrus to show the camera, then returned it to his gaze, and read: '"*Yo Yo Yo, Amen Amen, Yaoth Yaoth Yaoth* . . . Come secretly Jesus and Melchidesek, come secretly and bring the water of the baptism of fire, of the virgin of the light."'

He shrugged, to camera.

'To us it sounds a little ominous, and strange, like a black-magic spell mixed with Christian prayer; the way the names of power – the names of demons – are liberally sprinkled with biblical references is unsettling. But that is because, in a sense, it is *meant* to be unsettling: black magic and Christianity mixed. Here is another spell which actually threatens an archangel if he doesn't bend to the will of the magician: "If you do not do my bidding, Angel Gabriel, I shall always despise you, and loathe you, ask God to condemn you, *atha atha atharim, atha atha atharim.*"'

He gestured at the words on the papyrus. 'Notice how this spell concludes with another one of those repetitive, menacing incantations that the early Copts believed embodied supernatural power in themselves.'

Ryan picked up the second sheet of Coptic spells. 'Coptic magic could also be very strange, and brilliantly mad; here is a final example, written in Mesokemic. It is a love spell, or sexual enchantment, "Catch a blue-green iridescent fly. Write it with the first name of the prayer: you must prepare it on the sixth of the month. Make it full of vinegar. Throw it in the oven."'

Ryan laid the sheet on the table in front. 'What does it all mean? Why were these spells and curses included with the other older papyri? Again, that's a mystery we hope to unravel.'

His speech finished, Ryan looked to Helen for affirmation. She nodded briefly, and turned off the camera. The pause gave Ryan more time to think. He picked up the second sheet of spells, and spoke.

'Actually, Helen, there is something else. But I wasn't sure whether to mention it on camera.'

'Yes?'

'Have you ever heard of the Sacred Magic of Abra-Melin?'

'No.'

'It's a particular and notorious form of Coptic sorcery. Very ancient.'

She shook her head. 'Please explain.'

'I believe the spells on this page are from an authentic version of the Abra-Melin rite. Ultimately this magic comes from Araki, a little town near here.'

She shrugged, and glanced down at her camera. 'How do you know all this?'

'Because I was shown a similar, more complete papyrus a couple of years ago, in Cairo, by a dealer. He wanted my opinion. Their papyrus was a very early version of Abra-Melin, just like *this* papyrus. Though he had the full text. That complete version was sold at auction, to someone in Israel.'

Helen frowned, puzzled.

'Israel. OK. That is a connection. But what does it mean?'

'I don't know. It's confusing, isn't it? At the very least someone is unearthing lots of these documents. Perhaps they are all from the same cache?'

Ryan turned at a noise. Albert Hanna had opened the door, and was gesturing, his face concerned and frowning. 'A problem.'

'What?'

'See for yourself.'

Ryan stepped out and gazed across the foyer. There was a disturbance at the entrance to the hotel. People were crowded at the glass doors, peering out, straining to see something. They seemed excited, or deeply anxious.

Quickly, Ryan followed Albert Hanna to the entrance. 'Albert, what's happening? What is it?'

The Coptic dealer pointed a manicured finger

upwards. Ryan now realized that everyone was staring upwards. Across the street, people were gathered on the pavement also looking up. Some were shouting, '*La! La!*' – No! No! Others were heckling and jeering, angrily.

Or exultantly.

Ryan looked up. There was a grimy concrete apartment block opposite, with a large balcony on every floor. Most of the balconies were deserted, but the top balcony was crammed with angry men, waving fists, shouting, '*Allahu Akhbar!*' – God is great!

Then Ryan saw, in the middle of the crowd on the balcony, the focus of this anger and wildness. A young lad was being lifted up, carried towards the front of the balcony, hoisted by furious hands.

It seemed, appallingly and grotesquely, that the men were going to throw the boy off the balcony. The drop to the road was twenty metres.

Ryan gasped. They really *were* going to do it. Murder him, in front of everyone!

'Jesus, Albert. What the hell?'

Hanna shook his head. 'Listen! Can't you hear what they are saying?'

'What?'

'The crowd is chanting. The boy is a Copt. Apparently he walked into a Muslim house and assaulted a girl. So now of course the Muslims are going to kill him.'

'Is it true?'

Albert shrugged, contemptuously. 'The crowds believe

it, the family believe it. The boy has no chance. So now he dies. Maybe we can have some tea after.'

'Fuck this. We can stop it.'

'Oh please, my friend, not the American superhero. Are you going to fly up there in a special embroidered cape? This is Egypt. The Muslims kill us for their sport.'

Ryan didn't listen. He couldn't watch a young boy being thrown to his death, like this, in broad daylight – it was a *lynching*. He'd spent too many years in Egypt and heard of too many atrocities like this: for once he was going to do something. He was liberated from his job, now he could be himself. What did he have to lose? He was Ryan Harper.

And he was four inches taller than most of the men here.

He barged his way through the glass door, then the pungent giddy crowd. Seconds later he found the apartment door on the street – wide open – and pushed himself inside, and up the stairs. He was running now.

One storey, two, three, four. This must be it. Again the door was open, people skipping in and out excitedly. They stared at Ryan in astonishment. He pushed them easily aside and made for the main room and the balcony. He was going to save this kid. He had to. It was wrong, he could save him.

The balcony was heaving with people, but Ryan shoved, using his strength: the boy was standing on the railings now, the men getting ready to throw him.

Ryan flailed his way to the front, and reached out. He could save him. He reached for the boy's legs to pull him to safety.

But at that moment the boy fell.

18

Sohag, Egypt

Even as Ryan reached for the kid's cheap blue jeans, the Coptic boy fell from the balcony – and Ryan grabbed his ankle. The boy yelled, in horror and shock and surprise as Ryan employed *all* his aching strength to drag him back up over the balcony, to safety.

For a few seconds an epic silence prevailed, as if the entirety of teeming Middle Egypt had drawn breath.

Then the shouting started: angry, sweating men jabbing fingers at Ryan and the lad – *What are you doing, he tried to rape her! The Zarraba kid was a rapist! What right have you got?* It was very ugly and very dangerous. Ryan backed slowly away, moving into the room, protecting the kid with a fatherly arm. For several minutes he waited, with the boy, cornered, but trying to stay calm and still, his hands raised submissively, hoping the angry men would calm down. The Coptic lad whimpered beside him, hiding in his rescuer's shadow.

But the mood didn't abate; the mood was *worsening*. Now he saw why: dark shades in the corners, the women of the house, affronted by a strange male, hiding their faces like terrified ghosts.

This was worse than bad. Quite possibly the house was orthodox Muslim: Salafist. So in saving the kid Ryan had committed a cardinal sin by intruding on the family space, forcing the women to veil themselves in their own house. A terrible error.

A dozen men were shouting, one old man with half a row of teeth was tugging his hair.

'Someone call the police. Lock him in a room. The American. Let's put him in a cell. And the Coptic boy. Take them!'

Thrusting the old toothless man aside, Ryan grabbed the boy's hand and bolted. He pushed open a door and threw himself and the lad down the dull concrete stairs, feeling the adrenaline of panic, two stairs at a time, three, jump, run. The voices were coming after him.

'Stop him, stop the American, the dog, the fucking dog, the son of a pimp! Stop his dog of a boy!'

Five, six, seven stairs. Here was the door; half-closed. He kicked it open violently and the light outside almost blinded him.

But they were out, in the street. The crowds roiled as a platoon of policemen pushed through. A big police van was attempting to shunt the crowds apart, to drive them back. Where was Helen? Where was Hanna? What had happened to them? He could still hear the men behind him, still shouting, 'Fuck him, the American, the monkey's ass: there he is, by the hotel, there's the boy, go and get them—'

'Ryan!'

He swivelled. It was Hanna – gesturing. 'Quickly!' He was beckoning Ryan inside the hotel lobby whence they had emerged. There was little choice: Ryan dragged the boy inside.

The hotel lobby was quiet. Everyone was staring at them, the tall American and the small, scruffy Coptic lad: headscarved women were staring from their undrunk cups of shay, in contempt and dismay, as if *Ryan* had committed some awful crime, as if *he* had pushed the kid off the balcony, rather than saving him.

'*La.*'

The boy wrenched his hand free of Ryan's grasp. His eyes were filled with panicky tears.

Ryan spoke to him, quickly, in Arabic. 'You must come with us. They will take you again. They will kill you.'

Hanna intervened. 'This way.' He pattered down the steps of the lobby out onto the terrace overlooking the Nile. 'We have your bags. That was brave and very stupid. And now we have a boy to save. Let us go to the river.'

It clicked. Ryan realized, yes, of course, *the Nile*. There was a small flight of stairs leading from the grubby hotel terrace down to a pier. And yes, there was a small motorboat, with a tall Arab man in a white djellaba, frowning and anxious. Helen was already inside the boat with their bags. She waved urgently.

He didn't need further encouragement. Hanna led the way but Ryan swiftly pursued, pushing the bewildered Coptic lad along. The three of them jumped into the boat and the man in white tugged his outboard motor into life and the little boat began its puttering course across the mighty Nile.

Instantly, suddenly, amazingly, peace descended; the peace of the eternal river, the cool breeze of the blessed Nile. They were OK, *they had escaped.*

The nearest bridge was maybe a mile downstream and jammed with traffic, there were no other boats in sight apart from one big coal barge, floating upstream. Ryan sat back, watching the East Bank recede, the hotel and the horror, the crowds. The boy sat at the end of the boat, covering his face with his hands. He looked barely sixteen, hardly more than a child.

Helen shook her head. Her eyes were also a little red. Had she been crying? The sight must have been ghastly from below.

Hanna was talking to the boy. 'Why did you do it? What did you do in there?'

The Coptic boy said nothing. His T-shirt was an advert for a ten-year-old Batman movie. His teeth were very white, his eyes very dark. A handsome young lad, but just a boy. Shamed and cowering.

Helen interrupted. 'Give him a chance. He . . . they were about to murder him.'

Everyone was momentarily silent.

152

The West Bank of the Nile was nearly in reach, the white-robed boatman was standing. Ryan looked at the boy. 'What is your name? Please tell us. Where are you from? How can we help you?'

The boy shook his head; then he stood up and jumped from the boat onto the riverside, as the boat collided with some disused old tyres hanging from the dilapidated wooden jetty.

'Wait!' Ryan jumped on to the jetty. 'Please, wait!'

The boy paused. He nodded in an odd fashion, his eyes bulging, as he yelled, in Arabic, 'You do not understand. Why did you stop them? I did it. I walked into the house, I touched their girl. I knew they would find me and try to kill me. I wanted them to kill me. I wanted them to kill me. I am Zarraba.'

Then he turned on his heel, and ran.

Ryan looked at Hanna, who looked at Ryan.

Helen cried, 'What? What did he say?'

'He said he wanted to die. He said he went into the house, hoping they would kill him.'

'Then he was clearly suicidal.' Hanna smoothed his goatee. 'And your attempt to save him was egregious.'

The boatman had finished tethering his vessel. Ryan felt the snag of something nasty, tugging at his memory. 'But there's something else. The Muslim men. They called the boy Zarraba, pig person. That's another name for the Zabaleen, isn't it? And isn't that where it all began? Sassoon, in Cairo?'

It was Helen who answered. 'Yes. The murdered

monk, seen by Sassoon. Wasef Qulta. He was a monk at the Monastery of the Caves in Moqqatam. Where the Zabaleen live.'

The white-robed boatman was waiting patiently for payment.

Hanna frowned. 'A seductive mystery. But we're not going to solve it here and now. Nonetheless the documents in our possession become ever more intriguing. And potentially remunerative. Mr Harper, you will *have* to translate it, you studied under Sassoon. In London. You can do this.'

'It's impossible. I had a look – I don't know Akhmimic.'

'Nothing is impossible. Quantum physics says the moon is potentially made of Brie. If anyone can translate those papyri, it is you. But come – first you need peace. I know a place where we can hide, for a few days, here, in Panopolis, the ancient city of Min, the Ninth Nome of Egypt. *Akhmim.'*

Hanna paid off the boatman with a handsome wad of Egyptian pounds. The three of them crossed the quayside to the street, where Ryan surveyed the quiet scene: low houses, donkey carts, a few barber shops; it was all much quieter than Sohag.

A few minutes later they were climbing out of a taxi in the centre of Akhmim.

By Egyptian standards the town was pretty, if impoverished: distressed churches leaned against even older mosques; weavers sat in houses by large open windows, to catch the light. Weaving was an ancient trade here, as Ryan knew. Some of the oldest textiles in Egypt came from Akhmim: the town's lineage was extraordinary.

'I have friends here,' said Hanna. 'An old Coptic family, quite distinguished. We can rest and hide out, like fugitives! We are safe, for the moment, from all that unpleasant kerfuffle in Sohag. Just along here – yes.'

They had come to a large modern house overlooking a scruffy open space used as a haphazard open-air museum; even from here Ryan could see a statue of Bastet, the cat goddess, and Sekhmet, with his lion head.

The Egyptologist in Ryan would normally have been deeply intrigued: he'd always wanted to visit Akhmim, given its amazing history, and had never quite found the time. But right now he wanted to be in a room, with the air conditioning on. And the doors firmly closed. The memory of the boy's face wouldn't leave him. Why did the Zabaleen boy want to kill himself? Was it just coincidence that he was Zabaleen? Or did it connect – somehow – to Qulta's murder?

The door of the house swung open. They were taken inside by a smiling, attractive, unveiled, middle-aged woman, who chattered in Arabic with Hanna. She wore a crucifix, kissed Hanna on the cheek, teased him about his pot belly. Helen disappeared into the bathroom.

The peace and coolness of the house was an unutterable blessing. Ryan was beginning to see exactly why Helen had recruited Hanna: he really was an operator, a player. He calmed things down and got things done, smiling with his very white teeth, talking in charming French and Arabic and English.

The Coptic woman showed Ryan to a large clean bedroom, where he dropped his bags and fell asleep.

Two hours later Helen knocked on his door. 'Come. I want to film you.'

A few minutes later he was sitting in the large white-painted living room, clearing his throat, talking to camera.

'Akhmim is, for Egyptologists, a truly tantalizing little city, rich in historical and cultural associations. The history of the town dates back to the earliest traces of Egyptian civilization, the Badarian culture of the fifth millennium BC. The sixteenth-century historian, Leo Africanus, claimed it was the oldest city in Egypt.'

Helen nodded her encouragement.

But Ryan was getting used to this anyway, talking to camera. He actively enjoyed it: he was using his knowledge. Teaching things to an unseen audience was better than talking to bored kids from New Jersey. It was maybe better than mixing concrete in the Abydos sun. He continued.

'Religiously, Akhmim has played a role out of all proportion to its size. The family of the Pharaoh Akhenaten, the first monotheist in history, came from Akhmim. Likewise, alchemy was born in Akhmim: the greatest alchemist in history, Zosimos of Panopolis, of the fourth century, lived here. Indeed the very word alchemy, and the word chemistry, might mean "that which is from Akhmim", since the city was also known as Khemmis or Chemmis, hence "chemistry".'

He paused, and leaned an inch nearer the camera. 'Then there is magic: Pharaonic and Egyptian magic all came from Akhmim. The wizards who duelled with Moses in the Bible were traditionally Akhmimic. Moreover, Hermes Trismegistus, the founder of Hermetic philosophy, of Western occultism, was likewise said to have lived here. And Sufism – the great cult of Islamic mysticism – was formed here, in the ninth century, with Dhul-Nun al-Misri.' He sat back a fraction. 'The associations are therefore endless and outstanding. Arguably, this tiny desert town is the religious navel of the world, more Jerusalem than Jerusalem. And of course, our documents, the Sokar documents, are written in sub-Akhmimic, the local dialect of Coptic, the oldest and most impenetrable form of that Gnostic language.' He stopped, abruptly, thinking hard.

'Why have you stopped? That was OK.' Helen sounded aggrieved.

He put his hand up for quiet, then called across the living room to Hanna, who had been idly leafing through a book. 'Is there a monastery around here with an intact library? Dating back to the fourth or fifth century?'

'There are dozens of monasteries! This region is one of the cradles of Coptic faith. The White Monastery had the finest library in Egypt after Alexandria was burned. That is where Sassoon found the Sokar documents, as we know.'

'Yes, but the White Monastery was ransacked, pillaged.

I just need a library with an intact run of codices – it doesn't have to be huge, just intact, unbroken.'

Hanna stood up. His face was delicately flushed. 'Because, if you can compare one text with the one before, and the one before that, going back through the decades, you will be able to see how the language evolved. You will be able to decipher the papyrus! *Très audacieux!* I know exactly the place. The Monastery of St Apollo. The Holy Family were meant to have sheltered there, in the Flight out of Egypt. But then they sheltered everywhere: they had a strange need for constant shelter. We require a taxi. We must be discreet.'

The drive took twenty anxious minutes, into the desert to a tiny, humble monastery tucked under a large cliff, pitted with Pharaonic tombs, like the sockets of eyes in skulls; all of it next to a shallow, artificial and very ancient-looking lake-pool.

Hanna did the preliminary and ancillary work, subtly smoothing their entrance into the monastic precincts, making generous offers to the preserved body of St John the Dwarf, taking tea with the bearded abbot, and telling diverting stories. He made sure water and fruit was brought to Ryan, as Ryan toiled in the little library among the musty parchments and fragile codices and doddering manuscripts and cracked *ostraka* – writing preserved on potsherds.

On the first day, he worked back through the codices and parchments, comparing, annotating and decoding. The mental work was hard but rewardingly exhausting. He felt the kindly face of Sassoon smiling over his shoulder. 'Not bad, not bad for an amateur philologist. Not bad at all.' He deciphered the name of the author; he cooled himself by taking a swim in the salty lake next to the monastery.

Helen joined him in the lake, Albert paddled. Ryan couldn't help noticing her lissom, suntanned body, in her swimsuit; he wrenched his gaze away. It was a physical effort to do so.

Albert and Helen retired to the town in the afternoon; Ryan kept working. Then at last he commuted back to Akhmim in the dark, safe from sight, and slept in the quiet clean house. That night there were no bad dreams.

On the second day, he returned to the monastery at first light, when the old mud bricks were cold to the touch and the desert cliffs tinted a pale tangerine. This day, he began to examine their papyrus in particular, but it was desperately difficult: so much was illegible, erased and defaced, the peculiar sub-Akhmimic alphabet so intractably old and unusual. At moments he felt he was close to a breakthrough, but it didn't come.

The starlit drive back to Akhmim that night was melancholy. He sat alone in the kitchen and ate *fuul* and flatbread for supper, staring at a Coptic calendar on the walls, thinking about the boy and trying not to think about what he had said; remembering his wife and trying not to remember her death. *Rhiannon*.

His lonely meal was interrupted by Helen. She sat down opposite, over a beaker of water. And spoke.

159

'Tell me your story, Ryan. What happened to you? Why did you disappear?'

This was Helen's manner, of course: abrupt, but not necessarily rude. Just dispensing with preliminaries and seizing the information. He was getting used to it.

Ryan exhaled, and gazed in her almost flawless blue eyes. 'It ain't pretty.'

'Tell me.'

He told her. How he had met and fallen in love with a young woman when he was studying under Sassoon in London, at the beginning of his glittering career, after leaving Harvard. This was when Ryan Harper was the coming man – Sassoon's successor, the brilliant new Egyptologist.

He said the word 'brilliant' with an ironic grimace. Helen nodded. 'And so? Then?'

A deep long pause. 'We moved to Egypt. Working in Saqqara. We were very happy, the happiest I had ever been. What does Freud say is the key to happiness? Work and love? Well, I had both. Then Rhiannon got pregnant, and we were both overjoyed, literally, beyond joyous.' He swallowed some *fuul* and flatbread, swallowed the choke of grief. 'She died in childbirth. A local infection, perinatal malaria, from the Delta. And the baby . . . My daughter went first, she died too. And that's when . . . well . . .'

The silence in the kitchen was morbid. Ryan picked up his plate and took it to the sink and washed it, noisily.

Helen spoke behind him. 'That is terrible.'

160

Ryan scrubbed the plate clean, and stacked it. 'My parents were Baptists, but I was never ever religious. And yet, what happened to Rhiannon and the baby – that killed something in me, killed the hope. I hated everyone, resented everyone. Then I stopped hating the world and began hating myself. Blaming myself. Should I have brought Rhiannon to Egypt? Unsanitary Egypt? Maybe I made a mistake?' He shrugged. 'Then I stopped caring. And started drinking. I got into fights, messy arguments, insulting important people. In Egypt, as you know, you have to play the politics. Kiss the babies of bureaucracy. I didn't. I was sacked. They were right to sack me. I drifted for a bit, a succession of demotions. By the time I was twenty-nine I'd had enough: I gave up the academic work and got a simple job as a charity worker in Abydos, trying to save the temple there, the Oseirion, from drowning. They have terrible problems with the water table, because of Aswan.'

'You raised some money for this cause?'

'Sometimes. Mostly I just got stuck in – physical labour, digging ditches. Hard yakka, as the Australians say. I enjoyed not having to think.'

Helen gazed at the table, then at his face. Then she said, 'I did notice your hands. They are tough, bruised, not the hands of a scholar.'

'Well I'm not, not any more.'

'And also you *look* like a . . .' A brief, embarrassed smile. 'When we were swimming, you are . . . *stammig* as we say in Germany. More like a worker on a farm.'

161

Ryan looked at Helen. This was different. 'I also did a bit of teaching, to keep my income vaguely bearable. Bored American kids get to know their Anubis from their Horus. It's a Study Abroad programme. But the kids have stopped coming, there's hardly any work anyway. Because of the troubles.'

He stared at his glass of water. A few years ago it would have been whisky. But in the end he'd realized that hard physical work killed the pain better than any alcohol. Ryan sipped the water and looked at the German woman with her severe and high-cheekboned beauty. She had a hint of Nefertiti about her, the famous bust in the Berlin Museum. A slightly sad and Nordic Nefertiti. He decided to copy her curtness. 'So. You? What's your story?'

She was unfazed. 'Not as sad as yours, but it has pathos. My father is an academic, quite well known, he still teaches politics at Heidelberg. Mother: *hausfrau*. We come from rural Catholic Bavaria – it is a little like your Deep South, very religious. My sister is – was . . .' She blinked, the blue eyes blinked, twice. 'She was the favourite, the star, the bright one, not me. She was the beautiful daughter and so clever, musical, a brilliant concert pianist, she had the great career . . . the Germans worship music.'

Helen poured herself a glass of mineral water. 'She had a stroke, aged twenty-five. Ischemic. We do not know why. It can happen in teens and young adults, as well as old people. It can happen any time.'

'She died?'

'Yes and no.'

Ryan shook his head. 'I don't understand.'

'She lies in hospital in Heidelberg today, in a coma. Persistent vegetative state is the precise medical term. Is she alive or dead? Maybe God knows, I do not know. I know she will never recover, not now.'

'You believe in God?'

'No. But the reflex is there, I suppose. This is why I work now, work so hard. My parents were broken by Anna's stroke, so now I try to be her, the successful daughter. I am not, I fail, but I try. I do not have a husband, I rarely have boyfriends, I just work. I work to be someone else, to replace someone who has gone. There. My story. The End.'

Ryan sighed profoundly. 'I am very sorry.'

'Yes,' Helen said, lifting her glass. 'But at least we both understand. This is good. You know something, Ryan? Sometimes I do not quite trust people who have no tragedy in their lives. Now I can trust you.'

He lifted his water, they chinked.

The faintest sad smile on her lips.

'*Prost*.'

'Cheers.'

Ryan drank the last of his whiskyless water. And said, 'But do you trust Albert Hanna?'

Helen shook her head. 'Ah. Of course not, he is a serpent. But an amusing serpent. And we have no choice, we need him. And now I say good night. I hope it goes well for you tomorrow.'

Tomorrow came very early. He got up at dawn and

163

crept outside, and got in the waiting old taxi, and drove through the surreal shadows of the dawnlit desert. Then he worked for six hours without a break, eyes straining in the darkened old library with the flickering lamplight.

Then at last he sat back, massaging his aching neck. He had a bulging notebook, literally full of notes. He picked it up and stepped out of the creaking library, emerging into the stark desert sun of the monastery courtyard. He was almost content: he hadn't cracked the code, but he had definitely made a start. A very good start.

Helen and Hanna were sitting on a stone bench. Helen gazed at him – tense and waiting. Ryan regarded them both, and declared, 'The guy who wrote it is called Macarius. He's a sixth-century Copt. It's all about religion.' He paused. 'And we have to get going.'

Hanna shook his head. 'Why? Why can't you stay here and translate it all?'

Ryan had his answer. 'Because many times Macarius says I went to *this place* and I saw *this here*. But he doesn't *describe* it; therefore, we have no idea what he's talking about. How it fits in. We cannot solve the puzzle without following his logic – and his route.'

Helen was half-smiling. 'This is good. We will make a better film!'

'Or get arrested,' Hanna said.

A silence settled on them all. The sunlight glittered on the lake-pool beyond the open monastery gates.

Hanna broke the silence. 'Very well. The die is cast. Where then, Mr Harper, where are we going first?'

'To Bubastis.'

Hanna nodded. 'But of course. Bubastis. The city of cats.'

19

Bodmin, Cornwall, England

The winter weather up here was significantly worse than the drizzliness of the Cornish coast: the fierce wind carried flurries of snow and Dozmary Pool was showing shoulders of ice. The great granite outcrops that made Bodmin Moor visible from thirty miles away – Rough Tor, the Minions – sheltered the huddled, grey little sheep from the worst of the piercing gales.

Karen braked, slowed, and took a right turn off the A30, making her careful way down a narrow and sombre lane lined with high blackthorn hedges. The road was muddy, but the mud was frozen.

It was a suitably bleak landscape, a suitable place for a lunatic asylum. Except of course it wasn't called the Cornwall County Lunatic Asylum any more – it was now the Bodmin PCT Psychiatric Hospital and Mental Health Unit. But the Cornish still referred to it as they had always done: anyone who went mad, anyone who was sectioned and sent here, was said to have 'gone up Bodmin'.

The car park was empty. The car indicators blinked, obediently, as she locked her Toyota and walked towards the main asylum buildings. The architecture was a mix of ambitious Victorian Gothic and some 1980s wards and offices. The new bits were not ageing as well as the gloomy, redbrick grandeur of the old stuff. The Victorians built to last: they liked to incarcerate their lunatics in style.

The wind was biting. Karen was relieved to get inside the warm, brightly lit reception, where a sweet, plump nurse took her credentials and led her down maybe seventeen corridors to a large reinforced glass door with an elaborate system of locks.

The sign beside it read, SECURE UNIT and WARNING.

The nurse keyed a code, and they waited for something to happen. With nothing to do, the nurse made small talk, glancing at Karen.

'Bit blowy out there?'

'Freezing!'

'Yes. You get used to it, up here on the moor.' She smiled. 'Actually that's a lie, you don't. January is a shocker, every time. Here we go.'

The door was opened from the inside by a tall security guard: once again, Karen showed her police credentials. She was escorted to a desk in an open-plan office, and introduced to a senior staff nurse, Nurse Hawley, a thin woman with an even thinner smile. They shook hands. Nurse Hawley invited Karen to sit: and got straight to it, opening a file.

'Alicia Rothley, twenty-seven years old, white female, brought in by Bodmin police two days ago: she was in a café in Bodmin town centre, raving, throwing coffee.'

'At customers?'

'Everywhere, but mainly over herself. Swearing and cursing, tearing her clothes. A classic and severe psychosis. She has been officially sectioned, under the Mental Health Act. She is very . . .' For the first time, the thin, efficient woman hesitated. 'Well, she is very *unbalanced*, put it that way. Unstable. Labile. We can only give you a few minutes. Much of the time we are having to sedate her, and sometimes restrain her. She is unmedicated at the moment, so you can talk to her.'

'She's suicidal?'

'Quite possibly. She's certainly intent on self-harm. Please don't give her anything, not even a pen, that she might use – that way.'

'Has she said anything about . . . why she is like this? What brought her here?'

'Not really, no. Nothing comprehensible, at any rate. Perhaps you will have more luck than us. We are having her assessed for long-term care this week. But I'll show you to her room.'

'Room' was the wrong word, Karen thought, as she was guided down yet another corridor with a series of doors on either side. These weren't rooms, they were *cells*.

A card opened the electronic lock, like a hotel keycard; the door swung open. Alicia Rothley was huddled at the end of her spartan bed, her knees to her chest, staring at the two women framed by the door.

'Just a few minutes,' Nurse Hawley said. 'There's a panic button right here – for staff, not patients.' She spoke these last words very quietly. *'The code is three three four.'*

The door was closed. Karen was alone with Alicia Rothley.

The first thing she noticed was how pretty this girl was: she had fine, actressy cheekbones, dark hair, even darker eyes. The staff had dressed her in a white T-shirt and old jeans, no shoes, socks, no belt. A pair of white slippers sat neatly paired on the carpeted floor but the clean room was otherwise devoid of decoration or distraction. A small CCTV camera was positioned unreachably high in the top corner, a red light showing that it functioned.

The walls were padded. The single chair, which Karen sat in, was soft and plastic, like something from a kindergarten. The only window was high and barred: revealing the high branches of leafless trees outside, clawing at a very white sky.

'Hello, Alicia. I'm Karen.'

The girl said nothing though her eyes said a lot: fear, confusion, horror. Now that she was closer, Karen noticed there were tiny pink scratches on her face. From the cats? The scratches were all across her neck, and under her chin. Odd.

'Why are you here, Alicia?'

Nothing.

'What happened to you in Bodmin? Do you remember

that? Why did they . . .? What happened to you a few days ago?'

The girl averted her face, and shut her mouth tight, like a three-year-old refusing food.

This was pointless. Karen tried again, sensing her few minutes ticking away, but each question got the same blank, mute response. The frustration rose inside her; they really needed this girl to open up. Her elder brother, Mark Lucas Rothley – Luke Rothley to his friends – was possibly the key to all this. A few hours' research had told her Rothley was the son of a diplomat, from a fairly wealthy family. His father was dead, his mother retired to Spain. Rothley had attended Marlborough College, where he was 'popular and liked', though perhaps a little arrogant. He'd then refused a scholarship to Cambridge and instead gone north to Durham University, because of the more challenging rowing on the Wear, or so everyone said; he was definitely quite an athlete. He was also an impressive student: after taking a first in neurobiology and psychology, Rothley had gone on to do his postgraduate degree at Yale, where he had also excelled, if not quite so superbly. There were rumours of some drug use in America, as there were rumours that he had dabbled in the occult at Durham.

But then, his friends claimed, he had changed. He used the inheritance from his father to go backpacking for a couple of years – India, China, Egypt, southeast Asia. He went through a Buddhist phase, then a vegan phase, and then a phase of hard partying in Thailand.

170

And then, finally, he'd disappeared off the screen, moving into a kibbutz in Israel. That was the last place any of his old friends claimed to have heard from him. His Facebook page had stopped updating nearly two years ago. His mother said she got the odd email, supposedly from Israel.

Yet he was not in Israel.

Karen gazed at his sister. 'Alicia?'

Nothing.

'You can talk to me, it might help. We need help. A young man has died.'

Nothing.

Karen sighed. Although the UK Border Agency had no record of Luke Rothley re-entering the country, that was hardly a surprise: they didn't record the movement of UK citizens, as a rule. The only conclusion was that Rothley *had* surreptitiously slipped back into the country at some point in the last couple of years. But why? To do what? Just to torch all the cats in West Cornwall? Why? And where was he getting his money?

Rothley had, of course, used cash to rent the Lodge, so they couldn't trace him by his plastic. He also, apparently, owned no car, and no mobile – at least, not under his own name – so that route to his whereabouts was also blocked. Consequently their best and possibly only hope of finding him swiftly was his sister, Alicia. Who was struck dumb with madness. Or terror.

Karen pulled her plastic chair closer to the bed. 'OK, Alicia, let's try again. We need your help. Really. We think people might be in danger – your friends, the friends who were with you in the cottage. The night you burned the cats.'

The girl closed her dark eyes, and lowered her face, clutching her knees even more tightly to her chest. The interview was going nowhere. The girl was locked in: literally and emotionally. Karen had seen this before. But she couldn't give up.

'That was you, wasn't it? Alicia? You were up there, on Zennor Hill, that night? You burned the cats?'

Was that a shake of the head? A tiny response? Was she opening up?

'Alicia, tell me. Did you burn the cats? Did you?'

Silence.

'Did you? Did you burn all those cats to death?'

'Cats.'

A tiny little voice, girlish and sad; but she had spoken.

'What? Alicia? Tell me about the night, when you killed the cats.'

'Didn't.'

'You didn't kill them?'

'He killed them. Burning them, all night.'

'Your brother Luke?'

Alicia raised her face, and gazed hard and fierce at Karen. The policewoman got a sudden and intense sense of *threat*. Reflexively, she pushed her chair back. But the girl came closer, and now she was on all fours on the bed, her voice a low growl. 'He killed them, the Devil killed them.'

'What does that mean?'

'The Devil, my brother is the Devil. He killed the cats. The Devil came and entered him. Fuck you!'

The girl was almost snarling now. Karen tried to calm her. 'Alicia, it's OK, we just want to—'

'He will kill you, bitch. Luke will smell your fear. He will kill you.'

'Alicia?'

The girl was muttering.

'Lal Moulal. Ananias, Azarias—'

'*Alicia?*'

Her voice rose again. 'He did it! He killed all the cats one by one. They screamed. He did it, the magic, the Araki magic, the fucking Egypt magic. And they burned! *Atha atha atharim!* They fucking shrieked and he made us all do it!'

'We just—'

'He is the devil, he is. You think you can catch him, silly bitch! Luke will *rape you, he will rape the fucking smile off your face.*'

Karen stepped up, inching towards the alarm.

'He fucked me like a dog, made me pregnant, *atha atharim*, he is the Devil now!'

Karen was furiously pressing the panic code. The girl came across the room; she was on Karen in a second, tearing at Karen's jeans, trying to kiss her. Karen thrust her away, horrified and nauseated. Alicia Rothley was licking Karen's face; laughing, and licking—

Quickly, thought Karen. *Quickly quickly quickly!*

The girl's hand was inside Karen's bra, thrusting like a man, groping, her fingers were clawing in Karen's

173

groin, forcing their way inside; her pungent saliva was wet on Karen's face—

The door swung open and two security guards rushed in. A doctor grabbed Alicia by the waist and dragged her away from Karen, onto the bed. Straps were flourished, and tied around her wrists. The girl began howling, like a tortured dog.

'*Atha atharim, atha atharim!*'

Her heart thumping with horror, Karen stepped outside the cell. For some reason she thought of her mother, burning. The crematorium. The flames burning the flesh.

Deep breaths, deep breaths. Slowly, she did up her unbuttoned jeans, and her shirt, as best she could; one shirt-button had been ripped away entirely. Seeing a hand sanitizer on the wall, she grabbed it, pressed the button and rubbed the gunk on her hands and on her face.

She felt violated. She felt violated *by a girl.* The girl's tongue had licked her face. Like a dog.

The noise behind the cell door had subsided. Karen paused, inhaled, exhaled, then summoned her composure and made her own way back to Nurse Hawley's office.

The thin-lipped nurse gave her a sad and sympathetic nod. 'I was watching on CCTV.'

'You were *watching*?'

'I'm sorry. I sent security right away. You are all right?'

Karen sat down. And gazed at her trembling hands. 'Yes. I think so.'

The nurse picked up the file on ROTHLEY, ALICIA.

'As I said, it is an unusually pure and dramatic psychosis. We usually give her hefty dosages of anti-psychotics. The police at Truro, Sally Pascoe, gives me to understand she was involved in some Satanic rite? Some ritual?'

'Yes.'

Nurse Hawley opened the file. 'Whatever it was, it probably tipped her over into psychosis. Of course she may have been schizotypal anyway; but she needed a catalyst. And she got it. Did she give you any useful information?'

'No . . . not really. It was . . . sorry, I'm a bit shaken. She said her brother was the Devil. They did some magic, she said he got her pregnant. Just crazy stuff, I think. Then she went for me.'

'Yes.'

Karen closed her eyes, trying to forget. Then she remembered she had a job to do, and answers she needed. 'What are those scratches on her chin, and her neck? Have you checked them? Must be from the cats, right?'

Nurse Hawley shook her head. 'Well, no. Not exactly.' A slow pause. 'Many of the scratches are from, uh, shaving. She resists but we have to do it.'

Karen sat forward. 'What?'

'Yes. We have to shave her. Every day. Like a man.'

20

The Necropolis of Cats, Bubastis, Egypt

Ryan yawned. He was exhausted from the flights and car rides and nerve-shredding army checkpoints that had brought them here, right across Egypt, to the middle of the great reedy Nile Delta and the smoky modern city of Zagazig, with the ruins of Tell Bastet on its outskirts.

Helen's frown was visible in the darkness.

'How can you film down here?' Ryan asked. 'You can barely see the rat in front of your face.'

She laughed, briefly. 'Sense of humour? That is good. I have a portable light here, in my bag. It will be good enough. I just need to set it up. This will take two minutes.'

Ryan sat back, in the piles of dust. Exactly what kind of dust it was, what comprised this dust, he had no idea, and did not especially care to speculate.

They were deep in the dark heart of the great cat

necropolis, a labyrinth of tombs: surrounded by tiny three-thousand-year-old mud tunnels, each dotted with thousands of little niches in the walls. Almost every niche contained a mummified animal: a desiccated little corpse of a cat, wrapped diligently in special linens, and preserved with nitrates. Other niches probably contained jars of internal cat organs. A few most likely contained the mummies of less revered animals.

'OK,' said Helen, in the unsavoury darkness. 'Nearly ready. One more second . . .'

'Where is Albert?'

'He is still with the guards, bribing them, making sure we have time and that no one interrupts us. We need to be quick though. Half an hour, I think. OK, start by telling us what you have discovered about the papyrus.'

'Wait, you want to spend half an hour down here?' Ryan stared around. The idea of lingering for more than a few minutes in this stifling maze of tunnels was grotesque. The air was acrid with death. Ryan wondered how many ancient diseases were preserved here. He thought of his wife and child, dead of malaria, an infection bred here, in the Delta.

'Really, Helen. Can't we film up above ground? Just do an intro?'

'But here is better!' Her smile was brief but sincere. 'It is so atmospheric in a necropolis! A catacomb. Even the name is good. The catacombs of Bubastis. It will really work, trust me.' She looked at him, smiled again. '*Please?*'

She'd said *please*. For the first time ever.

Ryan nodded and obeyed. He rubbed dirt from his face and turned to the dazzling light that Helen held aloft. Shadows danced beyond the cone of light, the shadows of little cat corpses, as he spoke.

'We are now closer to unravelling the mystery of the Sokar Hoard. By comparing our pages with similar documents, in the archives of the Monastery of St Apollo, outside Akhmim, we now know a lot more about our papyrus. It appears to have been written in the late sixth century by a Coptic scholar from Akhmim named Macarius. Quite possibly, judging by the vocabulary we have translated, Macarius was a follower of Gnostic Christianity, certainly a scholar of religion. The papyrus seems to be an investigation into faith, in the form of a journey across Egypt, a very early travel book, if you like. These are not unknown in the ancient world. But most of this we have yet to translate. Yet we have already deciphered some of his sentences. For instance . . .' Ryan coughed some of the endless dust from his mouth. The dust of dead cats. 'For instance, in the very first passages, he says "I went to Alexandria, but there I found nothing, for there the great knowledge had been destroyed by the invaders. But it did not concern me as I had read all the books which came from Egypt. And so I went to . . ."' Ryan paused, and turned his notebook to show the camera. 'Here, Macarius uses hieroglyphics, as he often does when citing a place name. These hieroglyphics say Pr-3BST. As it happens, this is easily decipherable. Ironically, the demotic hieroglyphics are easier to translate than the obscure, archaic Coptic dialect. So. Pr-3BST is Per-Bast, the House of Bast. In other words, he means *here*, Bubastis, the city where the cat goddess Bast was famously revered.'

Ryan put down the notebook and gestured at the roof of the mud tunnel above him.

'So here we are in the necropolis of cats, the city of the dead cats, underneath the ruins of great Bubastis. From the first days of the Early Kingdom to the Persian invasions of the fifth century BC, this famous capital – at one time the capital of all Egypt – was the centre of cat-worship. As a result, Egyptians and others brought cats here, by the cartload, to be mummified; some cats were specially bred *just* to be killed, ritually drowned, so they could then be mummified.

'And it wasn't just cats. Many species of animals were mummified throughout Egyptian history: dogs, rats, rams, fish, ibises, baboons and sacred crocodiles. And beetles. Scarab beetles.

'The Egyptians were so obsessed with the afterlife they went so far as to mummify *insects*. The dust of Egypt is therefore littered with millions of these animal mummies: so many, in fact, they have since been used as fuel, or fertiliser, dug up by bulldozers and shipped abroad by the ton.' Ryan now gestured at a little niche close to his shoulder. 'But here in the Bubastic necropolis it is very definitely cats that predominate, as we can see. Here. If I just reach in . . .'

He slid his hands into the dark, dry, narrowing slot.

He could feel the three-thousand-year-old cat, preserved within its gangrenous swaddling. The papery corpse was repellent to the touch. Desiccated yet still faintly organic, dry yet moist, paradoxical and revolting. He swallowed his disgust and pulled it out.

'In my hands I have a classic example, probably a cat mummy dedicated by a poorer family or individual. The richer votaries would commission a coffin for the cat mummy, and Canopic jars for the organs. The poor would simply have their cat basically eviscerated and embalmed, like this one, as you can see.'

Ryan lifted the sad little corpse to the camera; the head was barely connected by the flaking spinal cord to the body, the fur was like dead ashes, the eyes were all rotted out, the greasy dark sockets gazing at him regretfully. Or accusingly. Disturbed from the sleep of death.

He was relieved when he was able to slide the tiny corpse back in its immemorial hole. And clap the noxious dust from his hands.

'So why did Macarius come here? The text breaks off at this point, tantalizingly. The following passage is illegible. But as he was researching religion, he was surely researching the religiosity of Bubastis, which was intense and famous. At one point Bubastis was home to the greatest religious festival in Egypt, described by Herodotus. Apparently *seven hundred thousand* people would gather for the annual festival of Bast, travelling along the Nile to the Bubastis temples and oracles in great barges. And they came to party. Herodotus describes the excited women in the barges hurling off their clothes and mocking the peasants on the riverbank with their exposed genitals. And then the drinking and fornication would begin, a Dionysiac ritual, a vast bacchanal, days of dancing and coupling above the necropolis. It was the greatest orgy of the ancient world, perhaps the greatest orgy in human history.'

Ryan paused. He didn't know why. Something was wrong, he was sure of it. The shadows of the cats danced around him. The dust was so thick. He cleared his throat and continued.

'We can only imagine what Macarius thought about this vivid history. He may, like a good Christian, have been scandalized. On the other hand, some strains of Coptic Gnosticism already had a very unusual attitude to sexuality. A Greek scholar called Epiphanius journeyed to Egypt in 335 AD, and met a group of Gnostics whom he thought were ordinary Christians but he later called them Stratiotics, or Phibionites. He describes a group engaged in orgies, a cult that consumed semen and menstrual blood at the peak of their rites. Epiphanius even claims some Gnostics cooked human babies for Passover dinner.'

No. Something *was* wrong. There was a shadow – there – it was there, looming behind Helen: she couldn't see it. He could hear it.

'Helen!'

The black shape emerged into the cone of camera-light: it was an Arab man in a black cloak and a black beard. His face was wrought with anxiety.

'*Run!*' he said.

Ryan lifted a hand. And yelled in Arabic, 'Why? What is happening? Who are you?'

The man pushed Helen in the back. 'Run. There are men coming after us.'

Ryan snapped back, 'Who? Who are they?'

But the man gabbled on, 'We couldn't stop them. I work in the gate. I ran for it. I was coming down here to warn you.'

His explanation was cut short by a blaze of noise and light at the far end of the tunnel. Their pursuers.

'They have guns. They are going to kill us.'

21

Bubastis, the city of cats, Egypt

Ryan grabbed Helen by the hand and they ran, and crawled, desperately, urgently, down the musty mud tunnel, knocking cat mummies to the ground, crunching them underfoot, backbones cracking at last, skulls kicked out of the way, black rotted eyesockets staring unseeingly into the momentary glare of the flashlight.

'They're still coming, I can hear them—'

Helen was panting, dragging her bags with the camera. Ryan twisted in the horrible, narrow tunnel and took her bag, hoisted it, and scrambled on. But even as he fled, the Arab man squeezed past so that he could show them a new route: a tiny, half-concealed, even narrower tunnel.

'This way.'

They had to duck under a low overhang of mud, rotten with age. The roof was unstable, Ryan realized.

It could give way at any moment: they were taking a terrible risk. They would be smothered with dirt and ancient mummies: mummified beetles and mummified crocodiles and mummified ibises, and tons of Bubastic mud bricks. Filling their mouths, stifling them, drying them out, until they too would become just another trio of human mummies – raising the total to half a billion *and three*, as if anyone would notice.

'Here, along here!'

The tunnel forked. Ryan could hear voices in the muffled distance, still coming after them. Who was this? The police? How could they have followed them? Was it the army? Come to arrest them? Had Albert betrayed them?

They took the left fork. The tunnel widened: the niches here were much bigger. Ryan glimpsed the shouting faces of dried-out baboons in large holes, grimacing, rigid and stricken.

The Arab man seemed suddenly confused. 'Here. No. No. Here? No?'

The tunnel divided into three: it was a labyrinth. The man was paralysed by indecision, his flashlight switching this way and that, picking out a dried ibis, squawking for eternity, a piece of rock, scribed with faint hiero-glyphs, and the endless passages of poisonous old mud bricks, dark and stained, soaked through with natron, wood-resins, animal fats. The salts of mummification had permeated the fabric of the tombs at this ancient end of the maze. This whole place was drenched and tainted with the liquors of preservation, the rancid juices of immortality; and now the voices behind them were audible.

'Stop! Or we'll shoot!'

English voices? British accents?

Helen pushed her way down the first tunnel, past the confused Arab man. But even as she did, a gun was fired. The bullet missed them, thudding into one of the niches down the way, shattering some ancient baboon skull.

Ryan put a hand on Helen's trembling shoulder and pulled her back. They were caught, they could not escape – running was pointless.

The lights got brighter as their pursuers – or killers – approached. Ryan lifted an arm to shade his eyes from the dazzle as he tried to make out their faces.

'We're trying to save your stupid lives, motherfuckers.'

This time a Canadian accent? The men were young, aggressive, wearing jeans and tight T-shirts, canvas jackets; their manner was soldierly.

The Brit barked in Ryan's direction, 'You, Harper? Tell the towel-head to get us out of here. Now.'

Ryan asked the terrified Arab man to show the way out. Once he had been calmed, the man obeyed. For several minutes they squeezed between narrow walls of mud, lined with mummies and coffins and broken and rotten bandaging; everywhere, little skulls peered from little niches, their eyesockets seeming to move with the flashlights passing. The silent journey was horribly tense, as well as grisly. Where were they going? Who were these guys?

185

At last the Arab stood and lifted some planking, throwing it aside, and they emerged, blinking, into the overcast light. A dampness tanged the air: a faint drizzle had evidently fallen. This was the autumnal Nile Delta winter, so different to the endless seasonless sunshine a hundred miles south.

The men with the guns shunted them around a heaped old ruin of mud bricks, and there was Albert Hanna, squatting morosely in the dust; beside the gateman of the ruin-complex. Two more white men with guns were standing over them. The man with the British accent, apparently the leader, snapped an order: 'Sit. We need to talk. Sit the fuck down!'

They sat in the dust like prisoners of war. Ryan gazed at his captors. The other man was looking to his left and right, like a trained soldier, like secret service. Ryan realized that *these* men were anxious, even scared. But scared of whom?

'You can call me Callum,' said the Brit, his gun casually levelled in their direction. A soldier perhaps? He had blond hair, shaved close to the skull, but wore a seriously expensive watch.

So not a regular soldier then. Ryan tried to work it out. The other men were similarly confusing: a mixture of military bearing and surf-dude demeanour.

'These are my friends,' Callum continued. 'We're here to save your bloody arses.'

Albert Hanna spoke up. 'Then why are you pointing guns at us? Are you going to burn a village to save a village?'

186

Callum chuckled mirthlessly, and slid his weapon into a holster. Then he crouched so that he was eye-level with Albert. 'Mate, listen. You *do not know* the trouble you are in – a whole lot of trouble.'

'But who are you?' Helen asked.

Callum waved away the question. 'It doesn't concern you. We are, for the moment, your only fucking hope.' He turned to Ryan. 'You have the Sokar documents – or part of them, right? And you are trying to decipher them?'

Ryan answered, his voice tinged with anger and suspicion. 'Yes. But who are *they*? How are they following us, how did they trace us?'

'The cops in Nazlet coughed. Gave your names to journos, names of mysterious Westerners sniffing around Nazlet when Sassoon was discovered. Bloggers picked up the story, spread it. Everyone knows who needs to know: there are plenty of rumours on the net. The people hunting you down have spies every-where, lots of spies and money. How many checkpoints have you been through? How many Egyptian soldiers on two bucks a day have they paid off? This is how *we* traced you, so this is how they are tracing you. Except they probably have satellites too. Satellites and drones, the full McFlurry. They could be here in a minute, so we need to get out. And when we go, Ryan Harper, you will decode that document for us. In return we will stop you getting killed.'

'But who is this terrible secret enemy?' Albert Hanna insisted, his immaculate dark suit powdered with mud. 'Who, precisely, is chasing us?'

187

Callum turned. 'You're the brilliant Coptic guy, Hanna, right? Famously smart? You not worked it out?'

'It is the Israelis. Is it not?' Helen said. 'The soldiers in the desert. They are coming after us.'

'Ten out of ten.' Callum stared at Helen. 'The Isrealis are coming after you. They have all the money they need, they have Mossad men with guns, and if they catch you with that papyrus they aren't going to be cuddly like us. They will take the documents, and shoot you dead, and feed your corpses to the pigs of Moqqatam.'

Helen stirred, and Albert too.

But Ryan stood his ground, arms crossed. All his life Ryan had detested being pushed around and, *mano a mano*, pound for pound, he reckoned he could take this Brit – if he could get hold of his gun. But the gun was holstered and well out of reach, for the moment.

Callum smiled. In the most unamused way possible. 'Fighter not a lover?'

Ryan shook his head. 'Need more information. Why should we trust you? More than the Israelis, more than anyone?'

''Cause we haven't killed you yet?' Callum sighed, aggressively. He reached in his pocket and pulled out a crumpled photo. 'You've obviously not seen this.'

He showed it to Helen and she flinched at the sight. Ryan grabbed the photo.

It showed the bruised face of an Arab man with a clean bullet hole in the dead centre of his forehead.

'I don't get it.' Ryan frowned.

Helen interrupted, and answered. 'That is the man, the Bedouin man, who first found the cave, with Sassoon's body. The man who guided me back there.' She turned to Callum. 'The Israelis did this?'

'Yes. They realized they didn't have all the documents. They came back for the rest. They located this poor bastard and when they realized he couldn't *assist* they shot him dead to make sure he couldn't talk. And they will do the same to *you*. *When* they find you. *Which* they will.'

Callum moved so close to Ryan that they were nose to nose. 'Now, we can either get the fuck out of here, before they catch us. Or you can linger and enjoy the historic sights, for the last few minutes of your life.'

22

Truro Police Headquarters, Cornwall

The owner of the witchcraft museum was frowning nervously as Karen reached in her bag for the recorder. Setting the machine on the desk, she sought to calm him. 'Many thanks for coming in, Mr Ryman, we know you are busy.'

'Oh, not at all, not at all.' He smiled in an unconvincing way. 'I was in Truro anyway, to see my mother. She's up at Treliske, the hospital.'

'Nothing terrible, I hope?'

'Her pacemaker needs changing. Marvellous what they can do these days. She is practically bionic: two false knees, replacement hip. I sometimes wonder if she will rust rather than age.'

Sally Pascoe popped a slice of Nicorette. 'What do you do, anyway, when the museum is shut?'

He shrugged, and straightened the knot of his tie. 'Oh, this and that. I pootle and potter, potter and pootle.

I suppose I am semi-retired now. The museum gives a reasonable income. My pension! Ah. I used to be a tour guide, to the Middle East. I had my own little company, quite upmarket, tailor-made trips to biblical sites, with academics and writers. That's when I became first, ah, interested in the occult. The belief in ghosts and miracles and the paranormal is so sincere there – the demons of Sumer are still with us! If you go to somewhere like Palmyra, it is—'

Karen raised a hand. She'd just remembered how much this guy liked to talk. 'Sorry, but can we get to it? This shouldn't take more than a few minutes. We just want your opinion on an interview I conducted.'

Ryman nodded, silenced.

Karen toyed with the digicorder as she quickly explained about Alicia Rothley's arrest, her transfer to Bodmin Psych Unit, her connection to the cat-burning and the possible chief suspect, her elder brother, Luke Rothley.

The pallid face of the man became even whiter as he listened. 'Good holy lord. That is, ah, that is something. Ah yes. Hm. Trevelloe Lodge, eh?'

'Yep. We think there were maybe eight or nine people staying there. For the whole month.'

'Well. Trevelloe. Yes yes, yes yes. I know that area, the standing stones there, of course, the Merry Maidens. And Men-an-Tol, the birthing stone, up by Ding Dong mine. And Madron well, the whole area is, ah, drenched with occult and supernatural associations, and let's not forget the fogous—'

'No. We mustn't forget the fogous,' said Sally, giving

up on her gum and throwing it in the overfull rubbish bin. Then she tilted her head at the digicorder.

Karen took the hint, picked up the recorder and pressed play. 'So, Mr Ryman, this is the recording of my interview with Alicia Rothley at Bodmin. Have a listen, and tell us what you think.'

The voices were quite distinct: it was a good recording. The sound of the faint winter drizzle on the police HQ windows seemed to recede as Karen's questions to Alicia echoed around the office.

Donald Ryman gazed warily at the little machine on the desk. He said nothing. Karen picked up the recorder, and fast-forwarded.

'She didn't respond at first, as you can tell. She just sat there, terrified, and mute. Kind of locked in. But then, eventually, she opened up. Here.'

She pressed play once again.

'*Cats.*'

'*What? Alicia? Tell me about the night, when you killed the cats.*'

'*Didn't.*'

'*You didn't kill them?*'

'*He killed them. Burning them, all night.*'

'*Your brother Luke?*'

Karen looked at Sally, and then at Donald. He was transfixed now, leaning close.

'*He killed them, the Devil killed them.*'

'*What does that mean?*'

'*The Devil, my brother is the Devil. He killed the cats. The Devil came and entered him. Fuck you!*'

On and on, to the crazed crescendo. Despite her best attempts, Karen failed to suppress a shudder. The words sounded all the more horrific for being relayed in this fairly anodyne environment – in this friendly, messy office with its empty plastic coffee cups and the Christmas-party photos on the wall, and the bin containing yesterday's *West Briton* newspaper.

And a girl screaming from a digicorder:

'*Ananias, Azarias . . . atha atha atharim!*'

The recording concluded; an awkward silence ensued. Donald Ryman seemed shaken, his nervous tics more pronounced as his hand adjusted the knot of his tie.

Finally Karen spoke. 'Mr Ryman, do you know of any magic that might, in some inadvertent way, induce sexual or hormonal changes?'

He gazed at her with a bewildered expression.

'I ask this because the girl, Alicia Rothley, is showing signs of *masculinization*. She is becoming a man. In fact, if you looked at her results, you would say this is someone having pre-operative hormone treatment for gender-reassignment surgery.'

Sally Pascoe interrupted Karen. 'We're not suggesting there is some spell that can simply do this, but maybe there is some kind of, you know, sexual magic, where people . . .' She shrugged. 'I don't know, where people have, say, testosterone injections. Does that happen in any magical rituals?'

Donald shook his head. 'No, I have never heard of such a thing; it is . . . ah, quite outside the canon. Most bizarre. Really . . .'

Karen and Sally swapped glances. Karen gestured at the recorder. 'OK, what do you think about the recording? Can you give us any context?'

This time he seemed more confident.

'Well the names, yes yes. I know the names. Ananias, Azarias, they are obviously the names of demons, hermetic demons, ah, ah, ancient Egyptian magic. She has obviously been witness to some . . . serious ritual.'

'What does that mean?'

He shrugged, a faint shine of sweat on his lined and anxious forehead. 'I mean a ritual from one of the old grimoires, one of the old books of magic. It could be the Key of Solomon the King, or the Grand Grimoire. But . . .' His voice faded.

'Go on,' Sally Pascoe urged.

'Well. Ah. One of the words she used, *Araki*, implies something a lot more . . . well, *worrying*. Have you ever heard of the Sacred Magic of Abra-Melin, Abra-Melin the Mage?'

'No.'

'Well, of course not, sorry, it is quite obscure. But to experts . . .' He seemed flustered again; the tie straightening was now almost pathological. 'The book of Abra-Melin is a magical manual which dates back to the fifteenth century. There are copies of it surviving from about 1700: in Dresden in Germany, in the Bodleian in Oxford, and one in the Bibliothèque Nationale, in France, I believe. It was written by a Jewish scholar, Abraham of Worms, who was apparently taught magic by Abra-Melin himself. A mage, or a sorcerer.'

'A wizard? A real wizard, with sleeves?'

Donald Ryman ignored Sally's question. 'Until recently it was thought the grimoire was merely compiled by Abraham of Worms, culled from extant sources: but a few years ago some German scholars proved that it is probably entirely authentic, that it really does come from a tiny town called El Araki in Upper Egypt, between Sohag and Luxor. The description of the village in the book is completely accurate: there is no way a Jewish Kabbalist from fifteenth-century Worms would have known about Araki, unless he'd been there. Moreover, Araki is near the, ah, epicentre of Egyptian magic, Nag Hammadi, where the Gnostic gospels were found, and Akhmim, which is the very home of alchemy and the occult itself. All in all it is a fascinating region . . .'

'Mr Ryman, what is the significance of this magic?' Karen asked. Specifically, the, what did you call it, the Sacred Magic of Abra-Melin?'

'Well now.' Donald Ryman shut his eyes for a second, as if praying. Then he looked at the window, and spoke to no one in particular. 'Please don't think me a credulous old fool. I am aware of the fatuity of much of this. I don't believe in pixies and Beelzebub. But even in sceptical circles the magic of Abra-Melin has a troubling reputation. The ritual involved for summoning demons is complex and ancient, extremely challenging, and, ah, truly evil. Some say the Abra-Melin ritual can only be successfully completed if several humans are sacrificed, culminating in the murder of a living child. Others believe it merely requires a symbolic sacrifice, or perhaps animal sacrifice.'

Sally interrupted him. 'You're saying this . . . this Abra-Melin thing, this *is for real*? You can get demons to appear?'

'No.' He gave a pained shrug. 'No, probably not. Of course not. At least, I don't think so. But I know that Crowley himself tried the magic in 1900, in Boleskine in Scotland and at his notorious flat in Chancery Lane, and even he found it too frightening. So it is reported.'

Karen asked, 'What you are *definitely* saying is that the girl, his sister, has been exposed to this particular ritual, right? Otherwise, why mention Araki?'

'Yes, that is exactly what I am saying! My educated guess is that her brother is attempting the difficult and ancient Abra-Melin ritual. And in all the history of the occult, that is the one solitary ritual that might give one pause, that could make one lie awake at night.' He flapped his tie again, agitated. 'Consider me an imbecile if you wish, but the rite of Abra-Melin is the only magic in history that, for whatever reason, and in some terrifying way, actually appears to work.'

23

Chancery Lane, London, England

'Chu, Kouchos, Trophos, Kimphas, Abraxas.'

Rothley tipped the silver salver of blood over her head: the liquid ran down her face in warm trickles, in dark, salty and delicious rivulets. Francoise looked up at his handsome face, and his glittering eyes. 'Yes, yes please. Please give it to me. Baptize me with blood.'

He wasn't wearing robes this morning: was this really the special day? He was just in his jeans and the T-shirt with the picture of Hendrix, but he was so handsome. His eyes glittered: she couldn't stop looking at them, looking at him. Like watching a film when she was a child, she was staring up and adoring something bigger, brighter, finer.

'These are the names of the six powers of death, those who bring every sickness down upon every person, those who bring every soul out from every body.'

He poured a little more of her blood. Some of it

ran into her eyes and it stung but Francoise tried to ignore it: she had to be strong, she wanted to be strong; this must be the end. She knew it now. This was the day; but she was so very faint, she was losing too much blood already, but she was going to be strong.

'I adjure you by your names and your names and your powers and your places and the security of death itself, that you shall go to Francoise, daughter of the father, and that you shall bear away her soul.'

Too much blood: how much blood could she lose without fainting? She wanted to lie down now but there he was, Rothley. He had seen she was in pain and close to fainting and he'd paused, he had set the salver down and he was tightening the tourniquets on each arm. Yes! He was fixing them like a doctor, he was a doctor, a healer, her Saviour, her Christ, no, *better* than Christ.

The light from the windows was wintry and glorious, she could hear the last sounds of the London traffic, a sweet muffled music.

Rothley's teeth were white and lovely as he bit on the leather straps of the tourniquets, cutting off some of her blood loss; she gazed patiently at him, yet she wanted him to bite her, she wanted him to bite her face, he could bite away her face, and kiss her too, like Jesus coming to kiss a child who says her prayers. She remembered the holidays in Normandy – her mother and her father, the sea and the sky, pearly-grey seas, and beautiful skies . . . long, long skies.

Mont Saint Michel and the oysters, her first oysters, grey as the Normandy skies in winter.

Rothley dropped the straps of the tightened tourniquets and gazed into her eyes. His eyes were so dark, almost black, like the Devil; he was a beautiful devil with his black eyes, like a demon in the desert, seducing.

'I adjure you, O dead one, by the manner in which you were seized. And by this punishment that has come upon you, which you have heard. And by the demons you have seen, and by the river of fire that casts wave after wave, you must bring your suffering down upon Francoise. As I place this bone here.' He pressed a bone to her face. A collarbone, was it a human collarbone? He took the bone away and she saw that it was smeared with the blood on her face, her own blood, from her beautiful wounds, wounds like Christ; yet *he* was Christ, the Christ of Death, coming to take her.

'Zarlai, Lazarlai, Lazai, Lazarlai.'

Burning leaves, burning cats, the burning cats, the way the cats burned, she could not forget it, ever, and then the Devil was Rothley and Rothley was Jesus, the Christ of the End.

'Samakari, of Christ, I call upon Lord Sabaoth, Adonai Adonai, O child with the flowing hair, I place an oath upon you, O dead bone, in order that you bring forth suffering, from this corpse Francoise whose true name this is. *Yaoth Yaoth Yaoth*.'

The intonation made her sleepy, she was ready to sleep

now. She gazed around the large empty room, at the altar with its saucer of severed rats' feet, and the small steel sword, smeared with her blood, staining the white altar cloth; she gazed along, and down, at the little dead birds scattered across the floor.

So many of them. So many tiny dead birds – and there was the skull that ate all the birds. The skull had fallen over. It lay on its side on the wooden chair, staring back at her, choked with grey feathers stuck between its yellow teeth. Yes, that was the smiling skull he fed with starlings and little baby pigeons and her blood.

'Iesseu, Mazareu, Iessedekeu.'

Francoise nearly swooned. In front of her was the hole.

She knew that was her coffin, she would have his child in the hole in the floor, which was her coffin: that was where she would give birth to his child, the child of death, a smiling dead baby, for he was the Father of Death.

Francoise looked down at herself. She had blood on her naked breasts and on her thighs; her whole naked body was soiled with blood and yet she felt cleaner than she had ever felt.

And now Rothley was writing words on her skin with her own blood.

'By the calling of four demons, written on the body of one. Aromao, Tharmaoth, Marmarioth, Salabaooth. Adonai Adonai Adonai. From the flame of which they are made, the wrath of the scorching wind.'

200

His fingers lingered over her breasts, writing the words in sticky red blood.

'By the fire of the scorching red river. The hatred that scattered, and the four hundred angels, scattered and written with hatred – and strife – and loathing.'

Delicate words, beautiful words, she was written with names and words, she was his page, her white skin was his parchment, his blank white page. Francoise murmured, in pain, 'I am ready . . .'

'You must char the face of Francoise, you must force the suffering from her.'

'Yes—'

'I invoke you today, Sourochcata, You who are strong in your power, who brings the rocks to dissolution, let my voice come to her.'

'Come to me, dissolving me—'

'You who dissolve the sinews and the ligaments and the joints, you who take her hands away, you are to dissolve the sinews of Francoise for all time, and give her this child, the child of her end, the child of her death, come now, and come forever.'

He was taking her by the waist, hoisting her to her feet. She was so unsteady she stumbled, the blood loss had been so great; but Rothley's strong arms held her fast, and guided her to the space in the floor, where she would be buried; where she would die.

'Yea, I adjure you, your names and your amulets. Lay her down here, inside this place, the house of death.'

The planks were scratchy on her bare feet as she

walked to the void where the floorboards had been ripped out; was there enough space for her in there? Under the floorboards? It was dark. For the first time a shudder of fear trembled through her. What would it be like to be dead, to be buried under these floorboards forever?

'As this daughter lies down, yea, yea, Jesus Christ, Beth Betha, Yao Sabaoth, Adonai, *Eloueiu*—'

Rothley pushed her head, he was pressing her into the crawlspace, into the dust and the darkness, under the floor. He was pushing on her body so she could fit under the floor; and now she was in, and he was putting the planks back over the space, and hammering nails, sealing the lid of her coffin, and as he did he called the words, still.

'Gemas, Demas, Gemas, Demas.'

Francoise trembled with fear and joy, she could not see anything except a few cracks of light; she was in her wooden tomb, and he was sealing it shut, and she was happy and all she could hear in the darkness, as she died, was his beautiful voice in the distance, the Jesus of Death, calling her, calling her . . .

'God who has bound the heaven and has bound the earth, must bind the mouth of Francoise, that she may not be able to move her lips.'

Francoise moved her lips, silently, repeating the words. It was nearly over now. The last nails were being driven in: she was in her womb of darkness. She fumbled to fill her mouth.

'Lazarlai, Sabaoth, Eloim, take your daughter, bring her suffering, bind her silence, make her perfect. Zothooza, Thoitha, Zazzaoth, the saints of darkness, come at once, at once, at once. Amen.'

24

Dokki, Cairo, Egypt

The Canadian soldier, Simon, twitched the curtains of their hotel room, gazing warily at the twilit street below. The cool of a January evening approached. His boss – leader – captain – whatever he was – called across.

'Anything?'

'Nah. Quiet here. For the moment.'

Callum nodded. 'Good.' He turned to face Ryan. 'So, Harper, tell me again. Pretend I have the IQ of a spoon. Why can't you just translate what you know, here and now, and tell us what the document says?'

'Because . . .' Ryan sighed, and looked at Helen, who sat on the bed drinking a Pepsi, her expression drawn, and unresponsive. Did he really have to go over this again? He'd already explained the problem three times, since they'd arrived in Cairo from Bubastis, ferried in Callum's dusty four-wheel drive, before hunkering down here, in this anonymous hotel in this anonymous Cairo suburb.

'You just want to film, don't you?' Callum pressed. 'That's why you want to actually go to these places, so you can make the movie, make money.'

'*Shakespeare* wrote for *money*.' Albert Hanna had returned from his trip to the bar in the lobby: he had fetched the drinks himself, as they didn't want anyone to see the Sokar documents.

Hanna sipped from his tumbler of Scotch, and continued. 'It is *quid pro quo*, no? We have our motivation. And you have yours. You want to know what is in the papyrus. Ryan Harper is the *one man* who might be able to do it, now that poor Victor Sassoon has gone to the western hills. Therefore, let him do it his way. Because you need our help.'

Ryan listened to the dialogue, impatiently. He still didn't trust these 'soldiers'; but the threat from the Israelis seemed clear enough. They had been kidnapped by Fate.

Callum turned to Albert. 'OK. Get it. Shakespeare wrote for cash. But Shakespeare didn't have Mossad trying to shred his Coptic arse with clusterbombs.'

'I've certainly never read that in the canonical biographies.' Hanna moistened his lips with more Scotch. 'Nonetheless the point is good, *mon brave*: if Ryan says he can't decipher the papyrus without visiting the locales, then you surely have no choice. We must go.'

'It's like this,' Ryan said, gesturing to the third sheet

205

of the papyrus, 'Macarius says here: "I went to Tell Amarna, the city of the Aten, and I saw the second *something* of Tutankhaten . . ." The *something* is illegible, or written in an even obscurer alphabet. What is he referring to – a stele maybe? Some column of hieroglyphs in a tomb? We need to go to Amarna and see. Look in the tombs.'

Callum gazed at the walnut finish of his expensive pistol, which was lying on the coffee table next to the papyrus. The juxtaposition was significant. Ryan recognized the distinctive shape of the gun. A Korth. Very pricey – and very professional. *Soldiers, definitely soldiers. Or mercenaries.*

'OK,' Callum said. 'OK. And this is just one example. Macarius does this several times, yeah?'

Ryan nodded vigorously. 'Yes. At Luxor. At Philae. Again and again. Indeed, this might be deliberate.'

'How?'

'It's possible he wrote the most significant remarks in code, or in some intractable alphabet which we have yet to crack, so that his deductions would be revealed only to the initiated. Like here, see, there's a passage in Greek – ΑΓΓΟ, ΑΕΘΗ, ΑΑΘ, ΒΕΖ, ΒΗΕ – but it seems to make no sense at all. It is maybe some kind of riddle, or a spell, in code. It is *deliberately obscure*.'

'Don't get it.'

Hanna sat in the largest chair, the tumbler of Scotch hanging from his hand. 'Krafft-Ebing, the nineteenth-century German physician, wrote his groundbreaking work, *Psychopathia Sexualis*, in Latin so that the common reader wouldn't be shocked by his accounts of men having sex with patent-leather boots. It is a leitmotif of literature: when the contents are very controversial or dangerous – *encode*.'

'You're saying the writer, whatsit, Macarius –' Callum gestured at the document – 'deliberately *chose* to be as obscure as possible because he didn't want people to be able to easily follow his conclusions? So only a select few would be able to get what he was saying?'

'Yes.'

'That's very annoying.'

'Yes it is,' Albert said. 'But also tantalizing, and further indication that what we have here is a unique and maybe explosive document. Combustible!'

Callum stood up, abruptly, and disappeared into the bathroom. For a few minutes the hotel room was silent, the only noise the faint murmur of the blond Brit talking on his mobile phone, apparently to some senior authority. This had already happened several times. Discreet phone calls, which produced a swift decision.

Helen was still on the bed, cross-legged. Staring into space. Simon was at the window, anxiously alert and plucking at the curtain like a prurient neighbour.

Callum returned, zipping his mobile into his jacket pocket.

'All right,' he said, sitting down. 'We'll do it your way. *For now.* There are some benefits: we keep moving. Less chance of us getting vaporized by a drone.'

Hanna nodded. 'Excellent decision.'

207

Callum pressed the questions. 'But where are we going? What's the route?'

Ryan sighed. He had a *kind* of plan: Cairo, then Amarna, and Luxor, then Aswan. North to South. Maybe. That seemed to be the path Macarius had taken, ascending to Upper Egypt, and the first Cataracts of the Nile. It made emotional sense, too: a journey along the Nile to its highest navigable reaches. But what exactly had Macarius seen, on that route?

Ryan shrugged and admitted: 'It's not quite that simple. To say exactly where we are going, I mean.'

'Why?'

'Because, after Bubastis, the papyrus becomes even more obscure, verging on chaotic. It mentions baptism several times, and also Bastet, the cat goddess. Most of all, from this point on it mentions Moses. So we know he is important to the puzzle.' He picked up his notebook and read: 'Here Macarius cites the Roman historian Tacitus, who wrote that Jews were a "detested race in Egypt", because they were unclean, and they brought epidemics, and that's why they were sent to the desert with Moses, and then on to Zion, where they instituted a new religion.'

'OK. And?'

'There are another half a dozen references to Moses on this page alone.' Ryan laid a gentle finger on the document. 'Here Macarius quotes the historian Manetho, who wrote an Egyptian chronicle under Ptolemy the Second. Manetho represented Moses as a rebellious Egyptian priest, and leader of a colony of lepers.'

Hanna interrupted, 'The idea that Moses was an Egyptian is not entirely startling, Freud made the same point; indeed Moses probably *was* Egyptian – the suffix *mose* is Egyptian, meaning *son* or *child*. As in Tutmose, the Pharaoh. Ptahmose. Rameses even. It is the same syllable.'

'Acts Seven, Twenty-two.' This time the interruption was Helen's. She elaborated. 'Moses is said to have been "versed in all the wisdom of Egypt".'

'So Moses is an Egyptian. Great.' Callum sat forward, aggressive and taut. 'What the hell does that mean?'

'We don't know,' Ryan confessed. 'No one is sure. Historians argue to this day whether Moses even existed, or if there really was an Exodus of Jews from Egypt, in 2000 BC or 1500 BC or whenever. There is no archaeological evidence, though there is quite a lot of documentary evidence. But Macarius is clearly obsessed with the idea, and in particular with the idea that a new Jewish faith threatened the ancient Egyptian faith.'

Finishing his Scotch, Hanna set the tumbler on the glass coffee table. The noise of glass on glass was jarring in the tense silence.

Ryan mused, aloud, 'You know, my guess is that Macarius must have first read some of the texts at the White Monastery in Sohag. Remember it was the greatest library in Egypt after the destruction of Alexandria, perhaps the greatest library *in the world* at that time. Therefore, something he found there must have inspired him, or troubled him enough that he undertook his journey. To find the real truth.'

'Like us,' said Helen.

'Yes . . . I guess.' Ryan was frustrated. Muscles taut. 'But remember we only have some of the Sokar documents here. And we need to go to Luxor and Philae, and Amarna.'

Callum raised a forceful hand. 'Look. Just decide where we are going *now*. What's our first stop?'

Ryan looked closely at the papyrus. 'According to Macarius, he says he next went to the place where "Moses was found". He means the place by the Nile where the baby Moses in the basket was found by a Pharaoh's daughter, somewhere in Lower Egypt, around here. He says this is the same place Jesus was washed as a baby, by the Virgin Mary, according to Coptic tradition. But I have no idea where: Coptic folklore isn't my speciality.'

'But it is mine,' Hanna intervened, eyes glittering. 'I know exactly where that is. Ben Ezra synagogue.'

'The synagogue in Maadi? *Coptic Cairo?*'

'Exactly.'

'But that's not by the river.'

Hanna shook his head. 'You forget, the Nile has *retreated*. The Romans built a watergate there, the so-called gate of Babylon: Coptic Cairo used to be on the riverbanks.' He sat forward. 'Coptic Cairo is one of the most lavishly historic quarters of the city, a walled city within the city dating back to ancient Egypt, when it was a suburb of ancient Memphis. More importantly, that little corner of Cairo has a remarkable *plenitude* of religious legends attached. There is a spring behind old Ben Ezra synagogue – itself inside the Coptic quarter – which is said to be simultaneously the place where baby Moses was found in his crib, where Jesus as a baby was baptized by his divine mother, during the Holy Family's flight through Egypt, and where Jeremiah preached to the Jews. And it is also where the Virgin Mary took a ferry. I've no idea why. Perhaps she needed to do some shopping in Heliopolis? The point is, this place, this spring in particular, is intensely significant and it *exudes* mythology. Shall I continue?'

'No.'

Hanna smiled. 'As you wish. But this is, without question, where we need to go. I suggest we do it at night.'

'At night?' Helen asked. 'Will it not be closed? It is a walled area, as you said.'

'The entire Coptic quarter has been shut for days.' Hanna replied. 'Because of the riots and troubles. The police are protecting it from our good neighbours the Salafists, who might otherwise be tempted to burn down the Hanging Church, and probably expectorate on the iconostasis.'

'So if it's shut down by the authorities,' Callum said. 'How the hell do we get in?'

'I have a friend.'

Ryan had expected this. Hanna had friends everywhere.

Hanna explained. 'But it will be dangerous. Less

211

dangerous if we do it under cover of darkness – but dangerous nonetheless. But then, everything is dangerous now, is it not? The sons of Abraham might be drawing a bead on us this very minute.'

Callum stood up. 'We do it tonight. Midnight.'

25

Coptic Cairo

A fine crescent moon rose above the tiny crucifix that adorned the dome of St Sergius. The symbolism was apt. Ryan stared around, sensing the danger. They were parked in a side street three minutes from the hushed white walls of Coptic Cairo.

Despite the curfewed calm of these deserted streets – the disturbances were miles north – the place felt surrounded. Besieged and frightened in the darkness. And perhaps facing its final doom, after two thousand years of remarkable survival.

Hanna pointed. 'Here's my contact.'

Albert's 'friend' was a Coptic youth of maybe fourteen or fifteen. The boy's expression was mute and defensive – but he led them through the shadows to a decrepit wooden door, set low in the perimeter walls.

'Hurry,' said Callum. '*Hurry up.*'

The boy fumbled nervily with an enormous set of

keys. At last the door swung open and they slipped inside. Ryan stared around. The Coptic boy had brought them to a Christian graveyard behind the churches. Large marble angels stared at the crescent moon; columns and pilasters recessed down pathways; a faint scent of dead flowers perfumed the normal Cairo smells of sewage and pollution and cooking oil.

Their *protectors* stopped inside the gate. Callum snapped an order: 'You guys go. We'll wait here. Do what you have to do. But do it quick.'

Hunched low, Albert, Helen and Ryan followed the boy along a gravel path that slalomed between the tombs and mausoleum, to the old buildings of Coptic Cairo. Dead faces in monochrome photos, affixed to the more recent graves, stared at them in disappointment as they slunk past. Helen had her camera switched on, filming their progress. Ryan squinted ahead, trying to make out their direction. He'd been here once before, as a young man: he'd walked this labyrinth of ancient passages and cobbled lanes, bewildered but seduced; by night the ambience was more troubling.

'Asre! Onzor!'

The Coptic youth was beckoning them into the very deepest shadows, between two high old walls: presumably the walls of monasteries. The moonlight was just sufficient for them to follow his progress, beyond another corner, past a brace of grim and shuttered tourist shops, where a more modern church rose up abruptly. It had no doubt been erected on the footings of a previous church, which was built on a synagogue, which was built on a Roman temple of Mithras, which was built on an Egyptian temple of Isis . . .

Ryan swooned a little in his thoughts as they approached this precipice of religious history, this vertiginous drop through time and faith. It was simultaneously marvellous and unnerving. Coptic Cairo was like an exposed fossil bed, showing the strata and the evolution: the fishes then the dinosaurs then the mammals. It gave him the same rhapsodic vertigo he'd felt in Saqqara, when he was happy, when he was a younger and better man, when his wife was pregnant, when they'd walked together in the sunset by the Djoser Pyramid, when they'd kissed—

'Ryan!'

It was Helen, grasping his shoulder.

He shook his head. 'I'm fine.' But was he?

'Let's get this done.'

They followed the boy once more until Albert pointed at a small but handsome stone building beyond a railing. 'The synagogue of Ben Ezra.'

The boy unlocked the railing; they crept quietly along the path and slipped inside the synagogue. Scratching a match into flame, the boy lit some candles, his hands shaking. Ryan picked up and carried his candle in its little candle-tray like a Victorian rector roused from sleep in his nightshirt.

In the guttering candlelight he plodded the aisles, scrutinizing the bejewelled and evasive interior of Ben Ezra synagogue. The glow of his candle showed Ottoman carvings in cedarwood and marble, palmettos and lotus flowers, rich and sensuous and distantly sad; the Jews of Cairo had gone, all the Jews of Egypt fled, making this more of a mausoleum than a living building.

But why had Macarius come here?

'Albert?'

Hanna materialized from the shadows.

'Albert, tell me, this place, the history, the synagogue.'

'It is ninth century, but it is adapted from a church that is older, maybe eighth century.'

'But our papyrus is probably sixth. So if he came here he didn't see *this*.'

Hanna nodded. '*C'est vrai.*'

'Where is the spring, where Moses was found?'

'I'll show you.'

The spring was behind the building. Outside, the candle in his hand guttered and died in a firm nocturnal breeze.

Ryan stared down. The great and famous spring, the place on the Nile where Moses was found, where Jesus was washed, where Jeremiah preached – was now a gurgling manhole with an orange gardening hose coiled at the side, and plastic rubbish stuffed in the grille.

Albert spoke. 'You know . . . I believe there was an even earlier church here which was demolished, so the bulk of the, ah, most venerable antiquities, from that time, would now be found in the museum?'

Ryan paused, and thought it through. This made sense. What should he do?

Helen was inside the synagogue, still filming, but the lad was at the door, his face wrought with anxiety. Ryan brushed aside his own doubts, and asked the boy to open the museum door. He quailed visibly. Ryan insisted. The boy shook his head.

Albert emerged like a genie from the gloom, flourishing a handful of dollars.

In the silent movie of the moonlight, the boy's smile was very white. '*La moshkelah!*'

The museum was apparently barely three hundred metres away, at the ancient centre of Roman Cairo.

The moonlight shone on the silent flagstones; the three of them kept to the shadows, until they emerged into an impressive courtyard. Hulking Roman watergates loomed above them, the path between led to a set of huge, intricately patterned doors. The museum itself, as Ryan recalled, had once been the Roman fort of Maser; the site had been lavishly reconstructed and restored, but the brooding quality of the military building remained.

It felt as if they were breaking into a prison.

Albert hurried the boy. At last the great wooden doors opened and Ryan stepped hastily inside. Echoes of darkness and nothingness answered him. He needed light: so this time he took the risk and used the flashlight in his phone. The boy shrank from the alarming and unexpected dazzle.

Ryan turned. Where was Helen?

Albert hissed at him from the shadows, 'We must be expeditious, Ryan. It is dawn soon, and Cairo wakes early.'

'Yes, yes, OK.'

He ran down the vast hall, from exhibit to exhibit, gazing in the sturdy glass cases: at ancient gold Coptic Bibles, at purple stoles of Akhmim weaving, at a pair of sultry Roman erotes – naked sex gods, carrying aloft the Virgin. It was all here. But what did it mean? Here was a truly strange icon: two dog-faced saints, Ahrauqus and Augan, approaching Jesus. Ryan recognized the iconography. Like the jackal-headed god Anubis? God of the mummy wrappings, baptizer of the dead.

And here was a tomb carved with *ankhs*, the Egyptian symbol of life, a cross with a head, next to the real cross. The *ankh* and the cross interchangeable. And over here was an entire wall painting. He turned his flashlight to read the explanatory text: 'Only two of these are known to exist; the other can be found in the small church at the Monastery of St Tomas, at the mouth of Wadi Sarga, sixteen kilometres north of Akhmim.'

The painting showed a coronation of the Virgin Mary. She wore a blue robe decorated with lozenges; just like the Egyptian goddess Nut at the temple back in Abydos, a goddess spanning the vault of heaven, her dress spangled with delicate stars.

Akhmim?

'Ryan!'

It was Albert, almost running.

'We have to go, now. My boy says someone is in the graveyard – trouble – we must go!'

It was intensely frustrating: Ryan felt he was on the

verge of something – a breakthrough – yet he was obliged to leave. Reluctantly, he followed the urgent steps of Albert Hanna. Helen joined them. They whispered as they walked quickly, sliding from shadow to shadow, fleeing the walled city, making for the cemetery, and the gate – and safety. 'I filmed the spring, did you get anything in the museum?'

'No – I—'

'What?'

'Jesus.'

Someone was indeed in the graveyard.

Wordlessly, Ryan pointed. Helen followed his gesture and her eyes widened.

An Egyptian peasant was sitting next to a gravestone, praying, or mumbling, but he was also hitting his head repeatedly against the gravestone: the noise of his skull impacting was audible and ghastly. *Clunk*. And again, he mumbled and butted the stone. Blood was now pouring down his face. *Slam*. And again. More blood. The sight was horrifying. The man was slowly killing himself.

'Stop him!' Helen cried, quite anguished. 'Can we help him? Look—'

'There is no time, he will attract others. *Come on!*' Albert's voice was fierce.

So they ran, openly and blatantly, to the gate where Simon was waiting, crouched, like a trooper in a street battle, keeping a low profile. 'Get in the fucking motor!' he spat.

The Hyundai was parked and revving and ready to

go, Callum at the wheel. Ryan glanced across. Waiting placidly at the gate to the cemetery was a donkey cart, piled with rubbish. The road was otherwise deserted, in the pallid light of the Cairene dawn.

The garbage and timing meant it was surely a Zabaleen cart: that was what the Zabaleen did, go round Cairo at all hours, picking up rags, in their donkey carts. Ryan saw the logic. The cart must therefore belong to that peasant in the cemetery. Therefore, the man slamming his head against the stone, trying to injure or kill himself, was a Zabaleen.

Just like the boy on the balcony in Sohag.

What did it mean?

Callum cracked the gears as they sped downtown. Ryan stared pensively out of the window. The traffic was light but growing, shop owners were yawning and stirring. They had rejoined the angry and eternal chaos of al-Misr, the Mother of Cities.

26

London

By the time Karen was buzzing her cousin's front door, in the frosty darkness of a January evening in suburban Muswell Hill, she realized she was nervous, like someone going on a date with someone very nice. Her heartbeat was raised, she was caffeinated by anxiety: the idea of seeing her daughter after two solid weeks of separation was exciting and disruptive.

That was one of the many things that surprised her about parenting: the way you loved your kids *and* missed them. She had, theoretically, expected to love her daughter when she arrived, but she hadn't been prepared for the overwhelming rush of conflicting emotions when she'd taken little baby Eleanor home from hospital, the overpowering sense of gratitude and sudden vulnerability, the desperate happiness tinged with fear, the hallucinatory levels of paranoia:

my God, my baby is choking on a grape; my God, she's blind; my God, she's like her father. Or her mother.

And as Eleanor had grown up Karen had learned that she actually *liked* her daughter, too. At six Eleanor was bubbly, good-natured and funny; sometimes deliberately, sometimes not. She could also be infuriating, and definitely headstrong. But she was a proper personality, a vibrant if tiny personality, and when Karen went to work she found she missed her daughter's *presence* even as she breathed a sigh of relief that she could get on with business.

'Hello?'

Karen pressed the buzzer for a third time. She could hear noises inside, the sounds of kids. Now the hallway light came on, the door was opened, and a tiny blonde tornado of love came shooting out of the door and jumped into Karen's arms.

'Mummy Mummy Mummy Mummy!' Eleanor squeezed her so tightly Karen felt as if she was choking.

Alan stood in the door with the twins at his feet, smiling. 'I see she missed you then.'

'Didn't!' said Eleanor, as Karen laboriously unwrapped her daughter's arms from her neck and set her down. As soon as Ellie was on the ground she wrapped her arms around her mother's legs instead and said, 'Mummy is cold, she needs some soup.'

Alan laughed, handing over several tons of kit. 'Here's her bags, and her clothes, they're mostly washed.'

Karen thanked her cousin several times; he waved

away her gratitude. 'It's been great, I told you: the twins love her.'

For several minutes the six-year-olds said goodbye to each other, mainly by lifting up their shirts and comparing the fake mermaid tattoos on their stomachs, then Karen kissed Alan, and Ellie kissed her cousins, Jake and Daisy, and mother and daughter got in the car and drove the few hundred yards to their smaller home, a garden flat, where Eleanor flung herself at her wooden toy train and the doll that said, 'Hell's bells'.

It was good to be home. With her daughter. In her pyjamas, reading *Winnie the Pooh*. When it was midnight, after two glasses of wine, Karen went into her daughter's room and listened to her daughter's breathing.

The sound was gratifying. Karen recalled an old Buddhist saying that her Detective Sergeant, Curtis, had once intoned to her:

'What is the definition of happiness? Grandmother dies, mother dies, daughter dies, *in that order.*'

There was a profundity there. So Karen's mother had died, but that was how it was meant to be; it wasn't a tragedy, it was the way the world turned, it was sad but it was right. Feeling angered by it was like feeling angry at the arrival of autumn, or taking rainfall personally.

And children were the purest solace. Karen brushed her daughter's hair from her frownless, worryless, six-year-old forehead, and wondered if she could give her only child a brother or sister. But doing that probably meant a man in her house, and something in her found that difficult. She liked the independence, she *liked* the need for self-reliance. *I can do this. I don't need anyone.*

'Goodnight, sweetheart.' Karen kissed her sleeping daughter in the darkness and shut the door.

For the first time since her mother's funeral, Karen slept properly and dreamlessly; and when she took her bonny daughter to school in the morning, Karen smiled at the other mums, and made a joke with the teacher, and when she arrived at work, in the busy offices of New Scotland Yard, she was very rested, and very eager to get on with the case.

DS Curtis was an affable red-haired Irishman of about her age, not entirely ambitious, but not lacking talent, either. He listened attentively as she went through the narrative. The cats, the suicide, the girl in the psych ward.

'So, Karen, er, it's not a homicide yet?'

Curtis always called her Karen. At the beginning of their working relationship they had experimented with his calling her 'Ma'am', but she'd decided that made her feel like an ancient dowager in a period drama, so they'd reverted to Karen.

He said, 'I'm not quite sure why we're concentrating so much on this.'

'I think it's going to get worse. Maybe homicide.'

'Why? How do you know?'

'I have a feeling.' She smiled. 'In my waters.'

'My nan used to say that, in Kilkenny. Turned out she had a bladder problem, from all the stout.'

Karen clicked on her computer. 'The suicide might

224

be manslaughter, the guy might have been driven to do what he did, or drugged, we don't know. But we do know there were seven other people in that cottage, burning the cats, staying at Trevelloe. Where are they? We need to trace them. They may be in serious trouble: of the only two we have located, one is dead and one is psychotic. What about the rest?'

DS Curtis nodded. 'OK, Ma'am!'

'Yes, yes. Let's start by chasing up Alicia Rothley. She had friends in London, we have a list. Get on that. OK? And I'll do my homework.'

The office was productively quiet for several hours. Lunch came and went with a flurry of supermarket sandwiches and hot coffee. At the end of it, Karen was decided: Aleister Crowley really *was* crucial.

They knew that the gang members were re-enacting magic associated with Crowley: Taghairm and Abra-Melin, in particular. They also knew the gang was using properties linked to Aleister Crowley: Carn Cottage, Trevelloe Lodge. Where were they now? If they were still in the country – and Alicia Rothley in her madness had implied that her brother was still here – then possibly they were staying in some other property with Crowley connections.

So who was Crowley? Karen had only read snippets, so far; now she needed the full works, all the details. They weren't hard to source. The web was full of 'Crowleyana', an entire industry of speculation and rumour, and even some hard facts – dedicated to this strange man.

One newspaper piece gave her almost all she needed to know:

Edward Alexander Crowley was born in Leamington Spa in England in 1875, to a wealthy brewing family who were hardcore Protestant evangelicals: Plymouth Brethren. The future Satanist was named Edward, after the father he came to adore. But Edward Crowley Senior died of cancer when the youngster was eleven, an experience so traumatic that Crowley lost all interest in the family's fierce religion.

The boy hated his pious mother, who sent him to a series of private schools where he was mercilessly bullied because he was fat. Having persuaded her to remove him by claiming he was being sexually abused, he was given a home tutor who, despite being a former Bible Society missionary, introduced him to such worldly pursuits as card games and billiards.

In 1895, Crowley, by now calling himself Aleister because of its Celtic overtones, went to Cambridge University to read moral sciences. Instead of studying, however, he boasted he spent his time on sexual experimentation.

Leaving three years later without a degree, he used his considerable family inheritance to take a flat in a large building in Chancery Lane, London, signing the lease with one of the many aliases he loved to use, Count Vladimir Svaroff.

The flat in Chancery Lane, in an area of London full of medieval resonances, was perfect for the budding Satanist, who was fast making it his mission to dispel Victorian hypocrisy by any means he could.

Crowley had just been introduced to the Hermetic Order of the Golden Dawn, a mysterious magical society which claimed to possess arcane truths handed down to the modern world from ancient Egypt.

He soon became an initiate, taking the name of Brother Perdurabo, meaning: 'I will endure'.

But Crowley rapidly came to despise his fellow brethren – who included the Irish poet W B Yeats – because of their timid approach to magic. Determined to conduct bolder experiments into the supernatural, he took as his personal instructor an impoverished magician called Alan Bennett whom he invited to stay with him.

And so a period of intense magical activity began, based on the invocations of a medieval Egyptian mage called Abra-Melin. Crowley and his followers believed that they could summon the spirits of the dead, and perhaps even the Devil himself, through animal sacrifice and pagan rituals.

Piecing together Crowley's writings and those of the impressionable acolytes that visited the place in Crowley's day, we have a good idea what the flat looked like, not to mention the unsettling things that went on inside.

The visitor passed from the cold stone dusk of the stairs to a palace of rose and gold that has long since vanished. Gold-black Japanese wallpaper covered the rooms and the place was lit like a brothel by an ancient silver lamp with a red bulb. The floor was covered with leopard skins and on the wall there was a huge crucifix in ivory and ebony.

There were two temples, one to good, the other to evil. In Crowley's 'Black Temple', actually more of a cupboard, a bloodstained skeleton sat before a sinister altar, made of a round table supported by the figure of an ebony Negro standing on his hands.

On the altar, a sickening perfume smouldered in a container and one visitor claimed the stench of previous blood sacrifices filled the air. In his delusions, Crowley used to feed the skeleton blood, small birds and beef tea in the hope of reviving it.

No wonder people were afraid of him. It was said that in the streets he could make himself invisible; others claimed that he was throbbing with so much magical power that his coat once burst into flames. Horses were generally frightened of him. However, despite these 'gifts', and in order to create real magic, Crowley believed he needed the use of a large remote country house with a terrace at the door facing north: the best direction in which to create a spell.

In Boleskine, in northern Scotland, he found the perfect house. He fell in love with it, and having inherited nearly five million pounds in today's money immediately bought it. There he claimed he invoked at least a hundred spirits. But he soon began to disturb his neighbours: villagers accused him of summoning ghosts from Boleskine churchyard, and a local butcher accidentally chopped off his fingers when he inadvertently handled a word square – a written spell – associated with the Abra-Melin ritual.

It was time to move on. Still honing his evil persona, Crowley travelled to Egypt with a young bride – whom he liked to string up naked in a cupboard. In Cairo, he claimed to have had a vision of himself as the new Messiah, saying he had received a message from an angel called Aiwass *who told him he was the herald of a cult which would have its own Bible, the Book of Thelema, the Greek word for will . . .*

Karen read on, amazed. From Egypt, Crowley had gone to America, India, Sri Lanka, China, then back to England, then Germany – apparently he went everywhere, spending the last of his inheritance from his ironically God-fearing parents. And the debaucheries got worse: whoring, heroin, cocaine, pederasty, coprophagy. The sentences blurred in front of Karen's eyes: 'he liked to bite the hand of his mistress until she bled'; 'at least five of his girlfriends committed suicide'; 'in Sicily, he fatally poisoned his friend by making him drink a glass of cat's blood'.

Karen googled a picture of Crowley. Fat, bald and unprepossessing. Apparently he seldom bathed. When Karen found a recording of his voice, online, it was impossibly reedy and unsexy, like a castrated Anglican vicar intoning the Acts of the Apostles.

Yet this man *must* have had some immense mesmeric potency. Despite his increasing corpulence and horrible demeanour he attracted followers and lovers – male and female – well into his sixties. And his cult was powerful to this day. What was it that he possessed? What hypnotic power? Was there really something in his magic that worked? Most importantly, had Rothley tapped into the same Crowleyan magic?

For another hour she researched the Abra-Melin ritual. As she did, she recalled the words of Donald

Ryman: *'the rite of Abra-Melin is the only magic in history that, for whatever reason, and in some terrifying way, actually appears to work'*.

'How's it going, Karen?'

Curtis had returned from the cold outside, bringing with him the faint smell of cigarette smoke. She didn't envy him these little smoking breaks: it was freezing out there. Minus two. A very cold January.

'I'm getting there, I think. I'm sure the key is wherever Crowley stayed.'

'Sorry?'

'We know Rothley likes to use properties associated with Crowley. Right?'

'Yes . . .'

'So I'm going through the main ones first, surviving apartments, hotels, et cetera. But we mustn't stop there. Remember Crowley was around a hundred years ago, and he moved constantly. We need to check out *every possible address*. Even if the site where he stayed has been demolished, and rebuilt, it might still attract – God knows – the vibrations Rothley likes. The spirits. That is what he believes.'

DS Curtis smiled.

'I'm serious,' Karen said. 'Make a list, and go there, even if it's been turned into a bloody car park. We need to get into Rothley's head.'

Her junior officer nodded, and sat down at his desk.

Once more she focussed on the facts. If the gang were staying in another property directly linked with Crowley, there were two serious and obvious options, as the biography told her. The first was Boleskine House near Loch Ness.

But, as Karen swiftly ascertained, Boleskine was, these days, privately owned by a perfectly upright family – a lawyer, his wife and four young kids. The lawyer was legitimate, and quite senior, and he didn't take kindly to being called a third time, in his Edinburgh office, to have his bona fides assessed. 'I can assure you the law firm of Macdonald and Griffiths is entirely unconnected with medieval demonic rituals. Now goodbye.'

That left the apartment in Chancery Lane as the only major property with Crowley connections still standing in the UK.

This time, her brisk research was more generously rewarded. The entire block of 102 Chancery Lane – once home to the 'wickedest man in the world' – was being redeveloped. But the slowdown in the property market meant this redevelopment *was on hold*; the place was a shell: unused, boarded up, empty, it hadn't been touched for two years. Anything could be happening in there.

Karen called the developers and was quickly put through to the site manager, Darren Glover.

'Chancery Lane?' he said, cheerfully. 'Yep, s'on our list. We're hoping to be back in next month, site's been a mess for so long, be good to get cracking.'

'When did you last visit the site?'

'Oh. God knows. Months ago. Like I say, it's been empty—'

231

'Does anyone ever go inside the building?'

The man paused. 'I guess not. We have security, but they patrol – you know – the perimeter, occasionally. Er. But why would anyone want to break in? There's bugger all in there. Place is gutted.'

Karen glanced at the darkening sky. 'Do you have a spare hour after work, Mr Glover? Could you meet me there?'

'You really want to go inside?'

Karen paused. For some reason she was suddenly reminded of Donald Ryman's words: *Some say the Abra-Melin ritual can only be successfully completed if several humans are sacrificed, culminating in the murder of a living child.*

'Miss Trevithick? Hello?' The man was still on the line. 'Hello, are you there?'

'Yes. Sorry.' She paused. For a few seconds. Resisting the faint tremors of dread. Then she said, 'Yes, I want to go inside.'

27

London

Karen got off the Tube at Blackfriars. It was a cold and rather drizzly evening. Tourists were wandering along the Thames Embankment. She called the school to make sure Eleanor had been collected by Alan, as arranged.

Her first day back as a mother and *already* she was neglecting her daughter. *Again*. The guilt burned but Karen did her best to ignore it.

As she walked along, Karen gazed about; she'd always loved this part of London. The exotic clash of ancient and modern, the surreal quietness at night. She used to walk here when she was a student in the big city, loving the hushed and medieval precincts of the Temple, tucked between the shining offices and bank HQs, the cenotaphs of money.

She passed one particularly glamorous and empty new office block. The darkness of a cold winter evening had sent the office workers home. Spires of Georgian churches loomed between chasms of glass. And then she found it.

102 Chancery Lane. It was a rundown Victorian building, a sooty old heap with greyed windows, yellow brickwork and an air of sickliness. It was also pretty much derelict, ripe for redevelopment. Surrounding the ground floor of the block was a palisade of wooden walls, with scaffolding creeping up the sides. KEEP OUT signs were everywhere.

But the builders were nowhere, of course. The whole block was desolate. Indeed this whole quarter of London was so very quiet: another enclave of historic silence amidst the monied and glittering bustle.

'Ah, hi. Darren Glover.' The young site manager came running up the road. 'Sorry I'm late, just got off the bus.'

He turned a padlock and pushed open a temporary wire door, and they squeezed inside the palisade. The last thing Karen saw of the outside world was a bus rolling down Holborn, and then she was inside. It was gloomy within. A couple of bare, shining bulbs were strung on naked wires, hanging from a cracked and corniced ceiling, but they didn't seem to work. There was an old chandelier covered in oil lying in a corner of the lobby. Karen and Darren switched on their torches.

The ground-floor rooms were bare and bereft, having been already stripped by the developers and then left to go damp. They offered no sign of life, and no sign of habitation in the recent past. Darren Glover put his hands on his hips, vindicated. 'I told you, it's empty! Nothing here.'

Standing in the dank and chilly hallway, Karen frowned. Frustrated. Maybe she was wrong. Or maybe she was right. She remembered the newspaper piece: passing *from the cold stone dusk of the stairs* . . . 'Let's try the upper floors.'

Around the stairs the dust of old bricks, and old life, was thick. Karen went first this time, guiding them with her torchbeam, which pierced the dust as if it were sea-fog. The grand Victorian stairway led to an old stone landing, and then she saw in the darkness a large door, its size indicating that it led to a significant apartment.

The door was closed, but the smell hit them at once. Something fetid and dead, but recently dead: something *rotting*.

'Jesus,' said Darren. 'That's disgusting. What the hell is in there?'

Karen walked to the silent, peeling door, and pushed. The door appeared to be locked. If Rothley had been here, how had he got hold of a key?

The affable site manager was now a lot less cheerful. 'Do you think someone is in there?'

Someone, or something? was the ludicrous thought that flashed across Karen's mind. *What was she expecting, a demon?*

Stupid.

She pushed against the door again but it did not

give. Even so, the door was old, and ill-fitting: there were cracks at the bottom, spaces between the jamb and the warped and peeling panels. Enough spaces for that ghastly stench to escape.

Another unwarranted thought intruded. The girl, on the bed, growling like a dog.

He will kill you, bitch. Luke will smell your fear. He will kill you.

'There's a box of tools downstairs.'

Karen turned to Darren Glover, their torchbeams crossing in the dust. 'Sorry?'

'Right at the foot of the stairs, there might be a crowbar. Let me go and get it.'

He disappeared into the gloom and the murk, leaving Karen alone with whatever was inside and beyond that door.

Was that a noise? She pressed her ear to the panel. Some kind of scratching? A rat? A pigeon? Something else?

'Darren?' Karen whispered. 'Mr Glover?' She wasn't sure why she was whispering but she didn't seem able to shout.

He will kill you, bitch

'OK, I got it.'

Glover re-emerged, illumined by his own torchlight, carrying a long black crowbar. He applied it boldly to the door, jemmying it behind the jamb. Just two savage tugs were sufficient, then the door snapped open and the full rotten scent flooded out: engulfing them.

236

Darren Glover pressed a sleeve to his nose. 'Jesus Christ. *Yuk.*'

Karen recognized the smell now. It was mammalian decomposition, probably human. She'd experienced it often enough: rancid, pungent, sickening, with a faint and eerie top note of sweetness. But there was a lot more in that smell, too, something . . . churchy. Incense?

Her torchlight pierced the room. One quick sweep told her it was empty, apart from a rug on the bare floorboards – and here, some red smears on the grey, wallpaperless walls. She stepped inside, and looked closer. Almost certainly paint, as if someone had begun to decorate the room then stopped. Were they trying to recreate Crowley's flat? The rose-coloured room? But then they'd abandoned the job for some reason?

Her shoes scrunched on something. She gazed down. She was walking on tiny dead birds. The floor was littered with little dead birds, and feathers. They really *were* repeating Crowley's rituals.

'What the fuck are they?' Glover yelped. 'Starlings? Sparrows? And this! What the . . . what's going on?'

'It's black magic. This room used to belong to a famous Satanist, Aleister Crowley, a hundred odd years ago. He would feed little birds to a skeleton. They are copying him.'

So now she had her proof. Someone had been in here, recently, and that someone was surely Rothley. But what was that smell? And where was it coming from? It seemed to fill the room, but it had no obvious source. A dead rat lodged behind the walls?

But she recalled Donald Ryman's words: *Some say the Abra-Melin ritual can only be successfully completed if several humans are sacrificed, culminating in the murder of a living child.*

Karen shuddered. Once again, her torchlight illuminated something odd. A fat red disc, like a hockey puck, lying next to the birds. She took some gloves from her jacket pocket and snapped them on.

'You think this is a crime scene.'

Ignoring Glover's nervous assertion, she knelt and picked up the disc. It was soft, and organic: the shape and consistency of fishcake, but purplish red. Karen sniffed at the disc. It smelled strongly of incense: myrrh, copal, storax, whatever they used in churches. It was also a little crumbly. They'd get no fingerprints from this; but it was worth analysing. She took out a ziplocked evidence bag from her other pocket and dropped it in.

She picked up one of the birds, and bagged it, too. And these, what were these? Dead wasps? A dead little lizard? They also went in the bags.

And these: rats' feet. Severed, and scattered beyond the birds. She remembered the moles' feet in the museum in Boscastle. Repressing her revulsion, Karen went across the floor on her hands and knees, methodically gathering all this evidence.

Glover said, again, 'You think there's been a crime here. Right? Those are evidence bags.'

Karen said nothing. Now that she was closer to the ground the smell was even more intense. She realized it was coming from under the rug. From under the floorboards . . .

She stood up, abruptly, and whisked away the rug. The smell surged out. Her torchbeam revealed that several planks had been recently and crudely hammered over a hole in the original floorboards.

'Help me,' she said, gesturing at Darren's crowbar. 'Let's get these floorboards up.'

His expression showed his absolute reluctance, but he obeyed nonetheless. Grunting, and tugging, he jemmied up the new boards one by one.

First Karen saw the legs: bare feet, bare human legs, dead and grey, gnawed a little by rats: the corpse had been here a few days. Then the middle planks came away and she saw the midriff. A young woman, naked, smeared with blood.

Glover yelped. 'Fuck. Look at the hands!'

The hands and arms were covered with bite marks. Two of the fingers had been severed, messily: as if *chewed* off. Tourniquets had been applied to the upper arms, which now hung loose and leathery. Dark purple patches in the cement underneath showed where the blood had soaked.

Glover backed away. But Karen pointed to the last plank. Covering the face. 'Please?'

He swore, in a low voice, but he applied himself. The final plank came away with little effort, the nails lifted, the wood cracked, and the woman's face was revealed.

Karen stared, shocked.

She had expected to see a face contorted with horror, or grimacing, or simply rigid with fear – as she normally found in murder cases.

But the dead girl was calm and open-mouthed. The open mouth was clogged with drying red blood – and something else. Something raw and strange. What was it? Karen stooped close, to look, then she recoiled.

The girl's mouth was choked with her own severed fingers.

28

Luxor

They sat in the sad little garden behind the Luxor temple. The distant *feluccas* twinkled on the Nile like silver-winged insects come to feed on nectar; the river breeze carried scents of jasmine and donkey dung.

The city was awakening, the shop owners unshuttering their stalls of bogus antiquities and phoney papyri, the horse-carriages – *caleches* – waiting, brasses jangling, for tourists who would never show up.

Ryan felt a little empty himself, translucent with tiredness. They were all exhausted – Helen and himself, their two protectors Callum and Simon – all of them yawned and drooped – all apart from Albert Hanna.

He had fuelled himself, during their manic desert drive from Cairo, with copious amounts of Scotch. And still he was as ebullient as ever.

Picking up a stick, Albert gestured at a scowling Arab shopkeeper. 'They're really quite moody in the morning, the Mussulman. I've noticed this, but can't explain it. Surely they should all be in a good mood, because they are so clear-headed. "Another morning without a hangover! *Allahu Akhbar!*"' He grinned. 'And yet I am in a better mood than them. And I got *exceptionally* drunk last night.'

'Albert, they are all going bankrupt: their industry is dying.'

The Copt smoothed his goatee and ignored Helen's remark. 'This proves the superiority of the Christian West. You people get so much *done*, despite being alcoholics.' He smirked at Ryan. 'That said, one simply *has* to wonder what the West might have achieved without the crippling effects of gin. The British would probably have invaded the moon.'

Callum interrupted. 'Guys. This isn't good. No tourists at all. Not even a Jap with a cameraphone.' He gestured at the square, and the empty *caleches* with the bored horses. 'We're way too conspicuous.' He turned to Ryan, who was once more poring over the Macarius papyrus. 'Any joy?'

'No,' Ryan confessed. He'd spent most of the arduous, checkpoint-avoiding desert drive from Cairo desperately trying to decipher the next part of the papyrus. They had hoped to go to Amarna, but it had proved too dangerous, sealed off from all visitors by the troubles; so they had come straight to Luxor, doubling their journey. Yet even this extra time had not been sufficient for him to crack this part of the text.

In his thoughts, Ryan could see Sassoon shaking

his wise and teacherly head; he could see Rhiannon, disappointed. Had he given it all up for nothing?

Helen gently nudged his arm. Sympathetic and half-smiling. Her attitude to him seemed to have changed over the days: she was warmer. She smiled more, despite the anxiety and fear. 'Tell us again, what exactly it does say.'

She was filming him, discreetly. Ryan was too exhausted to feel self-conscious. He gazed down at the papyrus. And spoke.

'The beginning is clear enough. "I travelled for many days, along the river, arriving at the Temple of Amun at Diospolis." But where is Diospolis? Well, the Greeks had a pretty logical system for renaming Egyptian cities: they simply said, this is the city where such-and-such a god was worshipped. Consequently, Diospolis means the city where Zeus – or Dios – was worshipped.' Ryan stood – and Helen's camera followed him. 'But when the Greeks said Dios they meant the supreme god Amun-Ra, worshipped here at the great Temple of the Sun at Thebes. The city now known as Luxor.'

He stretched his arm and Helen panned the camera, taking in the mighty stone pylons and the enormous, lotus-headed pillars of the Luxor temple. The whole place was glowing in the hot morning sun. The colossus of Rameses stared at Ryan, indifferent and supreme, and hiding its enormous secret. Behind them the avenue of sphinxes stretched for miles along the Nile, all the way to Karnak. A parade of royal cats, with human faces. What was the Egyptian obsession with the cat? Did it fit in somehow?

Ryan focussed. Face towards the lens. 'The question is obvious. What did our scholar Macarius find here? In his own words he says he went inside the temple, "and there I found the great secret . . . which I took with me up the river". But after the word "secret", Macarius reverts to obscure symbols, which I have transcribed here.' Helen focussed the lens on a sheet of paper in Ryan's other hand. Ryan had drawn the symbols double-sized, not that this had helped him interpret their meaning.

He showed them to the camera.

$$\Gamma \neg \cap \Pi \int \backslash X \ldots$$

'What language is this? What alphabet? The symbols are basic, simplistic, almost runic, the kind of symbols you would cut into stone. We cannot translate them. Whatever secret Macarius found here remains concealed.' Ryan stopped talking. A policeman was staring at them from the square, beyond the temple forecourt.

Albert Hanna muttered, 'That's it, *monsieur*? You don't know? You've given up?'

'I just . . . can't translate. Helen can't work it out, you can't work it out – we're stuck.'

'Let me, if you will, have one more attempt.' Albert took the sheet of paper and traced the symbols with his finger. 'Hmm . . .' The goatee-stroking implied that he was thinking hard. But then, abruptly, he handed the paper back to Ryan. '*Pff.* As you say, they look faintly runic. But they aren't Viking runes. I have seen the runes carved by the Varangian guards in the marble of Hagia Sophia, and these aren't runes. Perhaps we should just move on to the Cataracts of Philae: we are starting to attract attention from *les gendarmes*.' He nodded in the direction of the *caleches*, where three policemen were now staring at them.

'We do not have permission to film,' said Helen. 'It would not matter normally because there would be so many tourists. But we are standing out now. They might want a bribe.'

'Or they might have been asked to watch out for people like us,' said Callum. 'The Israelis have satellites. They could have followed us across the desert. Who knows? They are certainly *baksheeshing* half the fucking cops between Aswan and Alexandria. We're wanted. Dead or alive. Mainly dead. This is not a joke. What's more, we can't help you against the cops. We can protect you from the Israelis, but if you get in trouble with the Egyptians, in Egypt, that's different. We can't fight the fucking army. If you go in the temple and the cops stop you, you're on your own. If anything happens we'll meet at the next place on the list. What is it?'

'The Valley of the Nobles,' said Ryan.

'Yeah. There. At four p.m.? But this temple: that's up to you. We'll be just down the road. Somewhere very discreet.'

'But we do not know where we need to go in the temple.' Helen sighed. 'We are stuck.'

'No, you're not.'

Everyone swivelled. The Canadian guard, Simon,

who was normally taciturn to the point of muteness, was holding Ryan's discarded sheet of paper, with the transcribed symbols.

'It's a route map.'

'Sorry?'

'It's just a damn route map. It's the way you would write down a route – if you wanted to write a route like a series of letters. In a line. This is how you'd do it.'

Ryan stared down at the paper.

'Look.' Simon tutted. 'Here. Look. He's saying go straight on then dog leg. Next go right then ahead. Right? Then do a U-turn. Get it? It's a route into the temple. And the X marks the damn spot. *Capisce?*'

The solution was so simple and obvious it was somewhat crushing.

'We are a collection of ignorami,' said Hanna, but Helen was already dragging them in her wake to the gate of the temple. Callum and Simon remained behind, gesturing at their watches, as they slipped into the shadows.

For the moment, they really were on their own. *No protection*.

Ryan took the sheet of paper from Simon, as Helen paid the bored gateman for their entrance to the Luxor temple.

'OK,' he said. 'We have to go through the pylons, past the granite obelisk.' Helen filmed him as they hurried between the great, slanted stone pylons, ochre and magnificent in the desert sun. It was a temple of shadows and dazzle, darkness and sunburn; Arab men lurked in the shadier spots: depressed and hapless

246

guides, bereft of business, staring at their filthy sandals.

'Speed the plough,' said Albert. 'Those police are coming, and I think they're coming for *us*.'

'Past the colossi,' said Ryan. 'Then diagonally left across the peristyle court.' He glanced at the paper in his hand. 'No, wait, we go right *through* the peristyle court.' The shadows of the pillars had confused him for a moment. 'The door, here, then through again.'

Hieroglyphs adorned the walls: Anubis and Horus, Isis and Hathor, the cow-eared goddess; then a winged dove, like the Holy Spirit, hovering over the dead Osiris.

Ryan recalled the history. Maybe there was a clue in the history. This temple of Luxor was for many centuries the very centre of Egyptian faith. Once a year the divine image of the sun god Amun, with his consort Nut, the goddess of night, would journey in their sacred barques from Karnak temple to celebrate the yearly inundation of the Nile, the annual heartbeat of the Egyptian nation. Thus, the king and country were reborn. Every year, year after year, *for three thousand years* this had happened; except for that strange inter-regnum – the monotheism of Akhenaten . . .

'Ryan!'

His reverie was broken. Helen was gesturing. 'The police!'

Their time was almost up. Ryan ran into a dark side chamber, on the eastern side. 'This is it. This must be it. X marks the spot.' He gazed around frantically. The antechamber was dark, and smelled of rotting citrus fruit.

Probably the workmen took their lunch breaks here. But what was he looking for?

The walls were blackened with soot and obscured by scaffolding: restoration work had obviously begun, and then been abandoned, following the troubles.

'Ryan!'

He knew he had just a few seconds left. Whatever he was looking for was on this tall, pitted eastern wall, but it was covered with badly eroded friezes. Which one did Macarius see? What was the great secret?

Something caught his eye. It was up there, above head height. Horus? Horus and Isis? Thoth and Neph. *Yes!* Ryan climbed onto the scaffolding and looked closer—

'Ryan! They're coming!'

He knew the scene showed the birth of Amenhotep III, the Pharaoh of the Eighteenth Dynasty, father of Akhenaten; it had to be, that was the date of this part of the Luxor temple. But why was this particular frieze so important? Many of the symbols were so eroded that he had to feel them to understand their meaning: he had to read the Braille of Deep Time, going back through the centuries, reaching into the darkness, retrieving a concealed truth from thirty centuries ago—

'Stop!'

He was halfway through, more than halfway through. His hands reached for the final panel, a goddess with a baby—

'Stop now. You are arrested. Everyone is arrested.'

The police had pushed into the antechamber. Ryan

was physically hauled down from the scaffold by several rough and violent hands. He fought the urge to punch, because it was pointless; Helen and Hanna were already being handcuffed, and led out of the chamber.

Ryan was handcuffed too. The Egyptian policeman shoved him out into the sun of the courtyard, where the lofty, fat columns gazed down.

Ryan realized that one of two things could now happen. Either this was a regular arrest, for illegal filming, for trespass, for simply being one of the few tourists left for the police to shake down, in which case they faced a few hours of interviews, then bribes.

Or these cops had been paid by the Israelis, and they would now be taken somewhere quiet, to be silenced. Forever.

29

Police Headquarters, Luxor

Another concrete room. How many anonymous, rancid, badly drained concrete rooms could be found, just like this, across Egypt? How many pungent little hovels redolent of stunted ambitions? Tens of millions of Egyptian people lived in houses that weren't much better. Many were probably worse.

Ryan sighed. No wonder this country was breeding religious fundamentalism. God was the only hope in a country of the hopeless. Yahweh, Allah, the Lord God Almighty: He was the only light in the dark.

And yet, could he blame them? Sometimes Ryan envied the Egyptians – the Copts or the Muslims – the ardour of their faith. The great solace they possessed. Because he too wanted to believe. He too wanted to think that Rhiannon and their daughter were waiting, in the fields of God, amidst the flowers; waiting for him to come home. He wanted to dive into the clean waters of illogic, the cleansing and purifying absurdity, like a young man yearning for war.

But he couldn't make the leap.

Ryan gazed around the police holding cell. Albert Hanna was now being interviewed: he and Helen had already had an hour each of questioning, a questioning which in truth had been less than rigorous, probably just obligatory box-ticking, before the police sheepishly made their request for the inevitable and hefty bribe.

So the cops *didn't* want to kill them. They were just desperate, like everyone else in the Egyptian tourist industry: used to augmenting their pitiful salaries with tips and backhanders from the millions on the Tutankhamun tour buses, the Hurghada day trips, the bloated Nile cruise boats, now all empty.

Yet the questioning, however desultory, had still left Ryan shaken. Because the police had asked him the most unsettling questions of all: 'Why are you doing this? Why are you making a film? What is the point? Why risk your life? Egypt is dangerous now. Go home.'

In the hurtling drama of the preceding days, this most important query had somehow gone astray. But now, sitting here, Ryan had plenty of time to focus on it. Why *was* he doing all this? He'd virtually abandoned his job, he was indeed risking his life, he was trying to solve an ancient puzzle that might, in the end, turn out to be no puzzle at all: just the ravings of a sixth-century Coptic Gnostic, or some delirious monk. A circuitous maze with *no exit*.

Like life.

'Helen. Why the hell are we doing this?'

She said nothing. She was sitting across the cell, her knees up and her head rested on them. Sleeping? She was wearing a long black shirt over black jeans, and those somehow always-immaculate walking boots. Blonde in black. Ryan stifled any incipient feelings of desire. It was ridiculous. He was ten years older than her. She barely smiled at him.

Though she had been smiling more of late.

No. She was a young, striking woman with the brightest of futures: sharp, determined and talented. And sleeping.

Ryan sat back and stared at the ceiling. His mind went back to the papyrus. The Greek word-riddle, or spell: ΑΓΓΟ, ΑΕΘΗ, ΑΑΘ, ΒΕΖ, ΒΗΓ. It was next to the famous line from the Book of Revelation: *Here is wisdom. Let him that hath understanding count the number of the beast: for it is the number of a man; and his number is Six hundred threescore and six.*

Was the secret in the Sokar Hoard a spell for summoning the Devil? A spell that worked? Was it connected to the fragments of Abra-Melin magic?

'You are doing it because you want to be famous.'

Helen had spoken. Now she spoke again. 'You are doing this because you want the fame. And because, right now, you are a little disappointed in life. Because you are nearly forty and you think this could be your last big chance.'

This was possibly *too* much truth. 'Ah, OK.'

But Helen wasn't done. She stared at him with her

cold Nordic eyes and went on, 'You have no family, no children, nothing. Why not try and solve this amazing puzzle? Why not take a risk? What else is life for, if you do not dare, if you do not try and achieve *something*? Otherwise, it is just golf.'

He matched her unblinking gaze with his own. 'You think it's just vanity then. Male vanity.'

'No.' She stood up and crossed the cell, and sat on the same concrete bench as him. Close enough that he could almost identify her perfume. 'Without vanity, the desire for fame,' she said, 'where would we be? Why did men volunteer to fly to the moon? Because they wanted glory, and fame. Why did Columbus sail to America? Risk his life, sailing into nowhere? Because he did it for *fame*.'

'And gold.'

'It is human to seek glory, Ryan. And besides, *you* were a brilliant Egyptologist. And still are. You can still *do* this, Ryan. *You can do this*. You are halfway there already, you are thinking better, working better. Carve your name on the marble of history like Michelangelo signing his Pieta in St Peter's. *Ryan Harper did this*.'

He was struck dumb, for a second. Helen was rarely this loquacious. 'You've been assessing my *work*?'

'I watch you a lot.' She paused. 'I like watching you. I think the way you saved the kid in Sohag was brave. You are brave and sometimes, sometimes you are quite handsome, in a sort of slightly rusted way, like a nice old car.'

'You're teasing me now, Helen. Stop.'

'Am I?' She laughed, gently. 'Really? I do not think I am. I like watching you, and working with you. And I am bored of being alone, Ryan, being stuck in my own head. Thinking about my sister, feeling guilty.' She was sitting very close now. 'This will sound insane, but the last few days have been some of the happier days of my life. I have never been less alone than I am right now.'

'Helen?'

She stared at him. Defiant. Smiling.

'You should kiss me, Ryan. If it goes wrong, we shall say it was rape. After all, we are in a police station.'

Her face was near. Her beauty was close. He reached for her. And paused for a moment. And then he kissed her.

It was an awkward kiss, an amateurish kiss, the kiss of two people who had been alone for a long time. But she came back for a second, and this next kiss was better.

She smiled again. 'That was good. But I am not going to sleep with you. At least not here. The concrete is too hard.'

He stared at her, perplexed. And aroused. 'You know . . . you're a little unnerving.'

'Am I?' She stood up, backed away and crossed the floor to sit down on the opposite bench.

He asked, 'So why are *you* doing this?'

'I told you, because I want to be a success like my sister.' Her smile had faded. 'To make my parents proud of me as they were of her. To make them happier. I hate their sadness, their loss.'

254

'So it's just a different kind of fame, in a way.'

Her nod was accepting. 'Yes, of course.'

This time Ryan smiled, with something like gladness. They had kissed! – and it felt wholly correct. Perhaps, at last, the past was slipping away. 'But the—'

Their conversation was stilled by the door opening. Albert Hanna stood in the doorway, next to a tall policeman.

'We're free to go,' he said. 'The police captain is a Copt, and a seventh cousin. I have therefore spent another thousand American dollars to oil the wheels: the utility of the greenback remains undimmed. We are still, of course, in grave danger. So we need to move. Aren't we meant to be, ah, crossing the river?'

'Sorry?

'We have a rendezvous, do we not? The Valley of the Nobles, the next destination on the Macarius papyrus. Now we can make that rendezvous.'

Albert Hanna had rescued them; but his expression was morbid. Why? Helen and Ryan swapped glances, gathered their meagre possessions, and exited the police building. Ryan waited until they were out in the sun of the Luxor afternoon and sitting discreetly in the shadows of a tea-house, across from the Luxor temple, before he asked the obvious question. 'What is so wrong? What's happened?'

Albert gazed at him, quite distantly, and for once did not smooth his black and devilish little goatee.

'The police captain is an intelligent man. He studied in America. He is highly educated. He is not credulous. He is *sympathique*. He told me about the Zabaleen. He has friends in Coptic Cairo and he has heard reports, troubling rumours. The Zabaleen suicides, the self-harming, the strange behaviour we have witnessed – the young man in Sohag, the man in the cemetery – these are not isolated events.'

'And?'

'It is all quite violent and bizarre. There have been reports of Zabaleen . . .' He shuddered, visibly. 'Biting themselves. Self-mutilating their hands, their fingers, their faces. And there have been more murders.'

Helen frowned. 'It is some mental disease? Or a mass hysteria? What?'

Albert gazed at the avenue of sphinxes, smiling their feline smiles in the afternoon sun, serene and inscrutable. 'The story going around Cairo is that the Zabaleen have been bewitched by some archaic black magic, which has now been resurrected. The wilder rumours blame Wasef Qulta for bringing the Sokar Hoard to Moqqatam, the Hoard, with all its ancient spells. It seems the documents we carry with us, every day, may be the true and terrifying source of all this evil.'

Albert fell silent. A tourist *caleche* clip-clopped past them, chinkling and gangling. And entirely empty. Like a ghost of itself.

256

30

London

By the time Karen Trevithick had finished her business at Chancery Lane it was nearly eleven p.m. The Scene of Crime had been created, an SOC officer appointed, Pathology and Forensics had been alerted; the apartment was already being swept with infrared cameras and print-raising gels; the dead girl's face and body was photographed so many times the image of her eerie smile – fixed and serene – captured in stark and dramatic camera flashlight – was burned onto Karen's corneas, like a horror film you watch when you are too young that won't leave you at night, no matter how hard you close your eyes.

Given the lateness of the hour and her total exhaustion, the Met police budget generously offered Karen the option of a taxi rather than the Tube. Or so Karen decided. The warmth and peace of the cab was blissful after the horrors of Crowley's old apartment. Car lights flowed and ebbed, rather comfortingly, white and red and jewel-like in the cold.

'Here.' She tapped the cab driver on the shoulder as he religiously followed the instructions of his sat nav: like a minor Eastern king consulting an oracle. Karen tried again: 'Stop! I'm already here.'

'*Bear right after two hundred yards*,' said the pompous, disembodied female voice on the sat nav.

The cabbie shrugged and switched off the hectoring voice and pulled over. Karen stepped out of the car into the freezing cold, and the streetlit darkness; the suburban pavements were slippery and cracked with a determined frost.

She stepped carefully to Alan's front door and buzzed, trying to ignore the discordant chimes of guilt in her mind. First day back at school, and she dumps poor Ellie with the cousins, yet again. *That is poor, Karen, very poor.*

The lights in the hallway were dark. Probably everyone was asleep: it was nearly midnight. Karen pressed the buzzer again, half-yawning, half-swaying with tiredness. And entirely guilty. She'd make it up to her daughter, somehow. Perhaps she could take Ellie to the Aquarium at the weekend, with the twins; or maybe the petting zoo. Or just the zoo. Certainly, she wouldn't take her to the massive toy shop on the North Circular. No. That was bad. Karen was desperate not to become one of those hardworking professional *single* mothers who paid off the debt of guilt with endless gifts. Instead she would give Eleanor endless love. Hugs, not bribes.

The hallway light was finally switched on, and a shapeless monastic figure descended the stairs: Julie, Alan's wife, wrapped in a dressing gown, obviously just woken. Karen mumbled her conscience-stricken speech. 'Sorry, Julie, I'm so, so sorry. Did I wake you – the twins – I'm sorry. Thank you so much for taking Ellie.'

Julia stifled a yawn, her eyes deep-set with tiredness, and managed, just about, to answer. 'S'OK, ah, mm, Alan took Ellie to your place. Ellie wanted to . . .' Another enormous yawn. 'She wanted to sleep at home – she'll be there now.'

'Ah. OK. Sorry!'

This had happened before, more than once. Alan had a spare set of keys for Karen's garden flat and sometimes when he looked after Ellie he'd take her there, when she threw a tantrum because her mummy was late.

Guilt.

'God, did she kick up a storm?'

'Nnnno.' Julie yawned again. 'Well, a bit, anyway she's there. Gonna go back sleep – twins – school run . . .'

'OK, bye, Julie. Sorry. And thanks.'

Guilt.

The door shut in Karen's face but Karen was already turning, and walking – almost running – the few hundred yards to her own house. Just round two corners, she'd be there in ten. Poor Alan, he was probably desperate to go to sleep himself; yet he'd taken Ellie home, and fed her and put her to bed, and now he was stuck in Karen's flat watching late-night news or football on her crappy little TV, checking his watch and waiting.

Call him? She was only a few minutes from the door, but she could call him. Begin her apologies.

Karen whipped out her phone as she walked very quickly down Elmwood Lane, counting the house numbers. And dialling Alan's number.

The phone rang and rang, and then went to voicemail. Was it switched off to keep the peace? That was unlike Alan: he always had his phone on – he just set it to vibrate if he was in a house with sleeping children.

Karen dialled again to make sure she'd got the number right.

'Hello, you've reached Alan Wrightley, guess I'm not available so please leave—'

Voicemail. Again. The first creeping fingers of anxiety clutched at Karen's soul. No. This was insane. Maybe Alan had just fallen asleep on her sofa, lullabyed by some midnight football; with a newspaper fallen from his lap. Ellie would be safe and tucked in her little bed. That was it. Yes, that was it.

But Karen was running now. She ran the last few yards to her front door, her heart yammering like a Touretter, *worry worry worry worry stop stop stop stop.* She fumbled with the key as if she was a soldier being gassed, reaching for her gasmask . . . There! She was in.

The flat was dark. No noise, no TV, no sounds; nothing.

She tried to quell her worries with some logic as she raced down the corridor. She opened Ellie's bedroom door and snapped on the light, not caring if she woke her sleeping daughter. She was frightened now, stupidly frightened.

The bedroom was empty. The little bed, with its Hello Kitty coverlet, was flat and unruffled. Eleanor had not used it.

Karen yelled. 'Ellie! Eleanor! Alan!' She didn't give a fuck if she was waking Elmwood Lane, she didn't give a fuck if she was waking all of North London. '*Ellie!!!* It's Mummy – where are you?'

The flat answered with a contemptuous silence. Karen stood in the hallway, terrorized, yet trying to be rational.

Deep breath, *deep breath*. She approached her bedroom, the main bedroom. Perhaps Alan was here, in bed, with Ellie sleeping beside him. She opened the door and snapped on the light and gazed around: the bedroom was empty. Her bed was as she had left it this morning, down to the paperback book on the pillow, face down, halfway through.

Karen spun out of the bedroom and ran into the living room. This was her last hope. If they weren't in here – Ellie and Alan on the sofa in the dark, with the TV off, asleep, but why would they be doing that? – if they weren't in here, then she was gone, her daughter was gone, and the terrible *terrible* soundtracking nightmare of her every waking day, that something might happen to her daughter, had come true.

Luke will rape you. He will kill you.

The fear was so great, so chokingly huge and daunting that Karen actually didn't want to open the living-room door and see. As long as she kept the door closed she had hope; if she opened the door and saw nothing, that hope was gone.

Summoning the angels of her courage, Karen pressed the living-room door and entered the darkened silent room and in her despairing agony she knew, she already knew . . . but she turned on the light anyway . . .

And surveyed the total emptiness. There was a glass of beer on the table. Half-drunk. Only Alan drank beer. So he *had* been here. Next to it was a plate of biscuits and an almost-finished glass of milk. Eleanor's comfort food, when her mother was away. So they had been here, and now they were gone.

Taken?

The panic roared inside her. She dialled Julie's mobile as she pointlessly checked the last possible places – the bathroom, empty, the toilet, empty, the kitchen, empty. Even the wardrobes in Karen's bedroom. Empty. The phone answered.

'She's gone, Julia, and Alan too, they've gone – they've been taken—'

'What? *What?* Alan's with you!'

Karen was trying not to crack. She repeated, 'No, he's not. He's not here. Are they with you? Have I missed them? Did they come back when I—' Gulping air now, she only just managed to speak. 'When I was coming here, did they come back?'

'No. Christ, Karen, what are you saying. *Alan's gone? And Ellie too?*' Her voice was strangled with anxiety, and fear. 'You gotta call the police, Karen, I'm calling the police. Jesus, you're the police! Where are they? Who would take them? What are you saying?'

Karen mumbled her replies as she stepped into Ellie's bedroom once again. Hello Kitty smiled at her cheerily. A picture of Eeyore hung on the wall. Little pink socks lay balled on the floor. A toy that made a whirring noise sat next to her favourite books: *Mr Tickle, Russian Fairy Tales, Now We Are Six*.

The urge to crumple, to fall to the floor and give in to despair, was almost irresistible. Karen resisted and stepped forward, to look at the little pink Hello Kitty duvet, but as she did something scrunched, underfoot. She looked down.

It was a little bird. She'd stepped on the skull of a tiny little dead bird, and crushed its minuscule skull. There were several more of them distributed across the carpet, their eyes blank and white.

Rothley had been here. And he'd taken her daughter. And now Ryman's words tolled in her mind, like a bell: *Some say the Abra-Melin ritual can only be successfully completed if several humans are sacrificed, culminating in the murder of a living child.*

Karen gazed downwards, momentarily transfixed by pure horror. One of the little birds had a broken wing. She must have stepped on the bird, and snapped its little wing.

31

The Tomb of Ramose, Valley of the Nobles, Egypt

AΓΟ, AEΘH, AAΘ, BEZ, BHF. What did they signify? And the birth scene at the Luxor temple . . . how did they fit in? Somehow these random concepts, these shattered words, must form a beautiful poem. *Just put them in order.*

In the shadowy hallway Helen crouched in the archaic dust, slotting batteries in her camera. Albert Hanna leaned against a tubby Egyptian pillar, one of many in this wide, airy and rather beautiful old tomb.

Callum came in from the blazing daylight outside. 'You guys done?'

'Nearly,' Helen lied, looking up from her camera.

'OK, get to it.' The blond-haired Brit swept the room with his gaze. 'We're outside. The light is going, another hour maybe. We do *not* want to be here after dark. Got that?'

'*Jawohl!*' said Hanna, like an obedient Wehrmacht corporal.

Callum didn't laugh. Or smile. He looked at Hanna, and sighed. Then he spoke:

'You know, we've all got families, guys. We all want to go home. Please hurry the fuck up and find what you need to find.'

The speech was unexpected. For the first time Ryan felt a kind of empathy, maybe even pity for these men: their protectors. They were risking their lives to protect their wards; or protect the secret in the Sokar Hoard, if they found it. Ryan watched Callum as he strode determinedly into the sunshine, now slanting along the Valley of the Nobles. Ryan wondered how much these 'soldiers' were being paid by the voice at the end of those discreet phone calls. Paid to take these terrible risks. He presumed it was a lot.

Callum was also correct about the dwindling time available. Judging by the angle of light slanting into the tomb through the open door, the day was indeed expiring.

During his Egyptological career Ryan had been to this place several times. The Valley of the Nobles was a couple of miles down the West Bank of the Nile from the Valley of the Kings, where all the Pharaohs were buried. This particular cul-de-sac of dust and crumbling stone was notable for concealed tombs – like this one – constructed for the viziers and chancellors of ancient Egypt. There was also a workmen's village at the end of the Valley, where the keen traveller could find the footings and walls of mud houses: the poignantly humble accommodation of the men who built the tombs.

The Valley of the Nobles was less famous than the Valley of the Kings, or the mighty Ramesseum, or the Stalinist grandeur of the Temple of Hatshepsut, which were all just a few miles distant, across the desert that adjoined the Nile valley, yet it still, usually, saw plenty of visitors. Albert had told them that he also used to conduct tours here: tours in which he would escort hundreds of people a day through these very halls.

Yet today there was literally no one in the Valley. The little wooden ticket booths were padlocked. The empty car parks were patrolled by a lonely rock pigeon. Even the relentless hucksters with their cheap sunglasses, and bogus Books of the Dead, and chunks of Middle Kingdom Coffin Text made in China, had actually thrown up their arms to Allah, and returned to their homes in the ramshackle villages along the Nile. To fish, and smoke *shisha*, and talk of poverty and despair.

And so the echoing valleys of the Theban Necropolis had returned to their proper and immemorial silence, the silence that had been stolen from them so many centuries ago.

Ryan listened to that silence; he leaned against a pillar in the tomb and closed his eyes. And the silence rang in his ears. Nothingness. Nothingness, and death. Yes, Death was here, in these rocks. These valleys of secretive tombs, just like the Great Pyramids of Giza, were the jailhouse of Death, a place where death could be imprisoned: while the soul escaped.

And how would you escape a jail? By turning a lock with the key of life.

The *ankh*.

Ryan kept his eyes closed. The *ankhs* in the Coptic museum, that looked so much like crosses, that were used as crosses, could it be?

ΑΓΓΟ, ΑΕΘΗ, ΑΑΘ, ΒΕΖ, ΒΗΓ.

'I am ready now.'

He was snapped out of his reverie by Helen. She repeated, 'Ryan, I am ready now.'

'Sorry. Er, yes. I'm ready too.'

'So we film,' she said, gesturing to the place where she wanted him to stand. 'There, *ja*. Just in front of those wall paintings. They are beautiful.'

Hanna watched them, rather slyly, like a half-sleeping pet. His eyes glittered in the twilight of the tomb. Ryan wondered, aloud, 'You have enough light? To film?'

'I have all the light I need.' Helen smiled at him. Her smile had new meaning. Ryan smiled back.

'How touching,' said Hanna.

Helen and Ryan swapped a glance, then she pressed the button and began recording. 'So tell us, tell the camera, about this tomb.'

Ryan coughed, summoned his thoughts, and spoke to the lens. 'Immediately after his visit, and his revelation, at the Luxor temple, Macarius came here, to the Tomb of Ramose.' Ryan gestured at the row of portly, lotus-capped pillars beside him, and the windowless walls beyond, covered with fine reliefs and hieroglyphs. 'Ramose is a significant figure in Egyptian history, because he straddled two eras. First, he was vizier, the Master of the Secrets of the Palace – a sort of prime minister – to the great Pharaoh Amenhotep III, of the Eighteenth Dynasty. But he was also vizier to Amenhotep's son, the controversial heretic Pharaoh . . .' Ryan stroked two quote marks, with his fingers, around the word 'heretic'.

'This Pharaoh was first known as Amenhotep IV, but he changed his name to Akhenaten.' Ryan paused, for effect, then went on. 'Pharaoh Akhenaten is a deeply controversial figure in Egyptian history. Some say he was a tyrant, some a man of great enlightenment; many assert that he was the first monotheist in history. What we know for sure is that Akhenaten revolutionized Egyptian society, and that wrenching change is visible and tangible in this tomb.'

Ryan pointed at one wall to his left. 'See the differing styles in these reliefs? This wall at the eastern side is adorned with exquisite and detailed depictions of Ramose's funeral procession, but they are traditional: serenely stiff and formal, with weeping women in profile making offerings of fish and wine, and sledges carrying Ramose's placenta, and an image of Amenhotep IV rigidly posed, next to the goddess Ma'at. Yet over here –' Ryan walked a few paces across the tomb – 'on *this* side of the door, the Pharaoh Amenhotep IV has become the Pharaoh Akhenaten, and the artistic style is quite, quite different: the Pharaoh is rendered much more naturalistically, alongside his wife Nefertiti, acknowledging the adoring crowds at the so-called Window of Appearances, in his new capital of Amarna, in Middle Egypt.'

Ryan turned back to the camera. 'Akhenaten's strange and turbulent reign has provoked many theories. He seems to have suppressed worship of the old gods, and demanded worship of the one god: the great god, Aten, the sun – that's why he changed his own name to Akhenaten, which means "spirit of the sun", or "glory of God". In this painting –' Ryan knelt low down, next to the wall, and Helen tilted her camera accordingly – 'we can see the sun's rays, depicted with little hands on the end, blessing Akhenaten, his wife and family: confirming that the one new God approved of the Pharaoh, and saw him as his vicar on earth, a kind of pope, the infallible mouthpiece of the Lord. But look at Akhenaten's head and body, his pear-shaped torso, thin limbs and elongated skull, the way his costume sags below a protruding and rather feminine belly. Wherever it is found, in Heliopolis or Luxor or Amarna itself, Amarna art shows Akhenaten like this, with his strange head and feminine body. The peculiarities of his portraits have led scholars to wonder if Akhenaten was some kind of physical and mental freak.'

Ryan stood up and the camera followed him. 'One idea is that he was diseased, or afflicted in some way. Others have claimed he was actually an alien; one serious theory says he might have been a kind of hermaphrodite, born without genitals; but if this was the case he fathered an awful lot of babies for a man with no penis. One of his six children, Tutankhaten, succeeded the throne when Akhenaten died. But young Tutankhaten renounced his father's revolutionary faith, levelled the city of Amarna, returned to the old gods, and even tried to expunge his father's reviled name from history.' Ryan pointed upwards. 'There, you can see the so-called cartouche, or seal, of Akhenaten has been erased: someone has climbed a ladder and taken a chisel and chipped away the name of the heretic Pharaoh. The son, Tutankhaten, also changed his own name: he became known as the boy king, Tutankhamun.'

He paused. Helen waved a hand, *go on, go on* . . .

Ryan was thinking about the scene at Luxor, the birth of Amenhotep. Was there a way it fitted with the Amarna story? He could hear noises outside, distracting him. Yet the mosaic was slowly being restored, its ancient beauty would soon be revealed; he was ravished by the possibilities.

'Ryan, please, finish up.'

He stared at the camera.

'So why did Macarius come here? As ever, he does not specify, but it is now clear his great puzzle was focussed on monotheism. We know he was obsessed with Moses, the Egyptian priest who gave monotheism to the Jews, and we know he was obsessed with Akhenaten, the world's first monotheist: because he came here to the Tomb of Ramose, Akhenaten's vizier, and also he went to Amarna, Akhenaten's capital, and—'

WHUMP WHUMP WHUMP

Ryan stopped. The noise was now unmistakeable, and deafening.

WHUMP WHUMP WHUMP

A helicopter was landing right outside. Helen was already running to the rectangle of sunlight, the exit, but the wind from the copter rotor was billowing sand and dust into the hypostyle hallways of the tomb: it must have landed very close, dangerously close.

Hanna called out, 'Helen, get back!'

The dust was followed by a cracking sound, instantly familiar and immediately strange. An Egyptian wedding? No, of course not: *gunshots. And not in celebration.*

Someone yelled outside in the light. Was it Callum? Or Simon? It was the scream of someone in pain, someone shot? Maybe someone dying. They were being attacked.

'Helen!' Ryan now yelled at her and she edged back.

The gunshots outside were crackling now; a ricochet rang from the rocks. Another scream shredded the air in the tomb, this time a scream of command: and the words were in Hebrew. It didn't need translation.

'They will kill us!' Helen cried.

Ryan grabbed her hand and pulled her back into the deepest shadows. They were trapped, inside the tomb. They were going to die in the Tomb of Ramose: slain by Israeli agents, and robbed of the Macarius papyrus.

The secret would be taken, the mystery would go unsolved. Ryan was scorched by his own anger and sadness.

Hanna had disappeared down the corridor, to the end of the tomb, the claustrophobic final chamber where the coffin would have been kept. What was he doing? What was the point?

Callum stood at the door, silhouetted by the light. He was firing wildly into the setting sun. Simon was nowhere to be seen: Ryan reckoned he must be dead already.

The gunfire was fierce: the Israelis must have come in numbers. Callum was forced back inside the tomb. He stood with his back against the wall by the door, occasionally twisting to duck and dive and shoot out at the oncoming killers, but Ryan could see from Callum's face that he *knew* they were out of luck, out of options, trapped in here, trapped and doomed.

'Come.' It was Hanna, at the dark corridor entrance, beckoning. 'Come here – come now!'

Ryan grabbed Helen's hand and they followed, ducking low, because the stone corridor was so small, almost too small to squeeze through.

Hanna was in the final chamber, standing by a wooden trapdoor; darkness yawned beneath.

'What the heck?'

'It's a tunnel, it leads everywhere, a network – we can escape!'

As Ryan helped Helen onto the top of the indented

mud steps beneath the trapdoor, he heard the stomach-turning crack of gunfire *ricocheting down the corridor.* He gazed down in wonder.

Blood was spattered right across his chest.

32

Theban Necropolis, Egypt

It was Helen's blood: she had been shot in the shoulder by a rebounding bullet. She fell down the steps, crying with pain. The trapdoor flapped shut above them and the bitter crackle of gunshots was muffled. Callum was buying them time, up there, in the Tomb of Ramose.

Ryan stared urgently at Helen. Her injury was energetically pulsing blood; she had to lean on him like a wounded soldier, good arm slung around his neck as they turned and made a grab at their lives: lurching along the crude stone tunnel and away from the tomb.

'This way!' said Hanna, using his cellphone flashlight to illuminate the unpainted, unplastered, utilitarian tunnel with its ancient chisel marks showing on the walls. 'And here, hurry, yes, along here.'

'But they will follow us,' Ryan panted.

'No,' Hanna said. He flashed the light left, then right, in an explanatory fashion: the light exposed more tunnels, branching off into silent darkness. He was right, it was an enormous labyrinth, and now Hanna was taking them on a mazy, zigzagging route – making them unfollowable, as long as Callum bought them just a few minutes. Probably with his life.

There was no time for guilt.

'Ryannn . . .' Helen was moaning, her head lolling; she was semi-conscious with pain. Her blood dripped down Ryan's shirt.

He hoisted her close, feeling her heartbeat through her damp shirt.

'These tunnels were built by the workmen who constructed the tombs,' Hanna explained as they struggled on. 'They were also used by thieves. Only the local guides really know them well. When I worked here we'd take a hundred dollars from the very bravest tourists—'

Noises echoed, bouncing down the dark and indifferent corridors. Distant, yet menacing.

'They're in the tunnels,' said Ryan. 'They're coming – Callum must be dead. They're coming.'

'They *will not* find us.' Hanna calmed him with a gesture. 'Trust me, please. I know this maze better than most. The most obvious routes go to Hatshepsut's temple, and to Medinet Habu . . . we would have to be so very unlucky.' He turned, his eyes dark in the darkness. 'How is Helen?'

Helen was a sagging weight around Ryan's shoulders; almost a dead weight. He could sense her strength ebbing – she was being dragged under, by death. Ryan despaired. It was as if the Tomb of Ramose had *infected* her with death: all these mummies, all these coffins, all this Egyptian obsession with death, it was contagious.

The Egyptians were right: life was just a factory for making souls. They were all like the cats of rancid Bubastis, bred specifically to die, so what was the point?

The point was to live just one more hour. The point was to save Helen.

Ryan Harper did this.

He fought to focus so that he could help her. Once more he hoisted Helen, her limp arm over his shoulder, following the diminishing and barely illuminated figure of Albert Hanna. The noises echoed down the tunnels again. Faraway yet ominous. If death was caged in these rocks, so were they.

'Here, my friend, *mon brave*, not far now.'

The tunnel made another bewildering series of U-turns, junctions and dead ends, and then it switchbacked left and right and Helen groaned, and that was good, because it meant she was alive. But Ryan could feel the sweat from her body through his moist and bloodied shirt. A fever was rising inside her: they needed a hospital. If they escaped this labyrinth of cold stone, and bitter darkness, they'd need to get her proper medical care to have the bullet extracted. But how could they do that without alerting everyone – the authorities, the Israelis?

'This is it.' Hanna pointed to a wooden ladder, grey and ghostly in the dark. He climbed first, and pushed a trapdoor.

Ryan gazed up earnestly, hoping to see sky above . . . but there was just more musty darkness. Where were they? He glimpsed dim hieroglyphs.

Albert reached down as Ryan lifted Helen upwards; somehow they got her up and out, and Ryan quickly followed. He breathed the dank, clammy, unmistakeable air of what was surely another tomb; his life, it seemed, was now a series of tombs.

'Where are we?'

'The Tomb of Ay, successor to Tutankhamun,' Hanna said. 'Most remote of the tombs in the Western Valley. Quickly now, I know a place we can take Helen. St Tawdros. No one ever goes there.'

Ryan stared around at the stone chamber. The walls were decorated with scenes of hunting, and feasting, and the twelve baboons from the Book of Amduat. The centre of the chamber was dominated by a small, papery mummy, perfectly preserved in a glass box on a quartzite dais.

He looked again at the mummy. 'That's not Ay.'

Albert was already on the ramp that led out of the tomb.

'No, it is Tiye. She was moved here some months ago because of the Akhmim connection. They are restoring her tomb in KV. Come, quick—'

But Ryan didn't respond. Momentarily, he was transfixed. The Akhmim connection? Ay was from Akhmim. Queen Tiye was from Akhmim. And Tiye was the mother of Akhenaten, maybe the mother of Tutankhamun. All from Akhmim? This heretic family of monotheists.

He gazed at the mummy.

Even in the darkness, her vile and preserved little corpse showed the same curious, extraterrestrial head shape of Akhenaten and Tutankhamun. The elongated cranium. Yet the corpse was tiny. Like the unexpected shortness of a movie star, encountered in the flesh. What *were* these people?

'*Aiii.*' Helen was moaning in pain.

Ryan swore aloud at his selfishness: even as Helen was *bleeding*, he was trying to work out the puzzle. Hauling her dead weight, once again, he followed Albert as the Copt led them up the dark stone ramp. At last they pushed open a broken wooden door and he was breathing the fresh, dulcet air of the desert night.

The landscape was nothing but rocks and sand, lit by stars; and a beaten-up road leading down an incline. Very distant city lights must surely be Luxor.

Albert came close and lifted Helen's face by her chin. Her eyes were shut and she was trembling with pain and fever. 'It is very bad. But there are nuns there, they can help—'

'We need a damn *hospital*, Albert.'

His shrug was eloquent. 'You know that is not a

choice. They will have seen the blood – they will be well aware one of us is wounded. Every hospital and doctor for miles will be monitored.' He sighed, and detached himself, and walked up the hill. 'Come, my friends, let us throw ourselves at the mercy of St Didymus the Blind. It is only one or two miles – we must be mountaineers.'

It was only one or two miles of *hell*. First, up the hill, out of the side-valley, an ascent of pure pain; then, down a rubbly road, carrying an almost comatose Helen, who was seeping blood all the while. Halfway there, Albert took Helen's other arm, slung it over his neck, and together the two men helped her along, unspeaking and grim, until they reached a tiny crop of buildings, silent under the Pleiades.

'I will speak with the abbot.'

Hanna disappeared. Ryan leaned against a rock. Helen murmured, '*Warum . . . Wo ist . . .*' Then she fell into a feverish sleep.

They had arrived at the humblest of Coptic villages, just a tiny group of adobe houses surrounding a mud-brick monastery, lost in the starlit Theban desert. Albert was right: they were in the epicentre of nowhere. This was a good place to hide out, if Helen could survive without proper medical care.

Hushed and worried voices disturbed the stillness. A trio of nuns emerged, in black habits, accompanied by Albert, hurrying from the wooden gate of the monastery, St Tawdros. The nuns approached Ryan with compassionate smiles, then they took Helen in their arms. One of them had a flashlight, which she shone on Helen's face, then on her bleeding wound.

This nun shook her head, and gazed at Ryan. Her Arabic was soft. 'I fear we are too late, I am sorry.'

33

London

The Incident Room at New Scotland Yard was deserted. Apart from Chief Superintendent David Boyle and Karen Trevithick.

CS Boyle had guided Karen through her career and was certainly something of a father figure to her; Karen had lost her dad quite young. So she didn't remotely mind when he put an arm around her shoulder. And he didn't mind when she shed two or three quiet tears. Again.

Throughout the day she had been sneaking off to do her crying – like Curtis taking cigarette breaks. Now the working day was over she could cry in the office.

Luke will rape you. Luke will smell your fear.

Grabbing a tissue from a box on the desk, she wiped and dabbed, angry at herself for giving in once more to emotion. She might be a mother with a disappeared child, that child might even have been kidnapped by a murderer, *but she was also a police officer, a Detective Chief Inspector*. She could solve this.

But how? For the first time in her life the mysteries overwhelmed her. Maybe she should take CS Boyle's offer and remove herself from the case?

The idea was absurd. Wiping away the last tear, she said, 'We've got nowhere, have we?'

Boyle crossed to the whiteboard. He was nearly fifty, more grey than not, and she trusted him implicitly in almost every way; she trusted him to give her the unsugared truth.

'No, we haven't. It's bizarre, frankly. Let's try it one more time.'

Picking up a marker-pen, he wrote the word ENTRY at the top, followed by a big, flourishing question mark. 'If Rothley is responsible, how did he get into your flat? Your cousin Alan wouldn't have opened the door to a stranger, would he?'

'No.'

Boyle nodded, and lifted the pen. The buttons on his uniform, unusually, needed polishing. He was recently divorced. Karen idly wondered if the two things were connected. She was doing a lot of idle wondering today, anything to keep her mind off the girl buried alive under the floorboards. *Would that happen to Eleanor? What could this guy do to her? Put her in a coffin and . . .*

To her great relief, Boyle interrupted her meditations. 'So he didn't break in, and your cousin Alan wouldn't let him in, and yet he was in there, judging by the little birds.'

'That's about it. Yes.'

'Doesn't add up, Karen, just *doesn't add up*.' Boyle vigorously crossed out the word ENTRY.

Now he wrote underneath it, KIDNAP.

'Very well. Let's move on. Let's say he got in somehow. Now what? He's in the flat, and he is intending to – we presume . . .' Boyle's eyes were full of pity, but determination, too. 'His intention is to kidnap Alan and your daughter Eleanor.'

Karen resisted the urge to speak. In case she wailed.

'Yet we have no signs of struggle in your house. No upturned furniture, no evidence of resistance, no noises reported by the neighbours. Alan is, as I understand it, hardly the sort of guy to just give up and calmly let a stranger take him, and his niece.'

'No.'

'Therefore?'

'Rothley had a weapon.'

Boyle nodded. 'Either a gun, or a big knife at least. Probably a gun. Or Alan would have fought. He plays rugby, right? But there is a further mystery here.' Boyle put brackets around the word KIDNAP, and then a big question mark after it.

'We have not even the slightest trace evidence of Rothley being *in* your flat: no prints, no footprints, nil. Apart from, as I say, the birds.'

Karen gazed at the whiteboard, eyes blurred. In her mind she could see Eleanor running into her arms, she could smell her daughter's hair, see the toys she played with in the bath. She could taste the soup she made and they shared; she could see Eleanor laughing and jumping on the bed, seeing how high she could jump, with the twins.

The sobs came suddenly and this time were staggering in their ferocity. Doubling her over like a punch to the stomach, knocking the wind out of her. This was something new: it was the reality that gripped her, the terrible reality that this evening when she went home, *Eleanor wouldn't be there*. The flat would be silent. The little bedroom unoccupied. Karen would sit there alone in her living room, staring at a switched-off TV.

'I'm sorry,' Karen said, plucking uselessly at a tissue, as if paper could staunch her grief. 'I'm sorry.'

David Boyle came over and gave Karen another fatherly pat on the back.

Karen wished, right now, that she had a husband. She desperately wished she had a husband. She *should* have married. It was all her fault. If she'd married the father like a normal woman, none of this would have happened: but she'd had a fling, and she'd known it was a fling, and it was *her* idea not to use anything because she *wanted* a baby, but she didn't want a husband, and the guy was sweet and funny and smart and Australian. It was all perfect, if you wanted to be a single mother: the father existed and he was nice but he was elsewhere. That meant she could be Karen Trevithick, she could keep her name, and her career, but also have a baby, and be a mother, and yet remain independent: she could have it all. And now, because she had wanted it all, because she had refused to get married, she had lost *everything*.

Karen was so deep into despair and self-loathing and guilt she didn't realize Boyle was talking, but when she came back to herself, he was writing on the whiteboard again.

SUSPECT.

'What do we know about Rothley?' Boyle put a question mark next to the word.

SUSPECT?

'Not much,' Karen mumbled.

CS Boyle nodded. 'That's putting it mildly. Again, there is a striking lack of evidence. We know he was in Israel, then he apparently turns up in England, but we don't know how or why. He has money, but we don't know how or where he got it. He got a group of people to burn a truckload of cats. Where? How? Why?' Boyle was pacing now, back and forth. 'One of his accomplices kills himself. We don't know why, or who he is. He kills a young woman in Chancery Lane. We don't know how, or who she is. She even *bites off her own fingers*, and we don't know why: if he somehow persuaded her to do it, or what. Again, with no struggle at all. We know nothing. We don't even know how and why he got your address. It's absurd.'

'Not quite nothing,' Karen said. 'We have tracked down one of Alicia Rothley's friends, who said Alicia was acting very strangely in the last few months. Going off on her own, seeing someone unknown.'

'Presumably her brother, yes. Preparing the ritual, the month in Cornwall.'

'The magical stuff. We also know Rothley was apparently re-enacting everything Crowley did.'

Not quite everything, came the voice in Karen's mind. *He is trying to complete the magic by doing the one thing Crowley didn't: sacrifice a child.*

The sob choked in her throat. Boyle gazed at the whiteboard, apparently thinking along the same lines, but unable to articulate it. 'If he has . . . ah . . .' He coughed. 'We . . . we know he is trying to do this Crowley magic – this could be our way in.'

Boyle wrote the word CROWLEY on the whiteboard, and drew a large circle around it. The pen squealed against the board in the empty evening silence of the office.

'Crowley is our way in. We need to go back to the internet. Rothley must have recruited on the internet.'

'But there are dozens of sites dedicated to Crowley, and his world. The occult, Thelema, sex-magic, Crowleyana. All that.'

Boyle shook his head. 'So we check them all. I know your team have gone through this, but we need to go through it *again*.'

CS Boyle gazed past her shoulder, as if seeing the solution written on the wall behind, among the photos of the dead girl in Chancery Lane, the gashed face of the suicide in Cornwall.

'We're missing something. Tomorrow morning, hell, tonight maybe, we get the best bloody expert on this Crowley lunatic in here, and we give him seventeen coffees, and we threaten him with a brick over his head, and we find the forums or sites where Rothley *must* have got his disciples. We will find it, Karen. We will find this bastard.' Boyle walked to the coffee machine and poured two cups of over-stewed coffee. 'You know, if I was an idiot I'd say there is something, rather . . . well, haunting about this. The way Rothley *magics* himself into the flat, and *spirits* your daughter off. The way he appears and disappears. It's *unworldly*. But I don't believe in spells and witches. He has some shtick. Let's pin it down.' He handed one coffee to Karen, then sipped his own, wincing at the heat of the drink. 'That said, we know that *he* believes in this ludicrous magic. The Abra . . .'

'Abra-Melin ritual.'

'Yes. And it's complex, yes? Challenging and very complex?'

'Apparently.'

'So. If he is preparing some ghastly ritual, Karen, with . . . uh, with your daughter, it is going to take him time, it must take him time, which means we have time, we have time to find Eleanor.'

For maybe two minutes Karen felt a sliver of optimism, but once Boyle had left the office and she was alone in the room, the shuddering fear and guilt came dancing back in, mocking her.

Atha atha atharim.

Karen needed to get out. She was staying with Julie tonight, but she had to go back to her flat first. But there was no way she was lingering in that flat, not without Eleanor. And, moreover, she and Julie shared this misery: *Julie's husband was also missing.*

Out on the cold London streets a few infant flakes of snow were falling. Eleanor loved snow.

Karen made for the bustle of the Tube and the last of the rush hour; she wanted the crowds and the crush, she wanted to be just a normal person on a Northern Line train, reading a paper, nodding to sleep, chatting with a friend. Not a mother with a stolen child.

But on the Tube, people looked at her. At her red eyes. Could they tell? Karen exited the Tube at East Finchley with a small sense of relief and began the freezing walk home. As she did, her mobile shivered in her pocket. A message. Voicemail.

Her hopes leapt. A breakthrough? They'd found the house? They'd found Rothley? She clamped the phone to her ear. The voice was unmistakeable and it sent a spear of polluted ice into her heart.

'Mummy Mummy Mummy he is going to hurt me Mummy Mummy he is he is I'm scared Mummy Mummy please he is he is hurting me Mummy!'

The voice of her daughter ended there. Abruptly. How had he silenced her? Then, in the background, she heard a man's voice. Like a serene growling. An arrogant incantation.

'Ananias, Azarias, Lazarius.'

Then Eleanor screamed, and the voicemail ended.

Karen fell to her knees, then crumpled to the freezing pavement, quite broken. Snowflakes dissolved on her face, and in her mouth; she could taste their sad and silvery melting.

34

London

The little girl was sobbing.

'Don't cry,' said Rothley, leaning close. She was squashed in her wooden box, looking up at him. 'Why cry? Really. There's no point. Do you want to speak to your mother again?'

She nodded.

'OK. Here.' He held the phone close. The girl looked up at him, trusting, sweetly, desperately waiting for permission. Rothley held the phone to her ear and the girl listened to her mother's voice, and she sobbed and wailed into the mobile, entirely incoherent. Rothley waited for her to finish her futile lament. Then he killed the call and said, 'Good. Now, I hope you understand, I am going to do something to you, soon.'

'Yemm.'

'It is going to be very painful, and you will see horrible things.'

'No yem.'

'Yes. Say *yes*. It is for the best, in the best of all possible worlds.' Rothley smiled. The winter cold was piercing but they were all warm in here, in this sweet little chamber, that he had taken so long to prepare. All the months, all the years of training and dedication: from Buddhism to Zionism to veganism to Scientism to the final revelation – this. Here. This was it.

A faint smell of ammonia hung in the air. The little girl had voided her bladder with fear. Again. Rothley sighed. She also looked fairly ludicrous, roped and tied and kept in the box. But it didn't matter. The time had arrived for him to do the ritual, the very last of the Abra-Melin rite. Then the demons would come and the final revelation would be his. The ancient truth of the dark, dark magic, the Akhmimic magic.

The man strapped to the iron frame was groaning. He probably needed more Diazepam. Forty milligrams should do it. Rothley crossed the dark room and lifted the man's head. 'Do you want to say something? You want to say something important?'

But the man just sobbed. Twisting his hands in his restraints, twisting his mind against the drugs.

Rothley tutted. 'I thought we were friends.'

Reaching for his syringe, Rothley carefully injected his older prisoner with more Diazepam. Then he glanced at the clock. Seven a.m. He really needed to be careful about time: the ritual was so fastidious about procedures and protocol: turn north, turn south, write the SATOR square, wear only white, then complete.

Rothley turned and walked back to the child. She was still crying, and yet, through the endless, fizzing tears, she also gazed at him with that trusting look: wanting to believe that an adult knew what he was doing, that he wasn't going to *hurt* her again.

'I'm sorry,' said Rothley. 'It's not me, sweetheart, it's the Egyptians. And the Jews. Here.' He reached in his pocket and pulled out a plastic bag containing three vivisected rat hearts, smeared and bloody. Fingering the little bag, he extracted one heart, still warm, and offered it to her. 'Eat this.'

She shook her head. Defiant.

'You have to eat.'

She shook her head. *Mm-mnm*. Like a toddler. *Not eating.*

Rothley grabbed her and forced open her mouth and shoved the rat's heart in her mouth and clamped shut her jaw. 'Fucking eat it.'

The girl whimpered. But she refused to chew.

'Eat it or we'll do it again. Another turn around the block.'

Then he slapped her hard, having to reach down to do it. The slapping felt odd, because she was stuck in her box, just her head protruding. But it worked. She bowed her head, swallowing the rat's heart, and she cried.

Lucas Rothley exhaled in exasperation. 'OK.'

He had to stay in control. The Abra-Melin ritual was adamant about that: stay serene and pure, wear white, pray to the north. Now he had to say the words.

He opened the book.

'May the lady of fire shrivel your soul.' Rothley lifted the page to the dim wintry light. 'I beseech thee Lampsuer, Sumarta, Baribas, Iorlex. O Lord send Anuth, Anuth, Salbana, Lazaral, now now, quickly quickly. Come on the morrow night, and take this girl and this man, take them, shrivel up their souls, lady of darkness. Take them for your bitter food, chew them, and consume them.'

Rothley walked across the room. In the corner was a sack that writhed with vile energy. He slipped on his leather gauntlet, and untied it. The many rats inside surged, eager to escape, but he lifted the sack so that they fell back, seething, then he leaned in and grabbed just one by the throat. He knocked its head against the wall, rendering it semi-conscious, giving him a chance to retie the sack. Then he carried the lolling rat across the room, to the wooden box containing the girl.

Lifting the stunned rat over her head, Rothley extracted a pin from his pocket and jabbed it in the rat's eye. There was a faint popping sound. Liquid dribbled down on her.

'By a fire kindled with eyes, take her, Abraxas, Jesus, Adonai, take her. And feed her soul with offal.'

The little girl was whimpering, as ever. Rothley dropped the blinded rat onto the floor, where it writhed. Then he checked his watch.

The trap was closing.

35

The Monastery of St Tawdros, Malkata, Egypt

Ryan sat by Helen's bedside, in the bare monastic cell, holding her clammy hand. She sweated and moaned in her fever, and plucked in her dreams at her bandages. The afternoon sun was fierce and dying outside.

It was fitting, he thought, bitterly, that they should be where they were. These mud-brick church buildings, in this archaic mud-brick town, were situated where the ochre desert met the Nile valley: this was the very frontier where death met life. If he stood and looked out of the austerely small monastic window he could see the distant swaying palms of green Upper Egypt: life was that close.

But they were actually in death: in the desert, not far from the western hills, the place where all good Egyptians went to die. Where his wife and child had already gone.

Ryan held her hand.

'Anna, oh . . . *ja*. *Vater?*' Her murmurs were in German, incoherent to him, just shreds of unmeaning. Ryan wondered if the Macarius papyrus was the same: the ramblings of a man in the dream. Maybe he was chasing a dream.

ΑΓΟ, ΑΕΘΗ, ΑΑΘ, ΒΕΖ, ΒΗΓ.

Maybe that phrase meant nothing at all.

'*Wie ich im Geiste. Brannte.*'

The day of her fever turned into the evening of her fever. Ryan scratched a match and lit an oil lamp, casting its warm and fragile glow across the room. He thought of Rhiannon and death and wanted to drink whisky. He had no whisky.

A nun entered the cell with a metal bucket of cold fresh water. She used a clean rag to dab at Helen's hot and suffering face, muttering words in Coptic as she did so.

'*Shere ne Maria, to etchrompi.*' It was a prayer to the Virgin. The nun pressed the rag to Helen's forehead, who seemed to respond in her unconsciousness, half-smiling, half-frowning.

Ryan had already given Helen all the antibiotics he had in his possession, in a desperate bid to ward off further infection. A furtive local doctor had come in to stitch the wound; luckily the bullet had gone straight through the flesh and the bone was intact. The Coptic doctor had departed with a frown, and words of encouragement. So Ryan had hoped the nuns would provide whatever further medicine was needed.

But no. This was all the nursing offered by the nuns

of St Tawdros, this was all their medication: cold water and prayer. Let God do the rest.

And yet the nuns' compassion was clear. They had the most worryless eyes Ryan had ever seen: genuinely sinless, completely pure, entirely emptied. Their souls were vessels filled with the oil of love, and they poured it over Helen's face, anointing her with mercy.

Ryan left the nun to her primitive nursing. Outside, the desert night greeted him, and as he breathed deeply a jackal called out there, somewhere: a voice in the wilderness. Where was that line from? Ryan stood transfixed for a moment.

It was from the King James Bible of course. Isaiah 40:3. *The voice of him that crieth in the wilderness.*

Ryan groped for the meaning here, as he stood in the moonlit courtyard. There must be a meaning. He stared up at the high and endless sky, swirled with gleaming stars, the looted jewellery of a Czarina.

He needed to concentrate on the papyrus, to break the mystery open. What were the two direct quotes from the Bible in the Macarius text?

And the LORD brought us forth out of Egypt with a mighty hand.

Out of Egypt, out of the desert, out of the wilderness. And the other one?

Let him that hath understanding count the number of the beast: for it is the number of a man; and his number is Six hundred threescore and six.

They must be significant. Add them together and what did they produce?

The jackal howled again. A breeze blew across the monastic yard. And then the answer seemed to finally crumble in Ryan's hands, like a papyrus too old to be saved. Flakes of nothingness, flickers of light, then dark.

Enough. Needing to exercise his limbs and to shake off some of the sadness, Ryan strode from the nocturnal courtyard. A few short minutes brought him to a low hill. He gazed back. The village twinkled behind him, half a mile away, but in the other direction the light was stunning. What was that? Ryan stared, amazed. It was like an aurora borealis of the earth, great purples and greens; huge cyan and crimson lights were dancing across the mighty rocks and cliffsides of the Theban Necropolis. What *was* it?

'It is *son et lumière*.'

He turned, startled: and saw the dapper, slightly paunchy profile of Albert Hanna. The Copt waved his elegantly wristwatched arm. 'The lights come on every night, for the tourists: colours and music and pictures of Pharaohs. The lights are projected onto the rocks: you can see them for many miles.' He paused. In the stillness, Ryan could hear distant music now, that sadly danced with the lights. Albert continued, 'And yet, of course, there are no tourists, no one is watching. The cinema is shut, but the film plays on. It is poignant, *n'est ce pas*?'

'Yes.'

Ryan stared at the vivid scenes projected onto the mile-high cliffs. It was like the Macarius papyrus itself: for centuries the secret had been sitting there in its rocky

298

cave, in the western cliffs, a great work seen by no one, like an unvisited masterpiece in a shuttered museum. But now someone had come: to see and understand.

'It's . . . beautiful,' he said, to himself as much as Albert Hanna.

Huge translucent faces were now visible, projected onto the cliffs: Ryan could see the great golden death mask of Tutankhamun, the eerie elongated head of his father Akhenaten, then the Aryan cheekbones of Nefertiti, Akhenaten's wife.

'She was so beautiful, Nefertiti,' Albert mused. 'So very beautiful. You know, I sometimes believe that female beauty, in its highest form, like Nefertiti, offers a glimpse of the Divine.' Hanna's voice was pensive in the dark. 'Maybe this is why Muslims are so threatened by it? By the female face. So that they deface it, with the burqa and the niqab. And the early Copts were no better, always defacing the goddess . . .' He exhaled, long, and longingly. 'And yet human beauty, the face, is where God resides, no. Is it not so?'

'Albert, I must go back.'

'How is she?'

Ryan shrugged. 'The same. Every time I think she is getting better she relapses. The nuns are there this evening.'

'Well, my friend, if prayers have any efficacy she will be cured by the morning. Their piety is astonishing.'

Albert joined Ryan as they retraced their steps. 'You know, of course, this is one of the oldest monasteries?'

'In the world?'

'Yes. Fourth century. It is said that it was founded by Helena, the mother of the Emperor Constantine, when she was touring Egypt looking for places where the Holy Family sheltered. At this point I would traditionally make a cynical joke at the expense of faith, but somehow it does not seem right, not here.' He stared up at the little moonlit cross, on top of the gate of the monastery. 'This place has true spirituality. Such a thing rather unsettles me. As you may have noticed.' He pressed a firm hand on Ryan's shoulder. 'Good night, Ryan, I will see you in the morning. I sleep in the abbot's house.'

Albert Hanna turned and walked into the gloom; Ryan turned and entered the monastery. As he took his seat beside Helen, the nun stood, crossed herself and lifted her eyes to the ceiling as if to say: It is in the hands of God.

Helen mumbled. *'Wir wissen . . .'*

Ryan sat in his chair, and eventually slept too, his head resting on Helen's bed, beside her clutching hands.

The next twenty-four hours were the same, blurring into a fever of their own. Helen's bandages were replaced, the wound was uninfected, but the fever refused to quit.

On the fourth day, or maybe it was the fifth, Ryan could bear the attenuation of his grief and anxiety no longer, and he left her side for the entire afternoon. He trekked for half a mile across the melting tarmac roads and the bare and sunburned sands, towards the Nile. Albert Hanna had told him that Tawdros was

300

close to one of the great concealed sites of Upper Egypt: the ruins of Malkata Palace. Albert was correct: just six minutes of walking in the punishing sun brought Ryan to a series of muddy heaps and a pathetic line of walls, almost entirely rotted away. A solitary telegraph pole with no wire stood at an angle in the sand-blown centre of the site, as if marking the spot.

This was all that was left of the great palace of Amenhotep III: once one of the biggest palaces in Egypt, maybe the world. The higher spoil heaps at the side were the by-products of a great artificial lake, Birket Habu, built to Amenhotep's order in about 1360 BC. The dumps of spoil looked like modern rubbish heaps.

With his Egyptologist's gaze, Ryan surveyed the wider scene. The Nile was close here: the first fields of hibiscus and Moses-grass were just a quarter of a mile beyond. He could even see the silver glint of the great river itself, between the rustling date palms: it would have been easy to divert the river into this lake.

He stared down at his boots and the salty rocks beneath. This was the lakebed, or what was left of it. This was where the boy kings Akhenaten and then Tutankhamun played and swam and set toy boats to sail; here the young demigods grew to manhood, watched over by their Nubian slaves, tended by the parasolled concubines of the harem.

But now it was entirely dust. Ryan kicked a rock along. Three thousand years of desert sun had dried out the lake to a bitter, faintly saline basin of dryness;

three thousand years of desert wind and summer cloudbursts had eroded the splendid and mud-walled palace, virtually erasing it from the earth. Like the cartouches of Akhenaten, chiselled away by his angry son.

Ryan sat on one low course of adobe bricks, and mused. Amenhotep III seemed crucial to their puzzle. This Pharaoh of the Eighteenth Dynasty, in the fourteenth century BC, had built the rooms at the Luxor temple where Ryan had found the frieze; and what did they show, those friezes?

Ryan pulled out his notebook, and read his own notes:

The frieze shows, first, the goddess Hathor, in the middle, embracing the queen on the left, with the father god Amun on the right.

Second relief. Now Amun is on the right, with another figure on the left. Who is this? The god Thoth? King Thothmes IV?

In the next scene the god Amun is holding an *ankh* to the queen's nostril. Giving life?

7. Thoth announces to the queen that she is pregnant.

Scene 9. The queen is sitting on a couch surrounded by five figures on the left and four on the right, one in a group of three holding the baby . . .

The answer was a sudden voice in the desert.

Ryan actually started, and looked at the whispering dust: the answer had been so clearly enunciated, in his head, it was as if someone had spoken to him. But he was alone.

Now Ryan wrote his answer down:

The Luxor frieze shows divine conception. The birth of a son god from a father god: the father god comes down and impregnates the woman: then the god of magic, Thoth, tells the woman she is divinely pregnant.

His hand slowing, Ryan paused. Why would Thoth, the god of magic, speak to the woman? Who exactly was being born here? He remembered Albert's words about the Zabaleen: *They are bewitched by an ancient magic, something terrible has been resurrected.*

Ryan's thoughts were quicker than his handwriting, the words came too fast now. He wrote down the Bible quotes, again:

And the LORD brought us forth OUT OF EGYPT with a MIGHTY hand.

And, Let him that hath understanding count the number of the beast.

The shock of the solution was palpable. Ryan wrote the answer:

It isn't a god being born in Luxor, and brought out of Egypt. It isn't a Pharaoh. It is Jesus, and yet it is also Magic. Black Magic? The magic of Abra-Melin? Something even older?

For a full minute, Ryan stared at his own sentences, wondering if he was going mad. His reverie was only broken by a real voice, behind him. He swivelled to find Albert, puffing over the dusty spoil heaps, beckoning, urgently.

'Helen,' he said. 'It's Helen.'

36

New Scotland Yard

'Let's hear the first message again.'

Karen leaned forward and pressed play on her phone; the speakerphone relayed the sound of her daughter's voice, echoing around the Chief Super's office.

'Mummy Mummy Mummy he is going to hurt me Mummy Mummy he is he is I'm scared Mummy Mummy please he is he is hurting me Mummy!'

Then came the silence, then the incantation, then the scream, then nothing. *Nothing.*

CS Boyle steepled his index fingers, tipped back his seat and closed his eyes, thinking. On his desk sat a framed photo of *his* daughter, aged twenty-one, graduating from university, accepting her degree with a gown and a dazzling smile. Next to that was a photo of her brother, on a boat somewhere, laughing.

Alive.

Karen found it hard to repress a bitter envy. This

pointless, acidic hatred of happiness and normality, of happy people and normal people, had begun to consume her these last hours. How could they be happy and normal? How could they drive calmly to work and laugh in pubs and chatter away in restaurants when Karen's daughter was being prepared for death?

Yet she didn't cry. Karen had cried herself out last night, when she had been picked up from the pavement by kind strangers and driven to Julie's house. On Julie's sofa she had collapsed in on herself, like a demolished building. She had wept for an hour or more, continuously. And now the storm had passed; now the weeping was done, and the sterile bitterness, the fear, and the anger, were all that was left.

No, she didn't want to cry any more: she wanted to kill this man Rothley. Even if she got there too late, even if he murdered Eleanor, she would kill him: she would, she would slay him. Her ardour for revenge was biblical.

'And the third message. Can we hear that?' said the CS. 'We haven't heard the third one yet.'

Karen pressed the button on her phone.

There had been five voicemails in a row. This was the third. It began with Rothley chanting.

'Magoth, Asmodeus, Sebt-Hor, Ariton and Amaymon, I call upon you – here and forever – to return to this house, on the third day of the moon, when you shall take the child with you, unto the world unknown.' A serious silence followed this chant, tainted only by a strange, machine-like sound in the background. Then Karen's daughter

spoke up, calmly and lucidly. '*In cuius sunt vobis postulans hoc actus sacrificium?*'

CS Boyle dropped his hands, and stared, transfixed, at the phone. 'Good Lord. Is that Eleanor?'

'Yes.' Karen was almost used to it now. She stared at the window. Some small furtive flakes of snow were falling from a dark grey sky; she wished it would snow more, snow properly. Cover everything in whiteness and erase the world.

'But . . . she's talking *Latin*,' said Boyle, stating the obvious.

Karen nodded. 'Yup.' She'd heard these messages a dozen times, first with horror, then with sadness and panic, now with this dull gnawing fearfulness, and anger. Lots of anger. 'He goes on here, on the fourth message, it's the same.'

Once more she pressed the speakerphone. Rothley's firm, low and confident voice filled the office. '*It is on Eleanor daughter of Karen that I shall work a spell of final binding. Eleanor daughter of Karen must be cast into the outer darkness. Bind and fasten the flesh of Eleanor. She must not breathe, she must not be warm, she must not move, strike her and bind her, on the third day of the new moon, strike her, and bind her, and take her, at once at once at once, lift her up as a sacrifice to Satanael, Saoth, Seth, Satanoth. Amen. Amen. Amen.*'

Another pause. Then another tiny grinding, whirring noise in the background. It was surely some kind of machine? Yes. Karen recognized it. Like a drill, but muffled, as if someone in the background was making

306

something. Perhaps a table. Or an altar? Alan was good at that stuff. DIY. He used to come round and fix Karen's shelves.

Then Eleanor spoke again, her voice high and light, the voice of a six-year-old, quite calm and content. *'Nos facere iussa. Sumemus diem tertium mensis puellam. Amen.'*

The message ended. CS Boyle's face was, again, appalled. His gaze was watery as he stared at the phone.

'I don't understand how she is speaking Latin, I just . . . Could he have *coached* her?' His eyes desperately swept the room, looking at Karen, then Detective Sergeant Curtis, then at the grey sky through the window. He quailed visibly. Then he gazed at Karen once more. 'What does it mean? The Latin? Have you had it checked?'

'Yes.' She took out her notebook. She had talked to Ryman, the witchcraft guy, first thing. 'The first line is, apparently, "On whose authority are you commanding this act of sacrifice." The second line of Latin is, "We will honour your command, we will take the girl on the third day of the moon."' Karen closed her notebook. Her voice was level. She was in control of her emotions, if nothing else. 'The expert I consulted said these are the expected responses from the sub-princes in the Abra-Melin ritual.'

'The sub what?'

Karen explained, matter-of-factly. 'Demons, essentially. The first chant is Rothley first requesting the sub-princes, the demons, to do his bidding, and then the demons give their response, through my daughter, and then the second chant is Rothley's command for them to do the sacrifice, and the demons respond again.' She stared momentarily out of the window as she spoke. 'The demons agree, they agree to do the sacrifice. Apparently, this second chant, of Rothley's, is not from Abra-Melin directly – it's ancient Christian Coptic magic.'

'Sorry?'

'The expert, Ryman, thinks that Rothley may have got hold of a more authentic copy of the Abra-Melin ritual.'

'Authentic?'

Karen explained: 'It seems there are many disputes as to the, uh, authentic version of this Abra-Melin magic – different versions in different libraries, with varying spells and demands and suchlike. Ryman's theory is that Rothley has got hold, or thinks he has got hold, of a very ancient version, the authentic version, which has these Egyptian chants, from Upper Egypt, where the magic first came from. We know he is trying –' she had to force the words out – 'to do the ritual in the most authentic and challenging way. By taking a . . . a . . . a . . . a . . . child's life.' Keep going, she had to keep going. 'It makes sense he would do everything as correctly as possible. Including sourcing the most authentic version of the ritual. If he really wants it to work.'

CS Boyle's face was quite pale. 'I still don't understand how he's got your daughter to speak *Latin*. I mean, she . . . she doesn't speak, er, Latin, does she?'

'No. Of course not. She's six.'

'Then how? She's six years old, yet she's word-perfect.'

Karen had no answer. She simply wanted Rothley dead.

Boyle straightened his uniform: a man visibly struggling to master his confusion, and maybe his emotions. 'OK, the last message, you said there was one more?'

'Yep.'

'Let's hear it.'

For the final time Karen pressed the button on her phone. The voice of a grown man sobbing filled the office. DS Curtis closed his eyes as the sobbing went on, and on. A grown man crying. For a minute, or a minute and a half. It was, in its own way, the most terrifying of all the messages.

The sobbing continued but the message cut out, automatically. The full ninety seconds was used up. The office was silent. Boyle exhaled, long and slow, as if he hadn't been breathing. 'Is that your cousin Alan?'

Karen nodded. 'I think so. It's quite hard to tell because, well, I've never heard him cry before. He's not . . . you know, he doesn't cry like that. But yes, I am pretty sure that's him.'

'But why is he *crying*?' Boyle said, stupidly. Then he seemed to realize his stupidity and blushed and shuffled papers on his desk, to disguise his embarrassment. 'All right, let's reconvene here in an hour.' He looked at Curtis. 'How are we doing on the Crowley properties?'

Curtis began his explanation of their progress, combing through every address ever associated with Crowley. Karen knew all this stuff, so she excused herself and made her exit. She breathed deeply and calmly as she walked, fearing that otherwise she would faint. People in the corridor avoided her gaze; or so she imagined. Perhaps they didn't. Perhaps she just looked slovenly and they'd noticed and turned away in politeness. She was wearing last night's clothes; after the phone messages she had been too scared and distressed to go home to the flat and get her stuff.

How did Rothley get Ellie to speak Latin?

Back at her desk she sipped water, then clicked on her computer. She had an email to her personal account from an unknown sender. She opened it.

You have something I want.
Come tomorrow to the building on Chancery Lane, the basement. Come at 7 p.m.
Come alone or I will kill your daughter. If you do not come I will kill your daughter. You have a small tattoo on your ankle, of a mermaid. Your new shoes need cleaning. You are wearing the same skirt as yesterday.
Lucas Rothley

37

Tawdros, Egypt

'You're sure you are all right?'

Helen smiled, a little wearily. 'Yes. The fever has completely gone.'

She held his hand. The room was empty; the nuns had arrived and departed, whispering and smiling: their petitions had been heard by the Lord. Helen had first opened her eyes two days before. She'd looked frail then, but conscious at least. Today the youth in her face was fully restored.

And now Helen and Ryan were alone in her room; it was dark, and the desert night was purple and soft. There was nowhere to go. So she lay in the bed and Ryan held her hand, and he felt emotions reborn inside him, emotions that he thought had gone to the western hills.

'Make love to me,' she said.

He watched her: waiting for the joke.

'I am not joking. I haven't got anything to do but lie in bed. So you may as well get in. No?'

He kissed her hand. 'You're ill, you are recuperating.'

'No.' Her voice was firm. 'I am not. I just needed a day or two of rest. And then . . .' a sly pause, 'some sexual healing?'

They made love. It reminded him, bittersweetly, of the time he'd had sex with Rhiannon on holiday in Greece, and they'd both had terrible sunburn. They wanted to do it desperately, touching was painful, but it was also delicious and irresistible, even as it hurt.

Helen's eyes glittered in the dark, liquid and waiting; her kisses slurred. And her nakedness was pure and youthful: she was slender like the Pharaoh-queens in the paintings. He tenderly kissed the place where her wound was healing; he kissed the wound; he descended her suntanned stomach, he kissed the wound.

Sighing, and softly, she ran her fingers through his hair; her other hand twisted the thin linen sheet; then she pulled him to her face; kissed his chin, kissed his lips, then laughed, then stopped laughing – he turned her over, and she clutched at the pillow, clawing it, her arms extended, embracing the moon, like the night goddess, Nut. The undulation of her body, beneath him, was moving and arousing, and then she rolled over again and her tongue sought his; and the lamplight flickered over her breasts.

The dawn flush of orgasm rose to her throat; she closed her eyes and trembled, like the surface of water

312

disturbed; and her sigh escaped her, the *ka*, the *ba*, the soul that flees.

Then she turned on her side and she clutched his hand to her chest. 'Do you think this is the first time anyone has had sex in a monastery?'

'It feels like the first time I've had sex since my wife died.'

'No,' she said. 'You do not have to say that.'

'I do.'

They murmured for another hour, and kissed again; and she took him in her mouth until he shuddered. Then she fell asleep. Ryan didn't. He lay there thinking – thinking nothing. The jackal howled outside, out there in the desert, as Ryan listened to the nothingness, to the wilderness, to the desert wind, to Helen's breathing, to the faint, faint crackle of the wick in the oil lamp.

And what he did unto you in the wilderness, until ye came into this place . . .

Where was that from? Deuteronomy. And it was true. He had been wandering in the wilderness, afflicted, and lonely, for years and years; and now he was here, next to her, and he was lonely no more. Ryan kissed the nape of Helen's scented neck and she stirred in her sleep. And then he slept. For many hours.

They woke to enormous noise. The sun was high: it was almost noon. Something was happening outside, some ceremony: there was singing and chanting. Urgently Ryan threw on his clothes; Helen did the same.

He stared at her. 'What are you doing?'

313

Her smile was brave. 'I have been lying here for a decade, soon I will be a fossil. The wound is healed. The fever is gone. I feel fine. Come on.'

Slow and quiet, Ryan opened the door: he was engulfed at once by the urgent hubbub. There were laughing children and dark-haired Coptic women and priests who smelled of fortified wine, clapping and singing as they thronged the courtyard, and stepped into the church.

Albert saw him, and stole up, beaming. 'How is Helen?'

'Good. She wants to move on.'

'Ah yes. Yes, I think we must.' Albert nodded, eagerly. 'And this gives us excellent cover. The crowds! It is a special service, Saf El-Rouh: "send away the soul". A great Coptic businessman died, he came home from America very ill, he wanted to be buried here. This is the third day after his death. Look.'

The crowds were shuffling into the baroquely ramshackle old church, following a priest, assisted by a young deacon. The white-robed priest was reciting, 'Iftah laha yaruh Bab al-Rohena.'

Albert whispered, amidst the noise: 'It means, "Open the door for the soul, O God."'

Ryan couldn't resist a look. Inside the white-domed church many candles had been lit. Their light glittered off primitive icons, and flickered before the relics of St Theodore the Martyr. Handwritten signs in English hung on the white painted mud-brick wall: HOW DREADFUL IS THIS PLACE, THIS NONE OTHER THAN THE HOUSE OF GOD AND THIS IS THE GATE OF HEAVEN.

314

Some of the brickwork was obviously rescued from Egyptian palaces or temples, and retained the ancient decoration: Ryan could still see, low on one wall, the shape of an extended wing, the wing of Isis, next to a Coptic cross. In the middle of it all, the people were praying, and singing, and eating. Plates were piled on a table, with bread and watercress, alongside two symbolic glasses, one filled with water, one empty.

It struck Ryan at once: how closely the scene paralleled Pharaonic mortuary rituals shown in ancient texts. The only missing ingredient was beer, but even as he wondered this the priest reached in his robes and pulled out some brown grains, barley maybe, and crumbled them in the water. It truly was an exact copy of ancient Egyptian funeral rites. The Copts were the Egyptians: they had the knowledge, even without knowing it, they were the key. They were the *ankh*.

He stepped back into the courtyard. Helen was there, next to Albert. Her determined energy had returned.

'We must pack our bags.'

It took fifteen minutes. And they were ready.

In that short time the crowds had grown, and it was apparent a full-scale *moulid* was underway: a Coptic celebration, a saint's day, carnival and funeral all at once. Death was being celebrated because death did not sting. The Copts knew the soul had escaped the cage, and was flying to heaven.

'OK,' Helen said. 'How do we get to Philae? That's next, right?'

'Albert?'

Hanna was staring at the worshippers as they filed into the church. Abruptly, he crossed himself. And then his lips moved, murmuring. He was praying? The cynical and sceptical Albert Hanna was *praying*?

Ryan nudged him. 'Albert – Philae?'

'Oh, yes. *Aiwa!* I have bought us a car. It is perhaps the oldest car in the Theban Nome. A donkey would attract more attention, it is perfect.'

They stepped through the crowds to the monastery gate. But the crowds were intense; there were so many people. Some younger women, their dark hair streaming in the desert wind, were worshipping beyond the monastery walls. Ryan stared at them, in wonder. The wild noise of their singing was discordant, yet beautiful, as they raised their arms with palms outwards, like ancient Egyptians, again, doing the *orant*.

Still more pilgrims were chanting as they strode towards the monastery, others were clapping and drumming to sustain the beat. A large bearded man in black, episcopal and magnificent, was carrying a processional cross.

Albert stopped. 'We must pray,' he said. 'We must give thanks. Helen is alive: it is a gracious miracle; she was dead and now she has risen, like Jesus.'

'Albert, what the hell? Come on.'

The Coptic man turned and his eyes were shining. 'Are you surprised? Why shouldn't I be religious? I am a Copt. *This is my faith*.'

'But, Albert, we can't stay here. It is dangerous to

316

linger. You want the answer, make the film, you will make money. And we need your help, Albert.'

'What is money, to the treasures one stores in heaven?' Hanna smiled beatifically. 'You think I am joking. Ah yes.'

'Come on.'

Grabbing Albert by the arm, Ryan asked him where the car was. Albert shrugged, as if he didn't care, then pointed towards a rusty green Chevrolet, maybe thirty years old, at the edge of the crowds. They ran to it, Ryan dragging Albert, and slung their bags in the trunk.

Ryan took the key from Albert's pocket and Albert sat in the back. With wheels skidding, they took the desert road south. Philae was more than a day's drive, beyond Aswan, right through the wilderness.

The desert was empty here, as Egypt slowly descended into real Africa: burning Nubia. There were no army checkpoints. The drive was long and the sun was hot and the car was air-conditioned by several hundred holes in the bodywork.

They talked as they drove. Ryan mentioned the frieze. Helen said, 'I think it is just a Pharaoh. He is born of a god, is he not? The Pharaohs were regarded as divine.'

'But there's a hint of menace, or evil. Why is Thoth there, the god of magic?'

Albert spoke from the back. 'It is the birth of magic. And what is wrong with that?'

Ryan shook his head. 'But Macarius is saying, I think, that there is something magical at work in religion,

317

and maybe in Christianity . . . Dark magic. Not good stuff. Remember that whatever it is, whatever the truth concealed in the Sokar Hoard, it shook Sassoon so much that he killed himself.'

Helen nodded. 'It is all about magic: that would explain why the Sokar Hoard contained the Coptic spells. Religion is a kind of magic . . . But would that be enough to so unsettle a scholar like Sassoon? I do not think so.'

Magic. *Or voodoo*, thought Ryan. That was what he'd thought when he'd listened to the nuns in the monastery: they were doing *voodoo*, whispering their desert spells to heal the sick.

The desert stretched out before them, the sun quenching itself in the sand, struggling in the quicksand, dying all over again.

They pulled over at an anonymous hotel on the outskirts of Aswan. Helen and Ryan shared a room. Albert watched them sign the register and raised a saintly eyebrow, then retired to his room, complaining of a headache.

Ryan and Helen climbed the stairs. Their room was hot, stuffy and plagued by mosquitoes so big they wheeled, serenely, like condors. Helen wrapped herself with sheets to keep them away; but when it didn't work, she wrapped herself tighter. 'Do you think this is how mummies evolved? People just wrapped themselves in sheets to keep the damn mosquitoes away, then they wrapped themselves so tightly someone died. God.'

Ryan laughed. Helen was *funny*; beneath her stern exterior, her brusqueness, she was funny. He knew very well by now that he was falling in love with her. Quite passionately. As gently as he could, he kissed her wounded shoulder. And then he turned her over and kissed her properly.

They were back in the car before dawn and drove the last miles through a silent Aswan. The Nile shone like metal, the broad-shouldered rocks of Elephantine Island glistened darkly, the sails of the *feluccas* furled and sleeping.

Onwards they drove to the pier that led to the Philae temple on its little island: raised from the deluge that created Lake Aswan in the 1950s, when the Nile was finally stopped, after five million years, by the second Aswan Dam.

The sun was coming up. Birds swung in the violet air, snatching the last of the night's mosquitoes. It was beautiful and quiet and yet the emptiness was also menacing. There were no tourists, of course; but there were no people either. One of the great tourist sights of the world was desolate.

Just one Nubian man was sleeping in his little boat, which was tethered to the pier. His djellaba was filthy and his teeth were white and his skin was darker than black; his sneakers were fake Adidas. Albert woke him by the shoulder, and spoke. The Nubian frowned, hawked some spittle into the lakewater, and shook his head.

'Dammit,' Ryan cursed. 'The site is closed. The police

have shut down everything. Too much trouble to keep it open with no tourists.'

'So he is not going to take us?' Helen said. 'But we have to get there! Macarius says Philae is the key. We have to get there, we *must*!'

Ryan whispered, 'Hold on . . . Look.'

Dollars were passing between the two men on the pier. Then Albert returned, a shine of sweat on his forehead. 'I just about managed to persuade him. But he says it's dangerous. The police come every day: they are desperate for bribes. If they find us they will arrest us again, and if we get arrested again, ah, then it will not be so easy to extricate us from trouble.' He looked hard at Ryan. 'They will surely have our names, on a list, after what happened in Luxor. In the temple. And the tombs.'

'Then we have to hurry.' Helen had made the decision. She marched down the pier and jumped into the boat.

The little wooden vessel puttered across the glittering lake. The sun was rising now, and slanting through the great pillars of Philae, the mighty kiosk of Trajan, the walls where the last true hieroglyphs in history were written.

Philae.

'We need hours.' Ryan said. 'This temple is vast.'

Albert shrugged. 'The boatman says he will just give us ten minutes.'

'What?'

'Or we are stuck on the island. He will leave without

us. He is terrified of being caught by police. And, like-wise, we mustn't be stranded, it would be calamitous.'

Hanna was, of course, entirely right. If they waited they'd be swiftly arrested by the first tourist police patrol of the day. But swimming to escape would be way too dangerous: there was bilharzia in these Aswan waters: horrible parasites, the lake was notorious for it; and also water snakes, maybe even crocodiles. Swimming was insane.

'Ten minutes it is,' said Helen, grabbing Ryan's note-book. She pointed at the page, and showed him. The process was the same as Luxor. A series of turns and directions.

'OK?'

Albert said he would wait by the boat. He was hot and tired.

They ran through the mighty, silent pillars of the most beautiful temple in Egypt, utterly alone. Ryan yearned to linger: this was a unique experience, precious and memorable. Alone in Philae!

Eight minutes left: they passed the Nilometer. Six minutes: a glimpse of the Birth House. Four minutes: they saw the defaced images of Isis. Ryan had been here before but he'd never noticed it properly. Everywhere in Philae the face of the goddess Isis was brutally erased, chiselled out: by Copts, of course. And the inner halls were embossed with brutal Coptic crosses.

Ryan knew the history: in the fifth century the Copts had turned the abominable pagan temple, to the goddess of magic and fertility, into a proper Christian church. In doing so they had angrily chiselled out the visage of Isis herself, the mother of Horus, the tutelary deity of the entire Mediterranean. Isis the Beloved. Erased.

'Two minutes!' cried Helen.

Ryan searched the hieroglyphs in the Inner Sanctuary. This was the place. But where exactly? Where was it? What did Macarius come to see? Philae was the last place their scholar had visited, where he made his final conclusions. Tantalizingly yet predictably he had not written them down, not explicitly. But Ryan was sure he was on the very edge now, standing on the precipice. He was ready to make the leap of faith and discovery.

'One minute!'

But he couldn't find it. There was nothing here. He'd lost his chance.

Helen was tugging him. 'We have to go!'

'No—'

'Ryan! Please! If they find us – we cannot risk it!'

He stepped close. What was this? He reached up a hand. What *was* this?

'Ryan! We have to go!'

That had to be it. Right above Isis.

But what did it mean? Ryan turned, and nodded, half-despairing, half-exulting. He was so close. Helen sighed with relief and he followed her, climbing over soft limestone pedestals and fallen capitals, sprinting for the boat.

Albert was waiting at the temple pier, his face twisted with anxiety. The boatman looked angry, he was revving his outboard motor, the cordage was curled, the boat was unmoored: he was ready to go.

'*Alors*. Get in the boat!'

They jumped in. The boatman kicked the wooden piles of the jetty and fended off, thrusting them into the deeper lakewater. He leaned on the tiller and they puttered out, breasting the waters; Ryan stared at the lake, so beautiful in the rising sun. The sun that died, and was born again. Every day.

Helen cried out: 'The police!'

A police boat was crossing the lake ahead of them: in a few seconds they would be seen. And stopped.

Albert grabbed Ryan and Ryan grabbed Helen, and they threw themselves onto the damp planking of the hull, out of sight. Crouched and waiting, praying and waiting.

The boat crossed Aswan Lake. Ryan stared at Helen's tense and beautiful face, her virginal blonde hair. Beautiful Isis the Beloved.

Of course. Isis was key, Isis! *She* was the *ankh* that unlocked the secret. The strange bewitching smile of the goddess, that had shone across the ancient world, *was still radiating today,* from the Pillars of Philae, to all of humanity.

Ryan exulted, He had deciphered the hieroglyph. He had unlocked the Macarius puzzle. And he felt a surge of pride. He hadn't needed the missing documents, let alone the Arab gloss or the French concordance.

The few precious papyrus sheets rescued by Helen had been enough. Ryan had used the clues, and seized the prize.

And the answer wasn't remotely what he had expected.

38

London

Karen Trevithick told nobody about the email from Rothley. The necessity for silence, and secrecy, was a physical pain: another ache to add to the anguish that was her separation from Eleanor.

But she told no one. She just slipped out of the office at five, into the sleeting darkness and January traffic, and got a Tube home. It was the first time she had been there since the evening she had come back to Muswell Hill to find Eleanor gone. It was, of course, a scene of crime now. But it was also her home. And she needed stuff. But, nonetheless, she had to fight her own mind to get past the fear of crossing the door.

She didn't *want* to be here; the last place on earth she desired to be was in this place, with its intensity of reminders about Eleanor. And memories of that night.

Summoning all her resolve, she put her key in the lock. And heard a noise inside.

Eleanor?

Stupid hopes devoured her. Karen rushed into the hall, slapping on the lights, and pushed open Eleanor's door . . . The bedroom was empty. Of course. But the window was open: one of the Scene of Crime Officers must have lifted the sash window, left the curtain flapping.

Nothing, no one, nothing. Get a grip, *please*.

Karen pushed the window down and closed the curtain. She had to stay in control. So she didn't look left as she exited the bedroom, and she didn't look right, either: she didn't want to see the toys, the books, the clothes, the old plastic Thomas the Tank Engine bib that Eleanor used when she was a toddler; the tears were rising in her throat again, like bile.

'Get this done,' she said, to herself, aloud. 'Come on.'

Karen went into the bathroom and slipped off her clothes and showered, quickly, turning her face to the hot, hot water. Eyes closed. Think of nothing. Just get through, just do it.

But what exactly was she DOING?

It was impossible to exile these thoughts from her mind. Was she being insane? Going to meet Rothley? On her own? Perhaps it was crazy, but this entire scenario was mad, and cruel. Like one of those modern stories with an unhappy ending, where you left the cinema with an empty space in your stomach and a sense of grim despair.

Foisting off the emotion, she towelled herself down and then went for her clothes. She had to do this. She was being sensible, this could save Eleanor. Somehow.

But what should she wear? Karen opted for jogging bottoms and tennis shoes, two T-shirts, a zip-up top. Clothes for action, to give herself mobility. She was fit, she liked to run, she had done some karate: maybe she could tackle this guy. As she went for the jeans, her attention was snagged by a red hooded top, badly folded, waiting to be washed, ten sizes too small. It was Eleanor's. From the London Aquarium. It had a picture of a dolphin on it, smiling and drinking a cocktail.

Her reaction was reflexive. Karen's hand grabbed the top and hungrily, urgently, she pressed the fabric to her nose and inhaled the perfume of her daughter like a drowning scuba diver taking oxygen, deeply, deeply breathing Eleanor's life, her aliveness—

Karen hurled the top onto the floor.

No.

Zipping her top, she picked up her small rucksack and ran to the door, then sprinted to the Tube. She exited Temple Station at 6.45 p.m. Ten minutes later she approached 102 Chancery Lane.

Five minutes to the rendezvous.

Professional and adept, Karen checked the building, scanning it visually. Apart from the police tape marking the Scene of Crime it looked identical to the day she'd been here with the site manager and found the body of the girl with the severed fingers in her mouth. The windows were black sockets. The nicotine-yellow walls needed paint and cleaning. Classical motifs and capitals gave the place a bogus, faded grandeur. The ground floor was surrounded by the palisade of builder's plywood and KEEP OUT warnings. How would she get in?

Karen crossed the unbusy road. At night this part of Central London was deserted. No one lived in this tiny, mainly medieval quarter of lawyers' offices and bullion merchants. Five hundred yards away, there *was* active life, and bustling pubs, but here there was just the splash of an occasional taxi in the cold and the sleet.

Which meant it was a good place to choose if you were a criminal like Rothley. The idea that a villain returned to the scene of the crime was such a cliché that police now commonly ignored it: what villain would be that stupid? An obviously intelligent enemy like Rothley would not be stupid. Which meant that stupidly returning to the same place was actively *smart*. A double bluff. This was the last place cops would expect him to go. Especially to enact some elaborate ritual.

Karen found the wire door she had used before. It was open.

She paused for a moment and looked at her watch: 6.59. Should she go in? Was she just playing Rothley's sadistic game? What did *she* have that *he* wanted? She didn't know. Luke Rothley had all the power. She'd never met him but he scared her: his ability to enter and exit without trace, to take and do exactly what he wanted, to persuade a girl to bite off her own fingers.

And how did he know she had worn the same clothes twice?

Karen thought of Crowley. *It was said that in the streets he could make himself invisible; others claimed that he was throbbing with so much magical power that his coat once burst into flames.*

Rothley was Crowley. He was. The only difference was that Rothley was *worse*. He was doing the Abra-Melin ritual properly: sacrificing the life of a child. An act of evil at which even Crowley had shied. And now he was drawing Karen into this stupid and obvious trap, and yet she could not resist. Because it was her child he was going to sacrifice.

Karen Trevithick pushed the wire door and it swung open. She stepped inside and turned on her torch. The big dusty hallway was mute. Silent shadows fled across the wall, as if alarmed, when she flicked her torchlight down the hall. But it was empty. Then she tilted the beam at the iron banisters. Nothing. The silence was beyond funereal. Maybe there was no one here, in this vile old building. Maybe it was just a cruel joke, maybe Eleanor was being kept elsewhere. But Rothley had said to *come to the basement*.

'Come on,' she whispered to herself. 'Come on, you can do this, *come on come on come on . . .*'

The stairway to the basement was at the end of the ground-floor hall. Karen stepped over a fallen chande-lier, and walked the length of the hallway and then looked down. Her torch beam followed her gaze, down the stairs. The light was swallowed by the darkness.

There seemed to be a door at the bottom of the stairs. A black and dusty door.

Still, she could hear nothing – nothing but her own heartbeat, and her own breathing.

Karen went down the steps, counting them as she did. Trying to stay calm. 'One, two, three, four . . .'

The doorknob was slightly greasy. The hinges squealed in complaint, but the door opened. Her torchlight flashed up and down, left and right. The beam illuminated another narrow hallway, leading into darkness, with at least half a dozen doors that she could see. The dust was thick down here, and it smelled very bad. Rats, probably. Karen approached the first door, and listened. Eleanor could be locked behind any of these doors. Or she could be somewhere else entirely. Or she might already be dead.

'Eleanor,' Karen whispered. 'Mummy is here.' She wanted to shout it, loudly, as loud as she had ever shouted; but she didn't.

Enough. Karen turned the old ivory doorknob and kicked the door open. The room was bare and reeking and empty. A rat scuttled into darkness.

The next door. She kicked it open. Exactly the same: the nasty skitter of a rat-tail, whipping on floorboards.

She moved on, opening each door in turn. Speeding up.

Door three. Room three.

Empty.

Door four. Room four.

Empty.

Door five. Room five.

'*Mummy!*'

The blood in her heart stopped pumping. That was Eleanor's voice. It was loud and it was near.

'*Mummy! Help me! He's hurting me! Mummyyyy!*'

It was Eleanor in panic, in horrible pain, an Eleanor she hadn't heard before: agonized, desperate, terrified.

'*Mmymymymuummyy help me!*'

It was too much. Karen swallowed the sobs of anger and despair. The voice, her daughter's scream, was coming from the end of the corridor. Karen turned, and jumped over a heap of something, maybe carpet, old carpet, something rotten and damp and blackened and stinking, burned even, and then she found a turning – more doors, even more doors.

'*Mummmy . . .*'

The scream ended and died, in sad whimpers.

It was this door here. Door seven. Room seven. Light was visible at the bottom of the door. This was it. Eleanor was in *here*.

'Darling I'm coming I'm coming I'm coming—' She pushed at the door, and it swung wholly open. The light inside was unbelievably bright, shining directly in her eyes. It was so dazzling at first that she couldn't see anything. She shielded her eyes, trying to see. Then she saw.

39

Chancery Lane, London

Karen's eyes adjusted. The room was apparently empty. *Eleanor was not here.* The only obvious presence in the room was that dazzling white glare, emitted by a professional camera light on a tripod: and adjusted so that it shone directly at the door.

'Ellie?' Karen said. Then she shouted, loudly: 'Eleanor?'

Nothing. There was no one in the room. There was maybe no one in the *building*. Karen worked the logic. Rothley was surely tricking her, if not taunting her: that was certain. But how was he doing it? There had to be a speaker, concealed in the room: that was the only answer. A speaker relaying Eleanor's voice. So where was it?

Shielding her eyes from the intense glare, Karen walked to the camera light, and knocked it to the left. Urgently she scanned the walls, the grubby cornicing, the picture rail. Spiders shrank away in the corners. It was so dark and dirty, up there, she could hardly see *anything*. Maybe there wasn't a speaker?

She tried just one more time. 'Eleanor! Ellie! It's Mummy!'

A spider fell to the floor, near her feet, and fled into the shadows under the window.

These windows, Karen noted, were barred with black and rusted iron. What was out there? Some kind of basement stairwell, perhaps, leading up to the drizzly, empty, lamplit street. Perhaps Eleanor had been here and Rothley had taken her out that way. But how could he have done it so quickly? It was all mad, and it was cleverly menacing.

Karen stepped to the old sash window and looked out: it was indeed a stone stairwell. A wet, bleached pink copy of the *Financial Times* wrapped itself around the iron railings. The window-bars were flaking paint. And the glass of the window seemed to smell. Of what? How could glass *smell*?

'Eleanor . . .?'

Suddenly she saw it: just under the window, screwed to the wall, concealed by the sill, was a tiny metal box. Karen leaned down and examined the device. It was a relaying speaker, miniaturized and expensive, wired directly into the wall. A tiny red light showed that it was on.

So that was how Rothley had tricked her: by relaying the voice of her daughter, expertly tormenting her, seducing her with fear. But was it a recording? Or was it live? Was he here with her anyway? Was she somewhere else? Maybe even lost in this maze of dingy cellars?

Despair began to strangle Karen's feeble hopes. She was never going to find her daughter, the whole thing was a game, *his* game: he was playing her for repulsive fun. Probably there was some tiny CCTV camera in here as well, disguised by the plaster cornicing, or hidden in the grime, through which he was watching and revelling in her despair.

Karen spun around, shouting at the ceiling, at the high and peeling walls. 'Fuck you!'

She didn't really care if there were cameras or not: she was beyond reason now. She just wanted to shout. So she did.

'Where is my daughter? Give her back to me! I am here! Take what you want, but give my daughter back! Fuck you!'

A rat scuttled, somewhere – probably in a wall cavity – alarmed by her shouts; but the only other response was a shocked silence. As if this derelict and dying old building was affronted by her vulgar outburst.

Karen took deep breaths. 'Come on, Karen. Think.'

She was a policewoman; she needed a reminder of that. She could work this out, sort it, unpuzzle it. What clues did she have? It was clear Rothley *had* been in here, to set up this noxious and ornate charade. He must have left clues.

Stepping into the centre of the room she looked around. In the corner, opposite the lamp, stood four

334

foot-high stone jars, curvaceous and elegant, cream-coloured, neatly arranged. Only the carved stone lids differed: one was sculpted as a hawk's head, one as a serpent's head, one as a dog's head, and the last a jackal's. Karen had seen jars like this before . . . but where? She sieved her memories. Frantic and fast. Where?

At last it came to her. She'd seen jars exactly like this on her many visits to the British Museum with Eleanor. They went there often, because Eleanor loved the totem poles and Viking swords and big stone lions. And she really loved the mummies in the Egyptian rooms.

Karen did her best to ignore her intense, intense fear as she approached the jars. But the fear got her anyway. These, she now recalled, were *alabaster Canopic jars*. Special vessels used by ancient Egyptians for the preservation of human viscera, the internal organs of dead people. The lungs and lights were extracted from the body before mummification and kept in these ritual containers, to be left in the tomb alongside the disembowelled corpse.

Human remains?

Whose human remains were in these jars?

She knew. It would be Eleanor in here. She was going to open the jars and find Eleanor's vital organs: her little liver, her tiny six-year-old heart . . .

Karen trembled with the terror, and struggled to hold back the tears. Then she seized her courage. 'Fuck you, Rothley.'

She plucked off the top of one jar. It was empty. And the next? Karen slapped the lid away, with a clatter. This jar was empty too; so she flipped off the other two lids. And her heart paused. The final jar was not empty: it was full of some kind of viscous, amber-coloured oil. Black things floated in suspension.

Karen tilted the jar and poured some of the contents onto the floor. The black things were the severed heads and wings of beetles. Scarab beetles. The smell was sickly sweet.

She shuddered in horror, and relief. All this, she knew, was designed to unnerve her, to prolong and attenuate her terror; and it was working. Karen slapped the lid back on this last jar, sealing the dregs of liquor inside. Then she whirled around. What else was in the room?

Three white cats were lined up, stiff and dead, in the opposite corner. Karen crossed the room and knelt before them. Their fur was a pure, snowy white, unearthly in the dust. The only marks that blemished them were gory scarlet stains at the groin. Karen looked closely. No, they weren't stains, they were wounds. The cats had been crudely castrated. They had been tom cats, and someone had scissored off their genitals.

She stifled her nausea. And tried to work out the puzzle. Because Rothley, in his passionate and elaborate cruelty, might just have made a mistake. And left a clue.

The lights. The jars. The cats. The cats were key . . .

A noise disturbed her. A kind of violent flapping. She turned, terrorized. Her mouth quite open and dry.

The window was now wholly and instantly obscured, because some huge *thing* was trying to get in, something like a bat, but a monstrous bat, two yards wide, engulfing the window, flapping and growing, angry and maddened, attempting to get through the glass.

The flapping intensified. Karen backed away, consumed with horror, yet transfixed.

What the fuck was this? The animal – but it wasn't even an animal, it was a demon, a desperate horrible *thing* – this thing was scratching at the glass, with claws, or hands, and the flapping was so loud and so very intense, as if the thing was trapped outside, furiously trying to get in, to get at Karen . . .

And then it was gone. Disappeared.

Karen stood there in the room, panting with fear. What had she just seen? She could make no sense of it.

It was the last thing she wanted to do, but she had to do it. Gripping her emotions, Karen walked across the room to the barred window and stared out into the gloom, cupping a hand to the side of her face to shield the light.

A tarpaulin was flapping noisily over the window next door, snagged on the iron bars. It was vast and it was black, and it had obviously come loose in the wind and sleet, first catching on this window, then on the next. Maybe it had been used to protect a skip; perhaps it was something the builders had installed to shelter machinery, but it had come loose in the brutal cold wind and momentarily covered the window.

So in her heightened state of terror, amped to perfection by Rothley's hideous theatrics, she had managed to turn a humble sheet of black tarpaulin into a demon.

For a moment Karen breathed more easily. She wasn't going mad, she hadn't been bewitched, Rothley wasn't really a sorcerer or a magician: he was just a sadist and he could be found and she could save her daughter.

Then a tiny voice froze the thoughts in Karen's mind. A little girl's voice.

'Mummy?'

Eleanor? It sounded like Eleanor, but very, very far away this time. Or very muffled.

'Mummy . . .'

There it was again. It was real and it was agonized and it was coming from *below*.

Karen flung herself to the floor, pressed an ear to the cracks in the floorboards, and heard it again.

'Mummy, please help me, please, please come and get me.'

The voice was so tiny and muffled, and yet very near.

'Mummy Mummy Mummy.'

Karen shouted through the cracks, 'Eleanor, where are you?'

'M'under here, Mummy, I'm down here.'

Karen spun around, frantic. What was down there? Under the floorboards? The searching memory of the

338

girl with the severed fingers pitched her into a deeper panic.

'Where? Eleanor? How do I get there, darling? Tell me!'

'Here . . . here . . . down here. Find me . . .'

The voice was fading, and dying, fading into the sound of tears, then nothing.

Karen searched the floor, looking for newer floor-boards, nailed down, recently replaced, but there was nothing. Then she saw the trapdoor. In the far corner. By the threshold. She'd stepped right over it. Karen raced over to it; it had a finger hole in the centre and she forced two fingers in and lifted up. A black socket yawned. Like that old tin mine in Cornwall. Karen turned on her torch, and directed the light into the blackness. Wooden steps descended into the murk, tinged with faint orange, or yellow, like the shadow of firelight.

'Mummy?'

Eleanor *was* here. There was no mistaking that. Eleanor was down in this cellar. Alive. This was no relaying speaker. She could save her.

Then she heard another voice. A man's voice.

'*Atha atha atharim.*'

40

Aswan, Egypt

'It means the beloved,' Ryan said, looking at Helen.

She frowned, and gazed down at the hieroglyph.

Beyond her, outside the scuzzy internet café, central Aswan wilted in the noonday heat; empty cruise boats were moored and rusting by the riverside pier; unemployed taxi drivers sat yawning, in their white turbans, on the benches, waiting for the tourists who would never come. Other than them it was just Ryan and Helen in here, a couple of hardy backpackers, and the café owner. Albert had gone *to church*. His behaviour was becoming increasingly bizarre.

Helen traced the hieroglyph with her finger. 'I cannot read hieroglyphs, but these symbols refer to Isis?'

'Yes,' said Ryan. 'But the importance is the *sounds* that they also imply. M-ry. Beloved is pronounced M-ry. Egyptian has no vowels.' He wrote it down.

M-RY

'OK,' said Helen, and her expression showed her comprehension. She understood. 'And show me those other images again – the ancient Egyptian depictions of Isis with Horus.'

'Of course.' Ryan turned to his computer screen. 'Here.'

The screen showed a picture of Isis suckling a baby on her lap: her godly son Horus.

'So . . . it is just like the Madonna with child, on her knee. The Blessed Virgin with Jesus?'

Ryan nodded. 'Yes. Exactly. The image of Isis, M-ry, the Beloved, with Horus, is the template the early Christians used for Mary, the Beloved, with baby Jesus.' Ryan was feeling something he hadn't felt in many years: vindication, *triumphant* vindication. He had unlocked the Macarius puzzle, with only a half or a third or even a fraction of the documents: he had done it.

'This is why the Copts defaced Isis repeatedly and viciously in the temple of Philae. Especially when they showed her suckling Horus. Here, see . . .'

Helen stared. Ryan went on,

'They knew that the whole idea of the Virgin, of Mary, even the *name* Mary, had come from Egypt, not Israel, not from any historical event. They even stole her name. M-ry. Mary. The Beloved.'

'What else?' Helen asked. 'What else proves this?'

'The whole idea of the conception of Jesus comes from Egyptian mythology. That's what the frieze at Luxor is. A god comes down and impregnates a woman, she is told by an angel – a deity – that she is pregnant, and behold, she gives birth to a divine child. All of this written on a temple wall: *a thousand years before Jesus.*'

The café was dark, but Ryan felt as if he had seen the light.

'Once you make the connection, the evidence is overwhelming. According to some legends Horus, the son of Isis, was born on the winter solstice, in a manger. The birth of Horus was announced in the East, and he was attended by "three wise men" – they are shown at Philae. Horus was baptized by Anup the baptizer, *who was later beheaded* just like John the Baptist. In Abydos, at the temple of Seti I, his mother Isis calls herself "the great virgin" – I've seen it myself many times, so many times, it was staring me in the face . . .'

Ryan turned back to his computer, tapped the keyboard, and read out, 'The very scriptures are completely lifted: in Pyramid Text 1/5 the Sky Goddess, speaking from heaven and talking about the dead god, says, "This is my son, my first-born . . . this is my beloved, with whom I have been satisfied—"'

Helen interrupted. 'Matthew, chapter three, verse seven: "And Lo, a voice from heaven saying, *This is my beloved Son, with whom I am well pleased.*"' She shook her head. 'Again, impressive. Anything else?'

'Endless!' Ryan said, smiling. 'It's endless! Horus was also known as "the Way the Truth the Life", as the Messiah, and as the Son of Man. And as the Good Shepherd, the Lamb, the Holy Child, and as Iuse – Iusa! – Jesus! – which means the Holy One. He was also called "the anointed one". This is what must have shaken Sassoon to the core. This is why the Israelis want to destroy the Sokar Hoard. It proves that Judaism is descended from Egyptian faith.'

'And what about Moses?' asked Helen. 'How does he fit in?'

'Moses we now know was Egyptian, but monotheism was *also* Egyptian. Freud may well have been right: Moses was just an Egyptian priest, possibly a priest of Akhenaten. Consider the great hymn of the Aten: "I regulated the course of the sun and the moon". It's Genesis, but Genesis written by the Egyptians.'

'But the Exodus—'

'Never happened. There were no Jews in Egypt in 1500 BC: that's why there's no archaeological evidence for it. Which has always puzzled historians. Six hundred thousand Jews moving across Sinai, even six thousand Jews . . . I mean, you'd see something, right? Some evidence? Yet there is nothing.' He rushed on eagerly. 'Yet monotheism started in Egypt with Akhenaten. We know that for sure. So how did it reach Israel and the

Jews? It was taken from there by a heretic Egyptian priest, Moses, maybe with some followers. The Bible hides this awkward fact by pretending Jews were enslaved in Egypt, which is nonsense; but they can't admit that the central claim and narrative of Judaism, the story of Moses the Jew, is a total fraud. Yet there are hints in the Bible, in the Talmud, that Egypt is key. *All* the great biblical figures supposedly spent time in Egypt – Abraham, Moses, Joseph, Jeremiah, even Jesus in the New Testament – they were all in Egypt at some point. The Egyptian DNA of Judaism is still visible, there in the Bible, but it is concealed.'

'Wait.' Helen's smile was gentle, but her glittering eyes showed that she was excited too. 'Wait.' She turned and gestured to the café owner, bored and listless on his stool. '*Salaam. Kharkadil?*'

'*Aiwa.*' The man nodded, and went to his fridge. He took a jug of deep purple hibiscus juice and poured two glasses. Then he brought them over and set them down. Ryan drank. The juice was always good, but right now it was the most delicious drink he had ever tasted.

Helen sipped, and asked, 'So what about the Copts?'

'They are crucial. They are like archaeopteryx, in palaeontology.'

'Sorry?'

'The first prehistoric bird, which retains some reptilian features. Showing that birds evolved from dinosaurs.'

'OK.'

'The Copts retain features that show they are

345

descended from Pharaonic times: the hieroglyphs in the alphabet, of course, and the *orant* – their way of praying – that's ancient Egyptian. And that funeral rite we saw in Tawdros: that's Egyptian. Even their churches are often built out of Egyptian temples. Tawdros again.'

'But why are the Copts so important?'

Ryan smiled, exultant. Sassoon would have been proud of him. 'Because early Coptic Christian Egypt was the place where Christianity was codified, written down, *made up*. It was done in Alexandria, where all the great scholars lived, Jewish and Christian, Gnostic and pagan, right next to the great and famous library. The first evangelist, Mark, founded the Coptic church in 70 AD. In Alexandria.'

'The *ankh*!'

'Exactly. The cross only appears as a Christian symbol in, what, the late second century? Before that, the symbol of Christians was usually the fish, or the Chi-Rho monogram.' He was almost rushing his words now; he didn't care. 'Then the early Egyptian Christians realized the power of the cross – because they were no doubt inspired by the power of the *ankh*. The great Egyptian symbol, so very similar to a cross. I saw it in Cairo: that's what those antiquities in the Coptic museum reveal, the ankh evolving into the cross. And this fits with the documentary evidence, too. The first historical citation of the cross as a Christian symbol is made by an Egyptian – Clement of Alexandria – in the third century.'

Helen shook her head. 'So the entire Jesus story is a myth? It is just the story of Horus?'

'No. Well, no, not *entirely*. There probably *was* some charismatic Jewish prophet, or faith-healer, probably called Jesus, there is a bit of evidence for that; some agitator who annoyed the Romans and the rabbis, but the story of the Virgin Birth, the entire Nativity, that's pure Egyptian: the story of Isis and Horus. The Jewish and Christian scholars in Egypt must have folded it in, to attract and gather the faithful. They knew that Isis was wildly popular across the Mediterranean world, so they added in all the best bits of *her* story.'

'And the Resurrection?'

Ryan swallowed some *kharkadil*. 'Probably another Egyptian invention. The Resurrection doesn't actually appear in the authentic gospel of Mark, the first gospel: it's added later, but anyway it's just the story of Horus, and of the Aten, the Egyptian sun god, the sun goes down at the winter solstice, the three darkest days, then it re-emerges. It's the same mythology: Sunday, the day of the sun, Easter Sunday . . . Hello, Albert.'

The Coptic dealer had entered the café quietly. How long had he been standing there, behind them? It was a little stealthy.

He smiled at them. '"The Christian religion is a parody on the worship of the sun, in which they put a man called Christ in the place of the sun, and pay him the adoration originally paid to the sun." That's from Thomas Paine, I believe.' He pulled up a chair and sat down. 'Go on, please, I have been listening. It is fascinating. You have decoded it, my friend, decoded it!'

'Well, perhaps.' Ryan shrugged.

'No,' Albert insisted. 'This is it! Please, do not allow me to interrupt.'

Helen said quietly, 'OK then. Do we have any proof that it was all written in Egypt? Other than Macarius?'

'Yes.' Ryan suppressed his exultation, 'Oh yes. Remember how Macarius said, "I went to the great library, but it was destroyed"? That's because the early Christians burned the greatest library in the world, full of pagan and Jewish lore and knowledge: they sacked it repeatedly. And why? Why did they burn it down? Because they wanted to annihilate evidence for the Egyptian origins of the faith.'

'However—'

Ryan didn't give Helen a chance to interrupt. 'Remember also that Macarius said this arson didn't matter, because he had read all the books, all the books which came from Egypt?'

'Yes.'

'*He means it literally.* All of the New Testament came from Egypt. It's true. Let's play a game.'

'Sorry?'

'Open up your computer. Name a book of the New Testament.'

Helen tapped some keys. 'Gospel of John.'

'What's the earliest surviving copy or even fragment of John?'

She tapped again. 'Uh. Papyrus . . . uh . . . 52. From the second century. It is now kept in Manchester, England.'

'And where was it found?'

348

She typed for a few moments, then scrutinized the screen. 'Discovered in 1920, in Oxyrhynchus, Egypt.'

'Try another. Let's try Luke, the Gospel of Luke.'

'OK.' She typed, and then replied, 'Gospel of Luke, earliest extant copy is . . . written in Alexandrian Greek. Now kept in . . . the Bibliothèque Nationale, in Paris.'

'And it was discovered in?'

'Coptos, Egypt.'

'How about Thessalonians?'

She tapped. 'Papyrus 92. Third- or fourth-century fragment found in . . . Cairo, Egypt.'

Albert intervened. 'The Book of Revelations.'

A pause. 'Papyrus 115. Third century. Now in the Ashmolean, Oxford, England – but found in Oxyrhynchus. In Egypt.'

Albert tried another. 'Gospel of Matthew.'

'Papyrus 67. Late second century. *Found in Egypt.*'

The café was silent. Helen thrust her chair back. 'I do not believe it.'

'But it's true! It's almost miraculous. Try one more.' Ryan was verging on gleeful. 'Let's try something different: say, the Second Epistle of John.'

She keyed the names, then read the answer. 'The earliest surviving copy of the Second Epistle of John is a fragment of Greek script, on parchment, known as Uncial 0232.' She paused. 'It was found in Antinopolis, near Besa, in central Egypt.'

'You see? Every single book of the New Testament is first found in Egypt, and it's not just because they simply found one big copy – though the first surviving copy of the entire Bible is *also* Egyptian, from Sinai, the Codex Sinaiticus – but the first and earliest fragments and copies and papyri *are all Egyptian*. The entire Christian Bible was written and compiled in Egypt, mainly in Alexandria.'

'So Macarius was right?'

'Yes. And this is his big and frightening secret. Christianity was invented by Gnostic and Jewish scholars, slaving away in Alexandria, consciously inventing a new religion, taking elements of recent Jewish history: the story of some criminal magician, some local prophet, a suitably obscure rabble-rouser called Jesus, to ensure the Jews liked the new religion. But they wanted to spread the good news, they wanted Gentiles to believe too: this was a *global* faith they were writing, so they sprinkled in the Egyptian magic, added in the Nativity, the Virgin, the son of God, the miracles and the Resurrection, especially anything to do with the most popular goddess of the day, Isis. *In it went*. All of it derived from Egyptian sources. The *ankh*, the praying, everything. They even took the halo from the Egyptian sun symbol, positioned over the head of an Egyptian deity.'

Helen looked crestfallen. 'So. It is all a lie . . .'

Albert spoke, ponderously. 'Well, Helen, not so much a lie. More like a remake.' He was smiling. 'Christianity is a *glamorous* remake of a provincial original. Like, shall we say, a little European art movie turned into a Hollywood blockbuster?'

Helen's frowning face was illuminated by the glowing

computer screens. 'OK. OK. I do get it. This . . . this secret would terrify fundamentalists, Jewish or Christian, it would destroy their faith, or much of it – but it doesn't explain everything. It does not explain what is happening to the Zabaleen – why are they supposedly bewitched? And it does not explain what that quote about the Beast means, and it cannot explain what the Greek word riddle means.'

Ryan shrugged, exuberantly. 'Does it matter? We've just debunked Judaism and Christianity!' He chuckled. 'That's not enough, before lunch?'

'It's quite enough,' said Albert. 'Very impressive, exhilarating even . . . And now you must, I am afraid, accompany me.'

'What?'

He was holding something in his hand. Ryan stared down at it.

'I feel like a gangster. But there we are. Let us take a small but exciting drive. And then you can hand over the papyrus.'

'Albert—'

'If you do not, I am obliged to shoot.'

The gun was levelled at Ryan's stomach. Albert's hand was trembling. But his voice was quite firm.

'Now.'

41

London

The steps were so narrow that Karen had to descend them like ships' stairs, face to the rungs, carefully placing one foot beneath the other. What was she going to see at the foot of these steps? Her emotions spiralled but she closed them down.

Karen reached the bottom and turned around. She was in a kind of musty brick vault with a low wooden ceiling. It was empty, lit by the melancholy yellow light of a dozen little bulbs strung along the ceiling on dangling wires.

'Eleanor?' Karen called. 'Eleanor?'

Her voice echoed, and died. The only noise she heard was a dog barking along the passageways. The vault ended at a wall of thin red bricks, old and mossed, and then a further low door, barely four foot high, which, from what she could dimly perceive, led into another stone chamber.

It must be medieval, she thought. The whole of this corner of London was medieval in origin, threaded with narrow passages and wine cellars and storage vaults: that was one reason it was favoured by gold and silver merchants into the twenty-first century: they could store the bullion safely in stone-built chambers.

Her thoughts disappeared into the horror of reality. *Where was her daughter?*

Ellie's voice had seemed to come from directly beneath her, when she was in the room above. And yet – not.

He was still playing tricks.

Karen didn't even bother looking for the speaker. She knew it would be here somewhere, secreted in the dripping stone work, concealed behind a loose, five-hundred-year-old stockbrick.

'Mummy.'

It was Eleanor again. *Beckoning*. Muffled yet near, distant yet needy.

'Mummy, help me!'

The voice was inviting her into the next chamber, through the tiny stone door. Karen wondered, for a slice of a second, if she should resist, turn back, give up, refuse to play her ordained role in this satanic charade; but of course she couldn't. She had to go on. Rothley was probably elsewhere, with Eleanor, dead or alive. Yes. Halfway across London, halfway across the world, and this was all a joke. Yet the tiny scintilla of a chance that it wasn't a joke, that Eleanor might be down here, forced her to go on.

'I'm coming!' Karen called. 'Eleanor, I'm coming!'

'Mummy I'm in here, the door thing, help me. I'm scared, I, Mummy—'

Karen crouched through the door, having to kneel and squeeze left and push through sideways, the door was so small.

The next chamber was bigger. Wider and longer, and it had several doors. It was also empty. The ceiling was stone and low, Karen could not stand upright but had to bend and shuffle through. She looked left, down one yellow-lit passage. Water dripped. Shadows capered.

'*Lal moulal shoulal.*'

That was him. *Rothley*. The chanting was distinct; it seemed to be real. Just a few yards away, inside one of these doors.

Karen began to cry. She was bewildered and broken: it was too much: she was beaten. Rothley had beaten her. Maybe this was what he wanted. He desired her like this: defeated and sobbing, and then kneeling on the floor, tormented into submission.

The dog barked again. She looked right, and saw it: a small black dog, running across the doorway, down yet another passage, glimpsed and then gone. What the hell was a dog doing down here? Karen stepped through this door. The light was even dimmer here; there were passages leading on, some lit by yellow bulbs, others dark.

'Mummy . . .'

She could see something. The voice was coming from

a bundle in the next dingy brick chamber. Karen stepped inside.

The bundle was a roped and rolled tartan rug, lying on the damp stone floor. The voice was coming from the bundle. It was the shape and size of Eleanor: she was in here! Her daughter was here, wrapped in this rug!

'Mummy help me. I . . . Mummy!'

She leapt at the bundle. But it was roped and tied. And as soon as she lifted it, she realized that whatever was inside it was stiff.

Karen felt the dread creeping inside her. Stiff. She didn't believe in God but now she fiercely prayed it wasn't Eleanor. She would give her human soul for this not to be Eleanor. What was in this thing? Some dead dog? Some slaughtered animal? With trembling hands, Karen undid the knots. The thin grey ropes fell away and the rug at last fell open, and revealed a child's face.

It was Eleanor's face.

And it was as white as two-day-old ashes. The lips were faintly purpled. Eleanor was dead, stiff and cold. The eyes were half open but rigor mortis had set in. She'd obviously been dead for hours.

Karen clutched the body of her daughter to her breast. And now she wept, and wept, and wept, rocking back and forth, lunatic in her grief.

'Eleanor, Ellie, Eleanor, I was too late I was too late, I tried I tried I tried.' She kissed her daughter's cold lips, her cold face, her coldness. The stiffness was unbearable. Everything was unbearable now. From now and forever.

'Eleanor . . . Ellie . . .'

The feeble yellow lights glimmered above her.

42

London

The police arrived at the same time as the ambulance. Within ten minutes of Karen's phone calls, Chancery Lane was chock-full, from end to end, with police cars. Officers were streaming into the building, down the stairs and into the basements.

Karen's boss, CS Boyle, came straight over to her. She was sitting on the pavement, Eleanor's body in her lap. Stiff, cold, wrapped in the tartan rug.

'Jesus, Karen.' He sat down beside her, on the cold wet pavement. 'I don't – I just – I don't know what to say.'

Karen said nothing. She hoped he wouldn't cry. If he started crying she would cry again: she had already wept for untold minutes, before summoning what was left of her senses and ringing for assistance, drawing half the police officers in central London to 102 Chancery Lane. Half the cops, and one big ambulance.

The paramedics approached her cautiously. They had a stretcher. The young ambulancemen were in green hospital uniforms and they leaned forward to take Eleanor's body.

'No,' said Karen. 'No.'

'Karen . . .' CS Boyle put a hand on her shoulder, speaking very gently. 'Come on. They have to. It's their job. They need to . . . You know what needs to happen.'

'They don't have to pronounce her dead.' Karen snapped the words. 'I already know that she's dead.'

'Please, Karen, let them take her . . . Please. You can go in the ambulance, I'll come with you.'

'No. No! I'll go on my own.' She stared at Boyle, his kind fatherly face, his now-polished buttons. She wanted to hug him and she wanted to punch him, punch her dead father, punch *someone*. She was alone now. No mother no father no child. As solitary as a human could be. The cold winter rain was falling ever heavier.

'Miss Trevithick?'

Reluctantly, hatefully, grievously, Karen acceded: she lifted up the heavy bundle, the rug that contained her daughter's body; and the paramedics stooped and took Eleanor's body and put it on the stretcher. Karen followed them into the ambulance. The last thing she saw as they shut the ambulance doors was Boyle sliding through the wire door, entering the scene of crime. Where her daughter had been killed, or left for dead. Or whatever had happened. What did it matter? Nothing mattered any more.

The ambulance driver put the siren on, but it was only for show.

St Bart's was the nearest hospital. Grand old St Bart's, by Smithfield Market. The staff were kind and efficient: the doctor who pronounced Eleanor dead smiled in the saddest way imaginable, trying to be empathetic. The same doctor found bird feathers in Eleanor's mouth, and said she had probably been asphyxiated. So that was how Rothley had done it. He had put those little dead birds in her mouth until she choked.

Karen smothered her grief. She sat and stared at her fingers. Then she put a finger in her mouth – the knuckle of her index finger – and bit down. She wanted to hurt herself, to obscure the mental pain with physical pain. She closed her eyes and bit and bit hard, until the blood began to run from her knuckle and she tasted iron and she opened her eyes to see a doctor, in his white coat, staring at her, perplexed.

Karen trembled, and cried. The doctor came over and called for a nurse and the blood was wiped away. The same doctor offered Karen medication: a bottle of benzos for the grief. Rohypnol. Anything. She refused.

For several hours she stayed in St Bart's by her dead daughter's silent bedside. Quite, quite numb. Her finger hurt where she had bitten into the flesh. This was welcome. The pain was good. Nothing mattered. She wondered desolately when they would take Eleanor to the morgue. Or would they do the postmortem in here?

At midnight she could bear it no longer. The silence,

the silence of her daughter not breathing at midnight. She called Julie and was told they still had no news of Alan. And then she cut Julie off before she asked too much about Eleanor, and left the hospital. She took the Tube home, walked into her own flat and she sat on the sofa and stared at a switched-off TV.

The flat was so quiet. Hushed. Prayerful. Pin-drop and penitent. The silence had followed her from the hospital. All would be silent, now. Karen looked at the silent ceiling and then back at the silent TV. She realized she hadn't eaten in a day. But what did it matter? Why buy food just for herself? Why bother with anything if it was just for herself?

There were sharp knives in the kitchen. Very sharp knives. Karen gazed at her own wrists. Then she remembered the vodka in the kitchen cupboard. And all the many sleeping pills in her bedroom. Twenty would be enough.

43

Aswan, Egypt

Ryan drove the old Chevrolet north along the corniche, along the magnificent Nile, north out of Aswan, taking the Al Khatar road, leaving behind the towers of Elephantine and the mausoleum of the Aga Khan, perched absurdly on the opposite cliffs.

Albert sat in the back, his eyes bulging. Checking the mirror, Ryan could see there was something wrong with him: he was sweating, and wincing, as if at some inner pain. Ryan recalled the other symptoms: Albert's headache at the hotel the night before, his complaints of tiredness in Philae. Was he ill? The hand that clutched the gun was trembling; but Albert still had that gun. And it was still levelled at Ryan's neck, and sometimes at Helen, where she sat in the front passenger seat beside him.

'Albert, what's the point? Why are you doing this?' The Copt smiled forlornly, and stroked his goatee.

Then he caught Ryan's gaze in the mirror. 'It isn't obvious? Think about it.'

Even his voice was quavery. Not the confident and eloquent man of before; he was liverish, nearly croaking. But he still had the gun.

'You are going to sell it to the Israelis,' said Helen. 'You did all this for them. What was the point? You could have just taken it by force a month ago, saved yourself all this.'

'No.' Albert tutted. 'Not the Israelis. Disappointing.'

Helen tried again. 'Then who? Who? Why are you doing this? We have been through so much, we have helped each other, why turn on us?'

Albert did not reply, he just turned to stare out of the window, sweat trickling down his face, squinting hard, as if looking for something. It occurred to Ryan that Albert was seeking somewhere quiet, to kill them.

They were on an empty road now, the road north to Daraw, Edfu and Luxor. The last blue Co-op fuel station receded into the dust; a Bedouin man drove a camel alongside the road, whipping the beast with a merciless stick. Dogs yapped at nothing as they raced through the farmlands, past cane fields and wooden shacks. Ryan slowed the car to avoid a couple of kids, chasing the dogs.

'Keep going,' said Albert. 'Go faster.'

They sped up. The countryside blurred. Only the Nile stayed with them. The old man of Egypt, sluggishly ferrying its Ethiopian silt to fertilize the fields of the north, to feed the millions of the Delta. The Nile built

362

the Pyramids. The Nile was responsible for everything.

'Here,' said Albert. 'Stop here.'

It was an oasis of nothingness, just anonymous river-side countryside. A good place to shoot people. Coconut palms sheltered a broken-down car; there wasn't a human habitation to be seen. Vultures fussed and flustered over the corpse of a water buffalo that lay, bloated and grinning, on the riverbank. The smell was putrid. A small wooden boat drifted on its tether; lashed to another palm tree.

'Give me the p-papyrus.' Albert was stammering. 'Give me, give, give me the papyrus. And get out of the . . . car.'

They got out. Helen dragged her bag with her; Ryan picked up his.

Albert stood in front of them. He smiled, but the smile was twisted. He touched his hand to his face again, as if he were protecting a broken tooth. Tiny specks of froth smeared his lips, like a cocaine addict overtalking; and his breathing was laboured and slow. But he still had the gun.

Albert stared at the sky just above Ryan. 'Give me the p-p-papyrus. Now. Give. Give it. To me.' Every word was an effort. Albert was blinking fast, shaking his head. 'No!'

Albert was shouting. For no good reason. What the fuck was wrong with him?

Now he seemed to gain a modicum of control; he levelled the gun once more at Ryan's legs. 'I will kill you, I will. Give me it. Now.'

What options did they have? He was going to shoot them anyway. Ryan reached into his rucksack and pulled out the file containing the precious Macarius papyrus.

'Why?' said Helen, as Ryan sorted the fragile sheets. 'Why do you want them?'

'Because. You. Insult God.'

'What?'

Albert coughed his answers, his eyes swivelling, left and right, leery and panicking. 'You insult God. I am. Copt. A Copt. Copt. You insult, insult my faith. Give it.'

'No,' said Ryan.

The bullet streaked past Ryan's face. He actually saw its burning course, or the flash of sun on the metal.

The gunshot agitated the vultures feasting on the corpse of the buffalo. They clapped and flustered, flapping into the air; dirty airborne rags with talons.

'Give me now.'

Ryan yielded. He took the documents and handed them in their folder to Albert. Who reached for it. And missed. Albert's hand clutched at air, at nothing; then he reached again, and this time grabbed the file successfully and took it from Ryan.

He couldn't see it properly. Ryan realized that Albert was ill in some way, mentally or physically ill, in a fashion that affected his speech and *blurred his sight.* That was why he'd been staring at the sky above Ryan's head.

Slowly and quietly, Ryan stepped sideways, then

moved forward to take the document back, but Albert shot again. This time the shot missed by ten metres at least. He had shot at the last place he'd heard Ryan speak: he really was going blind, *but he still had the gun.*

'Ryan?'

It was Helen. Albert twisted violently and shot at the sound of her voice, the bullet missing her by mere inches. Now people were gathering: a boy on a moped had stopped to watch; a taxi was slowing down, the taxi driver gawping, quite terrified, at the scene.

The facts dawned on Ryan. They didn't *need* the papyrus. What were they doing, waiting to get shot? *They had the movie in the camera.* They had the solution in their hands. They couldn't get to the car – Albert was in the way – but they could get to that wooden boat.

'Come on!' Ryan dragged Helen by the hand towards the riverbank.

Clutching their bags, they scrambled down to the Nile. Swiftly, desperately, Ryan unloosed the tether of the little motorboat and they jumped in. Up on the riverbank Albert sent two more shots into the air, but he was on his knees now, his hands shaking. The bullets went everywhere and nowhere.

Albert had dropped the papyrus. Three or four cars had pulled over.

Ryan yanked the starter rope of the decrepit outboard motor. One tug, then two: it coughed into life. Helen kicked the boat vigorously away from the muddy river-bank and they were away, fleeing downstream.

Peering through the river-haze Ryan could see the fallen figure of Albert surrounded by cars and people. Was that a policeman, trying to handcuff him?

They were too far away to tell. For ten minutes neither he nor Helen spoke; they motored north in horrified quietness, trailing silvery plaits of brown river water, meandering around the vast corners of the riverine shore.

Peasant fishermen gazed, mildly confused, then uninterested. Two tourists on a boat on the Nile? Probably lost. Life was too difficult to worry about such a thing. Back to work.

At last Helen said, 'We have to get off this boat. The police will interview Albert.'

'If he can speak.'

'The police will talk to him,' she said. 'That kid on the little moto, he will have seen us: they will be looking for two Westerners in a little boat like this, we will not be hard to find.'

She was exactly right. Ryan scanned the next curve. The growing traffic on the riverside road showed they were near a town. It must be Kom Ombo – the City of Gold – with its great temple to Sobek, the crocodile god. There would be tourists here, if there were tourists anywhere between Luxor and Aswan. Maybe some backpackers, maybe some Russians undeterred by riots. And there would be cruise boats.

Yes. That was surely the answer. Going by train or plane was impossible: the airports and stations would be under surveillance. Travelling by road was equally risky: army checkpoints became ever more frequent the nearer you got to Luxor.

But a tourist cruise boat? That would be entirely anonymous. The few still operating would be desperate for business; and the cruise boats never got stopped. As long as they stayed on the boat, they could expect to reach Qena unmolested, and from there maybe they could hire a private vessel.

Ryan tillered the boat up to a small jetty. Rope tied, bags hauled, they climbed the steep riverside stairs, up the sandstone banks, and emerged onto the road.

As they watched for a taxi, Helen said, 'This is not the answer. We do not have the answer.'

'What?'

'We have *not* solved it. I do not believe our solution. Something very important is still missing. Think about Sassoon. Would he really have killed himself because of a revelation like this? Really? The discovery is not entirely new. We have more facts, more proof – but it is not revolutionary. And what has happened to Albert?' She shook her head. Angrily. 'Has he been poisoned?'

A cab pulled over. The driver was a headscarved woman – extremely unusual. She looked their way as Ryan leaned towards her window, asking in Arabic, 'Can you take us to the centre of town, to the main pier? We need a cruise boat.'

The woman nodded and they climbed in. The car joined the dinged and rusty traffic heading for the town centre. Donkey carts and Toyotas, bareboned horses and the odd gleaming limo. The car stalled at

367

a clot of traffic. A man, squatting on the roadside, in a filthy turban and an even filthier djellaba, leered at Helen and her blonde hair.

Helen was oblivious. She spoke, staring straight ahead. 'Let him who hath understanding reckon the number of the Beast.'

'What?'

'Reckon the number. That is it, Ryan. That is what he is telling us. About the Greek words. It's *isopsephy*. Numerology.'

'I don't get it.'

Helen turned. 'Numerology. It is a code. The Greek words are not a curse or a chant or a spell: the letters mean numbers. That is why Macarius left that clue on the line directly before. He was telling us straight out. *Reckon the number of the Beast*. We have to *reckon the number*.'

Ryan felt the flush of excitement. Helen was quite possibly right. And if she was right, what did that mean? What revelation could be worse, for a Jewish scholar, than what they already knew? That Judaism and Christianity were fake?

'Kom Ombo,' said the taxi driver, gesturing. 'You can take the boat.'

44

The Nile

The purser of the cruiser *Hypatia* took one look at Ryan's sweating face and tattered backpack and Helen's similar state of disrepair; then shrugged and said 'Sure.' He looked like a man who didn't care, whose business was dying, and so he might as well pocket the two-hundred-dollar bribe offered by Ryan and allow them on board. For another hundred dollars he would probably have let them enslave his children.

It no doubt helped, Ryan thought, that he so obviously desired Helen, giving her a sickly smile as she dragged her bag onto the deck.

The purser led them to a corridor of cabins. 'Take your pick. There are seventy to choose from.'

They chose the very first cabin. It was small and bright with a Victorian engraving of Abu Simbel on the wall and a brass-ringed porthole. Ryan couldn't help peering out, nervously, to see if Israeli commandos were pulling alongside in a fast black dinghy. Knives at the ready.

The purser was still watching, from the open door of the cabin. 'You are being pursued, *effendi*?'

It was obviously a joke. But it stung. Ryan shook his head. 'Ah no, just . . . it's just—'

Helen interrupted. 'We've been travelling by road for days, it will be a pleasure to sail on the Nile. When do we depart?'

The purser looked at his watch. 'Any minute. The dinner is at seven, the entertainment is at nine. You do not have to book.' He shut the door.

As became apparent, the purser was right: they certainly didn't have to book. This was a phantom boat sailing the Nile. The *Hypatia*, with its crew of dozens and its handsome mahogany fittings, was designed for one hundred passengers; and it had maybe ten. There were more staff than diners at dinner. The man who carved the ice sculpture seemed to be in tears.

But all of Egypt was in tears. There was a TV in the corner of the restaurant showing the BBC news in English from Cairo: tear gas and mayhem, a fatal bombing in a business district. 'Meanwhile, in Moqqatam, a Coptic quarter of the city, further violent clashes continued for the second day, as demonstrators burned down a clinic—'

The nation of Egypt was sickening; maybe it was dying. The Zabaleen, the Muslims, everyone. Ryan stared at the melting ice sculpture and remembered Rhiannon, in Cairo's Christian hospital, the day *she* died: clutching at his arm, her heartbeat fluttering. He remembered the way the malarial fever had risen inside her, like a remorseless flood, taking the baby, then seizing Rhiannon.

The memories were, still, unbearable. Even as he'd kissed her he had known it was probably the last occasion he would kiss her. Goodbye, goodbye.

The purser switched off the TV, with its distressing news. Ryan and Helen glanced at each other, and shifted into the ballroom. They had to act like *proper* tourists: they couldn't just stay in their cabin and work the code; so they sat in the big ballroom, and listened to the first few songs by the bosomy Egyptian singer in the disco room, where two old German ladies sat staring at the ceiling, and one young Russian couple danced by the tinsel-decked stage.

'OK. Shall we go?' She stood up.

'No. Upstairs on the deck.' Ryan gestured upwards. 'You have your phone? We can get better reception there.'

'But upstairs is dangerous? We agreed.'

'Not at night. No one can see us, no satellite, no one. I've been on these boats before, they keep the light subdued so you can see the stars. Come on, I need the air.'

The desert stars were indeed beautiful. Long-armed Nut, the Goddess of Night, had littered the lovely blackness with all of the family diamonds.

'You know, if we're going to die,' said Ryan, 'this is a good place to do it. On the Nile.' He stared at the passing scenery, barely lit by the moonlight. A few crackling woodfires glimmered in the fields. It was beautiful, even sublime. The banks rose in sandstone cliffs, then subsided to mud. The next stop was Edfu, tomorrow morning.

'We are not going to die,' said Helen, squeezing his hand. 'But if we are, then I am glad I met you first.'

He kissed her, twice. They were the only people on the deck of the *Hypatia*. The mystery was theirs. If they could solve it.

At last, Ryan extracted his notebook. 'Right, let's test your theory. Finally.'

'The quote about the Beast. We need to investigate that first.' Helen keyed her smartphone, and read: 'The Number of the Beast, from the Greek: Ἀριθμὸς τοῦ θηρίου, *Arithmon tou Thēriou*, is a term in the Book of Revelation.'

'And?'

Helen recited from the corresponding webpage: '"Theologians usually support the interpretation that the phrase 'the Number of the Beast' refers to pagan numerology, where every letter has a corresponding number."' She scanned the screen, and went on. '"For instance, 666 is the equivalent of the name and title, Nero Caesar, the Roman emperor; however, Protestant reformers have equated the *Beast of the earth*, of Revelation, chapter 13, with the papacy."'

'But what is isopsephy?'

Helen pressed her glowing phone and its light shone in the moonlit dark, like a tablet of illumination; the very stele of revealing. '"*Isopsephy*, from *isos* meaning 'equal' and *psephos* meaning 'pebble', is the Greek word for a special kind of numerology, derived from the fact the early Greeks used pebbles arranged in patterns to learn arithmetic."'

'But how do we know our guy would be using this . . . isopsephy?'

'Because,' Helen sounded a little triumphant, 'the very earliest example of true isopsephy comes from Philo of Alexandria, and the form was perfected by Leonidas, also of Alexandria, in the first and second centuries.' Her blonde hair was nearly white in the starlight as she gazed at Ryan. 'So, you see? If we presume our man is a Hellenized Coptic scholar, who saw Alexandria as his intellectual capital—'

'Which he did.'

'Then this *isopsephy* is what he would use, if he wanted to use numerology to encode something crucial. In the Greek riddle.'

Ryan smiled. But he was suppressing his resurgent worries. What if Albert had recovered, and the Egyptian police had interviewed him? The cops would definitely want to catch Ryan and Helen. Two people had probably died at Luxor. He and Helen had stolen the papyrus even if they had since lost it. And the Egyptians would want to know all about the Israeli connection. So far they had been protected by the chaos unfurling across Egypt.

'So. Am I right?' Helen pressed.

He tilted the notebook into the moonlight.

ΑΓΓΟ, ΑΕΘΗ, ΑΑΘ, ΒΕΖ, ΒΗΕ.

'If you're right, the first letter alpha, A, corresponds to 1. The second letter F, digamma, means 6.'

Helen wrote down the number 1 and 6 in her own notebook. Ryan continued, 'Then we have gamma, Γ, or 3. Followed by omicron, O, which usually means zero.'

Helen read out the number. 'So that makes 1630.'

'Let's do the rest.'

The cliffs and palms of Nilotic Upper Egypt paraded past them, in the nocturnal silence.

'So there are our numbers.' Helen read them out: '1630, 1598, 119, 257, 286.' She paused. 'They go down then back up.'

Ryan felt the initial tingle of understanding. 'They could be dates. Years maybe. What four- and three-digit numbers go down then back like that? I can only think of one obvious sequence: the years BC and AD. No? They're years. *They're dates.*' He pointed to her phone, as she swatted away a mosquito. 'Check those dates, see what happened in those years.'

Helen keyed the numbers in. '1630 BC – ah . . .' She glanced back at Ryan. 'The eruption of Santorini. That happened around 1630 BC, it seems.'

'Interesting, what about 1598 BC?'

She keyed. And paused. 'Not so much . . . Very vague. A Hittite king sacks Babylon. Senakhtere is Pharaoh. Maybe . . .'

'OK. OK.' Ryan was getting lost now. 'The newer ones will be surely more accurate. 119 BC: try that.'

'Hipparcus replaces Eumarcus as archon of Athens.'

She squinted at the phone. 'And the Han Chinese nationalize the production of salt.'

'Maybe it's 119 *AD*?'

'A rebellion against Rome. In Britain.'

Ryan pondered. A rebellion? Was this about rebellions? Eruptions? What? The solution dwindled even as they approached.

'Hmm. Don't see it. Try the next 257? 257 AD?'

'Goths invade Turkey.' Helen sighed.

'OK, let's do the last, 286 AD.'

The silence was brief, as Helen worked her phone. 'A new emperor in Rome, Maximian. The empire is divided between him and Diocletian . . . And that is it. I cannot see an obvious pattern. Can you?'

Ryan stood, truly frustrated, and walked to the railing. Where he gazed at the bulrushes, and at a very distant storm, way over in the western desert. With its tiny flashes of lightning, it looked like a storm for toys. 'Diocletian!'

'What?'

'Macarius was a sixth-century scholar. Are we sure he used the same calendar?' Ryan closed his eyes and tutted. *Stupid*.

'So these are not the right dates?'

'Helen, he's not using the damn Gregorian calendar. He's using the Diocletian calendar, that's what the Copts went by.'

'The, ah . . .?'

'Diocletian calendar, the Era of Martyrs: it was the Coptic calendar for many centuries. The year one is the year the Emperor Diocletian came to power, 284, the year he began to slaughter all the Christians in Egypt. For them it was the apocalypse, so it shaped everything – including the Coptic calendar.'

Helen was already tapping out the numbers, using her phone as a calculator. 'So we add 284 to each date if it is BC, and subtract it if it is AD.'

'Confusing, but yes. Try it.'

Helen scribbled in Ryan's notebook. An owl hooted as the boat slipped past. A harbinger of doom and death, thought Ryan. The Copts: they would deface them if they found them in Egyptian tombs. Chisel them away.

'So,' Helen said, 'when Macarius writes 1630 he really means 1346 BC; 1598 means 1314 BC. And 119 years before the Era of Martyrs, actually means, in our calendar, 165 AD . . .' She paused, frowning, and wrote the last digits. 'And 257 equals 541 AD. And 286 means 570 AD.'

Ryan was beginning to see something: he could sense the pattern or the logic. Part of him wanted to stop right here. Because what was dimly discernible was terrifying.

'OK,' he said, trying to hide the apprehension in his voice. 'Macarius was writing in the late sixth century: it must have been late if he included 570 AD. So whatever happened in 541 AD and 570 AD would have been recent history. Maybe it provoked him to write what he did, to go on his journey. I think I can guess already, but make sure I am right. What major event happened in 541 AD?'

Helen pressed the keys. She said, solemnly, 'The Great Plague of Justinian. Millions died across the Byzantine Empire . . . Egypt was sorely afflicted.'

'I thought so.' Ryan's throat was dry. Everything was dry. He wanted to dive into the Nile. 'Now, 165 AD. Try that.'

Her answer was sudden. 'My God.'

'What?' Ryan asked, though he could make a very good guess.

'165 AD. The Antonine Plague. Otherwise known as the Plague of Galen, brought back to the Roman Empire by soldiers returning from the Near East. Millions died.'

'OK. Yes. 1314 BC? Start looking for plagues now.'

'1314 BC? That is . . . the year before the Exodus, traditionally. The Exodus of the Jews.'

'Therefore the year of the plagues of Moses, just before Exodus. The ten plagues of Moses, in the damn Bible.' Ryan could see it all now: the entire appalling secret. With a sense of dread, he asked, 'And 1346 BC?'

'Akhenaten is in power, and . . .' she did another search, 'his reign is wracked by plagues.'

Ryan stifled his fear. '570 AD is the birth of the prophet Mohammed. But check it for something else, search specifically for plagues.'

Helen did as she was told. Then she spoke, very quietly. '570 AD. Europe and the Middle East are swept by another bubonic plague. There is a quote: "In 570 AD Greek soldiers who fought outside Mecca in 569–570 AD are said to have carried home a strange disease."' A silence. Helen shook her head. 'But I do

377

not understand, how does this prove anything? So, there were plagues, and Macarius noted them.'

Ryan raised a hand, and read from his own notebook. 'He doesn't just note them. Remember the passages that Macarius quotes at the beginning? It was there all along, written down, we just didn't see it.' He turned his notebook so that he could read by the fragile moonlight: 'Manetho, who wrote his Egyptian history under Ptolemy II, represents Moses as a rebellious Egyptian priest *who made himself the leader of a colony of lepers.*' He flicked the page. 'And here, further down, Macarius talks about the famous Tutankhamun Stela. I know what that says off by heart, so does every Egyptologist: "Now, when His Majesty was crowned king, the temples and the estates of the gods had fallen into ruin. The world was in the *chaos of disease.*"'

Another flick of a page. 'And here: Macarius quotes Chaeremon, an Egyptian scholar in Alexandria who became Nero's tutor. Chaeremon says the goddess Isis appeared to Amenophis in a dream and advised him to cleanse Egypt by *purging Egypt of lepers,* so the king gathered one hundred thousand lepers and expelled them, and their leaders were Moses and Joseph.'

Ryan waited for a second, giving his thoughts time to calm, and clarify. Then he went on. 'And again here, Macarius cites Pompeius Trogus's *Historiae Philippicae.* He doesn't give the quote but I know it: Moses is said to have quit Egypt to institute an Egyptian cult in Jerusalem, and the reason he leaves is because of *an infection, an epidemic.*' Ryan stared up into the starry sky. '"But when the Egyptians had been exposed to an infection and had been warned by an oracle, they expelled Moses *together with the sick people* beyond the confines of Egypt."'

Everything was silent. The only sound was the soft and gentle ploughing of the cruise boat in the river water, and the neighing of a donkey tethered in some little farmstead by the canefields. Hooting at their labours.

Helen was the first to speak. 'It reminds me. Of something I learned at Gymnasium.'

'What?'

'The name of the flea that carried the Black Death is *Xenopsilla cheopis*. Named for the Pharaoh Cheops. Even the Black Death came from Egypt. Or so people believed. The *pestis Aegyptica*. And after the Black Death there was an outbreak of great religiosity. An upsurge in faith.' She turned off her phone, and stared at the silent horizon of water and palms. 'Religion is therefore . . . just a psychological reaction. To the terror of plague, the horror of death, on an atrocious scale.'

Ryan shook his head. 'But maybe Macarius is being more specific than that. Perhaps *monotheism* is the psychological reaction. Whenever monotheism arises – Akhenaten, Moses, the first Christians during the Antonine Plague, the birth of Mohammed in 570 – we see epidemics, just before. The epidemics cause terror and great suffering, yet those that survive the epidemics become religious, monotheistic, because they have been terrified by such a powerful god that can wreak such

379

hell. That explains what was wrong with Akhenaten, and his relatives: he had some disease, it crippled him, gave him those weird symptoms, but when he survived he felt himself blessed. Selected. Elected. Perhaps by one great god. His illness made him a monotheist.'

Helen responded: 'So *that* is the story of the Exodus. There weren't any Jews in Egypt. There were people infected, like their Pharaoh, by a horrible disease, that killed many, yet gave the survivors belief.'

'It must be: these are the plagues of Moses, written in the Bible, the boils, the frogs, the flies and locusts.' He gazed at the moon. 'And this explains the slaying of the first-born, the tenth plague: they are trying to kill the disease by culling the afflicted, and stop the contagion. Create a firebreak. It *must* be, Helen.' Ryan rushed on, excited and horrified. 'But the culling doesn't work, it doesn't stop the plague, so in despair they expel the lepers and their great priest, Moses, and the priests and the lepers survive the disease, and start their wandering, and they finally reach Palestine, where maybe they infect the Israelis, who become monotheists in turn, after suffering the same psychological reaction to vast contagion. Because the surviving Israelites, instead of seeing this as a curse, regard this as a sign of God. It elevates them: they have been chosen. An elected people. But forever afterwards they are paranoid about further contagion, hence their dietary laws, the fear of unclean food, their detestation of impure and mentally different people, the Gentiles, the pagans . . .'

The stars shone down on the pagan temples of Edfu,

approaching them in the night. Helen shook her head slowly. 'Ryan . . . what if . . . we have got this the wrong way *round*?'

He stared at her. 'What do you mean?'

Her eyes sought his in the darkness. 'Perhaps the plague *is* monotheism.'

A fishing boat, with a solitary light, teetered in the wash of the *Hypatia*.

'Sorry?'

She hurried on. 'I have read enough Darwinists who believe religion is some kind of intellectual virus, a meme, or whatever. But, Ryan, what if religion is not an intellectual virus, what if religion or monotheism is an *actual virus*, which alters the mind. *And it strikes like a plague?*'

Ryan was silenced.

They both gazed out at the glittering river, reflecting the glory of Nut.

45

Upper Egypt

They passed Edfu, and Luxor. Then Dendera. Nearing his hometown of Abydos.

Ryan and Helen acted like tourists, but strange tourists who never left the boat. They read guidebooks and made love. They filmed each other in the cabin, talking over the theory. Excited, yet very anxious. Helen's phone had run out of juice – somewhere along the way they'd lost her recharger; they couldn't research it properly. Yet they couldn't leave the boat. But they needed to get out of Egypt. Maybe they could get a boat to Sinai from Hurghada, and cross into Israel? The Israelis might not be expecting that.

Better still, they could take a boat back to Luxor, and charter a hot-air balloon, and fly into Sudan. *Yes.* The tourist balloons were desperate for business. It was bizarre but it might work. The Sudanese had no love for the Egyptians. There was no passport control six hundred feet above Abu Simbel.

But if this was to have a chance of working Ryan needed all the cash in his little safe, a lifetime's humble earnings. And he also reckoned that dawn would be the best time to retrieve that cash. Abydos woke late: he could sneak in and get it. And he'd have an hour or two to sit at his desk and work alone, and work out the theory.

Helen was sleeping in their cabin, a little hot and irritable, kicking at the sheets.

Ryan seized the moment: he was going to take the gamble, and go to his apartment. He knew it was a risk, but it was necessary: he needed all of his spare cash.

Kissing Helen on her unconscious lips, he resisted the urge to say, 'I love you' – but the urge itself was very telling. Maybe, finally, he was leaving Rhiannon behind.

Quickly, he walked the gangplank down to the pier. Abydos temple was ten kilometres away from the Nile. He would need a taxi.

As he had expected, the Nileside township still snoozed. Horses drooped. Fuul sellers scratched on benches, and dreamed about a better day ahead. Even the pharmacists selling cheap Diazepam were shut. In the rising, blinding sun Ryan waited as patiently as he could by the riverside. Taxi drivers never slept in Egypt. They were the Waking Ones. You could always get a cab.

But no cabs came. Ryan squinted at the river. A mother was washing her naked baby in the river water, scooping water in a metal dish and dribbling it over the baby's head. He wondered how clean that water was, with all its attendant infections and parasites. He thought of Rhiannon. Dying of perinatal malaria: the parasite *plasmodium falciparum*, spread by the *Anopheles* mosquito, breeding in the torpid waters of the delta. The Nile had claimed her with one of its many parasites.

The words seized him. Parasites? *Plasmodium?*

A taxi pulled up. Ryan snapped, in Arabic, 'Abydos please. Fast as you can.'

The driver raced. The donkeys stared. The necropolis of kings and cats hove into view.

'Yes, here please, drop me here.'

Creeping through the morning shadows cast by the great temple of Seti I, Ryan keyed the door by the tea-house and climbed the stairs to his dusty, deserted apartment. The furniture stared at him reproachfully. Where have you been? Why did you leave us?

His thoughts accelerating, Ryan grabbed his money, then looked to his laptop: he had just enough time to do some research. But the room was too stuffy, a haze hung in the air. So he opened a window for a freshening breeze, then sat down at his desk. The robotic muezzin was singing the call to prayer from a mosque next door. As the first lyrics echoed across the city, and the empty Temple of Seti, he opened his laptop and typed:

Can a virus or bacterium or parasite affect human behaviour?

Two words leapt out at him: *Rabies* and *Toxoplasma*. Rabies made a kind of sense – the frothing, the Zabaleen, the mad biting? But rabies needed dogs and dogs had not featured in their discoveries.

Toxoplasma was different. *Feline toxoplasmosis.*

The cats. As Ryan squinted and scribbled in his notebook, the muezzin sang out his beautiful words.

God is the Greatest, I testify that there is no God except God . . .

The revelations came quickly now.

All the way through their odyssey they had encountered cats. There was a vast cat cemetery here at Abydos, beyond the drowned tomb of Osiris. Cats were likewise adored at Akhmim. The Egyptians venerated and even feared cats throughout their millennia of history: Egyptian cats were the origin of all domestic cats. And Ryan could, of course, never forget that grotesque hour in the catacombs of Bubastis, holding the cat mummy in his hand.

What could feline toxoplasmosis do to humans?

Ash hadu alla ilaha illallah . . .

Ryan clicked. And stared. 'Toxoplasmosis is a parasitic disease caused by the virus *Toxoplasma gondii*. The parasite infects most genera of warm-blooded animals, including humans; cats are the primary source of infection to human hosts. It is thought that maybe 50–90 percent of Europeans are carriers of the parasite; levels of infection in mankind are equally high in many other

385

parts of the world; most victims will never become aware of their status as hosts, unless the infection becomes acute . . .'

Ash hadu alla ilaha illallah . . .

Parasites. *Parasites.* Just like the malaria that killed Rhiannon. He clicked another article:

There is now no doubt that toxoplasma influences human behaviour in ways we are just beginning to understand. The effect of infection is also different between men and women. Infected men have lower IQs, achieve a lower level of education and have shorter attention spans. They are also more likely to break rules and take risks, be more independent, more antisocial, suspicious, jealous and morose, and are deemed less attractive to women. On the other hand, women tend to be more outgoing, friendly, more promiscuous, and are considered more attractive to men compared with non-infected controls . . .

More attractive? The parasite could make people *more attractive?*

I bear witness that there is no God except Allah. I bear witness that Muhammed is God's Messenger . . .

The headlines were just bewildering now.

A NATION OF NEUROTICS? BLAME THE PUPPET MASTERS
Today the Proceedings of the Royal Society of London is publishing a paper called, 'Can the common brain parasite, Toxoplasma gondii, *influence human culture?' The paper's answer? 'Quite possibly yes.'*

386

And another:

A common parasite found in cats may be affecting human behavior on a mass scale, according to a scientist based at the University of California, Santa Barbara. While little is known about the causes of cultural change, a new study by the US Geological Survey indicates that behavioral manipulation of a common brain parasite may be among factors that play a role. 'In populations where this parasite is very common, mass personality modification could result in cultural change,' said study author Kevin Lafferty, a USGS scientist at UC Santa Barbara . . .

There were more articles like this – many more. And this was just one parasite: toxoplasma. What else was out there?

Ryan sat back. If religion was not a virus, but specifically a cerebral parasite, altering man's behaviour, how would it work? It would have to be tiny, yet virulent, warping human minds like toxoplasmosis. And it would have to spread itself. How?

The call to prayer rolled on. As he stared out of his window, he knew he already had the answer.

The Oseirion was just beyond the great Seti temple. It had been filling with water over the centuries. Ryan had been trying to save it for years, save it from the Nile.

Ryan recalled the Macarius papyrus, and its constant references to baptism. And thought about that woman washing her baby in the river.

Baptism.

If the parasitic virus was born in water, then it would urge people to seek out water so as to continue its life cycle. Baptism would be a perfect way of achieving this, a superb adaptation. That meant that baptism was theoretically a behaviour *induced* by the parasite, so as to better spread itself. But could a parasite do this? Could a parasite make humans enact such specific and exact behaviourisms, such as to seek out water?

He clicked and searched. And one cold tear of sweat ran down his spine.

Hayya 'alas-salah, Allahu Akbar . . . The Guinea Worm.

The Guinea Worm is a particularly unpleasant parasite, endemic in parts of Africa and Asia, especially desert countries like Egypt and the Sudan. It spends its early life curled up inside a copepod, a tiny shrimplike organism, swimming in water. A person drinking that water swallows the copepod, and when the copepod dissolves in stomach acid the Guinea Worm escapes. The worm slips into the intestines and burrows into the abdominal cavity: the human stomach.

From there the worm wanders through the human's tissue until it finds a mate. The two-inch male and the two-foot female have sex inside the human body, then the male seeks a place to die. The female slithers through the human skin until she reaches the leg of her human host. As she travels, her fertilized eggs begin to develop, and by the time she has reached her destination, the eggs have

*hatched and become a crowd of bustling juveniles in her
uterus.*

*These juveniles need to get inside a copepod, to be swal-
lowed by a copepod, if they are to become adults themselves,
and so they drive their human hosts to water, by causing
a searing blister in the leg or foot, which the host tries to
cool – by dipping it in cold water, such as a pool or a
river.*

Ryan paused, and read that again.

The parasites can drive their human hosts to water.

The call to prayer had ended. The silence was absolute and monumental.

For another hour Ryan scanned the screen, adding
horrible information to his notebook: Ebola, eukaryotic
viruses, blood flukes, leishmania, trypanosomes. He
even found a curious paper: 'The Amarna Kings,
Aneamias, and Parasitic Liver Disease', by an obscure
scholar, Thomas M Simms, who openly speculated that
the strange behaviour and deformities of the monotheistic Pharaoh Akhenaten and his family were the
result of an *unknown waterborne parasite* that bred in his
artificial lake of Birket Habu. At St Tawdros. Where
Helen had caught a fever and nearly died.

Ryan had found enough evidence. Going to his safe,
he grabbed all his cash and stuffed it in a bag. Then
he exited his apartment, sprinted down the stairs, and
took a fast taxi back to the riverside.

He and Helen had done it. They had solved the
Macarius puzzle in a way they could not have conceived.

They had not only falsified Judaism and Christianity; they had not only proved that these faiths derived almost entirely from pagan Egyptian mythology: they had gone further. They now had evidence that monotheism – monotheistic religion, in its entirety – was nothing but an affliction, an actual disease, a pathology of the brain, a radical and epidemic mood alteration caused by a brain parasite.

The whole thing, the whole enormous glittering, imperious cavalcade that was monotheism – Judaism and Christianity and Islam – parading in its pomp through human history, was caused by a minuscule virus or microscopic cyst in the brain, maybe little bigger than a molecule. And it was waterborne, and spread by baptism, and in its acute stage it was accompanied by plague. No wonder Victor Sassoon had been driven to suicide.

The theory was terrifying, but it was *beautiful*; the answer was insane, yet the answer fitted so well. It was the truth. He had the truth.

Ryan walked along the pier, feeling the moment. But he had no time to relish this revelation. He had to tell Helen what he had discovered. So he sprinted the last few hundred metres, to the jetty, and the waiting *Hypatia*. He ran up the gangplank, but as he did, he stumbled, and fell.

What?

Hauling himself to his feet he reached for the rope. He couldn't see it properly.

Ryan spun around. The river was covered with a

weird muffling haze. But even as he peered at the mist the truth skewered him with terror. There wasn't a haze. It was an illusion.

His eyes were lying; his eyes were failing. He was going blind.

46

London

Karen woke up in her hospital room, quite alone in the world, desolate and childless. The TV suspended on the wall stared at her with its empty screen.

She groped for her memories: the bottle of pills, the alcohol, the sleeping pills, that agonized late-night phone call to DS Curtis – her poor friend! – the rush to the Whittington Hospital. After that: blackness.

But that was what she'd wanted – blackness – or she wouldn't have attempted suicide in the first place. Did she really want to die? Karen turned and gazed out of the hospital window. She could see bare winter trees, and a lightly toppling snow, falling on Highgate Hill.

Snow.

Always the snow, how Karen hated the snow. Because the snow equalled memories of snowmen and snowballs and laughing with Eleanor and the twins in the snow, and that equalled a sadness so intense it threatened, right now, right here, to turn Karen inside out with grief.

Indeed it was as if she was being sucked into nothingness, as if she was in a tumbling, broken spaceship with a gashed hole in the side; and the grief was that devouring nothingness beyond, sucking everything out of the spaceship. Pulling everything into the blackness. She had so nearly let go. So nearly let herself spin away and outside and into the silent, black, infinite space. Where her daughter had already gone.

Karen leaned the other way and grabbed a tissue from a plain little cardboard box. As she did, she noticed the bandage on her forefinger, the traces of dried blood on cotton. Now she recalled how she had gnawed at her knuckles. Consumed by anguish.

How long could she cry for? How long could this go on? How many tears did she have? Maybe she should refuse liquids, nil by mouth, then she would at least be unable to cry.

Eleanor.

No more tears. She cried. No more tears. She cried and sobbed.

Karen tried to sit up but she felt pinned to the bed by the grief: the terrible sadness was a rapist, lying on top of her, knife to her pulsing neck. *It gets worse, bitch. You think this is it? It will get worse.*

Eleanor.

He will kill you, bitch, he will smell the fear in you. The devil is in him.

Maybe the mad girl in the Bodmin asylum had been

right. Rothley was the devil. He had smelled the fear in her.

'Good morning?'

The voice was kindly, and authoritative. A doctor approached, with stethoscope and white coat, and sat on the end of the bed. His label read DR HEPWORTH.

He gazed at her. 'So you're awake. You had us all very worried.'

'I'm sorry,' Karen mumbled. 'I'm so sorry . . . stupid.'

'Well, that is a bit harsh. But, anyway . . . We'll need to do some tests – you've been, you know, elsewhere for two days now.'

'Two days?'

Hepworth nodded. 'Yes, I'm afraid so. Quite delirious. We had to restrain you at one point.'

'God, I'm just . . . sorry.' Karen stared at the shape of herself under the hospital bedsheets. Her legs. Her stupid body.

The doctor strode across, and came close. He shone a torchlight in both of her eyes, tilting her head back. He checked her pulse with two fingers. Then he sat down on the visitor's chair, and frowned, and asked her a question: the capital of England.

Karen mumbled, 'London.'

'The name of the prime minister?'

She told him that, too.

Hepworth nodded and jotted something on a clipboard. 'OK. Four times ten.'

'Forty.'

'Uh-huh.' He tapped the pen against his chin. Then said, 'Repeat after me, penny lion Paris bicycle.'

'Penny lion . . . Paris bicycle.'

He wrote something down on the clipboard, as if he was actually writing, PENNY LION PARIS BICYCLE. 'OK. Well. There it is.' He frowned 'We'll need to do more tests but you seem *compos mentis*. This is very unusual of course, though not entirely unique.' His frown softened. 'I'm sure you must be pretty keen to see your family.' He walked to the door and signalled down the corridor.

'No,' said Karen, desperate. 'I don't want to see anyone. I don't. I can't. I've already seen Eleanor, that's my family, I've seen the body, please, I can't—'

The doctor swivelled. 'Body? What are you talking about?'

Karen gazed at him.

She could hear footsteps running down the corridor. Light footsteps, running footsteps, a child's running, happy footsteps, a little girl's running steps. She saw a glimpse of blonde hair through the glass of the door. It couldn't be, it couldn't be, it surely wasn't, surely not, it mustn't be, it couldn't be; could it be?

Could it be?

Could it be?

The time and space surrounding her dwindled to a nothingness, and all that Karen was and all that Karen could be and all that Karen could ever be was Karen at this moment staring at the door and seeing the blonde hair and the smiling face and the little girl who leapt onto the bed, smiling, and hugging her. Hugging her mummy.

'Eleanor?' Karen's voice had never been so cracked. Cracked with sadness, and a terrifying happiness. 'Eleanor?'

Her daughter was lying on the bed, hugging her mother. Karen could smell her hair. It was Eleanor. She was alive. Karen had no idea how, but *she was alive*.

Now the tears came again, in their hundreds and thousands, and Karen didn't care. For ten minutes she rocked her daughter in her arms, weeping with happiness, crying and laughing so loud that nurses from the next ward came to stand and stare, and smile, and one of the nurses cried as well, and Eleanor didn't understand, and Karen didn't want to tell her. She just stroked her daughter's lovely, lovely, lovely blonde hair, and cried.

Three hours later Dr Hepworth pronounced her fit and well – as far as he was able. Karen barely let go of Eleanor's hand throughout the procedure. It was only when Julie and Alan and the twins had been in and out, and more tears had been shed, that she let Eleanor go and play with the twins. Even then Karen grimaced with anxiety. At the memory of her imagined yet very real terror.

As soon as they had left the room, she turned to Boyle and Curtis, who had been waiting patiently. 'So what happened to me, when did I start hallucinating?'

DS Curtis shook his head, as if he didn't know the answer, though he clearly did. 'Soon after the discovery of the girl's body in Chancery Lane, maybe ten minutes later. According to the site manager.'

'Glover?'

'Yeah, him: according to Glover you just dropped to the floor, like you had been drugged.'

'Yet I haven't been drugged, the tests show it.' Karen frowned. She wanted to get going, get out of bed, get back to the case. Get back to *living*. 'But . . . but the hallucinations were intense, just *intense*. Like the most lucid dream. Vivid detail. I imagined the abduction, I imagined case meetings, everything. I imagined Eleanor talking *Latin*. Yet it's not a drug . . . What could do that?'

Boyle was sitting on a chair in the far corner, but his voice filled the room. Confident and calm. 'We think it is a mental parasite, that induces hallucinations. One of the symptoms is, as you know, biting the fingers.'

Karen stared down at her bandaged finger. Then she looked at Boyle. 'But I dreamed that I did this. So . . . I really did this – but in my sleep? In my coma?'

'You really did it.' Boyle nodded. 'You had to be restrained.'

'That's what the girl did, in Chancery Lane, bite her fingers . . .'

'Yes. Clearly she was suffering the same – what is the word? The scientists told me, the same *parasitogenic* delusions. Remember the strange red *cake* you found at Chancery Lane?'

'Oh my God. I sniffed it.'

'We don't know if Rothley intended you to find it, or just left it by accident.'

Karen worked it through. 'So you had the cake examined, Pathology, right?'

'Wait.' Boyle came and looked her up and down, like a relieved but still-worried father. 'We have discovered more.'

'More?'

The confusion was back. Karen gripped the bedsheets. A sudden terror that she might tip once more into hallucination, psychosis, overwhelmed her; but then she thought: *Psychosis* – that's what happened to the girl at Bodmin. Except that Alicia Rothley's psychosis was much worse, and more prolonged. She had never come round, never recovered.

DS Curtis interrupted her thoughts. 'Karen, remember you told us to search every site that had ever been connected to Crowley? You were adamant: you said even if it's been turned into a bloody car park, search it?'

'Yes?'

'Well, we did. And your hunch was right, you were bang on. We searched and searched and eventually, yesterday, while you were in here, when you were, uh . . .'

'Raving mad. And strapped to the bed?'

Curtis smiled. 'Yeah. When you were tripping out we finally found that there had been a Golden Dawn temple—'

'Crowley's cult.'

'They had a temple, just off Howland Street, Fitzrovia, in an old Georgian townhouse. But it was bombed in the war and then it was shops and then last year they demolished that and built a brand-new office block, unoccupied for a year – economic conditions and all that – but of course, it wasn't unoccupied.'

'Rothley was there.'

'He was in there all right.'

The snow had stopped falling outside. A winter sun glimmered, feebly.

Curtis went on. 'We broke in straightaway, but we were too late, just a few minutes too late. Rothley must have had CCTV or something. He got out just in time to save his own sorry arse, but . . .'

The new horror evolved. 'He'd killed a child?'

Boyle came back, crisp and emotionless. 'Not yet. He's abducted her. Zara Parkinson, eight years old. Daughter of Nick Parkinson. We found *him*, still alive, just about. He told us everything. Rothley had kidnapped them both, and tortured them.' Boyle sighed. 'It's more of his so-called magic, I fear. Of course we are searching for the girl right now. We are hopeful we can save her. Rothley made mistakes, in his panic to escape with the girl. He left lots of evidence behind.'

'Such as?'

'For a start, his notes. He wrote everything down. He talks a lot about his – what do you call it? His *grimoire*. His book of magic, Abra-Melin. Apparently he believes that *his* version of Abra-Melin is *the* version.

It's from a town called Araki, somewhere in Egypt. Seems he bought it at auction a couple of years ago.' Boyle frowned. 'We're having it translated, but we've already got a handle on these blood-cakes, the cake you sniffed. They are apparently called "incense of tears".'

Karen flinched.

'That's the term used in his notes. It appears Rothley makes these blood-cakes from all kinds of organic compounds. We found various test tubes and samples. And we know that parasites must be in the example of incense that you found, in Chancery Lane.' Boyle put his police cap back on, getting ready to go. 'Because, after you flaked out, we got the evidence straight to Pathology. So far they have isolated one organism which closely resembles *Toxoplasma gondii*, the feline parasite which attacks the brain and causes visions and delusions. So we're pretty sure that your brief inhalation of the incense of tears was the culprit. That's what pitched you into delirium for a few days.'

'Kaz, if you'd actually *eaten* some,' added Curtis, 'you might have gone entirely nuts. Forever.'

'Like the girl in Bodmin.'

'Yeah.' A brief silence ensued. Then Boyle showed her a photograph of a late-middle-aged man, suave and suntanned, and wearing the smile of discreet wealth. He looked like a Silicon Valley software mogul. Jeans in the office, but a yacht at Malibu.

'Who is that?'

'Samuel Rani Herzog.'

'He's Jewish.'

'You guessed. We found lots more of these photos in Rothley's grim little factory of magic. Rothley even wrote the name of the man, in what appears to be rat's blood, on the wall. With lots of curses.'

'So who is Herzog?'

'Lives in Israel. And London. A billionaire, made his money out of weapons – Israel has a thriving defence industry. In the last decade Herzog has developed an interest in bio-weaponry. Five years ago he was recruiting parasitologists and neurobiologists. An odd mix. Since then his research has become more secretive, or at least low profile. This jars with his social image: he is a man with good friends in high places.'

Karen looked away. The snow had started again. Gentle, fairy-tale flakes. Settling on the near-dead branches of the winterbound trees. 'Rothley was in Israel?'

'Yes. That's the connection. So now we're looking for Herzog as well as Rothley. And of course the girl, Zara Parkinson.' Boyle glanced at Curtis, and hurried on. 'Herzog was last heard of in Israel, but he has many properties in England, and France and Egypt. A complex web. If he lands at any airport in the EU we're going to trail him. We suspect he is doing experiments, using parasites. He must have recruited Rothley. But Rothley went rogue, and now Rothley hates Herzog. That is our best guess. What the hell are you doing?'

'Getting out of bed, what does it look like?'

'But, Karen, you've just—'

'What? I've just woken up. Now I want some coffee. And then I want to get back to work. We have to save this girl, right?'

47

Egypt

Ryan's sickness and blindness worsened: by the evening he was slipping in and out of delirium. Sometimes he was lucid and calm, sometimes the parasite bit deep into his soul and the madness surged.

And the worst of it was that he enjoyed the madness. Because when he was mad he believed. As he stared through the porthole at the shining, hazy waters of the Nile he felt an influx of something, something greater than himself, a brilliance in the singing air, a surging oceanic beauty, supporting him. He felt the absolute conviction that God existed. It was all so true. It all made sense. Parasite or not, there was potent and emotional meaning to *everything*. It all mattered, it was all part of a plan, impossible to know yet irresistibly true. And death was a subtext. Just part of the whole, a mere petal of the rose.

Ryan nearly cried. Tears sprang to his eyes as he thought of his wife and their dead child and for the first time ever this did not make him sad. *Rhiannon*. He knew it was the parasite but it didn't matter. Helen stared at him and he loved her too, but it didn't matter.

'Lie back, Ryan. Lie down. Please.' She pressed a T-shirt, soaked in cold water, to his sweating forehead, as he collapsed onto the bed again.

The hours of darkness passed, in sweated madness, and then in calm. When the lucid hours arrived he thought the problem through. It was obvious that he and Albert had been infected by the same brain parasite that induced religious fervour: therefore he pillaged his memories of the last weeks to work out where. Luxor? Aswan? Philae? Bubastis?

Bubastis seemed the most likely. All those revolting cat mummies. But then he remembered Albert hadn't been down into the tunnels.

Helen had drifted into asleep, next to him. A frown darkened her beautiful face, as she dreamed. Gently, he stroked the pale curve of her neck. He loved her. He knew that. And if he loved her he had to let her go: he'd already worked that out, as well. If she stayed with him she was doomed.

By dawn, or maybe sooner, before the next attack of madness, he had to decide how they'd separate. Probably his only option was to take himself to a hospital, which meant certain arrest by the Egyptians, and possible murder by the Israelis: it meant the End.

And there was no guarantee Helen would survive even when they *did* split.

'Mr Harper?'

An American voice? Outside the cabin?

Ryan stood, and grabbed a Swiss Army knife. Unjacking the little blade, he opened the door.

A white-toothed, rich-looking, middle-aged man stood there. He had a tiny diamond stud in his ear. Gazing down at the pitiful little pocket knife in Ryan's hand, he said, 'Not sure that's going to liberate you from the *entire* Egyptian army.'

Behind him stood two other men, types Ryan now recognized: the surfer-dude soldier. Military boots, pricey tattoos, evident muscles, sunglasses at night. And beyond them all was the purser, wearing the nervous-yet-contented smile of a man who has been recently and lavishly bribed.

The rich guy spoke. 'I am Samuel Herzog. And that is . . .' He peered over Ryan's shoulder. 'That's Helen Fassbinder, isn't it? And one of you is infected? Or both?'

Ryan shook his head, but the lie was evidently feeble. He wasn't even sure *why* he was lying.

'Ah. It's *you* isn't it? You are infected?' The man smiled quietly. 'Then we better be quick. The cycling between mental states is increasingly rapid as the illness takes hold. You are clear-headed now?'

Ryan nodded. Mute but truthful.

'Good. We need to be good and honest friends – we really need each other. I have a car on the dock, and a private plane at Luxor Airport; there are two nurses on the plane.' His smile was dazzling: quite perfect. 'Come to England with *me* and we can save your life. You can't really go to Sohag Hospital, can you? They'd have no idea what to do. They'd probably feed you Tylenol and let you die like a toilet rat.'

Ryan looked from Herzog to Helen, sleeping on the cabin bed. He didn't trust this man, but he was also dying; what could he do? Perhaps the man could save them both. 'I need to know more.'

'Let's go on deck. My guys will watch over Helen.'

Ryan followed him to the deck of the boat. Where the eternal stars admired their faint reflection in the dark Nile waters. The river-haze was there, but it hadn't worsened. His blindness had plateaued; the fever of faith had abated. But he knew it would return.

Herzog spoke first. 'Here's what *I* do. I make weapons, and I sell them. I have always been interested in new weapons, especially bio-weaponry: the future. I have excellent resources. And I have been following your *situation* for a while. Very closely. And that is why I sent my soldiers to protect you.'

'Soldiers?'

Herzog nodded. 'My soldiers of *fortune*. Ex-SAS, ex-Navy Seals. They take big risks, because they need the money. I choose guys with debts and problems, and I pay them Homeric bucks. I told them to watch your back because I wanted to see if you, Ryan Harper, probably the globe's most gifted Egyptologist after Sassoon, despite your early retirement, could decode the Sokar documents. And prove my thesis.'

'You knew Victor.'

'He was my hero, for a long time. I loved him. Almost like a father. Yet he also annoyed me, he was so religious. Deluded. And he sold himself as this great Jewish figure – a survivor of the camps – yet he didn't make Aliyah, did he? He didn't go to Israel? No. But *I* did. I left America, New York, and went home, to help our Jewish homeland. Sassoon stayed in nice comfortable Hampstead in London. Where the Palestinians are less able to kill you with rockets. Sassoon and I remained in touch. I told him what my research was beginning to reveal: that monotheism was parasitogenic, and this was possibly the final secret concealed in the Sokar documents. He assured me I was a fool, and he went off to find the Hoard. And he found the *truth*. Poor Victor.'

'But why are *you* here? Why do *you* need to decode the documents?'

'I want to know if I am right about Sokar. But I also want the documents, or want*ed* them, for the purposes of science.'

Ryan looked at the sky. Was it blacker than before? It seemed so. His vision was deteriorating again. He trembled at the idea: even as part of him yearned to yield. And believe. He had to use his last moments of lucidity. 'So why come to us? Hanna has the documents.'

Herzog shook his head. 'Not any more.'

'Sorry?'

'We had people in Aswan who got to Hanna, in hospital, as fast as we could, before the Israelis got there. The Israeli zealots might not have known his identity but we *certainly* did. My men took the Macarius papyrus from Hanna before he died, in Aswan. Raving. *Meshugah.*'

Ryan was trying to see through the glass darkly. 'The Israeli involvement . . . why? I don't—'

'A section of the Israeli military is highly orthodox, and fundamentalist – they pray at Masada to Yahweh the night before they graduate as officers. Prayer vigils for soldiers? *Imagine.* They have growing influence, however, and the most senior of them knew Victor Sassoon, the great scholar of Egyptology and Jewish theology. We *all* knew Victor Sassoon.'

Ryan looked over Herzog's shoulder; he could see the green-orange lights of a city in the distance, across the lightless flats of the desert. But the haze was there as well. Like a sandstorm rising.

'Sassoon told *several* people before he died that he was going looking for the Sokar Hoard, these documents which would, rumour had it, damage the Jewish and Christian faith very badly. His suicide implied, therefore, that he had unearthed something truly *terrible.* Consequently, when his body was reported as found, the Israeli military – or rather, the maniac and rabbinical wing of our Israeli army – swooped down. They'd been waiting. They had men all over Egypt, ready for the moment. Just waiting to seize the documents. But you had already got part of them.'

'But it was Helen. She went to the cave first, and hid when the soldiers came.'

Herzog's eyes widened a fraction. 'That is why the Hebrews have been after you ever since. The Israeli fundamentalists just want the Sokar documents. They want them *destroyed*, because they prove that Judaism is a mere remake of Egyptian mythology, that Yahweh is a demon from the desert, and Moses was a goy. But, of course, they don't care about any cutting-edge *bioscience*.' He shrugged, as if to say, *What can you do.* 'So when we snatched the Macarius papyrus from Albert Hanna and he croaked about everything, then I was able to barter.'

'You gave them the papyrus? You just handed it over? To be destroyed?'

Herzog stared up at the stars. 'Because we didn't *need* it any more, Ryan: we needed you and Helen. I guessed that one or both of you would have been infected with the God Parasite, like Hanna. You are, therefore, walking Petri dishes of invaluable biochemical evidence. Invaluable.'

'Why not take Albert? Dead?'

'I prefer a live specimen. I need a live specimen. I also need information.'

'So the Israeli army—'

'Accepted the deal. We did a hook-up at the Cataract. They got Macarius and in return I got all their information on you. They have paid off every cruise-boat owner

409

in Egypt, as well as every airline. Expensive business . . . So here we are. We're saving your life; I am sure you are grateful. We need to get on my plane at Luxor. And quickly.'

'What will happen then?'

'You will be cared for. In England, our lab there. We are surely the *only* possibility of your escaping death and of Helen escaping Egypt. And now, in return, you can give me your information: tell me exactly where you have been – exactly, down to the last detail, the last plate of shwarma you have eaten. I need to know what you have been doing since you left the bones of Victor Sassoon in Nazlet Khater.'

Ryan told him.

Herzog raised a hand, and asked, 'Akhmim?'

'Yes.'

'Akhmim is crucial.' Herzog nodded to himself. 'I was convinced, when I began this quest, that it all came from Akhmim, *everything comes from Akhmim*. I've already looked into Akhmim. But I couldn't work out a source.' He scowled. For the first time. 'Where did you stay? In Akhmim?'

Ryan told him.

'What did you eat?'

Ryan told him.

'Did you go anywhere? Do anything?

'We just . . . I spent most of my time about fifteen kilometres outside Akhmim. The Monastery of St Apollo. That's where I decoded the papyrus.'

Herzog grunted. 'I do not know it. *Feh.*' The engines

of the cruise boat churned water in the darkness. 'Is there anything at the monastery? Anything, unusual? A spring maybe? A water source?'

'Just a library. And a lake.'

'A lake?' Herzog frowned. 'In the desert?'

Ryan touched a hand to his head. Like Hanna. He was acting like Albert Hanna. He had to stay calm. 'The lake was . . . very small, artificial maybe . . . Kind of . . . square.'

'Tiye's lake.' Herzog was smiling now, his white teeth perfect in the gloom. 'Tiye's lake! Everyone thought it was in the Delta.'

'You mean Amenhotep's wife, Tiye?'

'Of course. Amenhotep was always said to have constructed *two* lakes for his wife and his sons. One was Birket Habu, dried out, by Malkata.'

'We went there.'

'But all you Egyptologists told me the other must be near Heliopolis or in the Delta. I scoured the satellite maps looking for the remains of a square lake near Suez or Alex or Memphis. All the time it was near Akhmim!' His laugh was dry, and terse. 'So that's where you caught the parasite, that's where you were infested. Did you drink it?'

'No. We swam. Albert paddled.'

'Well there you go: you might as well invite a rabid dog to chew on your *arm*. You caught the cholera of Belief.'

Ryan stared at this man. He was starting to believe him; but then, he was starting to believe in God.

411

The sun was rising; the sun god Amun had risen again.

Herzog persisted. 'Helen is interesting, though. Why wasn't she infected? She swam too?'

'I think perhaps she *was* infected,' said Ryan, yielding to the truth. The struggle was almost over. He was so *tired*. 'She had a fever at St Tawdros, near Thebes. But then it passed . . .'

Herzog's smile was faint in the darkness. 'The God Parasite is quite unpredictable, it kills some, it converts most, a few are virtually immune.'

'But you said I am bound to die?'

'As far as we can see, once you reach the blindness stage you are going to die.'

'How do you know?'

'It's in the Talmud, and the Bible. Search the manuscripts of early Jewish history, or early Christianity, and you will find stories of saints and armies being blinded by Jehovah and dying like flies. The Jews were terrified of it, but they blamed *pork* – the humble *pig*.' Herzog smirked. 'Yes, the trichinosis parasite, in pork, causes blindness as well, but it wasn't the culprit. They didn't realize that Moses, the infected Egyptian priest of Akhenaten, and his infected followers, had already brought the God Parasite to Israel. And so history unfolded.'

The sun's rays were visible, the desert sky was bleaching. Ryan asked, 'How did it evolve? The parasite?'

'That is the fascinating area. Scientifically. We are still

such *infants* in this field. What we can guess is this: the God Parasite is tiny, possibly molecular. It may have been evolving in Egypt for thousands of years: the combination of desert conditions, reliance on a single water supply and continuous millennia of dense human civilization in one place are ideal for a water-borne parasite to make the leap from infecting animals to infecting people.'

Ryan inhaled the night scents of rural Egypt. The cooling Nilotic breeze on his face. The breath of God in the desert. He was remembering verses from the Bible, learned as a kid. It was flooding back: all those boring Sundays in church with his Baptist parents.

Nor for the pestilence that walketh in darkness; nor for the destruction that wasteth at noonday.

He gazed at the eastern wilderness, stretching to the Red Sea, and Sinai, and Israel.

For I will punish them that dwell in the land of Egypt, as I have punished Jerusalem, by the sword, by the famine, and by the pestilence . . .

Ryan struggled to talk. 'But how do, do, do these parasites affect behaviour?'

'Neuromodulators. The parasites subvert the normal function of hormonal neuromodulators – the things that order the brain around – and they manipulate them in their own favour, to encourage an abundance of crazy behaviourisms.'

'An example?'

Herzog shrugged. 'I have several million examples.

413

You know that one in four species on earth are parasitic? There are *two hundred thousand* species of parasitic wasp alone. One of the parasites that first seduced me into this field was Entomophthorales. It is an evil fungus that parasitizes the housefly. It glues itself to the fly's body then burrows inside and starts eating all its blood, at the same time as it tunnels into the brain, like Muslim terrorists heading for the cockpit of a 747.' Herzog glanced at his watch, then continued. 'In time, the presence of the fungus, by manipulating the brain of the fly, gives the fly an irresistible urge to relocate to a high place, perhaps a blade of grass, or the top of a door. There the brainwashed fly glues itself to its perch, lowers its front legs and tilts its abdomen away. And in this surreal position it dutifully dies, and the fungus is *ejaculated* from the exploding abdomen of the fly, its contorted position perfect for firing spores widely into the wind, to shower on more flies below.'

'Christ.'

'Well, precisely. And there's more. The parasitic control of the fly's brain is *so* sophisticated it makes sure the fly commits suicide in this flamboyant manner *just before sunset*: only at that precise time is the air dewy and sweet enough for the spores to develop quickly on the next unfortunate fly. And so the cycle continues.'

'That's horrible.'

Herzog smiled. 'Yes. And there are thousands of similar examples. It's one reason why I am not religious.

414

How could a good Creator conjure such monstrosities? There is a beetle which chews away the tongue of a fish and becomes its tongue, a parasitic *tongue*. There is a magnificently evil parasite which forces its poor host to change gender, yes – change *sex* – there is also a parasite which obliges its victim, say, a horse, to smash its head pointlessly against a rock or a tree: the Bornavirus.' He put a hand on Ryan's shoulder. 'But not all parasites are quite so malign. Many parasites thrive in a mutually beneficial way with the host. The God Parasite is one.'

'Beneficial? But . . . Akhenaten was diseased, his children died young?'

'Clearly in its earliest stage, the very first manifestation of monotheism, the God Parasite was brutal and harmful: it caused cranial malformation, strange bone diseases, bulging eyes – hence the oddness of Amarna portraiture. Those fearful plagues of Akhenaten and Moses. But Darwinism honed it. It got better. More user-friendly, more beneficial to the host.'

Ryan shook his head. As if he could shake the blackness from his sight. He was definitely going under now. He sat down on a wooden bench and closed his eyes. 'It's not benefiting me. And it killed Albert.'

Herzog's voice was lonely in the darkness. 'Ah, but only some people die. Those that survive do benefit, but *why*? Here is the genius of evolution: the parasite is, in fact, in its later forms, extremely beneficial – because monotheism is beneficial to the human host

415

– religious people live longer than atheists: they are less likely to drink and smoke, they are happier, healthier, and, crucially, *they have more kids* – look at teeming Islam compared with sterile Europe – the atheists die out, in their sad and childless despair, meanwhile the monotheists breed like the lesser rodents.' Herzog sighed. 'We are sure the God Parasite, once it gets into the human brain, and presuming the host survives the initial infection, is then passed harmlessly down from mother to child, probably via uterine hormones. Or just maybe it smuggled its way into our DNA. Much of our DNA was originally the DNA of parasites that we co-opted. Either way, that's why religious belief is partly heritable. A child who inherits the faith that infected his parents suffers no plague, no blindness, no insane epiphanies; he is just happy and monotheistic and devout, and he breeds more kids who have the same parasite.'

Herzog paused. 'It does, however, appear that the parasite is not invulnerable. Eventually it stops descending down the generations, unless the human hosts are reinfected. Hence, maybe, the rise of secularism and atheism in Europe.'

Ryan opened his eyes. He saw an egret fly over the boat, spectral in the moonlight. Like a ghost. Or an angel.

Herzog concluded, 'The parasite also evolves very quickly, we do not know how. It may become actively hostile to atheists, it may explain hostility to atheists.

The science is still experimental and unformed, which is why a living, breathing, intelligent, freshly minted victim like you is such a valuable *commodity*.'

The moment was coming. When Ryan would have to agree. Before he lost his reason again. It was fleeing him now. He grasped for the words. 'Commodity?'

'This is the *situation*.' Herzog clasped Ryan's shoulder. 'We are developing a cure for the God Parasite, a way of eradicating monotheism! Imagine the potential!'

'I can't. Why? Why are you doing this?'

'Because of my country, the survival of my people. Because Israel is *doomed* if monotheism survives: religion is killing us. If it isn't the Christians it is the Muslims – it is especially the Muslims, right now. Indeed, Israeli Jews will soon be outnumbered by Muslims even within Israel. There is no hope for the Zionist homeland, the Islamic nukes are *here already*. But ah! If only we can make the Muslims non-Muslim, make them nice secular liberals, take away the lunacy of monotheism around the world, then, *hava nagila*, Israel survives. And we get rid of the zealots at home.' Herzog smiled bleakly. 'Consequently we are, right now, developing a prototype parasite-killer; a parasiticide. We will use it on you. We do not know if it will work. It may cure you, it may not. But if it doesn't, you will die, and then we get to cut open your head and look at your brain.'

He extended a hand. 'Think, Ryan, think. While you still *can*. Doesn't that sound like a pretty good deal? In the circumstances? With Helen asleep downstairs? You love her, don't you? You want to save her. And yourself. So this is your only option. If you don't agree you will *definitely* die, and she will be arrested and jailed. So, therefore, use your last precious moments of rationality. Make the decision. Do it quickly. Or you will die a flailing and horrible death.'

48

Plymouth, England

The girl, Zara Parkinson, was weeping again. Rothley resisted the urge to smack her. She still had faint bruises on her face from the last time he had struck her: sad, violet contusions under her eyes, and some bruising on her slim, pale arms. This was not ideal. The Abra-Melin ritual was adamant that the final victim must *burn* in as pure a state as possible. Virginal, and perfect, and unsullied.

Besides, there was no real need for him to hit her again. He had done much of the hardest work, having successfully transported her across southern England to this old block of apartments in a rundown corner of Plymouth.

All the neighbouring flats were empty: they could not be detected. The flat was anonymous, and utterly context-less; the police in their dutiful slowness would surely be looking for him in some house connected to

Crowley and the Dawn. But Rothley was already beyond that – he had soared way beyond that.

'*Mnnggg.*'

The girl was whimpering, choking a little on her gag. Rothley leaned close, and assessed her half-naked body. She was quite dirty. He would have to bathe her and feed her tonight. Yes. Then put some ointment on her wrists where the ropes had grazed her skin, and dress her in clean white clothes. He had to get her right for the final ritual, for the great and dramatic denouement, when she could burn correctly in the 'incandescent fires'.

Staring out of the window, at the grey terraced houses of Plymouth, Rothley rolled the resonant Coptic concepts in his mind.

Burn the virgin in the scorching and incandescent fires of Hell. Before the eyes of many.

How fitting. It was rather magnificent in its own way. He had to burn the girl, and do it all in public. The writers of the Abra-Melin ritual had a gift for poetry, and theatre, as well as pre-Christian sorcery.

'*Mmmggnnn!*'

The girl was *still* mumbling, intruding on his thoughts. What did she want? Perhaps she was thirsty? He couldn't risk her dehydrating. He wanted her alive so that she could die. Pulling the rag from out of her mouth, he said, 'Yes? What is it?'

'Please . . . please . . .' The tears streamed abundantly down her bruised face. 'Please let me go. Please!'

She was sobbing. It was cruel. He sighed and shook his head. 'No.'

'I . . . I . . .' Zara sobbed some more, her lips trembling with fear, her eyelids opening and closing as if she were drugged. Soon she *would* be drugged. He would have to give her the last incense so that she was entirely bewitched; and of course he would inject some *Ampulex compressa*. Then she would walk into the incandescent flames virtually of her own volition. Her pure, virginal, eight-year-old's body would be taken by the sub-princes, and scorched and devoured. Wholly consumed, rolled in the mouth of Hell: a cruel and beautiful death, witnessed by many.

And so the great and noble ritual of Abra-Melin would be consummated, properly and authentically, for maybe the first time in centuries. And Rothley would be inviolable.

He exulted as he stuffed the grey dishrag in the girl's tender red mouth, silencing her pathetic whimpers. *He* had done it. *He* was enacting and completing the great ritual, he had done something Crowley couldn't, something no one had done for a very long time.

Maybe he should tell the girl why she was going to die? Perhaps she deserved to know her role.

Leaning close to her little white ear, Rothley told her in a gentle whisper how tomorrow morning she was going to be taken to a special public place, and burned alive.

Zara Parkinson wept.

49

The Clayzone, Cornwall

'Christ,' said DS Curtis, staring out of the window at the whitened landscape. 'It's like the moon.'

Karen replied tersely. 'This is a profitable industry. Brings jobs to Cornwall.'

'But all this white shit – on the roads and the cars.'

DI Sally Pascoe spoke up, from the back seat. 'It's China clay, kaolin, it gets everywhere, even inside the houses, people inhale it – but it's safe.'

Karen let Sally talk on; her mind was very much distracted.

Where was the girl? Zara Parkinson? So far they had made zero progress. They had finally exhausted the entire list of Crowley residences, extant and demolished, fictional and alleged – and found nothing. So their only route to the girl was tracing Rothley; and Rothley was after Herzog.

Which meant Rothley might just come here. To the laboratory in Rescorla. To find Herzog at home.

Karen got out of the car, put her binoculars to her eyes, and gazed down into the white-and-green valley. Either side of the great scoop of the dale were some of the biggest mountains of kaolin spoil in the clay district. At the far end of the valley was a lurid turquoise-green lake: coloured thus by minerals leaching into the groundwater.

This part of the kaolin district had been worked out decades ago. The English China Clay Company were already beginning the process of grassing over the mighty white Himalayas of kaolin tailings. Nonetheless the place still looked moonlike, as Curtis had said, or maybe like a landscape on a different, nastier planet: remote, swept by cold winds, bitterly sterile.

'So that's it,' said Sally.

'Sorry?'

'So that building there, that's Herzog's lab.'

'Yep. He has several properties all over the UK. But this place is a laboratory where he does research on stem-cell technology, or so he says.'

'Why here?'

'Cornwall is EU Objective One,' Karen said. 'High-tech start-ups get subsidies.'

'He doesn't need the money?'

'But he wants it. Billionaires love money.'

Karen lifted her binoculars again. The laboratory was situated bang in the middle of the vast disused claypit: a jumble of modern one-storey buildings. Steel containers stood outside them. Some cars were parked on the surrounding tarmac.

'It makes sense. The clayzone is remote. No one comes here, yet you're just ten minutes' drive from the A30. An hour from the motorway. And just twenty minutes from Newquay Airport. You can leave here after breakfast and be in London for coffee at eleven. Yet here you are, hidden away on the moon.'

'Maybe it *is* just a stem-cell lab.'

'Yeah, maybe,' said Karen. 'Yet maybe it isn't. He's not going to ask Kerrier Council if he can build a lab to manufacture mind-bending parasites, is he?'

Sally shuddered. 'What if . . .' She gazed down at the apparently innocent buildings. 'What if he is doing all that shit down there? I mean, imagine, imagine . . . the horrible stuff.'

'*Karen!*'

It was a shout from DS Curtis. Karen ran back to the car, and leaned in. Her hopes rose: had they found Zara?

Her detective sergeant was holding up the radio receiver. 'Herzog crossed into UK air space thirty minutes ago, seeking permission to land at Newquay. He's coming here, DCI. He'll be here in less than two hours.'

Karen got back in the car and shut the door. So, if Herzog was coming it was very likely Rothley would show up, too.

Frowning, and thinking, she said, 'Let's wait and try to catch him doing what he does. Pull back a few yards.

424

Make sure we're totally invisible.' She thought some more. 'Sally, call the armed-response team again – at St Austell. And the hazardous chemical people. Get everyone. Get them up here.'

'Why?'

'Rothley. I just have a hunch. *Rothley.*'

50

Cornwall

'It's just forty minutes,' Herzog explained, as they descended the wheeled steps and walked towards a big, black, newish SUV, waiting in the desolate car park of Newquay Airport. Ryan stumbled, Helen assisted him.

Ryan measured his sight, looking into the distance: the sea was visible over the green damp fields, a mile north. A pale January sun was failing to warm the freezing wind. But there was a darkness on the horizon, like an eclipse, and it wasn't bad weather.

Five hours' flying had brought them from sunburned desert to wintry western England. For most of it he had been delirious, stretched out on an extended seat, praying and sweating. Dying, like Albert.

Now one of those rarer hours of lucidity had returned. But the blindness was definitely worse. It was as if he was gazing through shrinking binoculars: the rings of darkness had tightened and soon he would be totally blind. In an hour or two he would be dead.

The passport officials at the tiny airfield hurried them through, just as the Luxor Airport staff had similarly hurried them through, seeing Ryan's condition. Everyone in Newquay appeared to know Herzog well: they bought entirely his story that he had rescued Helen and Ryan from the troubles in Egypt. Ryan was, allegedly, suffering from CS-gas poisoning: 'the terrible Egyptian police, you saw the riots in Cairo . . .'

Two of Herzog's men assisted him into the car. Ryan thought, in his darkening, despairing hours, this was all pointless: he was probably going to die.

Let darkness and the shadow of death stain it; let a cloud dwell upon it; let the blackness of the day terrify it.

The car began its journey south through dark woods of wet pines and more vivid green fields. Or maybe the forests weren't so dark, and Ryan's blindness was colouring everything. He stared, desperately, out of the window. Helen clutched his hand.

Little granite cottages shivered next to little granite pubs. The old chimneys of mineheads pointed accusingly at God.

'Moqqatam,' said Helen.

Herzog turned. 'What?'

'The Zabaleen, in Moqqatam, they are your lab rats, yes? You have been testing all your stuff on them.'

For a few seconds Herzog seemed atypically thrown. He said nothing as the car burned along the damp black roads, but frowned blackly. At last he spoke. 'You may as well know. Maybe you even deserve to know. Yes.' He shrugged, staring ahead. 'When I first became interested in parasites, I had no idea of the possibilities relating to monotheism. I was just interested in mind control, parasites that alter human behaviour. One such is *Taenia solium* – it causes bizarre behavioural changes that are just as subtle as those attributed to toxo: seizures, headaches, depression, but also psychoses.' He gazed out of the car at a drizzly field. 'Also restlessness, delusions of persecution, visions of divine fire and holy voices. Some versions of *Taenia solium* can give you hallucinations that are so bad and realistic you want to kill yourself. You see the worst things your mind can imagine.'

Helen insisted, '*Moqqatam*.'

'I'm coming to that.' The car accelerated onto a dual carriageway. 'If you ever get the chance, Google the name *Kevin Keogh*. He was a nice ordinary salaryman, in Arizona, but he became subtly infected with *Taenia solium. He* went totally crazy, jumped to his death and—'

'Moqqatam!'

'Isn't it obvious? All this evidence made me think. What if you could weaponize mind-altering parasites? Put them in aerosols you could broadcast from a cropsprayer. Hell, put them in a fucking *warhead*. Israel's ultimate defence. The Armageddon Bomb. So we started our initial experiments, in Israel, on animals. But we really needed human guinea pigs.'

'The Zabaleen.'

'Why not? Sassoon told me about them. They

428

sounded ideal. Because those poor rag-picking schlubs are despised by everyone: even the beggars of Cairo's cemeteries look down on the *Zarraba*, the pig people. The Zabaleen also needed a clinic in their City of Trash, and so we built them that clinic. And we also gave them real medicine: vaccinations, surgery, amputations.'

'But not just that!'

'What made the Zabaleen optimal for our purposes was that they do get a *lot* of strange diseases, from sorting through all that venomous trash.'

'So no one would notice if you experimented on them as well?'

Herzog seemed to smile. Ryan could not really tell. He was losing the ability to focus his eyes.

'The Zabaleen are therefore perfect cover. We look like charitable clinicians, yet in ten per cent of cases we give the Zabs a new and experimental injection, ostensibly for their hepatitis or their HIV. But really we're testing synthesized or weaponized parasites. Then we sit back and see what happens. Usually it's quite bad. But who cares? No one cares. Who would notice if another wretched Zabaleen went mad, or killed a priest, or turned out to be hosting a strange new screw worm? The Zabaleen get parasites and psychoses all the time, only my clinic assists them.'

Helen's voice was angry. 'This is just Nazi science. It is no better than Mengele.'

'No, it's better. So we turn a few into golems, sure. But we're not trying to wipe out the Zabaleen. We just

429

want to make sure the Jews are not wiped out ever again. Look –' Herzog pointed – 'we are nearly here.'

'But the Zabaleen burned down your clinic, we heard on the boat.'

'We had a few problems. They got violent. Maybe they suspected something. Anyway, we did our practical in-the-field experiments *there*, and we do our more intense research *here*, in Cornwall. We're going to move the lab but at the moment this is the place where we analyse results, process the data, manufacture the first weaponized parasites. And now we are on to the God Parasite, trying to defeat the worst parasite of all.'

'I could tell the world about this.'

'Really? Yes, you could. I suppose. If this was Hollywood. But then I could get someone to infect you with *espundia*.' The car turned onto a narrower road. 'That's an interesting organism. Eats away the flesh of the face, basically turns you into a living skull.'

Helen ignored this. 'You're moving the lab, why?'

Herzog gazed out of the window. The white spoil heaps dominated everything, it was an extra terrestrial landscape. Ryan could see whiteness ringed with black. And yet beyond it, something golden. Peace, at last; peace and reconciliation. He yearned for the quietness.

Herzog's voice was a comforting drone. 'Nearly there now. Yes, we're moving the lab. And it's not the first time. The Israeli government became hostile to my more interesting ideas vis-à-vis religion, and the abolition thereof. So, we decided to come to Britain, somewhere discreet, with access to English-speaking scientists. But now we're going to move the lab to an even *more* friendly regime. Singapore perhaps. We're working on it.'

Ryan spoke, for the first time in an hour. 'Cats. We know they are fundamental, a crucial link. How?'

The Israeli stared at Ryan. 'I was right to hire you.' He sat forward. 'Yes, there is a *second* Egyptian parasite which we have isolated. It also comes from Akhmim. We call it the Bastet Parasite.'

'The god of cats.'

'Because cats are the vector, as with toxoplasmosis. It's rare but you can catch it from cats, and the Egyptians were the first to suffer from it. We think it explains the association of cats with evil, magic and the Devil throughout history, because, you see, some cats really do pass on a parasite which makes the human hosts believe they have charismatic powers, and in a sense, as I said, the hosts *do*. It seems that human hosts of Bastet can unwittingly hypnotize people, or bewitch them, convince others they are sorcerers, with special powers.'

The car turned onto an empty car park in the very middle of the spoil heaps. Several glass-and-black-steel buildings broke the monotony of white clayspoil and grey sky. Ryan was lifted from the car. He was in the last minutes of lucidity; he knew the cycle now, the symptoms. Death approached, smiling.

And still Herzog talked, as Ryan was laid on another stretcher, and wheeled towards the lab.

431

'The Egyptians must have reacted, subliminally, to the Bastet Parasite: that's probably why they revered cats so much, worshipped them for thousands of years. They sensed that cats had some strange potency to transmit to humankind. And this is why all occult and all hermetic magic is thought to derive from Egypt, because Egypt is the origin of the domestic cat. Neat, no? Of course, we're not sure of the neurochemistry but then, we're not quite sure why feline toxoplasmosis makes women more attractive to men.'

Herzog was still talking. Always talking. Supremely confident; boastful. 'Indeed, I sometimes wonder how many wizards and holy men through history have simply been the unwitting victims, or lucky hosts, of the Bastet Parasite? We know of at least one example: an Englishman, Aleister Crowley, a Satanist who experimented with cat magic.'

They were heading into the laboratory, which was almost deserted. Chemicals in sturdy metal barrels with lurid haz-chem signs sat on large steel shelves. Glassware and machines lined the long walls, endless gleaming machines. Ryan lifted his head, and squeezed Helen's hand.

Helen was insistent. 'So why are you moving?'

'Bastet. Bastet is, indirectly, the reason we are moving. We had a worker here, brilliant kid, Luke Rothley, one of the best neurobiologists. I recruited him in Tel Aviv: he came asking for a job. I told him we were setting up a new lab, because things were getting uncomfortable in Israel. He agreed to work here in

Britain – but it was an error, my error. He couldn't resist trying the Bastet Parasite, taking a snoot of the Crowley cocaine. The poor guy went psycho, wanted to kill me. He *hated* the fact we were going to kill off God, and then he stole much of our data, most of our more promising samples, all the mind-bending parasites about to be weaponized, and he is still out there, doing his absurd spells with his real science. The police will catch him, but it's a warning. A siren.' Herzog opened the door. 'This is the main lab complex. OK, OK. Enough talking: these are my lab guys, my technicians. We need to get started. Hello?'

Ryan looked up at Helen; she was staring around, frowning. Something was wrong: something was even *more* wrong.

'Samuel.'

What? Who was this?

'Samuel Herzog. Hello.'

Ryan lifted himself on an elbow and squinted. A man had come from behind the door. He was in black clothes, tall, fair, athletic, holding a gun in one hand and a syringe in the other.

And next to him was a blonde girl, maybe eight years old, dressed entirely in white. Like a Victorian ghost.

The needle had already gone straight into Herzog's neck.

Someone cried, '*Rothley?*'

Ryan's sight was almost gone now: but he could see Rothley. Pulling out the steel needle. The girl just stood there. Barefoot in her white clothes, staring mutely into space.

The effect of the sudden injection on Herzog was quite extraordinary. His eyes were glazing over: the whites were occluding the pupils; he was hunchbacked. He lifted his dull eyes and gazed at Rothley.

The young man spoke. '*Ampulex compressa*. Ten millilitres. You of all people, Herzog, know what *that* means. Let's go to the safe room. Come with us, Zara.'

Rothley led the shuffling older man down some shallow steps; the girl followed like a loyal spaniel. Herzog seemed to have partly lost control of his limbs. Rothley was like a stern but caring parent, leading his children. The three of them turned a corner and disappeared through a mighty steel door.

It was all done so smoothly, so shimmeringly, so magically, that for a moment everyone was silent.

Then one of the white-coated lab guys spoke up. 'It's on CCTV.'

Another assistant was weeping. '*Ampulex compressa?* Really? I *can't* watch.'

Helen grabbed this assistant by the shoulder. 'You have to help. My friend—'

The woman shook her head. She was still crying.

'You mean he's infected? Herzog has the parasiticide. He keeps it locked away.'

Ryan lay back. So he was going to die.

And he didn't care.

But Helen did. 'You have to get Herzog out of that safe room. Get the cure!'

'We can't!' The second technician gestured, helplessly. 'It's lockable only from the inside: we *can't* get him out. Look for yourself. Rothley has him trapped.'

The big lab-entrance door swung open behind them. Police with guns came running in, hurling questions. Police? Ryan wondered if he was hallucinating. If he was, it was fine.

Because he was going to die. Rhiannon was waiting. Everything was as it should be.

Helen slapped him. Hard. 'Wake up! Ryan!'

The slap stung. Ryan felt a final, feeble surge of life force. He needed to *fight*. For a second the darkness cleared a little: he gazed around. The police were yelling questions, shouting about the girl, this girl, Zara, but it seemed they were as helpless as everyone else. The two men and the girl were locked in the steel cell down the stairs.

And so everyone turned: and watched the TV monitor. On the screen, Samuel Herzog was sitting on a metal bench behind Rothley, staring inanely into space. The girl stood at the back of the room, quite dumb. A mute little angel in white.

Rothley spoke to the CCTV camera, flourishing his syringe. 'In this syringe is a weaponized version of the neurotoxin of *Ampulex compressa*, the emerald jewel wasp. Also known, colloquially, as the zombie cockroach wasp. As early as the 1940s it was reported that female wasps of this species are in the habit of stinging cockroaches, usually of the species *Periplaneta americana*, or *Nauphoeta rhombipholia*. The wasps do this as part of a truly remarkable reproductive cycle. Later studies have revealed the precise procedure adopted by the wasp. As we now know, don't we, Samuel, the wasp stings the roach twice. Firstly, it stings the cockroach in the vicinity of the thoracic ganglia, so as to mildly paralyse the victim . . .' Rothley was frowning, distantly, as he spoke. 'This loss of mobility in the cockroach facilitates a second venomous sting, at a precise spot in the victim's brain, which removes what is left of the victim's escape reflex.' He squirted a little of the fluid from the syringe. Even with his diminished sight Ryan could see the silvery sparkle of the venom. The girl's eyes followed Rothley's actions, quite bewitched. Or hypnotized.

Rothley continued, his voice flat and laconic. 'In layman's terms, the magic of the emerald jewel wasp is that by injecting its mind-altering venom directly into the little brain of the cockroach it induces the much larger, more powerful roach to become a *slave*. And now, Sam, the second sting.'

Turning to his left Rothley slid the needle into Herzog's neck. The shining needle sank deep. The young man withdrew the syringe, then tapped it with a finger-nail, scrutinizing it carefully.

'With the neuromodulator injected in the roach's tiny brain, the wasp has total control over the cockroach. So what does it do? The wasp then proceeds to chew off a segment of the roach's antennae. Researchers believe that the wasp chews off the antennae to replenish its own fluids, or possibly to regulate the amount of venom in the victim.'

436

Rothley turned to Herzog. 'I'm going to cut your hand off.'

Herzog meekly lifted a wrist. As if he was a bride waiting for the groom to kiss her hand. But Rothley was brandishing a knife; and it was large and serrated.

'Oh *Jesus.*' The lab assistant turned away from the screen.

The police crowded around the TV monitor. One of them, a young woman, snapped angrily at the nearest assistant, 'Can we talk to him, to Rothley, in the safe room? Is there a speaker?'

The whitecoat nodded. 'This is the button. Press and talk.'

The policewoman pressed. And talked. Her voice carried electronically to the safe room. 'Rothley, I'm Karen Trevithick, I'm a detective, Scotland Yard—'

'Yes, I *know.*' Rothley's voice was lucid and distinct.

The policewoman snapped out, 'The girl, Rothley. Give us the girl. Zara Parkinson. Give her to us!'

Rothley seemed to shrug. 'I need her.'

'Rothley!'

But Rothley ignored the questions, turning to his hostage. 'OK, Sam. Lift your arm a little more.'

Ryan gazed, and squinted. The few degrees of vision he had left were quite enough.

Rothley was now sawing at Herzog's wrist. The job was laborious: the blood came in dribbles at first, but then it spat like stormwater from a gutter. The wrist bones split, and the severed hand fell to the floor. Rothley set the knife on a table. Herzog stared curiously

437

at the stump of his own arm, squirting blood. The girl also stared at the stump. Frowning.

Meanwhile, Rothley gazed at the camera with confident languor. 'OK. Having semi-paralysed the cockroach, the wasp completes the reproductive cycle. As the wasp is too small to carry the roach, it leads the cockroach victim to the wasp's burrow, by pulling at the severed stumps of the roach's antennae. Once they reach the burrow, the wasp lays a little white egg on top of the roach's abdomen. The emerald jewel wasp then, finally, exits.'

Now Rothley seemed to be looking in a bag. He spoke as he rummaged. 'With its escape reflex disabled, the stung roach will simply *rest* in the burrow, even as the wasp egg hatches on its abdomen. The new-born wasp-larva then grows by chewing and feeding, for maybe five days, on the exposed flesh of the living roach. After that it chews its way right *into* the roach's abdomen and proceeds to live as an endoparasite.' Still he rummaged, and talked. 'Over a further period of eight days, the wasp larva consumes the roach's internal organs in an order which maximizes the likelihood that the roach will stay alive, at least until the larva enters the pupal stage. Now it forms a cocoon inside the roach's body. Only at this juncture does the roach finally *die*. All that is left is for the fully-grown wasp to chew its way free from the cockroach's hollowed corpse, so as to begin its adult life.' He turned, and smiled faintly. 'Development is faster in the warm season.'

A lab technician slammed the button. 'Luke, stop it,

stop it, you're not an executioner! Let the girl go. Let them all go. Sam doesn't deserve to die like this! You're infected: you think you're Crowley, a magician, but it's delusional, the Bastet Parasite—'

The policewoman was also shouting. 'The girl! Just give us the girl – you don't need her any more – you've got what you want!'

From the safe room Rothley's voice was calm and distinct: 'Come here, Samuel.'

Ryan could see that Rothley was holding something – some kind of glass vial, or large test tube.

Rothley spoke again. 'Of course, I haven't got any wasp larvae. But I do have a scientific correlative: one of your own offspring, Samuel. The saliva of the parasitic blowfly maggot, *Calliphoria vomitoria* – remember we developed a weaponized version of this saliva as a flesh-eater in our early days in Israel? Samuel?'

Herzog said nothing. He was still staring at the blood that dripped from his severed wrist. The girl stood behind them, a hovering shade in seraphic white.

Rothley nodded. 'In sufficient quantities a synthetic version of *Calliphoria* saliva is equivalent to a Bronsted superacid. Dangerously strong, and formidably corrosive of mammalian flesh.'

He put on thick black rubber gloves. Flexing his fingers, he unstoppered the glass tube, paused and looked at Sam Herzog. 'It will burn out your throat as it goes down, and then it will dissolve your insides. You will, essentially, *melt*.' He lifted the unstoppered vial over Herzog's head.

439

Herzog obediently nodded. He leaned back, and tipped his head up. Rothley poured the pale liquid down his victim's mouth.

The reaction was immediate.

Initially, Herzog's lips burned, then his entire mouth appeared to smoke, as the liquid scorched into his tongue and his cheeks. Seconds later, the fluid reached his throat. Livid scarlet holes appeared in his neck, bleeding sockets of flesh. And now the jawbone collapsed and just fell away. Blood was dripping creamily down his chest even as fumes rose from the remaining half of his face. Herzog was disintegrating.

Rothley stood back to watch his victim's legs twitch and spasm as he lay, collapsed, on the floor. Half corroded. And surely dead.

His back to the camera, Rothley extracted another item from his rucksack, then he turned and held it up, so that everyone could see.

But Ryan couldn't see, the last degrees of sight had very nearly gone. The blackness was triumphing. He whispered, to Helen, 'What is it? What's he holding?'

'I don't know . . .'

A loud ticking emanated. 'The ticking is theatrical, the bomb is real.' Rothley told them all. 'The laboratory must also be destroyed. *In toto*. The girl's immolation is the final act. What is a man, that he should presume to kill God? This bomb is therefore big enough to level the entire building. But you have four minutes to evacuate.'

The policewoman, Trevithick, slammed the button.

'Stop it: stop the bomb. You're going to die first. This is suicide! Why not give us the girl?'

'Meginah, Elinala, Gelagon.'

Rothley intoned the strange words, slowly and deliberately.

'Stop the bomb.'

'Magid, Akori, Happir, Haluteb.'

'Rothley!'

'Sagal, Apara.'

It snapped into place. In his blindness, Ryan *recognized* the words. It was the Abra-Melin death ritual, *the same ritual inscribed on the second Sokar papyrus.* Ryan knew this spell, he knew it by heart. How many times had he read it these last weeks, trying to decipher the Sokar Hoard?

And the death ritual had a counter-spell. That was also on the Sokar papyrus.

If Rothley believed he was doing magic, he would necessarily believe in counter-magic.

Ryan shouted across the lab, 'Sizigos, Iporusu, Maregan.'

The effect was instant.

With the last of his eyesight Ryan could see Rothley's face, puzzled, frowning, staring intently at the camera. Angry.

Ryan continued: 'Dodim. Abala. *Darac.'*

Rothley shouted back, but he was stammering now. 'Sicafel, Sic – Sic – Iperige – Maregan—'

'Zara, run – please run!'

'Sizigos, KAILAH—'

441

'Run, Zara, get out!'

The policewoman was yelling. Ryan squinted. The girl appeared to be stirring, her bewitchment weakening. Maybe she could sense Rothley's faltering hold.

'Zara! GET OUT!'

Zara was running for the door of the safe room. Yet Rothley didn't even notice. He was staring straight ahead at the camera, his eyes wild and blazing.

'Situk, Irape, Situk, Irape!'

Almost the last thing Ryan saw was the blonde hair of the girl, *outside* the safe room, as she ran to save her own life, ran into the arms of the policewoman – and then *everyone* was running. Ryan could hear urgent footsteps all around. The entire place was evacuating, the bomb was still ticking. But Ryan was stuck on the stretcher. For the last time, he tried to move: but he couldn't move, and he couldn't see. And it didn't matter. He had saved the girl. He could die. Here. Listening to Rothley's manic chanting.

Ryan lay back, but then he felt arms and hands – Helen, lifting him up, assisted by someone else, hauling him off the stretcher, hoisting him over their shoulders.

How much time was left? Maybe sixty seconds.

Doors slammed open, the shouts of fear echoed, as they dragged Ryan down the corridor, as they kicked open the final doors.

Fifty seconds.

Now they were in the fresh air: he could feel it, as they carried him, painfully, laboriously, to some kind of safety.

Forty seconds?

They carried him upwards, maybe up the white slopes of kaolin tailings.

Twenty seconds . . .

Moving higher still: surely they must be looking down at the lab?

Someone shouted: *'Get down!'*

The explosion was so vivid it gave Ryan a final few seconds of sight: he glimpsed a monstrous fireball surging into the air, poisoned with chemicals, hellish and glowing, then evolving into a wild tornado of smoke, and flame, and kaolin dust. Ryan stared. The policewoman was cradling the weeping blonde girl, in her arms.

And then the God Parasite sealed the last chink of light in Ryan's mind; and it was just blackness. And silence. And infinity.

51

University College, London

'I never even knew there was a collection here,' said Karen, gazing across the sunny quadrangle. They were sitting on the great stone steps, almost alone. The college was largely deserted because of the Easter holidays.

Ryan nodded. 'It's the third biggest collection of Egyptian antiquities in the world. Flinders-Petrie gave it all to UCL.' He reached and fumbled for his plastic cup of coffee on the granite steps; Karen found it and handed it to him, wrapping his fingers around the cup.

With a smile, Ryan thanked her. 'I have partial sight now. It's no longer improving, but it's better than total blindness.' He gestured at the classical buildings to their left. 'We have the earliest example of metal from all of ancient Egypt, two magnificent lions from the temple of Min at Coptos, and a fine pair of socks from Alexandria. Probably Roman.'

Karen said, 'You like working here.'

'Yes I do. And of course, this is where I attended Sassoon's lectures, which is poignant.'

Karen gazed at him. It was four months since the explosion. 'Obviously you're not going to go back to Egypt?'

'Even if they'd let me in? No. I couldn't function anyway.'

'And Helen?'

'She's fine, she's great. She looks after me. We have very little money, but we are OK.'

'That's good.' Karen hesitated, then pressed on. 'The blindness. It was meant to be irreversible. And terminal. You were meant to die?'

Ryan sipped his coffee. 'Yes, but we worked this out. Acts, Chapter Nine.'

'Sorry?'

'Saul, the persecutor of Christians, is visited by a flaming vision of God. "And Saul arose from the earth; and when his eyes were opened, he saw no man: but they led him by the hand, and brought him into Damascus. And he was three days without sight . . ." But then a few days later he is visited by the Holy Ghost. "And immediately there fell from his eyes as it had been scales: and he received sight forthwith, and arose, and was baptized."' Ryan shrugged. 'It seems the blindness of the conversion experience can be temporary, even reversible. Or maybe it really is a miracle? Maybe God *works* through the God Parasite. How can we know?' He acknowledged her expression of surprise. 'Yes. The irony of it all is that I *do* believe. The parasite has done its work. And belief is good. I like it.' He sighed, but not unhappily. 'Anyway, Herzog *lied*. Guess he just wanted me in his lab to test his parasite-killer, the parasiticide, the one he intended to use against the faithful.'

The traffic of Bloomsbury rumbled beyond the railings. Ryan added, 'What's more, I can use disabled parking bays. So it's not all bad, not at all. Especially when you consider the alternative.'

Karen gently smiled. 'I suppose that's true.' She reached in her bag. 'By the way, I mustn't forget this: it's one reason I wanted to see you.'

He was gazing at her, frowning; she hurried on.

'You know we are still sifting the evidence at Rescorla, at the site of the explosion? Well, we found this digital camera. It was in the burned remains of Helen's bag. It looks quite intact, and it seems to work. We've finished with it, certainly for the moment.'

She handed it over, placing it carefully in his hands. Ryan squinted at the camera, with an astonished expression.

The pause was slightly awkward. Perhaps it was time to go.

Ryan threaded his arm through hers, and they strolled towards the gates of the quad.

'Eleanor is good?'

'She is. We're going down to Cornwall, for Easter.' Karen checked her watch. 'I'm picking her up from the childminder's, we're meeting the cousins down there. Should be a nice break.'

Ryan smiled. 'I'd like to have kids one day.'

'I hope you do. They are the very worst and very best thing that can happen to you. At the same time.'

For a few moments, the two of them chatted about families and children. Then Ryan frowned. 'By the way, how is Zara Parkinson?'

'She's fine. Considering. Traumatized of course, but alive.'

'That's good.'

'She owes her life to you.'

Ryan shook his head. 'No, she doesn't . . . I just . . . did what I could. I still wonder why Rothley didn't try and escape, once he'd lost the girl.'

Karen nodded. 'It is a bit strange. Best guess is he was just crazy, in the end – handling all those parasites, it must have got to him. We'd have liked to test his body for antigens, but there isn't a lot to go on; in fact, nothing. He was vaporized. It happens with big explosions.' Another silence. Less awkward, but a silence. It really was time to leave.

They said their goodbyes and Karen stepped into the urban melee of Gower Street. Her car was parked very close, by the university library. Turning the ignition, she drove to the childminder's, collected an excited and chirruping Eleanor, and they began the five-hour journey to Cornwall.

Leaving the day before Good Friday meant the traffic was not too bad. So they arrived at twilight, cresting the hill at Carbis Bay just in time to see the sun setting over St Ives, where she and Eleanor – and Alan and

447

Julie and the twins – had all rented a holiday apartment.

The following day dawned blue and fine. Ideal weather for a picnic on Maenporth Beach.

The children played on the sands in the sun, writing their names with big sticks. Karen sat on the blanket and chatted with Alan and Julie. As the kids chased the surf, Karen turned and gazed at the cliffs behind, where a small Cornish chapel, ancient and humble, stood in its seaside graveyard.

She recalled the comparison she had once made, between chapels and tin mines, both remnants of an exhausted industry, the ruins of what was no more.

But was that true?

This morning she had read in the local paper a report that claimed there was, supposedly, more tin under Cornwall still waiting to be mined than all the tin taken out so far. It was just inaccessible.

But one day they might find a way to tap into the seams.

52

Department of Parasitology, Imperial College, London

Graham Moffat almost dropped his rooibos tea as he stared at his laptop screen. There was no disputing it. The white detritus recovered from the air-conditioning units of the Rescorla laboratory was indeed TS.

Dead, but TS.

So far he and his superior had discussed this odd white detritus with no one, not even the Met police. There hadn't been any reason: the entire forensic analysis of the murder site in Cornwall had produced no real surprises; indeed, as the months had gone by what had initially felt like an interesting parasitological assignment had turned into a bothersome chore, and Graham had openly questioned – in staff meetings – whether Imperial College should be wasting valuable laboratory time in this way, even if they were assisting the police, and even if they were pretty well remunerated.

But this discovery? This changed everything.

He leaned forward, and tapped a few keys. The image enlarged, until the stained, purple, dried-out larva of the cyclophilid cestoid *Taenia solium* was several inches wide, like a lurid bruise.

It was unmistakable: Graham Moffat knew his parasites, he knew his chagas from his giardiasis, his loa loa from his pinworm. And this was *Taenia solium*. In some strange, new, aerosolized or even weaponized form.

Of course, Graham mused, sipping his cooling tea, they'd have to get this startling result confirmed. Perhaps they could take blood samples from anyone who was in the laboratory on the day of the murder, look for antigens or antibodies that signified brief exposure to this parasite. But he reckoned these would simply confirm what he was seeing.

Someone had introduced this mind-altering parasite into the air-conditioning unit, probably just before the laboratory had exploded. Someone with access to these parasites in weaponized form. That probably meant Rothley. And the presence of these parasites meant that all eye-witness reports from inside the laboratory were unreliable. They could all have been hallucinating. A brief but intense mass delusion. Anything could have happened. Anyone could have escaped.

Graham picked up his mobile phone. He could get

a better signal outside. It was time to call his boss, and then they would have to call the police.

The door slammed angrily shut as he exited the lab, making the table shake. And the purple larva on the laptop screen seemed to shiver, as if it were alive.

THE GENESIS SECRET

In the deserts of eastern Turkey, archaeologists are unearthing the world's most ancient temple. When journalist Rob Luttrell is sent to report on the dig, he is intrigued to learn that someone deliberately buried the site 10,000 years ago. Why?

Only one man knows the secret – a secret so shocking it may threaten the social structure of the world – and he is intent on destroying the evidence before it can be recovered.

THE MARKS OF CAIN

In America, a young man unexpectedly inherits a fortune. In Europe, a string of murders coincides with the disappearance of a brilliant scientist. Tying these strange events together is an ancient Biblical curse, a medieval French tribe of pariahs, and a terrible revelation: something that will alter the world forever. One couple is intent on discovering this darkest of secrets, but others will kill to stop them.

BIBLE OF THE DEAD

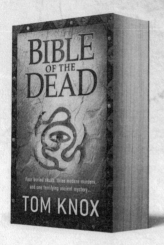

In France, young archaeologist Julia Kerrigan unearths three skulls, each with a hole bored through the forehead. In Laos, photographer Jake Thurby and Cambodian lawyer Chemda Tek are investigating bizarre finds at the ancient Plain of Jars.

As a series of brutal worldwide killings comes to light, Jake, Chemda and Julia must pursue separate leads to piece together the same terrifying puzzle. In doing so, they will be risking far more than just their lives…

THE BABYLON RITE

In Edinburgh, a famous Templar historian dies mysteriously at the Rosslyn chapel, setting journalist Adam Blackwood on a quest for the truth. In Peru, anthropologist Jess Silverton is digging up the world's most terrifying ancient civilization: the Moche. It seems that their ancient practices may not be entirely buried and forgotten…

Adam and Jess will both be thrown into mortal danger as they discover a global secret – that kills.

By Tom Knox

The Genesis Secret
The Marks of Cain
Bible of the Dead
The Babylon Rite